"The past doesn't matter."

His sexy smile loosened a sigh from her lungs.

"I see a woman who's stronger than she thinks she is. Brave, even," he said. "Wise. Hell of a gorgeous body." His gaze lowered down to her legs and back up. "I like you, Ruby. I'm attracted to you. And I was just hoping...you'd give me a chance."

The words were so sincere, so honest, that every defensive wall she'd raised came crashing down around her, leaving her exposed and open.

Sawyer was nothing like Derek, who'd only ever let her see strength and power and an unyielding control. *No.* Sawyer was okay with his vulnerabilities. They didn't seem to make him feel weak, didn't make him feel the need to assert anything over someone else.

"Sawyer..." There was so much she couldn't tell him. So many reasons she should ask him to leave. But the ache for him sank all the way into her bones. So instead of saying anything, instead of casting him out of her life, she leaned forward and pressed her lips to his, letting herself melt into him. Oh, lordy, lordy, lordy...the man could *kiss*...

ACCLAIM FOR *NO BETTER MAN*

"Richardson's debut packs a powerful emotional punch. [Her] deft characterization creates a hero and heroine who will elicit laughs in some places and tears in others."
—*Publishers Weekly*

"4 stars! Hot! Richardson brings us a modern read set in beautiful Aspen. Her brisk storytelling and the charming, endearing characters set within a solid, engaging plot make this sweet romance shine. A strong and vulnerable Bryce, coupled with a determined, lighthearted Avery, will appeal to readers, especially with their sizzling chemistry. This is a truly delightful read."
—*RT Book Reviews*

"Charming, witty, and fun. There's no better read. I enjoyed every word!"
**—Debbie Macomber, #1 *New York Times*
bestselling author**

"An enjoyable read. Richardson's spunky, baseball-lovin' heroine is delightful!"
—Katie Lane, *USA Today* bestselling author

"The perfect balance of humor, heart, and heat. I couldn't put it down! Sara Richardson will sweep you away."
—Christie Craig, *New York Times* bestselling author

MORE THAN
A FEELING

MORE THAN
A FEELING

A Heart of the Rockies Novel

SARA RICHARDSON

FOREVER

NEW YORK   BOSTON

Copyright © 2016 by Sara Richardson
Excerpt from *No Better Man* copyright © 2015 by Sara Richardson

Forever
Hachette Book Group
1290 Avenue of the Americas
New York, NY 10104

HachetteBookGroup.com

Printed in the United States of America

First Edition: March 2016
10 9 8 7 6 5 4 3 2 1

OPM

Forever is an imprint of Grand Central Publishing.
The Forever name and logo are trademarks of Hachette Book Group, Inc.

The Hachette Speakers Bureau provides a wide range of authors for speaking events. To find out more, go to www.hachettespeakersbureau.com or call (866) 376-6591.

The publisher is not responsible for websites (or their content) that are not owned by the publisher.

To every reader who has ever let the past define you:
You are stronger than you think.
Brave and capable.
Defined by love.
Of infinite value to this world.
Be free.

Acknowledgments

Every time I finish writing a book, I experience this overwhelming sense of gratitude because I know I could never do it alone. I am so grateful for the whole team of people who help me share my stories—Megha Parekh, the loveliest editor; my publicist, Marissa Sangiacomo; and the incredible sales and marketing team at Forever. Suzie Townsend and the team at New Leaf Literary are some of the best in the business. Thank you for being so good at taking care of the "other stuff" so I can just write.

I love my readers. Seriously. You have no idea how much your words of encouragement mean to me. Thank you from the bottom of my heart for taking the time to post reviews, to tell your friends about my books, and to send me messages that let me know you connected with one of my stories. Your words are a gift and I would not be able to continue this journey without them.

At times writing this book felt like an emotional roller

coaster, but I didn't have to ride it alone. Thank you to the
Downton girls—Melissa, Kimberly, Gretchen, and Jenna—
for giving me something to look forward to on those Sunday
nights. And for being real. Elaine Clampitt, thank you for
the regular coffee dates that keep me on track. I am blessed
with so many friends and family members who keep me
grounded and remind me that there is life on the other side
of the computer. Thank you all for filling my life with love,
laughter, and depth. And thank you to my sweeties—Will,
AJ, and Kaleb—for taking me someplace tropical after I finished a draft of this book. Even when we're not exploring
an island, you inspire me every single day.

MORE THAN
A FEELING

CHAPTER ONE

Morning was hands-down the most beautiful time of day in the mountains.

Ruby James stepped out of her Honda Civic and raised her face to the sky, closing her eyes, breathing in the fresh, sweet scent of the dew-kissed grass. At five o'clock the sky was still dark and studded with stars, but the frayed edges of the mountainous horizon glowed with the promise of light.

A new day. Fresh, clean air, a blank slate of possibilities. Each morning for the past year, she had been the first one to greet it at the Walker Mountain Ranch. And for the first time in her life, she had started to understand freedom. It manifested itself in the expanse of mountainous space, in the stillness of a world still asleep, in the opportunity she'd been given to take care of herself, to pursue a life she wanted, instead of one that had been thrust on her by a broken system.

The air's chill infused her with energy as Ruby tromped from her parking spot behind the Walker Mountain Ranch, lugging along a cloth market bag that held her very own personal set of stainless-steel measuring cups and a marble rolling pin. Elsie Walker, her boss and the head chef at the ranch, kept a set in the kitchen, but she preferred to use her own for baking. Then she'd take them home each night to polish them and bring them back the next morning. She imagined it was something akin to having a briefcase except instead of a laptop and a cell phone and whatever other devices were popular at the moment, her briefcase was filled with kitchen utensils. They were the best she could find at that gourmet kitchen store in town, solid and unbendable, the highest-quality materials for baking. And this morning she had to do her best baking because their best clients would be coming off the trail later this afternoon, and everything had to be perfect.

Each year in the spring, before things got busy, the Walker Mountain Ranch welcomed a group of foster kids from other towns in the area. They stayed at the ranch free of charge and went backpacking and horseback riding. They got to do the ropes course and zipline—why anyone would want to do that was beyond her. She preferred her feet firmly on the ground, thank you very much. But the best thing about the whole week was that the kids had the chance to just be kids without a care, for once in their lives.

She would've given anything for that chance back when she was being carted to foster home after foster home. So when Elsie had told her about the group—when they'd started planning—Ruby had decided she would do everything she could to make this week at the ranch the best of these kids' lives, cooking for them, volunteering to help out whenever they needed her—anything to make them feel wanted and accepted and free.

She approached the lodge's back door, the familiar scent

of wood stain greeting her. The massive logs stacked one on top of each other always reminded her of the Lincoln Logs she and her brother, Grady, used to play with before Mama went to prison. They'd build structures almost exactly like the one that stood in front of her, grand mountain palaces where magical things happened—where families gathered around fireplaces and drank hot chocolate. Where there were no drugs and no cops and no fears. They'd set up the fences and add in small plastic farm animals they'd shoplifted from the drugstore, pigs and cows and chickens, and even a crotchety rooster they'd called Slim.

Back then she'd believed things could turn around for them. She'd believed Mama would go to rehab like she always said, and then things would be normal. Once she'd even shoplifted an apron for Mama—a frilly thing that looked handmade. As if when Mama put it on she'd be magically transformed into the woman Ruby had always dreamed she would become. The mom who made chocolate chip cookies and drove the car pool and cut her peanut butter and jelly sandwiches into funny shapes that'd make her giggle at school.

But Ruby didn't believe in magic anymore.

Shaking her head at herself, she paused to study the Walker Mountain Ranch's lovely façade. Maybe that's why she'd ended up here last year. When she'd gotten in the car, she hadn't known where to go. She'd never had a place, and god knew Aspen, Colorado, was worlds away from Cherryville, North Carolina. But it was either stay there with Derek and live with the bruises that always splotched her skin, or go. Disappear. Build a new life, a new name, a new future for herself.

So she'd chased freedom. As she'd worked her way west, the mountains had called her name. She'd seen mountains before, of course, but nothing like the Rocky Mountains. Instead of mounded, green hills, they were massive and sharp, lovely but impenetrable. Exactly the refuge she was seeking. While there was a certain fragility to her new life—her new identity—this was the first time she'd felt rooted since before Mama'd been put away.

As always that thought burrowed deep in the tomb where she normally kept all those memories vaulted. That was where they belonged. Stashed away. Course with Mama's birthday being today, those crushed hopes and dreams were getting restless, feeling almost uncontainable. Was she still in jail? Had Derek contacted her mother after Ruby had run away? Cold dread washed over her and she plowed through the ranch's kitchen door before the tide of fear dragged her back into the currents of the past.

The kitchen was dim with only the under-cabinet lighting turned on, but it was warm, too, scented with cinnamon and yeast. Inhaling the familiarity soothed the tremble out of her hands. No one here knew a lick of anything about her past, and she had to keep it that way. She couldn't risk Derek tracking her down, not after the threats he'd made the last time he'd beat her up.

Holding her breath, she willed her heart to stop pounding so hard. She had to calm herself down. Derek couldn't find her here; she'd made sure of that. She'd been sad to hear of her old neighbor's passing, but Ruby James's death had given her the perfect opportunity to escape.

The woman hadn't had any children of her own, and she'd always had a soft spot for Ruby. Still, she'd been surprised to hear that Miss James had left her everything. Her house and her car. She'd never told Derek. She'd simply sold off the furniture, packed the sentimentals in storage, and loaded all of her things into Miss James's Civic. She used the proceeds

from the estate to fund her trip out west, paying cash for absolutely everything.

As a cop Derek had the means to look for her, to watch
for a ping on her credit card, to scan reports from all over
the country. That's why she'd been so careful. That's why
she'd used Ruby James's name. That's why she'd cut up all
her credit cards.

No. He wouldn't find her, she told herself again as she
marched to the other side of the room and set down her bag.
It was time to stop thinking about him. About Mama. A new
day. A new life. And she had cinnamon rolls to bake.

The Walker Mountain Ranch kitchen didn't open until
eight o'clock during the slow season, but Ruby and Elsie
made all the baked good from scratch, which meant Ruby
had to get an early start every morning. She preferred it,
anyway. Being alone. It was easier because she didn't have
to pretend. She didn't have to watch herself so closely, to
guard every word and thought so she wouldn't risk confusing her new identity with her old life. When she was alone
she could let down her guard, turn on some tunes, and put
her hands to work, rolling out scones and cinnamon-roll
dough and whatever else was on the menu for the morning.

Just the thought of that therapeutic process of kneading
and rolling and mixing was enough to set her emotions
right. Even though she'd left it behind, her old life was always there in the dreams, in the memories. Sometimes they
leaked out, spilling over into the present, but she could usually outrun 'em as long as she stayed busy.

And speaking of busy . . . she shimmied out of her fleece
coat and hung it on the hook behind the pantry. She had a
whole mess of baked goods planned for those kids—gooey
chocolate-chip cookies as big as their heads, fat, fluffy cinnamon rolls that would melt in their mouths. Smiling at the

thought, she started to unpack her supplies. First, the heavy marble rolling pin that had cost her a small fortune. Admiring the swirled gray-and-white stone, she pulled it out of the bag and—

Crash!

The jarring sound stilled her. A breath lodged in her throat. She strained her ears, listening.

A series of thuds and rumbles sounded again from the pantry.

Oh, god. A swallow tangled her windpipe. Something was *in* there. Her grip tightened on the rolling pin's handle. Was it a bear fresh out of hibernation? Scenes from that damn grizzly bear documentary she'd watched two days before flashed like a horror flick, the bear towering over her on his hind legs, teeth gnashing, claws slashing through the air. Aspen had a major bear problem. They broke into restaurants and homes, raiding kitchens, pilfering through trash. They were only black bears but still...

God. Oh, dear god. Her heart catapulted into an arrhythmia. Perspiration beaded on her skin. She stared longingly at the kitchen door, all the way on the other side of the room. It might as well have been Antarctica! There was no way she'd get over there without the *thing* hearing her! The pantry's half-open door stood between her and a clean escape...

More clatters cinched tension into her neck.

"Damn it!"

Ruby inhaled a gasp. Not a bear! Definitely not a bear. A muffled string of curses edged her back against the wall. A man. There was a man in the pantry! Except there were no other cars outside. Bryce and Shooter, the ranch's other guides, were camping with the kids out on the trail...

Wait a minute. She jerked her head and squinted in a futile effort to examine the kitchen door she'd walked through not five minutes before. It hadn't been locked. Holy Moses, it was *always* locked! If she wouldn't have been so preoccupied with the past, she would've noticed. Someone had broken in!

An icy sensation spread over her shoulders and locked them tight, the remnants of past trauma seeping into her.

Derek?

No, no. He couldn't have found her.

Another crash seemed to shake the floor.

Panic came in wrenching gasps, clouding her vision, prickling her skin. *Dial 911.* She had to call 911 before the man came out and saw her.

Still gripping the rolling pin, she reached her other clammy hand into the market bag and fished for her cell phone.

The pantry door creaked, then cranked all the way open.

It was dark inside, but a man's silhouette stood under the lintel. A large man. Tall, broad shoulders. The hood of a black sweatshirt obscured his face.

"Freeze, dirtbag!" Arm stiff with fear Ruby held out the rolling pin, brandishing it as if it were a gun.

"What the hell?" The man took a step toward her.

"I said freeze," she squeaked, because technically, there wasn't much she could do if he decided not to obey.

"Easy," the guy murmured in a patronizing voice, like he was trying to lure a scared puppy or something.

"You hold it right there, asshole!" She waved the rolling pin again. "I'm calling nine-one-one."

"Take it easy." Slowly the man held up one hand while the other took down his hood. "It's me, Ruby," he said, but *me* who? All she could see were the bright lights of panic shooting holes through her vision. Because she'd never been able to fight back.

She'd tried, once. Not long after she'd moved in with Derek. He was drunk and angry that she'd left the dishes in the sink after dinner. She could still smell the alcohol on his breath, still feel the ways his fingers had dug into the flesh of her shoulders. He'd shoved her hard against the sink, bruising her lower back. "Clean this shit up," he'd screamed at her. "Or I'll fucking break your arm." Terror had rattled through her, blurring her vision into a surreal haze like it was now. Out of sheer desperation, she'd grabbed the handle of a frying pan and swung it as hard as she could. Next thing she knew, Derek had her pinned on the ground, his fingers laced around her neck, cutting off her air...

Gasping for a breath, she realized her fingertips were tingling with numbness. *Oh, god!* How would she fight back with a *rolling pin*?

"Ruby!" The man shuffled a step closer. "Lower the weapon."

How? Her arms seemed locked in place. Her lungs heaved and gasped. *No!* Not here. Not now. She hadn't had a panic attack since she'd come to the Walker Mountain Ranch. But sure enough, her heart pounded so hard her head got light. It felt like her lungs were filling with water. She had to fight for a breath.

"Hey." A hand enclosed hers.

Fire roared through her. She would not let him hurt her. She would never let anyone hurt her again. "Don't touch me!" She ripped free and swung the rolling pin as hard as she could, feeling a thud as it collided with the man's body.

A winded groan punched out of his mouth and he sank slowly to the floor, clutching his groin.

"Holy Moses," she whimpered. She'd taken the guy down. What now? What the hell should she do now? Frozen, she stood over him, still clutching the rolling pin.

"You hit me with that again, I'm pretty sure I won't be able to walk for a week," the man said. "Kids'll probably be out of the question, too."

Ruby's vision cleared. She gazed down at him and stared into eyes so blue they put the Colorado sky to shame. "Sawyer," she panted. Realizing who he was didn't do much to curb the panic. Sawyer was Bryce's cousin! A cop! She'd nailed a cop in the balls with a marble rolling pin!

"I'm so sorry!" She dropped to her knees next to him. "Are you okay? I thought you were an intruder!"

"Obviously," he mumbled as he gingerly sat up and hunched over, resting his elbows on his knees. He shifted slightly with a wince.

"Why didn't you stop me?" Yes, it was perhaps a bit unsympathetic for her to ask that question when the man's voice was still cracking like a preteen's, but what the hell? With all of those bulging muscles of his, he could've immobilized her with one maneuver. He could've taken away the rolling pin and they wouldn't be in this situation now, would they?

"Didn't want to scare you," Sawyer mumbled. "You already seemed pretty freaked out."

Humiliation soaked her face. This was not good, him seeing her have a panic attack. Really not good. Out of everyone here, she'd avoided Sawyer the most. He was a cop. A little research and the man could bring down her entire fabricated life...

"You want to tell me why you didn't recognize me?" His tenor had settled back into the deep, gravelly voice she'd heard before. A tingle skittered up her spine. It was like having a conversation with Keith Urban.

"Because you looked right at me," he continued, locking his gaze on hers.

Oh, lordy, those eyes. So gorgeous. His face wasn't bad, either. Straight nose, strong, square jaw stubbled with a few days of growth. And there was an adorable faint line running down the center of his chin. Her heart started a traitorous flutter until she realized he was waiting for an answer; then the flutter turned violent.

"Um." She studied her hands, worry boiling up. "I saw you. Of course I *saw* you. I was just…a little panicked, that's all." If she told him the truth, that she couldn't control the panic, that it crashed over her and dragged her into a riptide of confusion, he'd start asking more questions.

"*A little* panicked?" Sawyer shot back.

"Well, can you blame me?" Her heart thumped in her ears. "I mean, I wasn't expecting anyone to be hiding in the pantry—"

"Hiding?" Sawyer laughed. "Why would I be hiding in the pantry? Bryce asked me to fix the shelves while he was gone."

She shot to her feet. "At five o'clock in the morning?"

He was slower to get up, but at least he wasn't grimacing anymore. "I'm on shift at eight."

Panic started to pump through her again, but this time it had nothing to do with fear and everything to do with the way he looked at her, the way his gaze drifted down her body. She crossed her arms so he couldn't guess her cup size. "How'd you get in here, anyway?"

Sawyer casually leaned against the kitchen counter, still looking her over like he appreciated what he saw. "I have a key. I'm staying here."

The room whirled. Not what she'd hoped to hear. That was bad. Very, very bad. It had been hard enough to avoid him before, but if he stayed here it'd be impossible! "I thought you were moving to Denver," she said, going for a casual, conversational tone. Damn the squeak of panic. But Sawyer was supposed to be leaving for good. Rumor had it that his wife had cheated on him with one of his friends. As far as she knew, he couldn't wait to get out of Aspen.

He shrugged. "The house sold faster than I thought. I still have a month left at work."

Fabulous. That was just her luck. The last thing she needed was a cop poking around the Walker Mountain Ranch.

"So what's with the panic attack?" he asked again, sounding more like a cop this time.

She busied herself with unpacking the rest of her kitchen utensils from her bag. "What'd you mean?"

"You know what I mean. I know what a panic attack looks like, Ruby."

"It wasn't a panic attack," she insisted, then focused on lining up her measuring cups so he couldn't read the flush on her face. "I was surprised. That's all. No big deal." She peeked over at him.

His eyes narrowed into skepticism. "Do you hyperventilate every time you're surprised?"

No. But she was about to hyperventilate right then. "Why do I feel like you're interrogating me?" she demanded in case he could see how weak she felt. Now that the adrenaline had drained away, her legs and arms shuddered with a growing frailty. The memories were closer, breathing down her neck. If she would've hit Derek with a rolling pin, he would've broken her jaw...

"Ruby? Is everything okay?" Sawyer asked quietly.

Crumpling the market bag in her shaky hands, she turned and smiled. "Everything's great." She'd learned how to lie, how to cover up the truth a smile. "I'm so sorry about your..." The blush made a strong comeback. "Um...do you want ice or anything?"

A smirk made him look less guarded. "Do I want to walk around with an icepack on my crotch? No thanks. I'll live."

"Suit yourself." She sashayed past him like nothing had happened, like her stomach hadn't tightened into a painful knot. "I should get to work, then."

"You're sure everything's okay?" Sawyer called behind her.

"Of course." She unstacked the stainless mixing bowls from the shelf above the sink.

"All right, then. Guess I'll get back to work, too," he said slowly. The pantry door opened and then clicked shut.

But something told her that wasn't the end of the conversation.

CHAPTER TWO

Sawyer shoved the hammer into his toolbox and latched it. He considered putting his sweatshirt back on but then thought better of it. Best not to risk spooking Ruby again. Who knew where she'd nail him this time. Another shot to the nuts like that and he'd need more than an icepack.

He just might need a massage...

Whoa. Easy. Those weren't the kind of thoughts he should entertain right now. And Ruby didn't need them, either, apparently. Didn't matter what she said—that whole scene in the kitchen earlier wasn't normal fear. When he stepped out of the pantry, he'd seen something almost primal come over her face, a sickening fear, the kind he'd only witnessed on victims. When she looked at him, she hadn't *seen* him. When he'd talked to her, she couldn't hear him. It was like she was somewhere else.

So never mind that the woman had long red hair, round

full cheeks, soft radiant skin, and the most perfect lips he'd ever seen. Never mind her Marilyn Monroe body with all those tempting curves. Something was off with Ruby. The whole panic-attack thing was weird enough, but add to that the fact that no one knew anything about her, and he had a good old-fashioned mystery on his hands.

Who was she? Where'd she come from? More important, what did she want at the Walker Mountain Ranch? One year ago she'd shown up in town. Aunt Elsie took her in, no questions asked. Even though he'd warned her about that kind of charity. She'd accused him of being jaded. How else was a veteran cop supposed to be? Being jaded was part of the job description. And since he was moving away, there'd be no one to keep an eye on things and make sure Ruby wasn't a liability to Bryce.

After the recent thefts they'd had, they couldn't be too careful.

He heaved his toolbox off the shelf. "Ruby?" he called through the closed pantry door.

"Yeah?" Her response was so soft he barely heard it.

"I'm coming out now. Just wanted to warn you." He gave the words a few seconds to sink in and then opened the door and strode into the kitchen.

Ruby stood over a KitchenAid mixer, which was whirring away with another one of her tasty creations, which he'd heartily enjoyed for the past year. Something must've been in the oven, too, because the kitchen smelled like the inside of a cinnamon roll, rich and buttery. He inhaled. "Wow. Something smells amazing."

She didn't look up.

Was it just him, or did those rosy apple cheeks suddenly look pale?

Somewhere a timer dinged. Clearly avoiding his eyes, Ruby brushed past him, the scent of vanilla and brown sugar trailing behind her.

Damn. Was it the kitchen that smelled so good, or was it her? He leaned back against the countertop and let himself watch her hips sway as she bent to slide the tray of cinnamon rolls out of the oven. When she turned around, he was still watching her. She paused, bracing the tray of fresh, plump cinnamon rolls out in front of her, and if he wasn't hard before, well... what could he say? He had a weakness for baked goods. And curves. It'd been a while since he'd let himself appreciate the finer parts of a woman. Kaylee'd put a stop to that last year when he'd caught her in bed with Jace. That'd been enough to curb his libido. Until he'd noticed Ruby, that was.

"Um. Do you need something?" the woman asked, her neck splotching.

"Yeah." Grinning, Sawyer pulled out a stool from the kitchen island. "I need a cinnamon roll."

Her eyes flared wide. "Excuse me?"

"After what you put me through earlier, I think I *deserve* a cinnamon roll." He gave his best puppy-dog look. The one that'd always worked with Kaylee. "Don't you?"

"Oh." She slid the tray on top of the oven and swiped the back of her hand across her forehead. "Sure. Yeah. That's fine." If her rigid posture was any indication, it wasn't fine. Not to her, at least. But that didn't bother him much. Hanging out in the kitchen would give him the chance to get to know her better, to figure out what she was hiding. For Bryce's sake. Not that it would be torture to spend the extra time with her or anything.

Without a word, Ruby hurried to the cabinet next to the fridge and pulled out a plate. Using a huge spatula, she scooped out a mountainous cinnamon roll, then smothered it with a creamy homemade frosting.

He'd be lying if he said his mouth wasn't watering.

When she slid the plate in front of him, he was pretty sure her hand trembled.

"Thanks," he said cheerfully.

She turned away. *Yeah.* She was definitely doing her best to avoid him, but he wasn't about to make it easy for her. "Can I have a fork?" he asked politely. Not to be a bastard or anything, but he was enjoying this more than he should've.

"Oh. Sure. Of course," she sputtered, her face glowing with a sheen of perspiration. Man, he'd seen a convicted felon hold up better during an interrogation in the box.

Ruby handed him the fork, then sprinted back to her mixer, which was still whirring away.

He watched her all the way. Damn, she had a nice ass. Especially in those tight jeans. Of course, analyzing the curve of her ass wasn't exactly part of his mission. Now was not the time for him to get sidetracked by a woman. Not after everything he'd been through with Kaylee in the past two years. If there was one thing *that* whole experience had taught him, it was how to recognize when a woman was keeping secrets. And Ruby definitely had something to hide. Which meant he had to keep himself in check. No matter how perfect her ass was.

Averting his eyes, he sawed off a bite of cinnamon roll and slipped it into his mouth. *Damn.* The woman could bake. The buttery frosting melted in his mouth and there it was again—that flare of desire. The one that had been hibernating in the cave of his disappointment. Doing his best to stuff it back down, he focused on eating.

Across the kitchen Ruby flicked off the mixer and detached the bowl. She peered into whatever it was she was making and frowned. He took the opportunity to get her talking. First thing he had to do was establish credibility. Interrogation 101. So he took another bite, moaning slightly for effect. Then he licked the fork. "Best cinnamon roll I've ever tasted. Seriously." That was no lie. "You've got a gift, Ruby."

"Glad you like it," she rasped, still studying the contents of her mixing bowl.

He set down the fork. "How long have you been working here again?"

"Almost a year." She dumped a mound of dough onto the countertop and pressed her hands into it.

"Where're you from?" he asked, trying to distract himself from the way her hands kneaded the dough roughly into a flat square. He'd be willing to bet those hands of hers were pretty damn capable.

She froze. "Um. I'm from out east."

"Out east" could've meant a thousand different things, but now he remembered. Months ago, when he'd pulled her over for parking illegally, she had North Carolina plates. "That's right. North Carolina."

"How'd you—"

"I pulled you over once, remember?" She'd been with Paige Harper at the time, who was once a guide at the Walker Mountain Ranch. Now she was married to Ben Noble, gazillionaire and one of Bryce's best friends. The two of them owned their own ranch where Paige did equine therapy.

It was weird when he'd approached the car that day. Ruby hadn't even looked at him. Hadn't said one word. He'd thought she was just shy, but that day she'd acted exactly the way she was acting now—her gaze shifting, her face flaming.

Sawyer finished off the cinnamon roll and chewed thoughtfully. He'd never gotten around to asking for Ruby's insurance information or registration. Come to think of it, he'd never even gotten a look at her driver's license.

"Can I get you anything else?" she asked with a squeak of insecurity. Yet another evasive maneuver.

"Nah." He stood and carted his dishes over to the sink, rinsing them the way Aunt Elsie had trained him to do. After securing them in the dishwasher, he turned to Ruby. She'd gone back to kneading the bread dough.

"So where in North Carolina?" he asked, leaning back, crossing his legs at the ankles.

"Charlotte area," she answered quickly, like this was an interrogation instead of a friendly conversation.

"That's quite a ways from Aspen," he observed. "Is your family still there?"

At the mention of family, a dark expression dulled her skin's radiant glow. "I'm sorry, Sawyer, but I don't have time to talk." She didn't sound sorry. The waver in her tone made her sound downright scared. "The kids will be back soon and I have a lot of work to do."

"Right. Sure." He straightened and gathered up his tools. "I should get ready for my shift, anyway." For another few seconds Sawyer watched her knead that dough, noting how stiff her movements were, how she kept her head down, her eyes lowered. Typical nonverbal cues of a guilty party.

What the hell was Ruby James hiding?

He obviously wasn't going to find out today. She'd completely shut down. Good thing he had one more month in Aspen.

"Guess I'll see you around," he said, then walked out the door.

Oh, yeah. He'd make sure he saw plenty of Ruby James.

CHAPTER THREE

Crash! A whole mixing bowl of flour hit the floor, resounding like the clatter of a cymbal. Ruby stared down at the white, powdery mess now scattered around Elsie's gleaming ceramic-tiled floors. *Damn it.* It was the third bowl she'd dropped since Sawyer left the kitchen three hours ago.

"Oh, my!" Elsie Walker yelped, rushing out from the pantry. She was the quintessential storybook grandmother, short and petite with coiffed white hair and those luminous blue eyes that seemed to run in the family. Though wrinkled from years of laughter and happy smiles, her skin had a radiant glow that Ruby envied.

"Are you all right, dear?" The woman flew to the cabinet underneath the kitchen sink and dug out the hand broom. Again.

"I'm fine," she assured her, but the words were hollow.

Her hands hadn't stopped shaking since the whole scene with Sawyer.

"You seem skittish today," Elsie probed as she swept up the pile of flour. "You've been acting like a spooked cat all morning."

Was it that obvious? Ruby shoved her bangs out of her eyes. "Sorry. Just tired, I guess."

"Why don't you go on home, then?" Elsie rose as graceful and composed as ever and scurried over to dump the flour in the trash. "I can take care of things today. It's high time you took a day off, anyway. It's been months."

Ruby sighed and fisted her hands so they'd stop throbbing with the hard pound of her heart. "That's okay. I have to finish up these cookies for the kids." And what would she do at home? Worry about Sawyer. Overanalyze everything she'd said that morning. Give herself an ulcer.

That's how her stomach had felt ever since he'd questioned her...*touched* her...like a hole was burning straight through her. Could he tell she was nervous? He sure seemed suspicious. And she'd obviously been flustered, with all of that sputtering and blushing. It didn't help that Sawyer Hawkins was utterly and completely gorgeous. Tall, dark, and hot. Lordy, he was the kind of man who would fluster her even without all the questions!

"Ruby?" Elsie waved a hand in front of her face.

She shook the image of Sawyer out of her head. "Sorry. What?"

"I asked you if you've seen the new pantry shelves Sawyer installed this morning."

Even the sound of his name on the woman's lips gave her heart a serious jolt. "Um. No. I mean, yes." Technically she'd seen the shelves, albeit very briefly when she'd hit him where it counts. "He's very nice." Heat engulfed her

face. "Wait. I mean the shelves. The *shelves* are very nice."
Holy Moses, what was the matter with her? She couldn't
even talk!

Elsie's lips pursed into a sly smile. "So you saw Sawyer,
then, did you?"

Ruby shoved up the sleeves of her thermal Henley. She
really had to start wearing tank tops to work. The hot ovens
in there practically boiled the air. "Um, yes. I saw him."
*Nailed him with my rolling pin, potentially damaging his fu-
ture ability to have children...*

She squeezed her eyes shut. She could just see the jokes
and comments that knowledge would draw from the rest of
the employees at their next Wednesday night dinner.

"He's a looker, that Sawyer. Isn't he, dear?" Elsie asked
in her innocent little-old-lady voice. As if she wasn't fishing
for Ruby's innermost thoughts. Which she had to keep
anonymous.

"He is nice-looking," she agreed, because she couldn't
deny the obvious.

"Nice person, too." Elsie's tone prompted her to agree.

"I wouldn't know—"

Elsie's phone went off, blaring "Rocky Mountain High."

Whew! Ruby turned back to the mixing bowl. Saved by
John Denver.

"This is Elsie," the woman said, sounding slightly disappointed to have been interrupted from such an important
conversation. "What?" Her shocked gasp spun Ruby
around.

The woman's face had gone white. "Oh, dear lord," she
seemed to choke out. "Is everyone all right?"

The burning sensation in Ruby's stomach sharpened into
a stabbing pain. The kids. It must be Bryce. Something had
happened. Legs numbing, she rushed to Elsie's side.

"We'll be right there," Elsie said, gesturing for Ruby to follow her out the back door. Jogging down the steps, the woman shoved her phone in her pocket. "There's been an accident. We have to get to the trailhead," she huffed out, and Ruby wasn't sure her legs would keep working.

"One of the kids?" she managed as she and Elsie raced down the dirt road at the back of the lodge. The sun seemed blinding instead of bright and warm, and the trees looked fuzzy.

"No. It's Thomas. He fell."

Thomas Richmond, the retired pediatrician who'd started a foundation to help foster kids develop self-esteem and a sense of worth. He organized the trips to the ranch every year. Such a kind man. Ruby had met him only a couple of times. He had to be in his late sixties..."Is he okay?"

"Bryce didn't say." Elsie yanked up the utility garage's door and hopped into the driver's seat of one of the ranch's two-seater ATVs. She snatched a black helmet off the dash and shimmied it onto her head, transforming her into something that resembled a badass biker grandma. "Get in, dear. We have to hurry."

"Are you sure we should drive? Maybe we should walk..." Nearly once a month Ruby heard a news story about some horrible ATV accident that'd maimed or killed someone.

"Get in!" Elsie turned the key in the ignition. There was a toe-curling grinding noise, then the engine roared.

"Okay, okay." Ruby carefully slid into the passenger side and fumbled with the buckle on her seat belt. Elsie plunked a helmet down on her head and cinched the chinstrap tight.

"Hold on!" The woman gunned the engine like it was a souped-up race car and peeled out of the garage in reverse, sending gravel and dirt flying.

"Holy Moses!" The momentum stole Ruby's breath. Her head jerked with Elsie's frantic tugs on the wheel. "Is this safe?" she yelled over the engine.

"Of course!" Elsie yelled back. "I've driven this thing once. How hard can it be?" She cranked the gear into drive and hit the gas.

"Once?" Ruby squealed, but the wind stole the words. The ATV shot straight up the side of a hill and through the forest. "Tree!" she screamed.

Elsie swerved. "I see it! Calm down, dear!"

Calm down? How could she calm down when Elsie was dodging evergreens like they were on one of those crazy closed slalom courses in all the car commercials that had *do not attempt* at the bottom of the screen. Her hands plunged to her sides so she could hold herself in the seat. *Oh, god! Oh, dear god. I don't want to die!*

Finally the machine skidded to a stop. The engine quieted, though the pound and swoosh of blood pumping through her still echoed in her ears. Ruby opened her eyes. Not far in front of them Paige, Bryce, and Shooter huddled around Thomas, who was sitting on the ground with his leg propped up on a backpack.

The kids were clustered a few feet away, each of them staring at their leader with expressions that ranged from concern to deep fear. That was all Ruby needed to see to get her stable enough to walk. She stood and pulled off the helmet, leaving it on the seat.

Elsie rushed to Thomas. "What happened? Oh, Thomas, just look at you!"

The man's silver hair was slicked with sweat and his face was pale. "It's nothing," he insisted, but the grimace gave him away.

"It's his leg," Bryce said. "He fell about a mile up the trail."

"Pretty sure it's broken," Paige added. "Shooter got him down."

"It's not broken," Thomas corrected in his gruff tenor. "Just a bruise, that's all."

Ruby stood back while Elsie knelt. "Let me take a look," the woman said, carefully rolling up his pant leg.

Knowing he was in good hands with Elsie and Paige, Ruby decided to check on the kids. They quieted as she approached. She'd met them briefly last week before they'd left for the backpacking trip, but she knew from experience they didn't trust easily. There were four boys and four girls, all ranging in age from eight to thirteen. In typical preteen fashion, the boys stood on one side of the circle and the girls stood on the other.

"Hey, how are you guys holding up?" Ruby asked, maintaining a distance that would make them feel comfortable. It had to be traumatic seeing someone get hurt out on the trail.

"Is he gonna be all right?" Javon, the oldest boy, asked. Though his pants were low enough to expose his red underwear, he seemed pretty responsible for a thirteen-year-old. Everyone else kind of looked up to him, and Elsie had mentioned he'd asserted himself as the group's spokesperson early on.

Ruby glanced over at Thomas, who appeared to be arguing with Elsie about something. "I think he'll be fine." He sure looked as feisty as ever.

"He couldn't walk," said a small voice from the back of the group.

Ruby stepped closer and noticed Brooklyn, the youngest of all of them at eight years old. She was a small beauty, with dark curly hair, thick black eyelashes, and olive skin. The sight of the girl's wide, scared eyes gouged at her heart.

She knelt in front of her. "He did hurt his leg, but I bet a doctor can fix it real easily."

The girl nodded, biting her lip, and Ruby wondered what those young, wise eyes had seen in her short eight years. Probably too much. Kids didn't end up in the foster system unless things were pretty bad.

The girl was still chewing on her lip as though fighting tears.

Ruby held out her hand. "I'll take you over to see him, if you want."

Brooklyn's eyes widened like she was scared, but she slipped her hand into Ruby's.

"There's nothing to be afraid of," she murmured softly. "Bryce, Elsie, Paige, and Shooter will take good care of him." From the looks of things, it appeared Thomas might not be making it easy for them, either.

"Brooklyn is worried about you," Ruby called over, mainly to warn him they were approaching.

In an instant the man's face softened. "Nothing to worry about, sweetheart. I'm fine. It hardly hurts at all."

Brooklyn eased her grip on Ruby's hand.

"See?" Ruby bent so she could look into the girl's eyes. "He'll be just fine, honey."

Elsie pushed off the ground. "Of course he will," she said. "But he'll definitely need to see a doctor about that leg."

Paige stood, too. "I'm afraid it could be a bad break." Ruby read the concern on her face. Her friend had her Wilderness EMT certification, so she'd know better than anyone. "I think we should call an ambulance."

"No ambulance," Thomas growled, but covered it up with a cough when he noticed Brooklyn staring at him, thank goodness. "I mean, there's no need for that," he said kindly.

Bryce and Shooter looked at each other, and even though Ruby didn't know them well, she could read their faces. He needed treatment.

Thomas may be slightly gruff and combative with other adults, but Ruby happened to know he melted like dark chocolate when it came to these foster kids. Hiding a smile, she looked down at Brooklyn. "Would it make you feel better if Thomas went to the hospital?" she asked loudly enough for everyone—especially him—to hear.

"Mmm hmmm," the girl murmured, nodding.

Thomas's sigh was loud and disgruntled, but a small smile tugged at his lips, too. "All right, then. If it'll make Brookie feel better, I'll see a doctor. But *not* in an ambulance."

"That's fine. We can drive you down to the truck in the ATV," Bryce said, lowering himself next to Thomas. He slung one of the man's arms around his shoulders.

Shooter got on the other side of him and together they hoisted him up, half carrying him to the ATV.

"I'll come with," Elise said, following behind them, and Ruby wondered about her connection to Thomas. She'd heard he'd lost his wife six years ago, and she happened to know that Elsie had been a friend of theirs for years...

"We'll get the kids back down to the lodge," Paige said, smiling at Ruby.

"Yep, no problem," she agreed. "I even just took a batch of double-chocolate-chip cookies out of the oven," she said to get them all smiling again.

Brooklyn squeezed her hand and smiled up at her, fear gone, those eyes sparkling.

That's exactly what she'd wanted to see in the kids' eyes. Hope. That was the hardest thing to hold on to when you were separated from the people you loved most in the world.

She'd lost hope for so many years, but now, this place—

these mountains—had given it back to her, and she wanted to share that same gift with these kids. Now that they were back at the lodge, she could be more involved. She could get to know them and tell them the safe parts of her story.

But most of all she could make sure they had nothing to worry about.

She could make sure nothing else went wrong.

CHAPTER FOUR

Every time Sawyer walked through the doors to the Walker Mountain Ranch office, it hit like a sucker punch to the gut. It wasn't the décor. Bryce and Avery had gone all out in that department. Massive log beams held up the vaulted ceiling. Custom prints by John Fields decked out the walls. To the right there was a black granite countertop set on pecan cabinetry—he should know; he'd helped Bryce build the damn thing. Then on the opposite side of the room leather couches sat near the solid black pub tables next to the coffee counter, complete with an espresso machine and Aunt Elsie's famous baked goods case. The place looked like something out of that *Million Dollar Log Homes* magazine he'd seen lying around at the station.

As posh as it was, walking into the place still got to him. Mostly because Kaylee used to work there. She'd stand at that very counter, taking reservations, checking in the guests. Damn, would that ever stop bugging him? Would he ever be able to walk in here and not think about her? Or maybe not so much her, but about the baby?

Now the reception area sat empty. They'd been looking to hire someone new since Kaylee'd cheated on him and quit, but they hadn't found anyone yet. For the time being, Avery was filling in.

Speaking of...she rushed out from one of the back storage rooms. "Oh, hey, Sawyer." A tired smile didn't meet her eyes. She always seemed tired these days. Not surprising, given the fact that she had a new baby.

"Morning." He made it to the counter and peered over at Lily, who slept contentedly in her bassinette behind the counter.

God, she was tiny. His baby boy would've been almost two by now. He would've been walking, talking, laughing, tossing the football...

"Everything okay?" Avery asked, breaking through the fog of memories.

He tore his gaze away from Lily. "Uh. Yeah. Everything's great." Forcing a smile, he attempted to loosen the tangle of grief that'd snagged in his chest. "Just wanted to talk to the boss before I head back to my cabin."

"He's in his office." She gestured to a door off to the left. "But beware, he's trying to figure out something on the computer. You know how that usually goes." Her grin poked fun at her husband. Those two were always doing that with each other. Teasing, flirting, touching. God, he couldn't wait to get out of here. Start over someplace else. While he was happy for them, it hadn't been easy to be around those two for the past year while he watched his own marriage disintegrate into nothing.

"Thanks, Avery," he said, then nodded toward the baby because he wasn't a complete dick. "She's growing fast."

"I know." Avery sighed. "Too fast. Sometimes at night I hold her extra long so I'll always remember how tiny she was."

A dull ache tugged at his ribs. Before Kaylee's miscarriage he'd imagined what it would be like to hold his child, and even though the baby hadn't yet been born, blood would flow through his arms, warm and thick. It would slowly seep into his body, like a craving about to be satisfied. He'd imagined a lot. He'd pictured doing all the things his own father had done with him—the horsey rides, the tackle football games in the living room, much to his mother's horror. Sawyer had idolized his father. Always had, always would, and he'd imagined he'd have that same bond with his son.

God, his son. For a long time he'd been able to ignore what he'd lost. But since Lily had been born, it'd gotten harder for him. Seeing her tiny face, the blond fluff on her head, those round blue innocent eyes...it made him wonder what his own child would've looked like. Would he have had blue eyes like his? Or dark, exotic eyes like Kaylee's?

"You want me to get Bryce for you?" Avery asked with obvious concern.

"Nah." He stuffed that grief down deep, where it belonged. "I'll stop in his office." Keeping his gaze safely off the baby, he walked away from the counter and pushed open Bryce's door. "Hey, Chief."

Bryce was three months older than Sawyer, and he never let him forget it. Now it'd turned into a joke. He always addressed his cousin with some superior phrase.

"What's the latest on Thomas?" During his shift Bryce had called him to ask if he could give Thomas a ride to the hospital, seeing as how the man refused an ambulance. Not that Sawyer blamed him. He probably would've done the same thing. Not like he'd been busy, anyway. Pretty slow day around Aspen. But that was spring for you. The shoulder season between skiing and summer hiking. Not many tourists. And hell, at least he'd gotten to use his siren for once. It'd been a while.

"We're still waiting to hear," Bryce said, kneading his forehead like it'd been a hell of a day. "Apparently some trauma victim came into the ER."

Yeah, Sawyer had heard there'd been some accident on Independence Pass, but he hadn't been put on the call.

"They've had Thomas waiting in a room all afternoon. At least Paige is with him. She'll keep on the doctors."

Typical day at the Aspen ER. "Sure looked broken to me," Sawyer said. He'd seen enough broken bones to spot one.

"Yeah. Which means I'll have to find someone else to help out the rest of the week. We've still got the ropes course and zipline coming up. And I wanted to take them to the rec center tomorrow night. A couple of them mentioned they'd never been swimming, so I thought we could teach them the basics before we open up the pool here."

"Sure. I can help out." Seeing as how he'd been on the high school swim team that'd be no problem. He might be rusty, but he could brush up.

"I'd ask Paige to step in, but she's already taking them horseback riding and Ben needs her at the ranch. Ruby's helping out, too, but Mom'll still need her in the kitchen sometimes."

Huh. Sawyer stepped into the office. Ruby was helping out, too. What luck. That might be the perfect opportunity for him to figure her out. "I should be able to get a few days off." He had plenty of vacation time to burn before his last day. "Just let me know when."

Relief eased the tension on his cousin's face. "Thanks.

That'd be great." Bryce's gaze drifted back to the computer screen in front of him. He clicked the mouse a few times.

He looked busy, but Sawyer had more on the agenda. "I got those shelves installed this morning." Not that he had to give Bryce a report, but it'd be the perfect opportunity to bring up a certain baker and the weird exchange he'd had with her before his shift.

"Nice." Bryce picked up a coffee mug and drank it like he was having a hard time staying awake. Which he probably was, considering he'd just been on a four-day backpacking trip with a bunch of kids.

"Thanks, man," he said. "Mom'll pay you with an apple pie."

"No need. Think of it as room and board." When he'd asked Bryce if he could stay at the ranch, his cousin wouldn't even consider taking rent. That was just the kind of guy Bryce was.

Thoughts of Ruby flitted back into his mind. Bryce was also the kind of guy who hired employees without doing background checks when someone desperately needed a job. And, while he wished he had Bryce's faith in people, he'd learned that when someone looked suspicious, there was usually a reason. Hence his increasing desire to figure out Ruby before something went wrong.

After a second of hesitation, he walked into the office and sat himself down in the chair across from Bryce. "Thanks for letting me hang here while I wrap things up."

Bryce turned away from the computer and leaned back in his chair, his eyes narrowed on him. "You sure about all this? Leaving town? Life in the big city?"

They'd had this conversation at least five times since Sawyer'd put the house on the market last month. It wasn't ideal, but Denver was the only place he'd found a job.

And he couldn't stay in Aspen. Not when the memories of Kaylee were everywhere. Their first kiss had been on the ski slopes. Elevation 8000 was where he'd proposed. And don't get him started on the ranch. Last Christmas, hanging around for all the holiday activities alone almost killed him.

"I need to get away for a while." Someplace where everyone didn't know what had happened. Someplace where five people didn't stop him to ask how he was "holding up" in one morning at the grocery store. He'd had enough of the "poor betrayed Sawyer" routine.

"I get it." A sigh contradicted Bryce's words. "Sorry things didn't work out for you and Kaylee."

Everyone was sorry. No one more than him. "Yeah." There wasn't much more to say.

But that didn't stop most people from trying, including Bryce. *Wait for it...*

"You want to talk about it?"

"Nope." He didn't worry about his cousin taking that the wrong way. After Bryce's first wife had died, neither one of them had said much. Hell, they'd sit across the table from each other drinking beer after beer, neither one of them saying a damn thing.

Unfortunately since Bryce had married Avery, who *never* quit talking, he didn't seem to take the hint.

"After Yvonne, I never thought I'd get married again," Bryce said. "Hell, I didn't think I'd ever look at anyone again." He leaned into the desk. "Kaylee did a shitty thing, Sawyer, but not all women are like that."

He hesitated. Everyone assumed the same thing. That he'd been screwed over...the devoted husband who'd been blindsided. But there was a hell of a lot more to the story than that. Now that the divorce was official, he'd had plenty of time to analyze it, and he couldn't let everyone believe it was all her fault. Fact was, he'd played a part, too. And it was time he faced it. "I don't blame her for ending up in Jace's bed."

Bryce's jaw dropped. "I sure as hell do. She knew what she was doing. "

Course she knew. But she had her reasons. And it was time to tell his cousin that. They'd been through hell together. If anyone would understand, it was Bryce. Sawyer's fists knotted, but he stared the man in the face. "Kaylee had a miscarriage a while back. At five months."

Bryce's hand let go of the computer mouse.

Yeah, he'd gotten his full attention.

"Damn, Sawyer. I didn't know. I'm sorry."

Again, not much to say. Not like sorry changed anything. "Yeah. Me too."

"Why didn't you tell me?" he demanded. "Man, five months. You lost a baby. We could've done a service or something."

That's why he hadn't told anyone. Kaylee didn't want to make it a big deal. "She didn't want anyone to know. It didn't seem to get to her as much." Pain worked its way up his body until it felt like someone had shoved his stomach up into his chest. "She didn't know if she ever wanted kids, anyway." At least that's what she said before they'd gotten married. *Let's not rush it, Sawyer. If it happens, it happens.* But apparently she hadn't thought it would happen. He glanced at Bryce. "I talked about doing a service. I mean, we saw him on the ultrasound." He'd had tiny little hands and feet. A beautiful face. He was their baby boy. At least, that was how he'd thought of him. They'd even talked about naming him Matthew, after Dad. "But she wouldn't consider it. I was mad as hell." That night they had the worst fight they'd ever had. She was screaming at him to get

over it. *Just get over it, Sawyer. Move on. There's no baby.*
Then…"I asked her why she'd miscarried, if it was something she did." Shame covered his face, hot and dry.

"Holy shit." Bryce's head tipped back with disbelief.
"She wouldn't have done it on purpose. Those things just
happen."

"I know. I lost my head. Wasn't thinking straight."
Truth was, it was easier for him to get mad, to blame her.
For a while it curbed the pain, the empty feeling left behind by loss. "A few days later, I told her I was sorry,
but things went south from there. She never looked at me
the same. And good ol' Jace was waiting in the wings."
Damn, the power of words. Those words he'd said to her
had broken something in both of them. That was on him.
He'd made a mistake that'd ruined his marriage, and he
had to own it.

"That's why you're leaving," Bryce said slowly, as if
putting the pieces together.

If anyone had earned the right to call him out on that, it
was Bryce. But the words still stabbed at him. Did he even
have a right to grieve? How could he grieve something he'd
never had? "I need a new start." A new place. New memories. A new focus.

"We'll miss you around here," Bryce said, but at least
he didn't try to talk him out of it again. "Don't know
who the hell is gonna keep an eye on the place with you
gone." He said it like a joke, but there was some truth to it.
Sawyer has consulted for him on the security system for
the ranch. He'd evaluated all their risk protocols.

Speaking of…

"Hey, what d'you know about Ruby James?"

"Not…*much*," Bryce said slowly, as though thrown off
by the fast change of subject.

But Sawyer had to plow ahead. Best to start his mission now or he wouldn't have time to complete it before he left. "Doesn't that concern you?"

Bryce waved him off. "Nah. Mom trusts her."

He gave his cousin a stern look. "She trusts everyone."

"She's got good intuition."

Yeah. Intuition never solved any crimes. Facts. Evidence. Those were the only sure bets. This whole thing with Ruby was simply highlighting a larger issue at the Walker Mountain Ranch. You couldn't just let some random person come and work for you. No wonder things had been disappearing. Last week about three hundred dollars had gone missing from the office. Then there was a diamond bracelet Avery couldn't seem to find. Bryce had chalked it up to them misplacing things, but Sawyer wasn't so sure. "Has Avery found her bracelet?" he asked nonchalantly.

"No. She thought she left it in the kitchen, but we've looked everywhere."

In the kitchen, huh? He didn't say it. "What about the cash?"

His cousin shook his head in frustration. "I can't figure out what I did with it. I swear it was in the bank bag, but..."

It had disappeared, too.

"You think someone took it?" he asked, hoping to plant the idea in Bryce's head. Because it was pretty obvious to him that someone had been stealing from his cousin.

"The thought's crossed my mind," he admitted, albeit grudgingly. Bryce, like Aunt Elsie, tended to see only the best in people.

Lucky for both of them, Sawyer had learned not to. "Let me look into it," he offered, not that he'd let Bryce turn him down.

"What'd you have in mind?"

MORE THAN A FEELING

"Well…" He had to tread carefully here. The Walker Mountain Ranch was known for unyielding loyalty to its employees. "What if it was an employee? Then it'll happen again." It would keep happening. And eventually three hundred dollars here and a bracelet there would add up.

His cousin shot him a skeptical frown, as if that was outside the realm of possibility. "You really think it's an employee?"

"I think it could be." There were plenty to choose from. This spring they'd hired three new guides, though they weren't full-time yet. Then there were the seasonal maintenance workers who'd just started back a month ago. And Ruby. "Did Ruby ever fill out an application?"

"It's not Ruby," Bryce said, shaking his head. "She's not the type."

Maybe not, but someone around here had to be open to all possibilities. "Most criminals don't seem like the type," he said.

Bryce laughed. "You're one suspicious SOB, you know that?"

"It's a hazard of the job," Sawyer reminded him. "Look. It doesn't have to be a big deal. I'll look around, ask some questions. No one'll even know." Especially the people he planned to investigate. All that would require is some good one-on-one time with them. He stood to leave. "I'll keep you posted. Let me know the report on Thomas when you hear."

"Will do," Bryce said, then looked up suddenly. "Speaking of Thomas…think you could hike up to the waterfall and get the gear we left behind this morning? After he fell Shooter and I dropped everything. I'd go but I've got to finish this injury report for insurance."

"Sure." Sawyer glanced at the clock on the wall. Just after four-thirty. It was only a mile and a half to the lake. That should give him plenty of time before dinner.

Bryce stood and came around the desk. "The gear is on the south side of the pond." He walked Sawyer to the door. "We left at least three packs behind. You might need help to lug it all back."

"Help, huh?" He almost grinned. He needed someone to join him on an hour-long hike to the waterfall.

And he knew just the girl.

CHAPTER FIVE

Nothing soothed the tension in Ruby like the rich scent of chocolate buttercream frosting. She inhaled the buttery cocoa and leaned closer to the cupcake so she could pipe the frosting in a floral design.

"I'm willing to bet those kids have never seen such a work of art," Elsie commented, coming to stand by her.

Smiling, Ruby piled the frosting as high as she could without the whole thing toppling over. "It's my favorite cupcake. Triple chocolate." She straightened and reached for the dark chocolate flakes she'd grated earlier.

"Well, it's soon to be their favorite, too," Elsie said, going back to the pot of Bolognese sauce that simmered on the stove. "As long as they eat a good dinner, that is."

"I'm sure they will." Warmth bubbled up, making her feel as excited as a kid herself. Talk about the perfect evening. Right now the kids were all getting settled into their rooms, freshening up, then resting until dinner. But then there'd be gourmet pasta, chocolate cupcakes for dessert, and a campfire complete with s'mores and songs. It would be the perfect evening, a way for them to forget Thomas's injury and have some fun.

Satisfied with the cupcakes, she turned to Elsie. "Can I do anything else to help with din—"

The back door opened and cut her off.

"Hey." Sawyer sauntered in, this time in a crisp navy-blue uniform that fit snug around his broad shoulders.

Ruby's heart dove straight into her molten stomach. What was he doing here?

"Sawyer!" Elsie rushed over to hug him. "That pantry's a miracle, I'll tell you what. You're so talented."

He seemed to brush aside the compliment with a shrug. "It was the least I could do, seeing as how that no-good son of yours won't let me pay rent."

"Rent! Don't be ridiculous. You're family, dear. You can't pay rent," Elsie gushed, and Ruby was grateful he had a distraction. Maybe he'd leave her alone.

"How about a triple chocolate cupcake?" the older woman tempted. "Ruby just finished frosting them."

"I do love Ruby's cupcakes," Sawyer said. The compliment had a formal ring to it. He could've been offering it to a complete stranger, but the words still stirred something in her heart. Her face heated again. She turned back to the counter so he wouldn't notice.

"Did you hear that, Ruby?" Elsie asked from behind her. "Sawyer paid you a compliment." Not responding was rude, and if there was one thing Elsie Walker didn't tolerate, it was rudeness.

"Thank you, Sawyer," she murmured, her throat thick with fear. Why had he come back? For the past year he'd hardly been in the kitchen at all, and now in one day, she'd seen him twice.

"You're welcome," he replied through a mouthful of cupcake. "Oh, and by the way, I'm sorry I scared you this morning."

"What?" Elsie broke in. "How on earth did he scare you?"

Knowing there was no way out of it, Ruby turned around, but she didn't dare look at Sawyer. "I wasn't expecting to see anyone when I got here." She shot him a quick glare but found it difficult to look directly into that beautiful, calming blue for too long. "That's all." She narrowed her eyes in a plea for him to agree. That was all. *Don't bring up the rolling pin incident. Please.* Then Elsie would wonder why she'd attacked him.

Sawyer shot her a small smirk full of understanding. When their eyes connected, it turned into a full-fledged tempting grin. Except she couldn't be tempted. Not by a cop. Not by anyone. She couldn't risk her secret.

Before he could say anything else, Ruby turned back to the cupcakes and started to stack them on the tiered cake plate.

"So what are you up to this evening, Sawyer?" Elsie asked as she clanged a spoon around the pot on the stove.

"Actually I'm going for a hike," he said, and why did it feel like he was still staring at her?

"Bryce asked me to run up to the waterfall and get the gear they left behind this morning."

Footsteps got louder behind her. Sawyer leaned into the counter and looked her over.

"Don't think I can get it all myself, so I thought I'd stop in and see if you could come with me."

"Now there's an idea!" Elsie chirped.

Ruby squeezed her eyes shut. Damn. Damn, damn, damn. "I can't," she answered without looking at him.

"Of course you can," Elsie insisted. "You never get out, and Sawyer needs help."

Somehow she doubted that. The man was built like a lightweight boxing champion. Surely he could handle a couple of backpacks.

"Yeah. I need help." Sawyer's smile grew like he knew he'd just trapped her.

The heat from her face traveled south. She looked around frantically. "But...I...don't have any hiking boots or anything."

"You can borrow mine!" Elsie retrieved a pair from the cabinet near the back door and handed them to her. "They might be a tad big for your petite feet, but they should work just fine."

Her lips stiffened into a plastic smile. Who the hell kept hiking boots in their kitchen?

"You'll absolutely love hiking, Ruby," the woman went on. "It's the best way to see the mountains. There's nothing like it."

Ruby stared at the boots in her hand. She'd been there only a year and for half that time, the ground had been covered with snow. She *could* like to hike, or at least it seemed like something she might enjoy. Possibly. The solitude, the quietness. But not with Officer Hawkins trailing behind her, asking her questions, digging into her past.

"You know, I actually have a lot to finish up here." She tried to hand back the boots. "I still haven't mixed the dough for tomorrow's cinnamon raisin bread."

"Nonsense." Elsie chuckled, shoving the boots back at her. "My goodness, dear. Don't be such a workaholic." She *tsk*ed. "I'll take care of everything. You need to get out and enjoy the day. You've been skittish since I came in. The fresh air'll do you some good."

Sawyer raised one of those dark eyebrows at her. She could hear the silent *skittish, huh?*

But she refused to give him the satisfaction of knowing he got to her. So instead of panicking and running out the door like the stove was on fire, she simply shrugged. "I guess I'll go. Might be nice to take a break. Thanks, Elsie," she said, lugging the boots over to a chair. She slipped off her clogs and laced up the boots; then she stood and posted her hands on her hips, glaring at Sawyer. "Ready?"

"I have to go change," he said with obvious amusement. "Be back in a few."

Can't wait. While he was gone, she'd have to devise a strategy for how to put him in his place. If she wanted to get Sawyer off her back, she'd have to toughen up.

Meek and mild obviously wasn't going to work.

* * *

He was late. Sawyer trotted out of his guest cabin and hiked down the hill toward the lodge. Okay, maybe he'd gotten carried away...taking a shower, combing his hair, putting on extra deodorant. If he wanted to get to know Ruby—to know *about* her—he'd have to make a good impression. That was the only reason he'd actually bothered to shower.

Yeah. Keep telling yourself that. Cleaning himself up had nothing to do with that fact that his mind kept drifting back to Ruby during his shift, back to the way that red wavy hair of hers draped her narrow shoulders, back to the shy smile that plumped her full cheeks. Wasn't like there'd been much else to focus on while he'd gone on patrol. It'd been a slow day, besides giving Thomas a lift to the hospital. Not even one parking ticket.

So in the absence of anything else to focus on, he'd thought about Ruby. For some reason she was temptation wrapped in an apron. He knew she had something to hide. That was obvious, but she also didn't seem calculated or manipulative the way Kaylee had been. There was this underlying vulnerability to Ruby that he found hard to resist.

And yet he *had* to resist. Because he was leaving. And for the next month, he'd be investigating her. Giving in to temptation would be one big conflict of interest...

At the edge of the ranch's expansive back patio, he stopped.

Ruby was reclined in one of the lounge chairs, her head tipped back, sunglasses on. He edged into the shadow of an evergreen tree, taking the opportunity to study her. Daaamn, she looked like an Irish goddess. She'd shed the thermal shirt she'd had on earlier and was lying out in a tight green tank top, the sun making her hair and skin glow...

What was that nonsense about resisting temptation again?

Her head turned in his direction.

"You ready?" he called impatiently so she wouldn't catch him checking her out. He might have a hard time focusing on anything besides her body, but she didn't need to know that.

Ruby scrambled to her feet and tipped her shades back on her head. "Of course I'm ready." She marched down the steps to meet him. "*I've* been ready for twenty minutes."

"That's a slight exaggeration." It couldn't have taken him more than eighteen to get showered and everything...

"So where are we going?" the woman asked in that rigid new tone she'd adopted. It was a complete turnaround from this morning's mumbling and squeaking. Feisty. Kind of a welcome change. It'd be easier to keep her on the suspect list if he didn't feel sorry for her.

He slipped in front of her, brushing her shoulder along the way. "Up to the falls. Trailhead's not too far. We can walk." The waterfall hike was one of the best-kept secrets at the ranch. All the employees and good friends of the Walkers knew about it, but none of them publicized the small glimpse of environmental perfection.

It left him awestruck every time he saw it, a mountain creek cascading down the side of the cragged slope, splashing and gurgling into a deep spring, clear as the glacial waters in Alaska. It was their place, not a place they wanted to invite just anyone. If word got out, there's no way they'd be able to keep it quiet. They'd have tourists driving up there in droves. It was a gorgeous hike, but more than that, it'd take them a good half hour to get up there, which should give him plenty of time for a proper interrogation.

"How far is it?" Ruby demanded, eyes narrowed into annoyance again.

"A couple miles round trip." He slanted his head and gazed at her. "Why? Have you changed your mind?"

"Nope." She smiled, but her lips were stiff and tight. "Lead the way." She hoisted a small backpack off the ground.

"What's in there?" he asked, not wanting to turn away from her. He could look at the woman all day. But not touch. No. Touching.

"Elsie insisted on packing us some food," she answered, all cold and formal, like she was talking to a used-car salesman.

"Perfect." He tried a friendly smile. Judging from the way she was icing him out, one little push was all she needed to stomp away, get in her car, and drive home. "We can hang out and have a snack at the falls, then." That'd give him a good extra half hour to pry the woman open. "Shouldn't be a difficult hike." He stepped off and led Ruby down the narrow path that curved past the pool and hot tubs, then through a small aspen grove. Her footsteps were steady behind him, but she said nothing.

They passed the stables, then hoofed it up to the modest trailhead he'd helped Bryce build last fall. The whole way Ruby trudged behind him, silent and tense.

Guilt made his skin prickle. He didn't want her to be afraid of him. He only wanted to learn her story. He *had* to learn her story for Bryce's sake. And maybe for his own, too. Because after her panic attack that morning, he couldn't get that vacant look in her eyes out of his head. Why had she automatically assumed he was there to hurt her? He almost didn't want to know the answer.

Where the path wound into the woods, he paused to wait for her. "So how'd you get into baking?" he asked, because he had to start somewhere.

"I got a job at the ranch," she muttered, keeping a good distance between them.

Knowing she wouldn't allow him to walk by her side, he started up the trail, crossing from the sun into patches of shade cast down by the pine trees. He let a few seconds of silence pass before trying again. "What'd you do before the ranch?"

"I was a waitress."

At Hooters? Why did he suddenly have a desire to examine her full chest? He cleared his throat, looked away. "What kind of restaurant?"

Ruby sighed, deep and pained. "A bar."

"Why'd you move to Aspen?" he asked, all friendly and

casual, like he wasn't picturing her in that tight orange Hooters uniform.

"I wanted a new start, okay?" Weariness soaked through the words.

He could relate. That's all he'd wanted for the past year. But he wasn't moving across the country to a place he'd never been, to a place where he didn't know anyone. Even with as ugly as things had gotten with Kaylee, he still wanted to stick close to his family.

Why didn't Ruby?

"So out of all the places in the country, you picked Aspen?" He slowed and snuck a glance back at her.

As far as he'd heard her car had broken down and she had no job, no home, no place to go. Sounded to him like she needed money. So how desperate was she?

The footsteps behind him stopped.

He turned, taking in the reddish hue on her cheeks, the flash of anger in those green eyes.

"Look," she spat. "I'm sure you've heard Elsie took me in. I know how people talk around here. So don't pretend like you don't know anything about me."

It was true. The Walker Mountain Ranch did have a rumor mill. What small business didn't? But even though Ruby worked in the kitchen every day, she seemed to stay on the fringe of everything, rarely attending the staff dinners or the gatherings out by the fire pit. Somehow, in the close-knit community that was the Walker Mountain Ranch, she'd managed to keep to herself.

"I haven't heard much," he said carefully. Because no one seemed to know much. Not even the Walkers.

Blazing past she left him in an angry wake. "Here's the short version of my life story—" She huffed between breaths. "I've been on my own since I was eighteen. No family. No mom or siblings or cousins or aunts to help me out with anything." Her boots pounded the packed dirt trail and he practically had to jog to keep up with her.

"So, yeah. I didn't have much of a reason to stick around North Carolina."

No one? She had no one? Sympathy weighted his gut. How could she be alone in the world? "Sorry," he muttered. He couldn't quite imagine what that'd be like. He'd been raised to live for family. Dad and Mom were the poster children for traditional, loving, supportive parents, despite the fact that they now spent most of their summers traveling. After raising three kids, he supposed they deserved it. His two sisters both lived in Denver now, but he chatted with them a few times a week and they both brought their families to visit as often as they could. Besides all that, he'd grown up with his grandpa and grandma and Aunt Elsie and Bryce, not to mention about twenty other cousins who'd drifted in and out of the area over the past thirty years.

Thinking back now, he couldn't even remember a time where their house wasn't full of loud, obnoxious people sharing a meal or playing Bullshit or celebrating someone's birthday...

Ruby stopped ahead of him. She turned, but her eyes focused on the ground. "When I left North Carolina, I was headed to California." One of her graceful shoulders lifted into a halfhearted shrug. "Thought I'd start over on the opposite side of the country, you know?" Her head lifted and she gazed into his eyes.

The look there nearly stole his breath, so much sadness she almost looked lost, but as quickly as it'd come the expression steeled into determination.

"When my car broke down on Independence Pass, I kind

of loved it here." She looked past him, out at the mountains, and her face took on a gentle softness. "I've never been somewhere so beautiful. So I wanted to stay."

"I can see why," he said, but one thing bothered him. She'd walked away from her life and no one had followed her. No one cared what happened to her.

Sawyer didn't move, didn't divert his gaze away like he should have. A plane could've crashed right behind him and he wouldn't have been able to look away from her. She was so complex, with that fragile strength covering a deep vulnerability.

She didn't look away, either, so he gambled with a few steps closer. "What happened to your family?"

Pain gripped her delicate features before she turned away and resumed a steady climb up the trail. She stepped over a tree branch. Red splotched her neck and ears, but he couldn't tell if it was from the physical exertion or anger. "Why do you care?" she asked.

He wasn't sure how to answer that question. He cared because he wanted to protect his cousin, sure. But... that pang of sympathy was deepening into an ache. What would it be like to have no one?

Thud, thud, thud. Her footsteps moved faster, like she wanted to outrun his question. Except he wouldn't let her.

"So where are they?" Even as the words came out, he hoped to god her family hadn't died in some terrible car crash or something. Talk about feeling like an ass.

"Why are you curious now?" she called over her shoulder. "You've never cared before."

She had a point, but he hadn't bothered caring much about *anyone* during the past year. He'd had other things on his mind. He'd definitely noticed Ruby, though. He may have been pissed off at everything, but he wasn't a robot. A man would have to be blind not to notice Ruby James. She had a memorable face...not to mention that sexy body.

But she sure didn't talk much. He'd never met a quieter woman. Which meant if he had any hope of learning more about her, of assessing her motives at the ranch, he had to open up, too. It was a strategy he'd used a number of times with a suspect. Tell them something about yourself. Get them to trust you. Build rapport. So he chased behind her. "It's not that I didn't notice you," he said. "I just didn't have my head on straight. Divorce'll do that to a guy."

Her steps slowed. She didn't stop, but she peered over her shoulder, the late-afternoon sunshine making her eyes glow. "Right. I heard about that. Sorry."

That actually meant something coming from her. She'd lived a loneliness he couldn't even begin to fathom. "Yeah, it pretty much sucked. I became a hermit for a while there." But lately it'd felt different. Maybe because he knew he was leaving. It was easier to face everyone knowing he wouldn't have to do it much longer. "It's pretty lonely to live that way. Shutting everyone out. I know from experience." The words left an opening, but she didn't take it. That fair skin of hers deepened into crimson. Seeming to ignore the comment, she spun and pumped her arms, keeping a pace that he found hard to match, even though his legs were much longer.

Damn. He'd gone too far. "Hey. Wait up."

But she didn't even turn around. He followed her up a steep series of switchbacks, sweat itching on his forehead.

At the top of the ridge, he jogged up to her, passing her and turning to walk backward. "What did I say?"

Something flashed in her eyes, but before he could read it, she looked down. He turned back around so he could see where he was going. The trail bent and wound through a grove of pine trees, the sweet scent of butterscotch thick in the air.

Then the trees opened into a clearing.

Ruby stopped suddenly. "Wow. Oh, wow."

Sawyer paused next to her to take in the view. It never got old. The creek cascaded over a series of rounded, water-eroded rocks, pooling into a beautiful azure spring surrounded by boulders.

"I had no idea this place was here," she breathed. "It's incredible."

She turned away from him and wandered toward the pool, stepping on the rocks and peering down at the water.

"What makes it so blue?" she asked as though mesmerized.

"It's glacial runoff," he said, working out his footing on the slippery rocks. "That and the pool is much deeper than it looks," he warned. "You might want to be careful." Although he wouldn't mind seeing her go for a swim in that thin green tank top she had on...

Ruby ignored him and moved her foot to the next rock.

"Might be slippery, too, with all that rain last night—"

Sure enough, her boot slipped and she pitched forward, splashing right into the pool's deep water.

CHAPTER SIX

Ruby opened her mouth to scream, but the cold muted it to a muffled squawk. *God!* It was like an ice bath! She gasped. *Oh, oh, oh.* Her feet flailed to find solid footing, but she couldn't touch the bottom. "Help!" she breathed out, bubbles bobbing to the water's surface, arms flailing, legs kicking. But it wasn't enough. Her head sank under the surface, strangling her throat, freezing her muscles. Her lungs burned. Light glowed above her, fading, fading. She kicked her legs, arms waving clumsily with the water's resistance. Her head broke the surface. *Air!* She sucked in, coughed and choked.

Her eyes opened. Sawyer was running at the water. He yelled something…

"Can't swim," she gasped, then choked on the water. Sinking. She was going down again.

A huge splash crashed, rolling waves against her body. His large hands gripped her shoulders and pulled her up and in, against his strong chest. He wrapped his arms around her, those solid muscles tightening into a shield, keeping her up until both of their heads broke the surface.

"Are you okay?" he asked in that gruff way fear had.

The burning sensation in her throat stung her eyes, but she nodded. Except tears built and ran over, mingling with the drops of water that slid down her cheeks.

Wrapping her in tighter, Sawyer hauled her out of the water like she was a child.

On the bank he let her go, but he stayed close, crouching to look into her eyes. Water glistened on his browned skin, and his thick dark hair stuck to his forehead. "You're sure you're fine? Nothing hurts?" Jagged breaths lowered his voice.

"Yes. I'm fine. Really," she said through chattering teeth. But the tremble of fear still reverberated through her bones.

"Hell, I don't know if I am." He exhaled and stood straight, squeezing his eyes shut in a long blink. Then he opened his eyes wide. "You scared the shit out of me, Ruby."

"I can't swim." And she never dreamed the pool would be that deep. It was so deceiving. She'd seen the rocks at the bottom before she fell in...

"Yeah. I got that," he practically growled. But he didn't look mad. He looked...scared.

Humiliation warmed her. "I never learned to swim." When would she have? Between Mama's four-day binges? "No one ever taught me." She hadn't grown up like him, likely going to swimming lessons while his mom snapped photos and cheered him on. Once Ruby'd waded into a creek that ran in a canal down the street from her house. When she'd made it up to her waist, the current swept her away. Grady had run along the bank, screaming at her. Finally their neighbor, the real Ruby James, had heard the commotion. She'd come running and pulled Ruby out of the creek, just as she was losing her breath. On the bank the woman had made sure Ruby was okay, then lectured her about the dangers of water the whole way back to her house. When Miss James had prodded her up the crumbling sidewalk and rang the doorbell, Mama answered. She was in her typical stupor, giggling and stumbling, those eyes red as a snake's. Miss James had taken one look at Mama, then knelt, her face soft and her eyes droopy with sadness. "You promise you'll be more careful, girl?"

She'd nodded, still shuddering from the fear. And from the humiliation of Mama's spectacle.

"All right, then," Miss James had said, without looking at Mama again. "You stay away from that water."

And she had. She'd always stayed away from water because she knew she wouldn't be so lucky next time. She knew she might not have anyone to rescue her. She'd never had anyone to rescue her...

Sawyer swiped a hand down his face. "You have to learn how to swim. You really have to learn," he huffed as though still out of breath.

The throb of fear still pulsed through her, forcing her to reach for his arm. Despite the fact that they were both soaked, his skin felt hot. She glanced up. The sun lit his eyes with a soft warmth.

"I'm sorry. I shouldn't have gotten so close to the edge." It'd been so beautiful it lured her in.

His eyes lowered to stare at the place where her hand clutched him. "No problem." Slowly his gaze worked its way back up her body. "Not every day I get to save a pretty girl."

Despite her better judgment, her lips fumbled with a smile. When was the last time someone had called her pretty? Besides Elsie. She didn't count.

"And this happens to be your lucky day." Sawyer hooked an arm through hers and slowly led her over rock after slippery rock until they'd made it to the grass.

"Why is that?" she asked, feeling the chill of her wet clothes dissipate. Sawyer made her warm. Very, very warm.

"Because I'm teaching the kids how to swim tomorrow night," he informed her. "Not to brag or anything, but I was an all-American swimmer in high school. College, too."

Why was she not surprised? From the little she'd seen of Sawyer, he was incredible at everything he did. Perfect, some might say. Perfect family. Perfect hero on the job. Perfect gentleman whenever a single woman tried to flirt with him. And she couldn't touch perfect.

"Are you planning to come?" One brow raised.

Her lungs contracted as though she'd started to drown again. "I don't know…" It didn't seem smart to spend more time with him than absolutely necessary.

"Don't you want to learn?" Sawyer's head slanted as though he was trying to figure her out. "In case you're hiking and accidentally slip down an embankment?"

"I'll think about it," she promised.

But he shook his head. "No need to think about it. I'll plan on you being there, too. You can help with the lesson."

She knew there was no point in arguing, even if she didn't intend to show up.

"You're okay, right?" Sawyer gazed down at her, still close enough that she could see the faint smile lines around his mouth. And what a perfect mouth…

"I'm fine." She studied the dip in his upper lip, the curve of his small smile.

"Uh...good." He broke away from her. "Okay. I guess we should get Bryce's gear." He started to walk away, but she tugged on his hand until he stopped to face her. Because he'd pulled her out. And now she owed him something.

She inhaled, trying to grasp the courage she always wanted but found so hard to hold on to. "I don't talk about my past because there's a lot I'd rather not remember."

His lips folded, poking a shallow dimple into his right cheek. "Understood."

For a second he looked like he wanted to say something else, but then he shifted behind her and prodded her toward the backpacks. "We should hurry. Get you back to the lodge so you can put on some dry clothes."

Confusion muddled her thoughts. That was it? After all of that questioning earlier, he didn't want to know more? She watched him gather up the bags.

"Ready?" he asked, keeping his distance.

And she couldn't help but wonder why he suddenly seemed desperate to escape.

* * *

Sawyer could've belted out a cheer when the lodge finally came into view. Dry clothes...had to get Ruby into some dry clothes. Any other clothes as long as they weren't thin, wet, and see-through. Because he was definitely seeing through and that made it difficult to think. His gaze slid sideways for another shameless glance. What could he say? She had plenty to show off.

Most of the time he prided himself on keeping his thoughts clean. Not like his buddies who'd gather at the bar and discuss the female anatomy in great detail. He'd always been a one-woman kind of guy. When he was with Kaylee,

he hadn't even wanted anyone else. He'd see a blond, sur-
gically enhanced bombshell who his buddies were lusting
after and she wouldn't do much for him. Because she wasn't
Kaylee. They'd been together so long he'd known every
curve and bend on her body. Instead of getting old it only
made him want her more. It made him feel like they belonged to each other.

But now...seeing Ruby's red hair, wet and curled
against her shoulders, the perfect shape of her breasts underneath her shirt...well that made it a little too easy for him
to imagine all the places he could lick her famous chocolate
buttercream frosting off her body.

"Are you okay?" she asked him as they passed the
ranch's glistening swimming pool.

"Great," he lied. Had she noticed the faster pace? Seriously, he couldn't keep looking at her or he'd be in big
trouble. The outline of her body—of her perfect, creamy
skin underneath that shirt had started to make him ache.
"Just don't want you to get too cold."

"I'm not cold." She smiled back at him.

Neither was he. Not one cell in his body was cold. In
fact, blood rushed hot and fast to every part of him. He
could really use some cold right about now. Maybe a cold
shower...

"Did I even thank you for pulling me out of the water?"
Ruby asked as he hustled her up the steps and across the
lodge's wraparound deck.

Oh, sure. Bring him back to that moment, when he had
her in his arms, crushing her body against his. That was all
he needed to keep his thoughts neutral. "No thanks necessary," he muttered.

She stopped abruptly and hooked her hand around his
forearm, forcing him to face her.

"Seriously, Sawyer. Thank you." Her green eyes glowed with earnest sincerity.

"Sure." *Eyes on her face. Keep your eyes on her face,* he reminded himself. Because underneath that wet shirt the woman had on a lacy bra that hid absolutely nothing. Not that she *should* hide anything, because damn...

Footsteps scuffed the ground behind him. He peered over his shoulder.

Bryce sauntered across the porch.

He let out a breath. Saved by his cousin.

"What the hell happened to you guys?" Bryce asked, his eyes following the trail of water they'd tracked across the porch. He shot Sawyer a hearty smirk. "You take her for a swim or something?"

Ruby's face brightened into a neon glow. Her chin instantly dipped toward her chest. She crossed her arms—covering herself—and stared at the ground, suddenly shy and unsure again.

What made her do that? Retreat into timidity?

Bryce was looking back and forth between them, a wrinkle deepening across the center of his forehead, so Sawyer decided to lighten the moment. "Ruby was desperate for a swim in the spring."

That snapped her head up. "I slipped," she corrected. "And I couldn't find my footing."

Sawyer puffed out his chest in an exaggerated strut. "So I pretty much saved her life."

Her glare could've incinerated him. And it'd be a lie to say he didn't like it. Sure beat the passive Ruby. Something came alive on her face when she got all fired up...

"Anyway." Bryce looked at Sawyer like he knew exactly what he was thinking. "Thanks for grabbing the gear."

"Not a problem." Sawyer handed over the three backpacks he'd insisted on carrying so Ruby wouldn't have to.

His cousin slung them down on the ground. "I heard from Paige."

Uh-oh. From the look of his grim frown they hadn't gotten good news.

"It's a bad break. Thomas is headed into surgery."

"Oh, no." Ruby's face paled. "What about the kids? What about the rest of the activities they're supposed to do this week?"

Sawyer studied her. He hadn't realized she cared that much.

"They've been looking forward to the ropes course all week," she said.

"I know." Bryce looked at Sawyer. "Paige can fill in with the horseback riding, but I'll need you for everything else."

"No problem. I'll call Chief tonight. Ask him for a couple of days off."

"Thanks, man." Bryce clapped him on the shoulder. "Ropes course is scheduled for Tuesday and the zipline tour is Thursday."

"Perfect," he said, glancing at Ruby with a smile. She didn't smile back. Was it just him, or did she suddenly look worried?

"I should go change," she said abruptly. "Thanks again for the rescue and everything." But she didn't look at him, and she definitely wasn't smiling at him anymore.

"What's with her?" Bryce asked as she walked away from them.

"Don't know." But he planned to find out.

CHAPTER SEVEN

*U*nbelievable. Ruby stalked to her beat-up Honda Civic and slid behind the wheel, still fuming. What was with Sawyer, anyway? A year. That was exactly how long she'd been there, and that whole time he'd left her alone. He'd hardly even looked at her. Now all of a sudden it was like he didn't want to let her out of his sight.

She cranked the keys and started the engine, coaxing the gas. Sawyer still stood on the porch watching her like he half expected her to peel out and speed down the driveway at a hundred miles per hour. He'd probably run right to his patrol SUV and chase her down to give her a ticket.

Well, she wouldn't give him the satisfaction. Yes, she couldn't get away from him fast enough, but she eased her car down the gravel road with the uncertainty of a granny who was worried about her brand-new Caddy. *So there.* Right after he'd pulled her out of the water, the man had been charming and kind, but the closer they'd gotten to the ranch, the more withdrawn he'd become. By the time they stood on the porch, he would barely look at her. Then he'd jumped right in with the volunteering thing.

Had she said something that made him suspicious?

As she drove down the highway, her hands tightened on the wheel. He hadn't questioned her on the way back to the lodge like he had during the hike up to the waterfall, but he still watched her like he was analyzing everything she said.

Damn it. She'd let herself get drawn in by his charm, by those captivating blue eyes, and yes, by those rippling muscles—she *was* a woman, after all. But she wouldn't fall for it all again. She'd have to do her best to keep her distance, even though she'd be spending the next couple of days working with kids alongside of him.

On the outskirts of town, she slowed the car, winding through the quaint streets, and even though she'd made the drive every single day since she'd arrived in Aspen, the views still stunned her—the manicured town avenues, the peaks rising over them, hemming them in like a shield of protection. To the south Aspen Mountain glowed emerald green, the last spring snow only recently melted, turning the slopes into flower-dappled meadows.

She took a left on Third Street and followed it all the way to the end, to the side-by-side two-family duplex she shared with Elsie. The woman wasn't home, but she'd be coming over for a girls' night along with Paige and Avery later. Maybe Ruby could get their read on Sawyer, since she hardly knew the man at all. Maybe they'd help her sort this all out.

Cheered by the thought, Ruby pulled into the driveway, noticing that a couple of weeds had popped up in the rosebushes. Elsie treated those rosebushes like they were her children, but she'd been so busy planning and grocery shopping since the kids had arrived, she probably hadn't had time to pull weeds. Dropping her stuff on the ground, Ruby walked over and yanked out a thistle, pinching it between the thorns like Elsie had taught her.

"Yarf! Yarf!"

Across the street an older man she recognized from the next block over walked his dog.

Aw... what a sweetie. The dog almost looked like a cocker spaniel, with longer beige fur, but it was smaller. Ruby loved dogs. She'd always begged for one of her own, of course, but Mama couldn't even take care of two kids, let alone an animal. So instead Ruby would beg neighbors to let her play with their dogs. They were soft and sweet and best of all, they hadn't cared that she had ugly, ratty clothes and unwashed hair. They'd loved her anyway.

Smiling at the memory, she rose her hand to wave. "What a beautiful—" she started to call out, but the man yanked on the dog's leash, dragging it down the street by the neck.

"Hey," she almost whispered, rising higher on her knees.

The dog caught sight of her and yipped with joy, tugging at the leash like it wanted to come greet her.

"Damn it, Nell!" The man yanked again. Harder. "Come on." He dragged it by the neck again, and the dog yelped in pain.

White-hot fury flashed against her eyes. She jumped to her feet, her hands shaking. He couldn't treat a defenseless animal that way!

The man jerked the leash again, pulling the dog behind him, making it gasp and choke.

"Hey!" she yelled, her cheeks tingling.

The man didn't look back.

"Stop it!" She was running across the street now, legs and lungs blazing like they were on fire.

The man walked briskly, then turned into a driveway. "Come! Nell. Come!" he yelled, jerking the leash until the dog was choking again.

Just as Ruby reached the edge of his yard, he opened the front door. The dog tried to make a break for it, but the man kicked it.

He kicked it!

"You can't do that!" Fire roared up her throat in a scream. "You can't kick a dog!"

Ignoring her the man slipped inside his house and slammed the door.

Her head got light. Rage blurred her vision the way it always used to when Derek hit her, like she wasn't seeing things right, like she was detached from her own body. *Oh, god.* She knew. She knew how it felt to be abused, to be unable to fight back. The poor dog was helpless. But she wasn't. Not anymore. She couldn't let this man get away with hurting an innocent animal.

Frantically Ruby blinked the world back into focus. She dug her phone out of her pocket and started to dial 911. But...if the police came, how many questions would they ask her? Would they take her name and information? Would they ask for her driver's license? Her fingers froze over the numbers. She couldn't risk it. She'd have to call someone else. Someone who already knew her.

She hit the first number on her list and held the phone up to her ear.

"Walker Mountain Ranch," Avery answered in her professional, bubbly tone.

"Hey, Avery, it's Ruby." Her voice hitched and she cleared her throat. "Um...have you seen Sawyer around?"

"Nope. Haven't seen him."

"Do you have his phone number?" She hoped she sounded casual, even though the threatening tears were stinging her throat.

Avery rattled it off. "Gotta go, another call. I'll see you tonight!" The line clicked before Ruby could answer. Tensing the shakes out of her hand, she dialed Sawyer's number.

On the third ring, the line clicked. "Hello?"

"It's Ruby," she squeaked.

"Ruby?" There was a shuffling, like he'd switched the phone to his other ear or something. "Is everything okay?"

In other words, why are you calling me?

"No. Everything's not okay." The words unleashed furious tears because she couldn't do anything. She couldn't help the dog alone. "I need you."

"Uh..."

"Please. There's this horrible man..." Her voice disintegrated as the tears clogged her throat.

"A man?" Fear roughed his tenor just like it had when he'd pulled her out of the water. "Where are you? Were you attacked? Are you hurt?"

She tried to talk but could only manage to whimper out the address.

"I'm coming," he growled. "I'll be right there. Call the police. Do you hear me? Call nine-one-one."

"No!" Her vision blurred. "No cops. Please, Sawyer. Just you."

She clicked off the phone and steadied herself against the white picket fence that ran the perimeter of the yard. Images flashed. Derek grabbing her by the neck and throwing her down onto the bed...

Nausea roared through her stomach. She knew how it felt to have someone squeeze the breath out of you. She couldn't let that man hurt the dog. She had to get it away from him. She had to help it the way she'd never been able to help herself.

* * *

This horrible man. Ruby's panicked gasps echoed again and again. A reel of worst-case scenarios flashed through Sawyer's mind. Had she been sexually assaulted? God, he felt sick. On the way out the door he snatched his holster off the entry table and buckled it around his waist, still debating whether he should call the station.

No cops. Just you.

But if she'd been attacked they could get there faster than he could. *Damn it!* He threw open the door to his Tahoe and dug out his phone again.

Ruby answered after one ring. "Sawyer? Are you coming?" She wasn't crying anymore, thank god.

"Yes, I'm on my way. Are you okay?" Because if she wasn't, he didn't give a damn what she said, he was calling in the big guns.

"I'm okay. I need your help." She still sounded shaken, but not panicked like she had been minutes earlier.

"I'm on my way. Hang tight," he said, then peeled out of the ranch's winding driveway and used his authority to blitz down the highway well over twenty miles per hour above the speed limit.

He skidded to a stop in front of the address she'd given him. Ruby stood next to a white picket fence staring at the house, which he knew for a fact wasn't her house. She lived in Elsie's duplex down the block.

She was still wearing the clothes she'd had on earlier, but they seemed to have dried.

"What happened?" he called before he'd even slammed the door.

A blank look had taken over her eyes, and for the first time it occurred to him that she could have mental problems. Maybe that's why she was on the run...

"That man in there..." Her voice wobbled. "I saw him choke his dog."

Sawyer stopped halfway to her. Heat simmered in his gut. "His *dog*?" *Holy shit.* He'd thought someone had threatened her, or attacked her...

"He choked it and yelled at it." Fat tears rolled down her cheeks, deepening the green hue of her eyes. "Then he kicked it into his house."

A *dog*. He didn't open his mouth. Couldn't. Instead of speaking he marched over to her.

"It was horrible," she continued, and when she looked up, when his eyes met hers, he saw a brand of heartbreak he'd witnessed only a handful of times. Usually on a victim's face. The stern lecture building in his brain poofed into a fog of sympathy.

"Sawyer, he choked it," she moaned, then hid her face in her hands and sobbed.

"Okay. It's okay." He gathered her into his arms, unprepared for the way it seared his heart. *Whoa.* Maybe touching her wasn't the best choice, considering it was so easy to recall the image of her in that wet tank top. And that vanilla scent of hers... it made it hard to think a clear thought that didn't involve him pinning her against the side of his SUV.

"We have to do something," Ruby insisted against his chest. "We can't just stand here and let him hurt that dog."

The way she clung to him tempted him to draw his weapon, storm in there, and take the guy down. But he couldn't. He couldn't barge in and arrest some guy for animal cruelty with no hard evidence. He ran a hand over her soft hair. "Maybe it only looked that way," he murmured over her head. "Maybe you couldn't really see."

"No!" She thrust her palms into his chest and pushed him away. "I saw him. He kicked the dog. And when he dragged it with the leash, the dog whimpered like it was in pain."

Sawyer heaved out a sigh. He looked back and forth between her and the house. The broken look was gone from her eyes. Now they were steeled, daring him to argue again, to offer other possibilities. Determination screwed her face tight. She knew, damn it. And he didn't have to be a genius to figure it out. This guy might not have hurt her, but someone had. Was it a parent? A boyfriend?

"Please," she whispered. "We have to get the dog away from him. Before he hurts it again."

"I can't arrest him. And I can't take the dog away from him, Ruby." It wouldn't be that easy. But he couldn't do nothing. Not with her staring at him that way. He battled a sigh. "I'll check on it. Okay? But I don't have the authority to do anything based on one accusation."

She nodded, clasping her hands under her chin.

Leaving her on the sidewalk, he trudged up the front walk to the man's door and rang the bell. Inside a dog barked, then was silenced. A minute later the door opened.

An older man poked out his head. He looked completely harmless. Short, somewhat bent over. Bald head with a rim of white hair.

"What d'you want?" he asked in that crotchety old-man way.

Sawyer looked back at Ruby. Her posture was rigid, hands posted on her hips like she was giving the man a silent reprimand. He turned back to him. "We're concerned about your dog."

"My dog is fine," the man snapped, and Sawyer had to admit he wasn't the nicest guy in the world. He could see this man going after a harmless dog.

He stood taller, looking down at the man, and pulled out his wallet to flash his badge. "You mind if I see it?"

With a scowl, the man opened the door wider. "Nell, come."

The dog trotted out and pranced around Sawyer's feet, licking his boots happily. It didn't cower, didn't seem to be afraid of Sawyer at all.

"The dog is fine," the man growled again.

Sawyer knelt. It really did look fine. Pretty dog. Expensive, too. Looked like a Cavalier King Charles spaniel. The coffee shop owner in town had the same kind hanging around all the time.

The dog sat obediently at Sawyer's toes. He scratched its head.

"Nell. Inside," the man commanded. This time the dog's ears lowered. It stood, tail low, and slunk into the house.

"That all?" the man asked, already closing the door in Sawyer's face. But he had no warrant, no probable cause.

"Yeah. Thanks." When he turned he read Ruby's crushed look all the way from across the yard. *Damn.* She wasn't happy with him. He took his time getting to her, trying to figure out what to say, how many questions to ask. If he pried too hard she'd shut down again, not telling him anything about her past, about who she was, and he didn't want that.

He wanted to know who she was. Sure, it might help Bryce, but the more time he spent with her, the more he just wanted to know her.

"I didn't imagine it," she spat when he stood across from her. "I saw him. I heard him yelling."

Sawyer nodded, but then stopped when it seemed to patronize her. "I believe you," he said instead. "But, Ruby, I can't do anything about it. Not today, anyway."

A look of anger cinched her lips tight, but her eyes filled with tears again.

"Hey." He reached for her, clasping his hand around her forearm, but she jerked back like he'd burned her. Like he'd *hurt* her.

Then her eyes widened with surprise as though she couldn't believe she'd done that.

But he could. Because something terrible had happened to her. Someone had done something terrible to her. It was evident in the way she guarded herself.

"I'll keep an eye on it," he promised. Because, damn it, those eyes of hers were so intense, so intense he had to touch her. He couldn't stop himself. Instead of touching the dangerous territory of her body, he gently reached a hand to her face and tucked that gorgeous red hair behind her ear. "I'll drive by. I'll watch out for the dog." His hand lingered by her jaw. "And the first time I see anything weird, I'll get a warrant."

She reached up and held his hand against her skin, closing her eyes, taking a deep breath. "Thank you," she whispered.

Then she rose to her tiptoes and pressed her lips to his, melting his joints, warming his blood, thickening it, like honey running through his veins. Desire flooded him, loosening his hold. But he forced himself to keep his hands on her cheeks instead of wandering to all the places they wanted to go. He had to be careful with her. So instead of parting her lips with his tongue, instead of plunging deeper into her, crushing her against his body, tasting more of her, he pulled back. He let her go.

Shock froze her eyes wide.

Still close, he whisked his thumb down her cheek, his eyes following hers as they shifted back and forth.

"It'll be okay." He smiled a little.

A smile flickered on her lips before she backed away. "I should go. I have to go." She swayed. He could relate. The whole world suddenly felt off balance. What the hell was he doing? He'd just kissed Ruby in a way that made him ache for more. God, he wanted more. He couldn't help himself. She was so soft and tasted sweet, mysterious, but somehow so familiar, too...

"Thank you," Ruby called as she jogged away. "For coming. I'll see you tomorrow."

Suddenly he couldn't wait until tomorrow.

CHAPTER EIGHT

What was she thinking? She'd kissed Sawyer. She'd *kissed* him. On the lips and everything. Oh, lordy.

Ruby peered down at her reclaimed kitchen table and started to set out the plates. She and Elsie had found the table in a trash bin at a mansion down the road from the ranch. Though it was obviously custom-made from a good quality cherrywood, the surface was damaged and scarred. A diamond in the rough, Elsie had called it. Together the two of them had hauled it out of that Dumpster. They'd tightened the screws and sanded until their fingers were raw. Then they painted it an antique white, somehow making the imperfections and natural striations stand out in a lovely, unique way.

She'd like to think her scars were hidden as well as the ones on that table, covered and transformed into something lovely. But then every once in a while something would happen like it did a half hour ago when she saw that man abusing his dog, and suddenly they weren't scars anymore. They were open wounds, festering and bleeding. Panic would set in, boiling emotions back to the surface, and she'd lose her hold on the present, feeling only the fear, the humiliation, the shame that covered her every time he'd hit her. Every time she told herself yet again it didn't matter.

And once those emotions took over, she did crazy things. Like kissing Sawyer. She'd kissed Officer Hawkins. Even more disturbing than that, he'd kissed her back. And it didn't feel like it was out of obligation, either. His lips were tender but guarded, like he was holding back. And while that had been a bit disappointing in the moment, it was also somehow selfless. In that highly charged second he could've ravaged her right there in front of that house and she would've let him. When he'd pulled her close, sheltered her against his solid body, the storm inside of her had quieted.

The thrill of it still hummed through her in dizzying waves. But he was a cop. He was her boss's cousin. He thought she was Ruby James the baker. Not Kate McPherson the domestic-violence victim.

All he knew were the lies she'd told, lies that were meant to protect her, but they were lies all the same. And the truth would ruin everything.

A spoon fell from her hand and clattered onto the table. She looked down at the place settings. She'd done it all wrong. One place setting had three forks and no knives, while another had two knives and a spoon. *Nice.* She shook her head and righted everything. She had to get it together before the girls came over. Stop thinking about Sawyer; stop thinking about poor little Nell...

The doorbell chimed. It was a sweet and charming sound, delicate, like wind chimes waving in the breeze.

"Coming," she called, trying to flush out memories of Sawyer with a long gulp of water. Fair Irish skin did little to hide the violent blush that seared her cheeks.

She swung open the door and greeted Paige, then Avery, then Elsie, who all paraded in chatting about the foster kids.

"They're so sweet," Avery gushed.

"And you should hear all they experienced on their back-packing trip," Elsie added. "Sounds like those dears will never be the same after seeing all that beauty."

Thinking about the kids brought a smile back to Ruby's face.

Elsie carted a stack of takeout containers to the table and spread them around. Already the wonderful aromas of her delicious cooking wafted around them. Smelled like she'd made her famous pumpkin ravioli with sage butter sauce.

"Hanging out with the foster kids has always been my favorite week at the ranch," Paige said.

Avery clasped onto Ruby's arm. "Bryce said you and Sawyer are helping out on the ropes course together."

Elsie's sparse eyebrows shot up. "Oh, really?" Surprise gave way to a knowing smile. "They went for a hike together this afternoon, too." She cozied up to Ruby's side. "And how was that hike, dear?" she asked as innocently as a dove.

The blush Sawyer had ignited after that kiss flamed into an inferno. "We kissed," Ruby blurted, and everything stopped.

Three pairs of wide eyes stared at her.

"He *kissed* you?" Avery finally asked, clasping her hands as if it was the best news she'd heard since her healthy baby girl was born.

"*Sawyer* kissed you?" Paige echoed. "The one who hasn't looked at another woman since he met Kaylee?"

Elsie simply chuckled. "Well, I wonder what took him so long."

Before Ruby could stop them, tell them all that she'd actually kissed him, chairs were pulled back from the table and she was ushered into one of them. Paige, Avery, and Elsie all sat, too, scooting their chairs as close as possible.

"Details, please." Avery swiped the bottle of pinot noir off the table and uncorked it.

"Was it on the hike? Where'd he take you? How'd you even end up going on a hike with *Sawyer*?" Paige asked while she held out the glasses for Avery to pour wine. "How was it? Is he any good? Because I've always thought Sawyer would be a pretty good kisser." In typical Paige fashion, the woman hardly took a breath. "I mean not as good as Ben, of course, but still pretty good with those sexy lips of his."

"Now, now, you two," Elsie reprimanded. "Give the poor girl some room to talk." Face beaming, she opened the food containers and started dishing up the plates.

"So?" Paige demanded, handing Ruby a glass.

She took it and bought time with a long gulp. Where should she start? "He didn't kiss me on the hike." Though she couldn't deny a slight attraction had taken root when he'd swiped her out of the water all manly and in control. She hadn't thought the feeling was mutual, but now she wasn't so sure. "He came over."

"Get out!" Avery swatted her shoulder. "He came over to your *house*?"

"Oh, baby!" Paige scrubbed her hands together. "This is getting good."

"Not exactly." Another sip of wine didn't submerge the fierce flutter of deranged butterflies in her heart when she pictured Sawyer's face. "I called him an hour ago because a man across the street was abusing his dog."

A collective gasp affirmed her decision to call him. No one should get away with something like that. She'd done the right thing.

"What happened, dear?" Elsie asked.

"He was dragging it by the neck," Ruby said, tears threatening again. "The poor dog was choking. Then, when I yelled at him, he kicked it inside his house and slammed the door."

"Grayson Collins." Elsie said the name like a curse. "That old bully has treated every pet he's ever owned that way." Her palm smacked the table like she'd like to smack him. "The man doesn't deserve to have a dog, if you ask me. He's downright mean."

"Exactly," Ruby agreed. "Which is why I called Sawyer. But he said there was nothing he could do without evidence."

"He could kick that guy's sorry ass," Paige offered, but they all knew police brutality wasn't exactly an option.

"Kicking his ass isn't Sawyer's style," Avery said. "But he'll watch for the right time. Then he'll figure out how to take him down. That's the kind of man he is. Good. Smart. Thoughtful…" She emphasized the words as if reciting all his good qualities for Ruby's benefit.

A sigh opened her chest. Yes. It was obvious that Sawyer had a lot going for him. "Anyway, after he went to the door and checked on the dog, he could tell I was upset, so he gave me a hug, and…" She closed her eyes, remembering the way his hand had gently brushed her jaw, the way he'd looked at her long and steady, seeing much deeper than most people, it seemed. "I kissed him," she muttered, still astonished at herself. But it was true. She'd stood on her tiptoes to reach his mouth and then she'd kissed him.

"Way to go." Paige raised her wineglass. "Gotta say, Ruby, I didn't think you had it in you, but a man likes a woman who'll take charge."

Avery gasped. "Maybe you can convince him to stay in Aspen!"

"Oh, yes!" Elsie clasped her hands. "That would be wonderful, dear." The older woman nudged Ruby's plate in front of her, a silent *you'd best eat before it gets cold*. Obediently Ruby picked up her fork. "I doubt I could convince him to stay in Aspen," she said around a creamy bite of ravioli.

"Oh, but he doesn't belong in Denver," Elsie said sadly. "He's a mountain boy. He'll hate it down there."

Ruby tried not to smile. She'd almost forgotten that he was moving away. One month. She wouldn't have to worry about avoiding him if he was leaving in a month.

"You two would be *so* perfect together!" Avery sighed. "I mean, he's *such* a great guy, Ruby."

"And he deserves a stellar girl," Paige added. "After what he went through with the bitch."

Every one of their expressions darkened. Well, except Ruby's. She'd been careful to keep to herself. She'd overheard snippets of Sawyer's story, but she didn't know much about him, other than he'd gotten divorced. "What did he go through, exactly?" she asked, then casually sipped more wine even though her insides radiated in a warm pulse. Because she couldn't stop thinking about that kiss...

"Kaylee cheated on him with a friend of theirs," Paige said matter-of-factly.

Elsie shook her head sadly. "He was devastated, the poor dear. Oh, but he loved that girl."

Avery put down her fork, an uncharacteristic anger flashing in her blue eyes. "He forgave her and took her back, but less than a month later, he caught them in bed again."

Ruby sipped her wine in between bites of ravioli. No wonder the man seemed suspicious.

"And this time he wasn't so nice about it." Elsie giggled. "Rumor has it he threw the guy out into the snow without even letting him put on his skivvies."

There was a hearty round of chuckling, but Ruby didn't feel like laughing. Regret burned in her chest. She had no business kissing him like that, letting her emotions take over. The last thing Sawyer needed was another woman lying to him. He didn't deserve that.

"So?" Paige demanded, heaping more ravioli onto her plate. "How was he? Good? Average?"

"Well, it wasn't a bad kiss," she admitted, even though that was putting it mildly. "But I'm not looking for a relationship right now."

Paige laughed. "Watch out. That's the same tune I was singing last year when Ben came into town." With an impish grin she raised her left hand and wiggled her ring finger, flashing the monumental diamond she now wore. "And look what happened to me."

"Pretty sure I don't have to worry about that." Ruby's lips froze into a smile, but the familiar pang of fear stabbed at her. To her, a ring had a different meaning. She'd almost committed her life to a monster. "Sounds like he's all set to move, anyway."

Avery and Elsie exchanged a look.

"He's running away, if you want the truth," Elsie harrumphed. "Sawyer doesn't belong in Denver. He belongs in the mountains."

"True, true," Avery agreed, licking the back of her fork.

Running away. Ruby glanced at their empty plates so she didn't have to look into their eyes. "Who's ready for dessert?" she asked, hoping to change the subject. Nothing distracted these three women like the prospect of dessert. Since Elsie did the cooking for their weekly girls' nights, Ruby always made dessert. Tonight it was a salted caramel chocolate tart.

Avery's hand shot up. "Me! Me! I'm ready for dessert! I've been waiting for dessert since breakfast." Ruby tried not to glare at her. For having such a serious sweet tooth, Avery was the best kind of thin—toned and curved but still skinny enough to wear a size two. Even after giving birth a month ago. As opposed to her healthy size six. Such is the life of a baker, though. How could she possibly serve desserts to people without tasting them to make sure they were perfect? Sighing, she stacked the plates and stood.

Paige hopped up, too. "I'll help you dish it up." She followed her into the kitchen.

As soon as the door closed, Paige faced her. "What's going on, Ruby?"

"What d'you mean?" she asked, engrossing herself with unwrapping the foil from around the torte. Out of everyone here, she'd spent the most time with Paige. The woman had never pried into her past, but Ruby knew she wondered.

Paige slapped her hands on her hips. "Any woman in her right mind would be ecstatic to get attention from Sawyer Hawkins. He doesn't give it out easily, trust me."

The memory of him kissing her back so carefully inflated her heart. He'd been so unexpectedly tender...

She turned to look at her friend and leaned against the counter for support. "Sawyer's great." That was the understatement of the year. "But I can't have a relationship right now. With anyone."

"Sawyer doesn't go around kissing random women." Paige went to the cupboard and dug out the dessert plates. "He's not that kind of guy."

She turned back to her torte. "*I* kissed *him*. Remember?"

"But he kissed you back."

Yes. That was true, her body reminded her in a tingling shudder. He'd definitely kissed her back, not fast and hard, but slow, stroking her cheeks with the backs of his fingers, letting his lips rest against hers...

Her heart lurched at the shock of it. *Whoa.* Carefully, slowly, she cut the torte into sections. "He's leaving in a month. And I...I'm not ready."

"Why, Ruby?" Paige asked quietly. "Why won't you give him a chance?"

"I can't." Her eyes got hot, glazed over with tears. Ever since that morning, when she'd let the past in again, she'd felt so much weaker. For a while she'd been able to ignore it, to shift her focus, but she knew she wouldn't be able to run from those emotions forever.

Hard as she tried to stop them, the tears spilled over. "I was in a relationship a while ago." She kept her voice low so the others wouldn't hear. "It was bad. Really bad. I had to get away." That was all she could say. She would never risk putting any of her new friends in danger. The last time Derek had beat her up, he'd threatened to kill her. This was her problem. Her past. And she wouldn't let anyone else get caught in the middle.

Paige gave an empathetic nod like she got it. She didn't seem surprised by the revelation. "Some men are so pathetic that they feel like they need to prove their strength." She clamped a hand onto Ruby's arm, filling her with warmth and hope. "But Sawyer's different. He just *is* strong. And trustworthy. And good. I've known him forever. He'd never hurt—"

The door burst open. "What d'we have to do to get some chocolate around here?" Avery demanded, looking offended. "I mean, I'm six weeks post-birth, girls. I'm not having any sex. I *need* chocolate."

Ruby forced a laugh. "Coming right up."

"I still think you should give him a chance," Paige whispered as they headed for the dining room. "Sawyer's one of the good guys, Ruby. Whatever it is you're running from, maybe he can help you."

"I don't want help. I just want to move on with my life." She couldn't risk Derek learning where she was, hunting her down. And who knew what he'd do to Sawyer if he found out she was attracted to him.

No. She had to keep the secrets locked safely in the past. Letting them out was too big of a price to pay.

Even for someone as wonderful as Sawyer.

CHAPTER NINE

Morning used to be Sawyer's favorite time of day. When he and Kaylee were married, he'd sneak out of bed before she woke up and brew the coffee, get breakfast started. He might suck at cooking overall, but frying eggs and bacon, or flipping pancakes, was his specialty. Kaylee would stagger into the kitchen, all bleary eyed and gorgeous with her dark hair knotted on her head. She'd hug him—cling to him— and depending on where he was at with the food, they'd end up kissing, or, if it was a really good day, he'd make love to her right there on the kitchen floor.

Now the memory made him pull the covers over his head, as if the darkness could make it disappear. He turned over in the empty king-size bed that Bryce had put into all the ranch's guest cabins. Would he ever open his eyes as the first rays of sunlight beamed through the window and not think of those mornings? It wasn't so much that he missed Kaylee. Well, he missed who she had been then. Losing the baby changed both of them; he wasn't naïve enough to deny that. They'd gone from being best friends and passionate lovers to being strangers who coexisted in the same house. He'd stopped making breakfast. She'd started going out to dinner with her friends after work most nights of the week.

Distance yawned between them, and it wasn't like he didn't see it happening; it was just that he couldn't find the energy to care. Truth was, he'd fallen in love with an idea— Kaylee as a devoted and loving mom, just like his mom. In some ways Mom had set him up to believe that all women were as perfect as June Cleaver, cooking gourmet family dinners every night of the week, baking cookies for him after he came home from school. Hell, she'd even clean his room, fold his laundry, and leave him treats under his pillow when she made his bed every day. But for Mom it wasn't an act. It was her life. It was what she'd loved the most in the world. Her family. Her kids.

Apparently that wasn't reality for everyone.

It wasn't like he'd expected the same out of Kaylee. He only wanted a wife who'd love her family, who'd never take one day of it for granted. After he told Mom Kaylee had cheated on him, she'd looked at him sadly. "Not every woman wants to be a mom," she'd said. "It doesn't make her a bad person, Sawyer. You just want different things in life and she was feeling trapped."

So yes, maybe it was his fault. Maybe he'd trapped her into his vision for the future, thinking she would change, that her biological clock would start ticking. Wasn't that a real thing? He'd thought it—

A loud knock interrupted his thoughts. Sawyer rolled over again and glanced at the clock: 6:00 a.m.? Who the hell could be standing on his doorstep before the sun was even up?

The knock turned into a pounding that lurched his heart into reaction mode. Sawyer jumped out of bed and pulled on the rumpled pants and shirt he'd had on the day before, then shoved his feet into his tennis shoes. He jogged out of the bedroom and across the small kitchen and living room. By the time he reached the door, he was out of breath.

Bryce stood on the porch. "Hey." His face was grim. "There's been another incident."

Sawyer blinked the sleep-induced fog out of his eyes. "Incident?"

"A thousand dollars is missing from my office," Bryce said, his jaw tight. "I was there until three o'clock in the morning working on some bookkeeping. So it had to be sometime between three and now."

Sawyer stepped out onto the porch and resisted the urge to shake his head. How many times had he told his cousin to install a surveillance system? "Sure wish you would've taken my recommendations," he said, giving in to the temptation to be the asshole who says *I told you so*.

But Bryce took it in stride, simply shrugging like *what the hell do you want from me?* "It's a family ranch. We've never needed security cameras."

Even though he was in the mood to argue, Sawyer silently stepped back inside, pulled on a fleece, and followed his cousin down the porch steps.

"I wouldn't be worried if things hadn't been disappearing," Bryce said, keeping a brisk pace. "I don't keep the cleanest office in the world."

"You're not stupid with your money, either." Bryce counted every cent, made sure the books weren't even a nickel off. It was a trait they'd both inherited from their moms. "Someone's stealing from you." He wanted Bryce to acknowledge it this time.

"Yeah. I should've realized it before." His cousin led the way across the ranch's massive front deck until they reached the office.

They stepped inside and Sawyer glanced around the main room. Nothing was broken. "How'd they get in?"

"No idea," Bryce said, jiggling the doorknob. "It's always locked up."

Locks didn't mean much when you trusted everyone's mother and their dog with a key. "Who has access?" He did his best not to sound impatient. It wasn't Bryce's fault he was so trusting. Elsie had raised him that way—to always see the best in people, and he hadn't been jaded by years of police work.

"Employees only," Bryce said, as if that meant something. "Most of them have a master key."

Don't roll your eyes. Later he would suggest that Bryce put a different lock on the office and not give *anyone* the key. Instead of launching into a lecture, he walked to the check-in counter, noting that nothing else was out of place. It was like someone knew Bryce kept the money in his office. Someone knew exactly when they could take it without anyone seeing. "How many employees are around between three and six o'clock in the morning?" He moved to the doorway that led into Bryce's office.

His cousin didn't answer, so Sawyer turned to face him.

"You know I need names," he said in his official-police-business tone, because now they were dealing with a repeat offender and the stakes were getting higher. A couple hundred dollars and a missing bracelet were minor offenses. But the suspect had gotten away with it, and now they were after more. "If we don't catch this son of a bitch, they'll keep stealing from you. You can't afford to keep losing money."

Bryce heaved out a sigh. "Ruby is *usually* the only one. She sometimes comes in between four and five." He raised a hand as if to slow Sawyer's thought process. "But any of the maintenance guys could've been here. A guide, maybe."

Not likely. Sawyer knew the maintenance guys, and none of them ever got up before ten, though he'd love to blame one of them. It was easier than considering the alternative. He did another sweep around the room, taking time to inspect the desk. "I could call in CSI. Have them dust for fingerprints."

"You promised we'd keep this quiet," Bryce reminded him. "I don't even want Avery to know about this. She's already worried enough, being a new mom. This would freak her out."

Pretty much the answer he'd expected. "Fine. Show me where the money was."

Bryce led him back to the desk. He opened a drawer and held up a brown zipper pouch. "I keep it in this and put it in my desk until we make the deposit."

Sawyer shot him a look. "That's some high-tech security you've got there. A real fortress."

His cousin tossed the empty envelope down onto the desk. "We've never had to worry about it before."

"But you admit it's a problem now. Maybe a security system would be a good idea."

Bryce shrugged off the idea like he always did. "I'll try to work it into the budget."

Leaving the desk behind, Sawyer bent to examine the door handle on Bryce's office. "Someone definitely had a key." There were no scratches on the metal that would indicate a picked lock.

He straightened and looked around again. "You sure nothing else was touched?"

"Not that I can see," Bryce said, pulling open drawers. "Laptop's still here. Credit cards are here. It's like someone just wanted the cash."

Because cash could never be traced and whoever took it knew that. They didn't have to sell anything and risk someone else ratting them out. They knew they'd get away with it.

Damn. Sawyer strode back into the lobby, noting the baked goods cases were full of fresh donuts and croissants. "Ruby was in here," he said, nodding toward the food. "She fills the cases every morning."

"What're you gonna do?" Bryce asked like he dreaded the answer.

"What I have to do," he replied, already opening the door.

"You're gonna talk to Ruby?"

He stopped. "Do I have a choice?" The thought of confronting her like this made his stomach twist, but there were no other leads. No one else was around.

"I hope she didn't do it," Bryce said, following him across the porch. "Mom would be crushed."

"I hope not, too," he admitted.

But he had to be open to any possibility.

* * *

Humming. She was actually humming. Ruby whipped the batter for the individual carrot cakes she was making for that evening's dessert. A smile snuck onto her lips. She'd never meant to kiss Sawyer, but the warmth of it still bubbled up and made her smile like a silly girl. Yes, she knew she couldn't indulge again, but somehow that one kiss was tempting her to defy logic. God, it'd been so long since she shared a kiss with anyone. Let alone someone as debonair as Sawyer. Okay, that would be never. She could still feel the soft stroke of his fingers against her skin...

The kitchen door pounded open. Sawyer and Bryce marched in. And there went her smile again, as if by simply seeing him, her body decided she was happy. How could she not be when he looked like that, all rumpled and sleepy with his untamed dark hair and the stubble across his jaw? "Um...hi there," she said, going for casual, but instead her voice sounded as light and airy as her body felt. Was she already blushing?

Sawyer wouldn't look her in the eyes. And maybe he didn't look sleepy...maybe he looked...grumpy?

Was he mad about the kiss? He hadn't seemed to be at the time, but a whole night had passed since then...

"Ruby." He looked over, his gaze focused above her head like he wanted to avoid her eyes. "We have to ask you some questions."

Glancing between his solemn expression and Bryce's, she set down the mixing bowl. "Okay." She drew the word out into her own question. Was it about the dog?

Sawyer crossed his arms, making them bulge. "What time did you get here this morning?"

The rush of heat that'd made her blush spread down her neck. "The same time I always do. Just before five. Why?"

He shared a look with Bryce. "You see anyone else around?"

The pulse point in her neck throbbed. Something bad had happened. "No," she croaked. "It was just me." But she couldn't be sure of that. She'd been distracted all morning, humming and thinking about that man right there. Who now looked at her with an accusation in his eyes.

"There was no one else?" he asked again. Slowly this

time. Like he wanted her to really think about it. "No cars? You didn't hear a strange noise?"

She tried to think, tried to flash through the scenes of that morning, but the growing pulse of panic blurred the images. What had happened? Had someone been hurt? Murdered? A cold prickle across her forehead made it feel like the blood was draining from her face.

Had Derek found her?

"I didn't see anyone," wisped out of her mouth on a breath of fear. She leaned against the counter to support her weak legs. "Why? What's wrong? What happened?"

Sawyer and Bryce shared another coded look, seeming to fight over who would tell her.

"Sawyer, what's going on?" she demanded, because her mind was entertaining only the worst possible scenarios.

"Someone broke into the office and stole some cash," he finally said. "Bryce locked up at three this morning and when he got back at six, the money was gone."

"Oh, no," she uttered, doing her best not to sound relieved. But no one was hurt. No one was being stalked. "How much did they take?"

"A thousand dollars," Bryce said.

Sawyer stepped close to her, his eyes seeming to analyze her face. "But not many people have been around. And whoever it was had a key."

"Oh." The word came out like a punch. It made her stomach hurt the way he was looking at her, talking to her. "You think I took it." Humiliation crowded out the infatuation that had inflated her heart. Now it felt cold and flat.

"I don't think anything yet," he lied. She could *see* the lie in those cold steel eyes. He suspected her. He thought she'd stolen money from the Walkers.

Tears rose up, blurring his face, blurring everything, the

MORE THAN A FEELING   89

happy, warm glow of the kitchen, the mixing bowl on the island in front of her.

Sawyer's rigid jaw went soft. "We only wanted to know if you've seen anything suspicious," he said gently.

"I had nothing to do with this." Disregarding him with a shake of her head, she turned to Bryce. Because, really, who the hell cared what Sawyer thought, anyway. She sure didn't. Not anymore. "You have to believe me, Bryce. I'd never steal from you. After everything you guys have done for me—"

"Of course you didn't," Bryce said, shooting Sawyer a look that clearly said *back off*. "We only came to ask if you'd seen anyone else around."

"Sorry." Inhaling to dry the tears in her eyes, she lifted the mixing bowl back into her hands and started to whisk again, working out the sudden onslaught of anger that flexed her hands. "I wish I could help." Batter splattered onto the counter, but she kept stirring, hard enough that her wrist ached.

"Okay, then." Bryce said after a hollow silence. "I'd really appreciate it if you didn't mention anything to Avery. She's already sleep deprived with the baby and everything."

"Of course," she replied without looking up. Now the anger had ballooned into righteous indignation.

How could they even ask her if she'd stolen money? She'd worked her ass off to thank them for giving her this opportunity. Did Sawyer think she was stupid? That she'd ruin her chance at the ranch—her chance at a new life—for a thousand dollars?

"Guess I should head out," Bryce called, cruising to the door like he couldn't get out of there fast enough. "Let us know if you see anything suspicious."

Her silent nod sent him out the door, but Sawyer hung around across from her, as if by standing there, he'd get her attention.

Ha. Well. She'd learned how to ignore bothersome men when she'd been a waitress, so he could stand there all day, and she'd still make sure she saw right through him. To prove she could, she glanced up, but the second her gaze rested on his face, her heart twirled in happy circles. *Okay.* Apparently her traitorous body was having a hard time letting that kiss go. Steeling her shoulders, she bent her head to inspect the batter, which was likely now over-whipped. Just like her heart.

Ruby turned and walked to the other counter. She simply wouldn't look at him. She had to focus, anyway. And he was so not worth—

Sawyer swooped in and stole the bowl from her hands, setting it on the counter out of her reach. "I didn't mean to imply anything."

The hell he didn't. She shook her head instead of speaking because they both knew that was exactly what he'd meant. That was why he'd asked her to go hiking yesterday. That was why he'd taken a sudden interest in her. He didn't trust her.

"Come on, Ruby." He slipped in front of her and stood too close. "What'd you expect? I don't know anything about you. You won't share anything with me. About who you are. About your past. Then you *kiss* me—"

"*That* was a mistake." Obviously. She stalked to the other side of the island and retrieved her bowl. "But don't worry, Sawyer. I don't make the same mistake twice." Not anymore. She'd stay away from him now that she knew where he stood.

"Don't be like that. I never said I minded the kiss." He

walked over and nudged her shoulder. "This is my job, Ruby. I have to ask the tough questions."

But he hadn't asked anyone else questions. Just her. Her chest pulled so tight she couldn't breathe. "And I answered your questions. So you can go now." She braced for an argument, but he simply nodded and shoved his hands into his pockets.

Then he turned around and left.

CHAPTER TEN

The towering stack of stainless-steel mixing bowls and cups teetered precariously on the counter next to the sink. Eyeing it, Ruby finished scouring the fourth muffin tin in a row and shut off the water. Her fingers stung—nearly raw from all the scrubbing, but at least the anger that had singed her skin didn't burn anymore.

"Oh, my!" Elsie walked in and gawked at the leaning tower of baking equipment.

"Yeah. Don't worry. I'll put it all back." Ruby wiped her hands on her apron and squirted some lotion onto her skin, rubbing it in until the cracks in her fingers stung. "Thought I should do some spring cleaning." So she'd scrubbed every single bowl and measuring utensil in the entire kitchen. And now that her hands weren't busy, the whole scene with Sawyer replayed again.

Had she imagined it? Or had he really accused her of stealing from the Walkers?

"Is something the matter?" Elsie asked, watching her closely.

"Oh...no." She bent to retrieve a towel from the drawer so she could dry everything and put it away. And stay busy.

"Does this have anything to do with what happened this morning?" Elsie dug out another towel and started drying alongside Ruby. "With Sawyer?"

"How did you—"

"Sawyer told me all about it," Elsie said, slipping the largest bowl back into the cupboard. "He asked me to check on you. To make sure you were all right."

Of course she wasn't all right. He must've seen the tears in her eyes when he came in and accused her. Was he too afraid to come and check on her himself? "I had nothing to do with it, Elsie. I swear." This woman had changed her life by taking a chance on her, and it would kill her if Elsie thought she didn't appreciate it. Tears pricked Ruby's eyes again, hot and infuriating.

"Well, of course you had nothing to do with it, dear. I'm sure they didn't mean to imply any different," the woman said, smoothing a comforting hand down her arm. "Sometimes Sawyer is a bit harsh, being a policeman and all. That's what it was. He takes his job very seriously." Looking concerned at the way Ruby's tears were now slipping, Elsie took her towel away and dropped it in a heap on the counter.

"There, now. Not to worry. I know you'd never do something like that, and so does Bryce. You sit, dear. I'll make you some tea. We can put away the dishes later." Elsie bustled away from her, humming while she filled up the teakettle and set it on the stove.

The reassurance should've salved the wide, gaping crack in her heart, but it still hurt. She shouldn't care what Sawyer

thought about her. He was leaving in a month. So why did
his suspicion bother her so much? Elsie might believe he'd
questioned her solely because of his role as a police officer,
but she'd seen something else in him. It was almost like he
was looking for a reason not to trust her.

And what had she done to deserve that?

"Here now." The woman set a delicate china teacup in
front of her. The soothing scent of lavender curled off the
top. Sighing deeply, Elsie sat across from her. "Why do you
think Sawyer suspects you?"

Wasn't it obvious? "Because I don't like to talk about
my past." No one else seemed to hold that against her.
When she'd first met Elsie, Ruby told her that she'd just
gotten out of a bad relationship and needed a job. That's
all. Though something in the woman had seemed to sense
Ruby also needed protection, they'd never talked about it.
But even without knowing anything about her, Elsie had
never treated her like a criminal. "Sawyer doesn't trust
me." For some reason, that was the hardest part. She knew
she hadn't spilled her guts to the man, but couldn't he see
that she was a decent person? That she would never inten-
tionally hurt anyone?

"It's not just you, dear. Sawyer has a hard time trusting
anyone right now." The soft gleam in her eyes spoke of
an endless ocean of patience. "Betrayal works its way into
you and alters the way you see everyone. You can't take it
personally."

So what was she supposed to do? Tell him everything?
Risk her whole future so that Sawyer would trust her? He
was a cop. And she was living under a false identity. Ruby
lifted the mug to her lips, inhaling the steam, sipping the
warm, honey-sweetened tea. "I don't even want to remember my past, let alone talk about it." Especially with anyone

at the Walker Mountain Ranch. The less they knew, the safer they would all be. The safer *she* would be. Maybe after more time had passed, after she was sure Derek had stopped looking for her, she'd tell him everything. But not right now.

Elsie nodded as though she understood. "If you can't tell him, then show him who you are now." She patted her hand. "You are such a beautiful woman, inside and out. Whatever you went through has made you stronger." The woman's eyes were so intent on her, like she was doing her best to infuse that into Ruby's mind, into her heart.

They were words a mom should've uttered to reinforce her daughter's shaky self-confidence. Words she had never heard directed at her. Before she could wipe away the tears, Elsie's hand squeezed hers.

"Spend time with Sawyer. He'll see the truth soon enough."

That was exactly what she was afraid of. "He seems to have made up his mind." Even though he'd kissed her back so tenderly the night before...

"The more you avoid him, the more suspicious he'll become," Elsie said with that motherly undertone. "You need to show him you have nothing to hide."

Except she *was* hiding. Behind a fake name, a fake persona. Ruby looked away, but Elsie caught her wandering gaze.

"Let him know you so he can see the truth. So he can see what a good person you are," she insisted, and Ruby knew the woman was right.

If she convinced Sawyer she was a good person, he'd move on to the next suspect. No more questions, no more suspicion. And maybe he'd find the person who was really responsible for the thefts so the Walkers wouldn't get robbed again.

"Isn't Sawyer teaching the kids how to swim tonight?" Elsie asked with a subtle arch in her eyebrows.

"Think so." She'd made a mistake telling Elsie he'd invited her to go. Now, judging from the way the woman looked her so brightly—like a lightbulb had just turned on above her head—she might regret that. "I'm not going." How could she? She'd planned on it until he'd stood across from her this morning, looking at her like she was a criminal. It would've been nice to learn how to swim. She was twenty-six, after all. If she finally took the plunge, maybe she could take Paige up on that rafting trip she was always offering.

"Of course you're going." Elsie chuckled. "It's the perfect chance to show him you have nothing to hide, dear."

Nerves sparked in her stomach. Yeah, she'd really have nothing to hide behind parading around in front of him in a swimsuit. Which, conveniently, she didn't even own. "I've never bought a suit. Never had a reason to." And now she was thanking god for that.

Her sweet, motherly, charitable boss whipped out her cell phone faster than Avery could whip out a credit card. Warp speed. "I'll call Paige and tell her to bring over an extra." She held the phone against her ear. "The woman must have twenty bathing suits."

Of course she did. "Fabulous," Ruby said, but Elsie was already busy explaining the situation to Paige.

Containing an uneasy sigh, she downed the rest of her tea. Between the deep water and Sawyer's mistrust, she only hoped she wouldn't drown tonight.

* * *

If there was ever a night he didn't want to be late, this was it.

Sawyer sped into the rec center's parking lot, fully aware

that he was breaking the law—*really* breaking the law—but for once he didn't care.

The big swimming lesson was supposed to start in ten minutes and he couldn't let the kids down. It'd been quite the adventure on his shift today. He'd wanted to get off early, but then he'd gotten held up with a report of a shoplifter at the gas station. Once he'd caught up with the suspect, he'd discovered the kid had only pocketed some napkins from the snack bar, which didn't exactly consist of stealing, seeing as how they were free.

Try explaining that to an outraged gas station owner.

He cruised around the front of the building and slowed the SUV. A woman stood by the entrance. He'd know that red hair anywhere. What was Ruby doing just standing there staring at the doors? He didn't know, but at least she'd come. First thing he'd smiled about all damn day. After the interrogation in the kitchen, he didn't think he'd see her tonight.

Not that he deserved to. He'd come on too strong. It killed him the way his suspicions always got the best of him. When he'd looked into her eyes, he knew it wasn't her, but it was too late. He'd regretted ever bringing it up. Now he had the perfect opportunity to tell her that.

He swung the Tahoe into a parking spot up front and jogged over to her before she decided to leave.

She watched him approach, her face expressionless.

"You came." He let genuine happiness breeze through the words. He hadn't even realized how much he wanted her there until he'd seen her. As bad an idea as it was, he *wanted* to spend time with her. He wanted to know her. And tonight he was willing to screw practicality.

Ruby looked around as though noncommittal. "I'm actually still trying to make up my mind."

"Would it help if I apologized?" He owed her that. She might be secretive, but she hadn't done anything to him. Or the Walkers. He wanted to trust her, despite her secrets. He wanted to believe everything she said, that she was as good as she looked, but he'd been lied to before, and that made it hard.

Ruby eyed him. "You don't owe me an apology. I know you're only looking out for the Walkers."

He stepped closer to her, gazing into her eyes until his pulse kicked up. "No." He wasn't about to let her excuse his bad behavior. "I shouldn't have confronted you like that. I'm sorry." He sensed a fearful vulnerability in her, and he'd been too harsh. Interrogating her wouldn't help him scale her walls. "Sometimes I let my past color the way I see things," he admitted so she'd know it wasn't about her.

Her lips parted and she looked up at him, letting her gaze rest directly in his for maybe the first time. "That I can understand," she murmured.

"So you'll come in and help me teach the kids how to swim?" he asked, wanting her to hear the hope in his voice.

Her lips quirked. "I'm not sure how much help I'll—"

"Sawyer?"

The voice he'd once known so well turned his shoulders to lead. Not now. *Please not now.*

But sure enough, Kaylee paraded through the rec center's glass doors clad in black workout pants so tight they had to be cutting off her circulation and a hot pink sports bra. Jace followed right behind her.

Of all the nights. Of all the moments. Of course he'd run into her now. When she could properly humiliate him in front of the only woman he'd had any interest in since the one standing in front of him made him look like a fool.

"Hi there!" Kaylee chirped like nothing had ever hap-

pened between them. Like they hadn't lost anything. Like
the ugliness of lies and angry words didn't fill the space
between them. She'd always been much better at pretending than him.

Jace at least had the decency to look awkward. He
hung closer to the parking lot like he wanted to avoid a
conversation. Not surprising, seeing as how the last time
they'd talked, Sawyer had ended up throwing him out of
the house in his underwear.

"I didn't realize you were still in town," Kaylee said to
him before glancing at Ruby.

Ruby's head tilted slightly, like she was figuring everything out. No introductions necessary, he was sure. She had
to have heard all about Kaylee from Avery and Paige.

He shifted his gym bag to the other shoulder. "Haven't
left yet. Still have a month left at work." And if he'd needed
a reminder of why he should leave town, here it was. At
least in Denver he wouldn't run into Kaylee and his old
friend, who was now her lover. Humiliation simmered beneath his skin.

Not taking the hint that he didn't exactly feel like chatting, Kaylee started to babble about how quickly the house
had sold.

"It was such a great house. I knew we'd have multiple
offers," she bubbled. "I told you those upgrades would help.
You were so against them, but..."

He almost laughed. Leave it to Kaylee to make small talk.
Like they'd never known each other intimately. Like all the
years they'd invested in their relationship meant nothing to
her. He almost wished he could feel the same way. But like it
or not, that history was a part of him.

"I can't wait until the check is in my bank account,"
Kaylee went on. "I think I'll book a vacation to Mexico..."

Before he could answer that he was glad their divorce would benefit her so much, Ruby's soft, strong hand rested on his forearm.

He glanced at her, captivated by the way she smiled up at him, like the two of them had a secret. It might have been the first real smile he'd seen on her face, full of both compassion and understanding.

"We should get going. Don't you think?" she asked in that lovable way she had. "The kids are waiting."

Kaylee's chin lifted as she sized up Ruby. She'd never liked being interrupted. "I'm sorry. I don't think we've met." Her smile bordered on a sneer.

"No. You're right. We haven't," Ruby said in her sweet melody. Then she turned and tugged him through the rec center's glass doors.

It was so unexpected that he laughed. Once they'd cleared the doors, he stopped and faced her. Searching her eyes, he saw more there than he'd bothered to see before.

"She didn't deserve you," Ruby said simply.

It was the nicest thing—the most genuine thing—anyone had said to him since the divorce.

"I'll go change. Meet you in the pool area?" she asked.

He could only nod. She amazed him. In one moment she'd managed to do what no one else could've.

Every time he saw Kaylee he remembered what he'd lost. But Ruby's touch had reached out and pulled him from the past. And now he remembered he still had a future to gain.

CHAPTER ELEVEN

Wasn't hard to pick out the group from the Walker Mountain Ranch. Sawyer heard the kids talking and laughing and squealing all the way inside the locker room. He followed the noise out to the pool area, where eight kids were bouncing next to the water like they had springs on their feet. They were about as diverse as any group he'd ever seen, covering every genre of the typical junior high scene—preppy, Goth, punk, jock, and maybe even one drama queen with perfect hair and makeup.

They seemed normal enough, except for one thing. Each one of them was separated from their parents, and not by choice, either. Bryce had mentioned there were a variety of circumstances. Neglect, drugs, prison...things he never would've considered as possibilities for his parents growing up. Things he couldn't understand even now. He'd give anything to have his son with him. Their parents had their kids, and yet they weren't fighting for them...

"Hey, thanks for being here, man." Bryce walked over and whacked him on the back.

"Wouldn't miss it." He'd actually been looking forward to this more than he realized. "Can't wait to meet 'em." He knew it'd take time for them to trust him, and they had to work on it right away. The rest of the week's activities would require trust.

Avery trotted over with Lily, who was snuggled in some sort of contraption that was strapped to her shoulders. "Hey, Sawyer." A sly grin raised her eyebrows. "Is Ruby coming?"

"Think so." He glanced toward the entrance to the women's locker room. He thought she was. She hadn't changed her mind, had she? "I ran into her out front. Maybe you should go check on her." He'd love to do that himself, but that might frowned upon.

"I'm on my way home anyway. I'll go through the locker room and send her right out," Avery offered a little too happily as she hurried away.

"Come on." Bryce waved him over to kids. "I'll introduce you."

Everyone quieted as they approached.

"Hey, guys, this is my cousin Sawyer. He'll be helping out in the water today," Bryce said.

One of the boys, short but stocky with a pretty sweet afro, looked at him warily. "Aren't you a cop?"

Sawyer laughed. "Off duty today," he said, but the kid eyed him like he was a Catholic headmistress. Great. Being a cop wasn't going to help his cause with the trust thing.

Bryce cupped a hand onto the kid's shoulder. "This is Javon."

Javon raised his hand in a cool-guy wave.

"And this is Neveah." Bryce moved to the blond girl who

wore more makeup than a drag queen, despite the fact that she was about to jump into a swimming pool.

Her head tipped in a nod, but her eyes wouldn't meet his.

"Brooklyn." He pointed out a younger girl with curly black hair and dark skin. She was the only one who smiled at him, and it was impossible not to smile back. Though her dark eyes were too serious for her age, something about the hope in her expression made him want to prove to her that world really could be a good place.

"And this is Wyatt." Bryce moved to stand behind a kid who wore dark eyeliner and had more piercings than Aunt Elsie's pincushion.

"They'll be in your group," Bryce went on. "I'll be teaching Denny, Mikey, Char, and Samantha in the deep end." He pointed out another group of kids who were already bobbing up and down in the water.

"Great to meet you guys." Sawyer walked down the line, slapping each of the kids a high five, which all of them returned somewhat unenthusiastically. Except for Javon. He didn't bother. "You all ready to learn how to swim?"

No answer. So Bryce had given him the group who weren't exactly thrilled about getting in the water. Actually he preferred that. Give him one hour with them and he'd change all their minds. Including Ruby's, if she'd ever get out here. Yet again, he glanced toward the women's locker room. What was taking her so long?

"Let me know if you need anything," Bryce said, then dove into the pool to join the other group.

"Will you really teach us how to swim?" Brooklyn asked.

He turned his attention to her. She looked to be maybe about eight or nine, and even though her eyes were round and afraid, they had a spark, too, like she wanted to believe she could learn.

Sawyer knelt to her level. "Yes. I'm going to teach you how to be safe in the water." He grinned at her. "By the time I'm done you'll probably be able to beat me in a race."

Her unsure smile tugged at his heart.

Before any of them could chicken out, he eased himself into the water. "Next one in gets an ice-cream treat after the lesson," he tempted.

There was a burst of chaos as all four of them pushed and shoved their way down the steps and into the pool.

"Guess that means everyone wins," he said, and they all cheered. While he had their attention, he quickly talked through what they would be learning—how to hold their breath, front floating, back floating, all the things that would help them be more comfortable in the water. Then he showed them how to do the warm-up bobs he'd always loved when he'd done swimming lessons as a kid. They picked it up right away, plugging their noses and plunging beneath the surface, then bursting up and gasping in a breath.

"Is this where I'm supposed to be?"

The sound of Ruby's voice jarred him. He raised his head, caught sight of her standing a few feet away from the pool, clutching a massive beach towel around her body like there was a blizzard inside the pool room.

"Yep. Sure is." He pulled himself out of the pool, keeping a close eye on the kids, who were well on their way to becoming professional bobbers.

"Everything okay?" he asked, because a half hour had to have passed since their little run in with Kaylee.

"Sure. Yeah." But she hugged her towel tighter. "Just not a big fan of water. Or swimming suits. That's all."

"Neither are any of them." He gestured to the pool, where the kids had stopped bobbing and were now holding on to the wall, looking up at him expectantly.

"So it'll be perfect," he insisted, resting his hand on her arm the way she'd done for him. "I've already pulled you out once. Wouldn't mind doing it again." He'd gladly rescue her every day if it meant he could pull that soft body of hers against his...

"This is boring. What d'we do next?" Neveah demanded, rolling her eyes.

Holy shit, he was gonna have his hands full this week.

"Hold on. My assistant and I are coming." He grinned at Ruby. "You in?"

She gave him a sideways glance, then trudged to a chair and unraveled the towel from her body.

Holy smokes. Sawyer cranked his jaw tight so it wouldn't hit the ground, because damn...the woman could pose for the centerfold of any magazine she chose. The bikini she wore was far from skimpy—looked like one of those athletic suits Paige wore on the river—but on Ruby it looked downright provocative. He let his gaze sweep over her body. None of those hard angles and bony features that plague skinny girls, but rounded curves that looked like they'd fit his hands perfectly.

Ruby walked back to him, her arms tight at her sides like she'd never been more uncomfortable.

"Like the suit," he said casually, as though complimenting a winter coat.

She looked down at herself and crossed her arms self-consciously. "I had to borrow it from Paige. I don't even own a swimming suit."

"After today, you'll want your own suit." Sawyer turned away and led her to the pool so the sight of her body wouldn't derail him again. "Trust me. You'll love swimming." If he had anything to say about it, that was.

"I wouldn't get your hopes up," she answered drily.

"All right, gang." Sawyer pretended he hadn't heard and lowered himself into the pool. "You know Ruby, right? She'll be my assistant today."

Their faces lit up, even Wyatt's, whose lined eyes usually held a flat expression to tell the world he'd rather be anywhere else.

"Ruby!" Brooklyn splashed over to the stairs, bouncing up and down with excitement.

Of course they already liked *her*. She was the one who fed them sugar.

"Are you guys married?" Neveah asked.

"No." Ruby answered quickly, still standing on the top step so that the water lapped at her ankles. "We're *not* married."

"We're just friends," Sawyer said. Just friends. Was it possible to be just friends with Ruby when his body reacted to her this way?

Trying to ignore her curves, he faced the class. They really had to get started. He needed a distraction. "How many of you know about the two most important floats you can learn to help you swim?"

All four of the kids blinked at him.

Okay. They'd have to start at square one. "The front float and the back float are the most important things you'll learn tonight." He hoped, anyway. "If you can float, you can learn how to swim. So first Miss Ruby and I will demonstrate the front float."

She gaped at him as if he'd just told a bunch of preteens the two of them were going to have sex. What was she so afraid of? Him touching her? Because it wouldn't be all that safe for him, either, feeling her body underneath his hands, but if she helped him teach, it would take her mind off her fears. That's why he wanted her to demonstrate. *Yeah. Sure.*

It had nothing to do with touching her. That was his story and he would stick to it.

"Come on, Miss Ruby." He beckoned her down the stairs. "Everyone cheer for Miss Ruby," Sawyer said with a grin.

The kids clapped and whooped.

"All right, Miss Ruby!" Brooklyn squealed.

"Don't be scared!" Neveah added.

But the deeper she waded into the water, the wider those expressive green eyes got.

"Hey," he whispered, laying a hand on her shoulder. "Don't worry. I won't let anything happen to you."

"I can't put my face in the water," she hissed close to his ear. "It makes me panic. I always gasp for a breath and inhale."

Hmmm. That would be bad. Couldn't have her choking in front of the kids. "Change of plans, gang," he yelled over the excited drone of voices. "We're going to start with the back float instead." Before she could find another excuse, Sawyer positioned Ruby in front of him and rested one hand high on her back while the other lingered as low as he could get away with. "Okay, Miss Ruby, all you have to do is lie down and relax. I'll hold you up."

Her lips formed an O and a hiss of air escaped, but she started to lower her back toward the water.

"Easy." He prodded her lower and lower until she was lying on her back, his hands underneath her, holding her up.

She stared into his eyes with a look of terror.

"Good. This is perfect." He looked up at the kids. "See how relaxed she is?" *Yeah. Real relaxed.* Underneath his hands her body felt like a two-by-four. "Because she knows there's nothing to be afraid of. Even if I took my hands away, her body would float."

Ruby's breaths were punchy now. And her face had paled.

She'd trusted him to hold her up. It was a good start, but she obviously needed a break. He stood her up, keeping his hand firmly on her back as a silent reminder that he wouldn't let anything happen to her.

Even though her body trembled slightly, she wore a determined expression that proved she was stronger than she gave herself credit for.

He could see it in the way her face steeled, in the way she held her breath, in the way she didn't give up. Ruby James might be timid, but she was strong.

And he wanted to find a way to help her believe it.

CHAPTER TWELVE

God, this was so humiliating. She was more terrified of the water than a bunch of kids. Ruby took in her peers, who were happily bobbing up and down, watching with a determined mix of awe and excitement while Sawyer instructed on the mechanics of a good back float.

Why hadn't she simply agreed to watch from the bleachers? There was a whole cluster of women over there—most likely moms who were watching their kids swim and go down the slide. Of course, at the moment every single woman in the place seemed to be staring in Sawyer's direction. The shirtless Sawyer Hawkins was obviously a main attraction.

And yes, okay, sure. Sawyer happened to have a body that could rival an Olympic swimmer's, the toned arms and chiseled pecs and dented abs. Smooth and tan, too, so the guy had apparently won the genetic lottery. But, really. Did they have to be so *obvious* about watching him? It made her feel like they were watching her, too, and that was the last thing she needed when she happened to be facing one of the biggest fears of her life. It wasn't the water so much as the breathing thing. Whenever she couldn't breathe, panic broke loose the same way it had when Derek's hand would squeeze her neck and steal her ability to take a breath.

Funny how you didn't realize the way trauma stored itself up in your subconscious.

"Good job, Brooklyn." Sawyer braced his hands under the young girl as she stuck out her belly and struggled to stay afloat. "You've got it! You're floating!"

Brooklyn sprung to her feet, giggling and squealing. "I did it! I can't believe it! I'm swimming!"

"You're a natural," Sawyer informed her, tousling her hair. That one small gesture of tenderness melted away some of the fear that had walled off Ruby's heart. He was so good with them. Encouraging and positive, but also challenging them to try their best. It was like he knew exactly what they needed to hear. And her, too. He knew when she needed him to touch her, to ground her against the trembling fear that rose up when she thought about going under. Somehow Sawyer helped her stave off the panic. He made her want to let go of the fear...

"Hey, gang. Great job on those back floats. Now we're gonna move on to front floats."

Crap. That meant face in the water. Ruby's stomach pulled tight. Maybe he wouldn't pick on her this time. Maybe he'd let her sit on the stairs and observe...

"In order to do a front float, you need to put your face in the water." Sawyer looked right at her and she knew she couldn't escape him fast enough.

"Miss Ruby and I will show you how it's done," he said,

swimming close to where she sat on the stairs. Under the surface of the water his hand found hers, squeezing it in a silent *you can do this.*

She wasn't so sure.

He tugged her to her feet, so that she stood directly across from him, their faces a foot apart. "On the count of three, we're going under," he said to her, then glanced at the kids. "And you guys can count and see how long we hold our breaths. We'll have a little competition."

A murmur of excitement went up from the kids, but Ruby started to hyperventilate.

"You can do this," Sawyer murmured so only she could hear. "We'll do it together." He squeezed her hand harder. "Take a deep breath, Ruby."

She sucked in a lungful of air, but there was no way it was enough.

"One, two, three." Sawyer pulled her under, still holding her hand. She suspended her chest, squeezed her eyes shut.

Her butt hit the ground and panic broke free. She couldn't breathe. Her lungs burned just like they did when Derek had his fingers laced around her neck. She'd squirm and try to fight him off, sure she was going to die.

God, she was going to die if she didn't get air...

She tried to let go of Sawyer, to get away, but his free hand cupped her cheek, both calming and firm. The strength of his touch stilled the chaos in her mind. *You're not going to die,* his touch assured her. *Because I'm with you.* And he was safe...

She opened her eyes, the chlorine stinging like crazy, and saw him smile at her. His eyes connected with hers and held her there, submerged under the water, heart beating hard with the courage he was offering her. Through the murky water, Sawyer looked straight into her, grounded and sure. He would never hurt her. She believed him. No matter how badly her lungs ached, she would believe him.

Bubbles rose from her lips. Her lungs continued to shrink, but Sawyer squeezed her hand, zapping his energy into her weak body. When the ache in her lungs threatened to collapse her chest, she shot him her best pleading expression and he nodded.

He broke the surface first, pulling her up after him.

Her mouth opened and she drank in enough air to fill a hot-air balloon. Her lungs heaved in a pleasant exertion.

The kids cheered.

"Twenty seconds! Twenty seconds!" they chanted, as if somehow they sensed what an incredible accomplishment that was for her.

"Wow," she gasped, their elation baiting a smile. Twenty seconds and she hadn't panicked, she hadn't felt the need to inhale a gallon of water.

"See?" Sawyer said, raising his brows at her, and if the man was tempting before, now he was downright enticing. "No problem."

Except there was a problem. Despite the damp cold of the pool, her body radiated this tantalizing warmth that only intensified when she looked at him. What he had done for her just now planted a connection in the rocky soil of her heart, rooting itself deep. How could she risk letting it grow?

"Your turn, gang." He grinned a challenge to the kids. "Try to beat twenty seconds."

Another burst of excitement buzzed around her.

"Ready. Set. Go!" Sawyer clicked the stopwatch that hung around his neck as four little heads dove under the surface.

He stared into her eyes again, in that perceptive, tender way of his, like he might reach up to touch her cheek, but Ruby backed away from him. She never should've come. Elsie was wrong. Spending time with Sawyer wouldn't make things better. It would only make things worse for both of them.

One by one the kids came up for air. Sawyer congratulated each one of them with a hearty high five, then turned back to her. "Front float time," he announced, beckoning her over.

The kids waited, their eyes wide, and she couldn't let them down. At the prospect of Sawyer's hands on her again, her body hummed all high notes, hands tingling, face flushing. Somehow, with Sawyer holding on to her, she didn't fear the water as much, but she definitely feared him. She feared how he made her feel, how he made her let go, how he made her forget her secrets.

"You can do this," he whispered, holding his palms up on the water's surface.

She didn't doubt it, not with him helping her, but she did doubt her ability to hold on to reality when those hands molded to her body.

With great hesitation, she eased herself down until his hands supported her upper stomach and lower hips. Her insides rippled as much as the water. Gasping in a breath, she submerged her face, focusing on the feel of Sawyer's steady hands underneath her. Heat radiated from the places he touched her, strengthening the beat of her heart, and it was too hard to fight the way she wanted him. So she gave in, letting her body rest in his hands, closing her eyes tightly to savor the feeling of being guarded and protected and...held.

Muffled cheers tempted another smile.

Sawyer slowly pulled his hands away from her, and, as shocking as it was, her body really did float. For the first time in her life, she felt completely weightless. It could've been ten seconds or a year, she wasn't sure, but then Sawyer's hands slipped back underneath her, one of them grazing her breast in a way that made her jump. She jerked up her head to stare at him, trying to look offended, but losing the battle against a smile.

"Sorry," he mouthed, and his face *did* appear slightly red.

She tried not to laugh as he stood her up.

"I didn't mean to," he whispered over another round of cheering. "Seriously. Not that I wouldn't want to or anything, but..." He trailed off like he wasn't sure exactly how to finish that sentence.

For both of their sakes, it was probably best if he didn't.

"You did it!" Brooklyn swung her arms around Ruby's neck.

Laughing, feeling lighter than she had in years, she pulled the girl in for a hug.

"She was amazing," Sawyer agreed, smoothing his hand down her hair in a way that made Ruby dizzy with the desire to fall into his arms so his hands would be on her body again.

She released Brooklyn and gazed up into Sawyer's tranquil blue eyes, trying to tell him everything she felt.

Eyes focused on hers, he inched closer to her...

"What's next?" Javon interrupted. It was the most enthusiasm she'd heard in him since she'd offered him a cinnamon roll.

The rest of the kids crowded them in.

"Oh." Sawyer's face went blank, like he'd forgotten what they were supposed to be doing. She knew the feeling. It was hard to focus on anything else when Sawyer was around, when he was touching her. It was so intense, the connection that drew them together. But they couldn't be together. Ever.

"Why don't we split them up into two groups?" Ruby suggested after a hearty throat clearing. "You can help half of them with the front float and I'll help the other half."

That way she wouldn't be so close to him. She wouldn't long for something she couldn't have. Spending time with Sawyer tempted her to forget what she was running from.

And she couldn't afford to forget.

* * *

After the lesson had ended and Bryce had herded all the kids outside, Ruby busied herself with retrieving the diving rings that Javon and Wyatt had launched around the shallow end of the pool. When she got back to the stairs, Sawyer was waiting at the top with her towel.

Impossible to avoid him now.

Droplets of water glistened on his skin, running down his defined upper body, and she could see why all those moms in the bleachers had been so distracted by Officer Hawkins in a swimsuit.

Goose bumps bristled her skin as she crept out of the pool, but they had nothing to do with a chill and everything to do with the way he watched her, his gaze working down her body.

When she stood across from him, a nervous energy swirled through her and weakened her legs.

"So what'd you think of the class?" Sawyer wrapped the towel around her shoulders, his fingers brushing her skin.

"Um. It was great." Fighting a serious swoon, she tore her gaze away from his chest and focused on wrapping the towel tighter. "The kids had so much fun." Because of him. Once they'd all mastered their floats, Sawyer had played Marco Polo with them. It was amazing to see how they opened up to him, how they'd laughed, especially Brooklyn. She'd attached herself to Sawyer most of the night. "You're great with the kids. Really." Seeing them relax like that had made her heart so full.

He reached up to push a lock of hair off his forehead, slicking it back. "You had fun, too?" he prompted with that tempting grin of his.

She relented with a sigh. "I'm glad I stayed. Even if it was slightly humiliating." At least the kids hadn't seemed to pick up on her fear, but still...

"You were brave." His hand lifted to her face and he touched her cheek, sending her heart spiraling out of control again.

Because of him. He'd made her brave. But now she was scared. She knew he wanted her as badly as she wanted him. She saw it in the way he looked at her, felt it in the way he touched her.

And she was losing the will to fight it.

"You're shivering," he said, sweeping a hand down her arm. "Here." He shoved an ASPEN POLICE sweatshirt into her hands. "They're closing so we don't have time to change. But you can wear this home. It'll keep you warm."

That wouldn't be the only thing keeping her warm. Because when Sawyer was nearby, her body turned up the thermostat. To keep up appearances, she pulled the sweatshirt over her head while he pulled on a faded green t-shirt. They both wrapped towels around their waists, slipped on their flip-flops, and then he led her out into the parking lot and walked her to her car.

"I'm glad you came." His voice was low…

"Me too," she managed to say through an infatuated sigh. "Thank you." For showing her she could do more than she believed she could. For not thinking she was ridiculous to be so afraid of the water.

The dim moonlight shadowed his face, but she felt him searching for her eyes.

"Do you remember when you kissed me?" he asked with a slight tease.

A warm rush of desire pooled low in her belly. "Um. Yes." She definitely remembered that. Feeling his solid chest against hers, his hands cradling her cheeks. Not like she'd forget that anytime soon.

"I didn't kiss you back properly," he murmured, his face lowering closer.

"You didn't?" she whispered, feeling his breath mingling with hers. Somehow the darkness made his eyes even more beautiful. They were clear and glistening, deep enough to get lost in.

One corner of his mouth lifted in a smirk as he slowly shook his head, his lips inches from hers.

Anticipation gripped her body in that tantalizing hum. It'd been so long since she'd felt it, so long since her chest threatened to burst open this way…

She wanted his mouth on hers, his hands on her body. She wanted to lose herself in him.

He took his time touching his lips to hers, so slow and sensual that her legs threatened to give and she had to lean her back against the car. This time his hands didn't move for her face. Instead he worked them up her sides and underneath the sweatshirt, pressing her against his solid strength as his mouth opened to hers. The seductive rhythm of his tongue took her over, quieting every hesitation, conquering her last line of defense. She gripped his shoulders and pulled him over her, until his body pinned hers to the car.

He smiled against her lips as he kissed her again, his fingers fused to the bare skin of her stomach. She let her head fall back so she could breathe, so she could clear the stars out of her eyes, and Sawyer took it as an invitation to trace his lips down her neck. She ran her hands through his hair, which was still damp. And gorgeous. So thick and soft.

Sawyer's arms slipped around her, holding her as his lips found hers again.

Oh, god, this was so much more than a kiss. So much deeper. So much more dangerous…

"Come back to the ranch with me," he murmured. "After I deliver ice cream to the kids, we can open a bottle of wine…"

She wasn't sure her lips could form words. They had to be swollen, pulsing and tingling like that.

She wanted to go home with him. Lordy, she wanted to. Saying no would cause her physical pain. But if she slept with him where would that leave them tomorrow? She couldn't forget the expression on his face when Kaylee had approached him earlier. It wasn't anger or hate. It was hurt and humiliation. She couldn't do that to him. She couldn't be another woman who lied to him.

And she couldn't tell him the truth.

"If you need more convincing, I'm happy to try," he said, kissing her again, and the only way she would be able to resist him was to tear herself away.

She let his lips cling to hers for a second more, storing up the way it felt to have his body against hers, then pried herself away, heart thumping, chest throbbing. "I can't. I'm sorry," she wheezed, stumbling to the driver's-side door. "I can't do this, Sawyer."

Then she got in the car before he could convince her to stay.

CHAPTER THIRTEEN

Ruby drove out of the parking lot like she was escaping a fire, turning onto the main road so fast the tires screeched. Night had settled in, making the world look colorless and stony. Reaching down, she blasted the heat in a futile attempt to soothe the tremble in her shoulders. As warm as she'd been in Sawyer's arms, it hadn't taken long for a cold, empty darkness to set in like a heavy morning fog. It clouded her under a haze of memories that seemed to belong to someone else.

She wished they belonged to someone else. She wished she were free of them so she could've gone back to the ranch and spent the night in Sawyer's bed. Even though she'd left him, Derek still held her prisoner. He still had that control in her life.

The night she'd met him, it'd felt like the tide of her life had finally changed. She'd been on her own since the day she turned eighteen and could walk out of the foster care system. For so long she'd believed that once she was on her own, things would be better. She'd tracked down Grady, who'd been placed in another foster home, and hoped they could be a family together. But life wasn't any easier on the outside. Grady up and joined the Peace Corps, so she was alone in the world, struggling to pay rent in a studio apartment, waitressing as many hours as she could to keep the lights on.

One night Derek came into the bar with some friends, and she always hated waiting on tables like that one because inevitably one or two of the men would get sloppy drunk and grab at her or make some disgusting comment that made her feel small.

But Derek was so polite, calling her Miss and thanking her every time she refilled their glasses or brought out a new appetizer. He'd stood out from the rest of the men, not only because of his sandy blond hair, soft brown eyes, and muscular build, but because he didn't drink too much or talk too loud or laugh at any of the crude jokes his friends told. Then he'd paid the tab for the entire group, not in a showy way, but quietly, leaving her a thirty-percent tip to make up for his friends' obnoxious behavior. She remembered holding the receipt and smiling at the note he'd written, the first buds of hope blooming in her chest.

He came back in a couple of times a week until they'd gotten to know each other, then he took her on a real date—fancy restaurant, a movie, a walk in the park—the whole deal. He was good-looking, had a steady job, and seemed to know what he wanted in life. For the first time she wasn't alone. It wasn't that she was afraid to be alone. She'd learned to take care of herself early in life, but she'd never had anyone to share the passing moments with—the happiness and the sadness and the mundane.

Maybe that's why she let things move so fast. Six months after they'd met, he asked her to marry him while they were spending a day at the beach. She'd said yes, gotten rid of her apartment, and moved into his house. Then everything changed. He convinced her she didn't need to work anymore, that her friends were "trash" and she didn't need them anymore, either. Not when she had him. Not when they had each other.

Without realizing it she cut herself off from the rest of the world. After that Derek started to yell. She'd seen men yell when they were drunk, but Derek rarely drank. He just got angry.

The first time he hit her he'd looked about as shocked as she'd been. Then he'd fallen to his knees in front of her, begging her to forgive him, saying he never meant to hurt her, promising it would never happen again. God, she'd loved him. And he'd been the first person to love her.

But it happened again. And again.

Everyone had thought Derek was the epitome of the southern gentleman. But now she knew he was just brilliant in his manipulations. It was like he'd waited until their lives were entangled, until she had nowhere to go, no job to support herself, and then he took off the mask. He'd push her to the ground for talking back to him, pin her up against a wall with his forearm, crushing her windpipe if she spent too much money at the grocery store. She'd tried to fight back, more than once, but he would hit her so hard in the stomach, she would lay sprawled on the floor for an hour, silent tears leaking from her eyes.

While he continued to be promoted by the local police force, she'd holed up in their house, doing her best not to set him off. Once his mama had come to stay a few weeks. She'd always liked his mama, and figured the woman must know how to make a marriage work, since she'd been married for thirty-five years. Ruby had worked up the courage to say something. "Sometimes Derek pushes me around. I get so scared...I don't know what to do about it."

"Oh, honey." His mama had patted her hand. "He doesn't mean nothin' by it. That's how men are. You need to watch that you don't get him all muddled and upset and things'll be fine."

She wished his mama would've told her the truth...*it's not your fault, honey. He's a violent and disturbed person. You don't deserve it.* Maybe then she would've been strong enough to leave earlier. Instead she'd spent months believing she deserved every bit of it. Until she knew she couldn't take it anymore. She was losing herself, disconnecting from the world, going through daily life like a robot. And when he'd knocked her to the ground that last time, she knew she wouldn't survive another week.

"I'm gonna leave," she'd told him, and he'd squeezed his hand around her throat until the pain of asphyxiation shot through her neck.

"You leave me, and I'll find you. I'll fucking kill you and make it look like an accident."

But she had to go. She would've died any—

A flash of something darted in front of the car, shattering the memories and thrusting her back to the present...to Aspen...to her neighborhood street.

"No!" She jammed her foot onto the brake pedal and her body whipped forward. The tires screeched to a stop, filling the car with the acrid scent of burned rubber.

What was it? An animal. It had to be some kind of animal. Oh, god, had she hit it? Her hands shook so hard that it took her three tries to free herself from the seat belt and push open the door.

Something whimpered from the other side of the car. Dread crammed her stomach as she walked around...

A dog sat a couple of feet away from the tire, licking its paw.

"Nell?" Ruby called, crouching and holding out her hand. It had to be Nell. She must've gotten out.

"Hey there, sweetie." She took slow steps, and though the dog's tail wagged, it didn't walk to greet her. "What's the matter, girl? Are you hurt?" Oh, lordy, had she run over Nell's paw?

With a forlorn look Ruby recognized all too well, the dog peered up through those slightly buggy but adorable eyes. She held her little paw in the air like it hurt too much to rest it on the ground.

"Good dog." Ruby knelt and reached over to pet the soft fur that sprouted from the dog's head. She was the most beautiful dog in the world, soft and white with chestnut spots. Gently she took the dog's paw in her hands and searched for a wound, but it must've been some sort of internal injury she couldn't see. "He hurt you, didn't he?" she asked quietly.

Nell licked her hand.

Looking around to make sure no one was watching, Ruby carefully lifted the dog into her arms and cuddled it against her chest.

Nell didn't fight, didn't even flinch, but instead settled right in and went back to licking Ruby's hand.

"It's okay," she whispered, sliding into the car. She drove the rest of the way home with the dog lying contentedly in her lap. After she parked in the driveway, Ruby hid Nell in Sawyer's sweatshirt, making sure the dog could poke out her head. Hurrying up the front porch steps, she kept an eye out for the neighbors. "It's not your fault, Nellie," she whispered as she unlocked the front door. "You don't deserve to be treated like that." No one did. Not her, and not a defenseless animal who offered nothing but love.

"Everything'll be okay now." There was no way in hell she would return the dog to that horrible man. Instead she'd keep sweet Nellie and take care of her so no one would ever hurt her again.

* * *

Sawyer drummed his fingers against Bryce and Avery's dining-room table, listening to Bryce yammer on and on about why they didn't need more security measures at the ranch. Aunt Elsie had taken the kids over to the hospital to visit Thomas, so he'd come over to Bryce and Avery's for a late dinner and a discussion about the ranch's security protocols...or lack thereof, but his mind kept backtracking to Ruby. That kiss. Shit. He couldn't stop replaying it. One minute Ruby had been in his arms, kissing him, threading those long, slender fingers through his hair, then some switch had flipped and she'd disappeared. And to think, he could be in bed with her right now instead of sitting here with his cousin. The thought killed him.

"I trust my employees," Bryce said firmly. "They're good people."

Good people don't always make good decisions. He didn't say it. While there were plenty of flaws in Bryce's argument, Sawyer opted for the diplomatic approach. "Still I don't think it's a bad idea to do background checks on the employees. You never know what'll come up." Guilt niggled. Okay. So maybe he had ulterior motives. If he conducted background checks, maybe he'd find out more about Ruby, about where she came from, about why she seemed to run away from him whenever he got too close to her. "Background checks are standard. Trust me. No one'll be offended."

"Dinner is served." Avery sailed into the room somehow balancing three bowls of chili in her hands. She slid one in front of Sawyer, then Bryce. "Why all the talk about background checks?" She settled into a chair at the head of the table. "You didn't mention anything back when we were hiring people."

Bryce gave him a warning look.

Actually he *had* mentioned something to his cousin, but like always, Bryce brushed it off. He wasn't worried, he'd said. Most of the people who worked for him had been around for years. Most, but not all.

Avery widened her eyes, demanding an answer.

Sawyer shot Bryce his own dark look. If he told her the truth, Avery would likely be on Sawyer's side.

Even if he didn't tell her anything, there were still ways to get her on his side... "I've heard about some break-ins in town. Figure it can't hurt to beef up security around this place." Judging from the worried look on her face, she'd agree with him.

"I think it's a great idea," she said. Then a devious smile narrowed her eyes. "Why don't you start with Ruby?" she asked a little too innocently.

He tried to ignore the comment, but his face got hot, and it wasn't only from the jalapeños in the chili.

The woman slurped chili off her spoon, taking her time to chew. Then she dabbed her mouth with a napkin. "I mean, seeing as how you *kissed* her and everything. Maybe you should do a strip search, too, Officer Hawkins."

"What?" Bryce gaped at him. "You kissed her? When? Where?" He looked back and forth between Sawyer and Avery. "How come I didn't know about this?"

"Because unlike women, I don't discuss every detail of my life," he muttered. Was it possible that Ruby had already told Avery what had happened between them an hour ago? No. No way. She must've been referring to the first kiss...

"Every detail?" Avery squeaked. "Honey, this isn't a small detail. This is huge! You're finally moving on. That's nothing to be ashamed of."

"Not ashamed," he corrected. "Just not broadcasting it to the world."

"Sorry," Avery said, but that grin on her face branded her a liar. "I can't help it. I'm so happy! Ruby is the sweetest person. She'd be good for you, Sawyer."

Ouch. He shook his head and shoveled in more chili. Bison and black bean, his favorite kind. "You married people. Always trying to fix everyone up."

"Is it wrong that we want you to be happy?" Avery shot back.

"I am happy. And I'm moving. Remember? Not exactly the best time to start a relationship." It was true, but that wasn't the real problem. The scene in the parking lot played again. "Besides, you can't have a relationship with someone who won't tell you anything about themselves, anyway." Who ran from you every time you tried to touch them.

Avery studied his face, those blue eyes intent and focused...like she could read his mind. "So you're not attracted to her?"

Damn that women's intuition thing. "It doesn't matter if I'm attracted to her or not. Things can't work out right now." Especially if she kept pushing him away.

"Things definitely won't work out when she finds out you're doing a background check on her," Bryce said through a laugh. "I can only imagine how that'll go over."

"It's not like I'm singling her out. We'll cover everyone. Guides, maintenance workers, housekeeping staff."

Bryce raised a skeptical brow.

Yeah. His cousin knew him too well.

"So she doesn't talk about her past," Avery said, waving it off. "She obviously wants to get away from it. And who are we to judge that?"

"Yeah," Bryce chimed in. "Running from the past. Hmmm. Kind of reminds me of someone else I know."

"That's different."

"Oh really?" Bryce taunted.

Avery scraped her bowl with her spoon. "When you get to Denver, are you planning to tell everyone what happened between you and Kaylee?" she asked with a counterfeit innocence.

"No," he admitted. So was that it? Was she running from the bad memories of a divorce? A betrayal? He'd love to believe that, but his instincts told him it was much darker. "And I'm not moving across the country. I'll only be four hours away," he reminded them. "Not like I'll cut ties and never see anyone from my past again."

"Four hours away might as well be across the country," Avery whined. "You're Lily's godfather. And now she won't get to know you."

"Of course she will." The words came out flat and awkward. Because, god, it was hard for him to hold her, to feel that warm weight in his arms. It always made him wonder about his son. He loved Lily, but holding her, staring down at that tiny nose and perfect little face reminded him of what he'd lost, of what he might never have…

"Speaking of Lily…" Avery hopped up. "I should go check on her. She should be waking up for her night feeding. Gotta stay on schedule!" Avery had the baby's life—

MORE THAN A FEELING   129

feedings, naps, poops—all scheduled to the minute. She was pretty type A. Guess he could see why Bryce preferred to keep the thefts quiet.

She gathered up their bowls. "I bet Lily would love to say hi to Uncle Sawyer." Traipsing away in the happy gait of a proud new mom, she left him and Bryce facing off over the table.

"Seems like Ruby's not the only one keeping secrets," his cousin commented in his direct style. "When are you going to tell Avery about the baby you lost?"

Sawyer had a hard time swallowing. "Why would I tell her?"

"Take it from someone who's lost a lot…" Which would definitely be Bryce. His first wife had died in a Jeep accident.

"Acknowledging the loss helps. Talking to people helps. You'll never deal with it if you keep it to yourself."

He reached for his water glass, wishing it was a beer. But seeing how Bryce was a recovering alcoholic, he never drank in front of him. He sure could use a beer now, though. "I've dealt with it."

"That's bullshit and you know it." They never hesitated to call each other out on anything. Hell, when Bryce was spending his days drinking nonstop, Sawyer had given him an ultimatum on more than one occasion. *Straighten yourself out or I throw your ass in jail.* So even though the flames of his temper flared, he didn't argue.

"Here she is!" Avery announced like she was introducing the queen of England. She hurried over with Lily nestled into the crook of her arm. "Would you mind holding her while I warm up her bottle?"

"Of course not." He didn't want to mind. He didn't want that burning sensation radiating in his chest, but it came anyway. Even so he held out his arms and Avery gently transferred Lily.

Those huge blue eyes peered up at him, round and content. He moved the blanket away from her face and her little hand latched on to his finger.

"Hey there, Lily." He tried to submerge the rising grief with a smile. She was amazing. So tiny. Fragile. Every instinct in him wanted to protect her. Is this how it would've felt to hold his son?

"Are you over Kaylee?" Bryce's quiet question stole his focus from Lily. It wasn't as hard to answer as it'd once been.

"Yeah. It's not her I miss. Not anymore." They'd had good times and he'd loved her, but they wanted different things, and he wasn't stupid. "It's being with someone." But it had to be the right person. No way did he want to go through another year-long divorce.

"Then maybe you should put yourself out there with Ruby. Take a risk."

"I take risks all the time." Hell, just last week, they'd gone rock climbing. Besides, he'd put himself out there with Ruby an hour ago and she'd bailed on him. What else could he do?

"You know what I'm talking about, jackass." Bryce tossed a wadded-up napkin at him. "Did it ever occur to you that Ruby might be more comfortable talking to you if she knew she wasn't the only one who'd been through something shitty?"

"I'm sorry. I didn't realize I was talking to your wife," he said, just to razz him. Even though…that made a lot of sense.

"Just sayin'." His cousin leaned back with a shrug. "You can't expect her to spill her guts if you're not willing to."

The man had a point.

CHAPTER FOURTEEN

Hold *still*, Nell." Ruby tried not to pinch as she brought the tweezers against the dog's paw. Closer inspection had shown that there was a massive thorn stuck in one of Nell's pads, which is what had likely caused the limp.

Thank god she hadn't run over the poor thing.

"How long have you been wandering around, anyway?" And had she run through a field of thistles or what? Squinting, Ruby pinched the thorn in between the tweezers and plucked.

The dog yipped and squirmed, but Ruby held her tight, finally removing the sharp thistle, which was much longer than it had looked. "There, now. See? All better." She patted the dog's head.

Nellie plopped into her lap, exposing her belly as if that had been the most exhausting five minutes of her life.

"It wasn't *that* bad, was it?" Ruby swept the dog into her arms and carried her over to the kitchen counter. Having no clue what could be wrong with Nellie, she'd driven to the only drugstore open and asked the clerk if he knew anything about dogs. The man was so kind, taking the time to answer her questions. He'd asked if the dog had been outside a lot recently. When she said yes, he suggested that she try searching Nell's paws for thorns. His dog got stuck with thorns all the time, he explained. Then he showed her everything she might need as a new dog owner. A fluffy round pillow bed, toys, treats, food, even some ointment and bandages for her paw. She'd never had a dog herself, but the clerk was happy to fill the cart with everything she might need.

Half an hour and about two hundred dollars later, here she was... proud owner of her very first pet.

Well. Not exactly *her* pet, really. But she refused to feel guilty. She was only protecting Nellie. If the dog had had a good family, she'd have brought it back to them in a heartbeat. As it was, neither one of them had anyone to love them, so they needed each other. A dog was the perfect distraction after what had just happened between her and Sawyer. The guilt over running out on him like that still burned like embers of regret. She knew she couldn't protect herself from having feelings for him. It was too late for that. But she could protect both of them from letting it go any further. If she could just wait it out a while longer, he'd be on his way to Denver.

"And now I have something to keep me busy." That would make it easier. "Isn't that right, Nellie?" she gushed, giving the dog Eskimo kisses before she set her on the counter. "We have to fix up that owie so you don't get an infection." Holding up the dog's paw, she dabbed ointment onto the wound and coiled the bandage around Nellie's leg. Then she set the dog on the floor. "How does it feel?"

Nellie took shaky steps before prancing with her head high.

Ruby swiped a chewy stick out of a box and dropped to her knees. "Good girl, Nellie." She held out the treat and the dog bounded over, sitting like a princess, somehow still wagging her tail across the floor.

How could that man have hurt Nellie? She was such a good dog...obedient and quiet and...

The doorbell chimed.

"Yarf!"

"Hush, Nell!" Blood rushed to her face. It was well past ten o'clock. Which meant that it wouldn't be a friendly neighborhood salesperson.

Heart thrumming, she scooped up the dog and jogged across the living room to the master bedroom. "You stay, honey." Ruby set Nell gently in the brand-new doggie bed and straightened. "Stay and I'll give you another treat, princess."

The dog cocked her head but didn't move.

"Good girl," Ruby said, closing the door tight.

Smoothing her hair, she crept to the door, trying to see through the drawn curtains. If it was the man from down the street, she'd simply tell him she hadn't seen Nellie. Hopefully the dog wouldn't bark and give her away.

She paused in front of the door. Oh, lordy. Her heart felt like it was about to implode. Bracing herself, she unlocked the dead bolt and swung it open.

"Sawyer." It was a half gasp, half question. Dear god! Had the man reported Nell stolen? Was Sawyer here to arrest her?

"Hey," he said, and she let out the breath she'd been holding because he wasn't in his uniform and she couldn't see any handcuffs anywhere. He couldn't arrest her in civilian clothes, could he?

"Um. Is everything okay?" She stepped out onto the porch, closing the door securely behind her. *Please don't let Nell yip. Not now . . .*

Sawyer shoved his hands into his pockets. "Everything's fine."

It should've made her feel better, but Ruby still couldn't breathe. Had he come to ask why she'd run away from him in the middle of such an exquisite kiss? Or maybe to finish that kiss? Because right now, looking at him in those worn jeans and faded blue ASPEN POLICE t-shirt that fit snugly over his broad shoulders, she couldn't remember why she'd run away.

She must be out of her ever-loving mind. Why would she *ever* run away from this man?

Sawyer shifted awkwardly. "I just . . . I wanted to tell you something. Can we talk inside?"

"No," flew out before she could think. "Um. Actually, things are a mess in there right now." It wasn't a lie. The dog paraphernalia had been scattered everywhere. Who knew a dog required so much stuff? "Why don't we sit on the swing instead?" she suggested, because if Sawyer came in and found Nell in her house, he'd force her to take the dog back to that awful man. And she couldn't let that happen.

Before he could argue, she led him to the porch swing Elsie had purchased as a housewarming gift when she'd moved in. She'd loved the front porch from the first time Elsie had brought her over to see the house. It spanned the entire length of the duplex and was homey and quaint, complete with white columns and intricate molding. The swing was made from two white antique doors that Elsie had rummaged out of someone's trash. She'd had Bryce build them into a swing and it fit the house perfectly.

"Sorry to barge in like this," Sawyer said, sitting close enough that she could feel his thigh against hers.

Oh, lordy. His thigh was so solid. As were his arms. And chest...pretty much everything, actually. "Don't apologize. It's fine." That unfinished kiss lodged between them; she could feel it charging the air. She cleared her throat and tried to breathe like a normal human instead of a sex-starved woman. "About what happened earlier..." What could she possibly say? "It wasn't that I didn't *want* to come home with you..."

"That's not why I'm here." Sawyer hunched over slightly, staring out at the night, gazing around as though looking for something. Courage, maybe?

She looked, too. It was a beautiful night, the air soft and cool, scented with the neighbor's overgrown lilac bush. The swing creaked and the crickets chanted a calming melody. Her fingers fidgeted with the swing's chain. The metal was cold and soothing against her skin. She looked up at the crescent moon, just a skinny slice in the black sky with stars sparkling all around it. She still couldn't believe how many stars you could see in the mountains. They were so vibrant, so plentiful. Her first night in Aspen had convinced her it was a magical place, and it still felt that way every time she saw it. Somehow, sitting here with Sawyer, taking in the magic of the night, it felt even more enchanted.

"Kaylee lost a baby. Before the divorce," Sawyer said, his normal commanding voice dulled by pain. "*We* lost a baby."

"Oh, god." A familiar knot of grief pulled tight under her ribs and hitched her breath. She'd never lost a baby, but she'd lost the chance to ever carry a baby, to ever have a baby of her own.

But this wasn't about her loss. Swallowing against the

cloud of sadness that rose in her throat, she rested her hand on his and turned to face him, pulling one leg up on the swing. "What happened?"

Sawyer faced her, too, looking into her eyes like he wasn't afraid to let her see the pain that resided there. "Kaylee was five months pregnant and the baby died. The cord had wrapped around his neck."

Ruby closed her eyes against a warm rush of tears. "I'm so sorry." The words couldn't touch that pain, she knew. She knew how it felt to give up on the dream of ever holding your baby...

"That was when our marriage started to fall apart." He moved his arm so that her hand slid down into his.

She threaded their fingers together, desperate to give him something to hold on to. "I guess I wanted to tell you because..." He turned over his hand, so that his palm rested against hers. "I don't want you to be afraid of me, Ruby. We all have things in our pasts we'd rather not talk about."

She pulled her hand away, resting it in her lap, looking for the stars again. "Are you here to ask me about my past again?" Is that why he'd come? To tell her something about himself so she'd swap secrets with him?

"No." He scooted closer and reached his hand to her cheek a gentle caress, turning her head slightly until he could look into her eyes. "I won't bug you about your past anymore. You don't have to tell me anything."

It should've calmed her, but instead her heart did flips. His eyes were so intense...

"The past doesn't matter. Because I know what I see now." That sexy smile loosened a sigh from her lungs.

"I see a woman who's stronger than she thinks is. Brave, even," he said. "Wise. Hell of a gorgeous body."

His gaze lowered down her legs and back up. "I didn't think I was being subtle, but in case you haven't noticed, I'm attracted to you. I can't say I've felt that way about anyone since I met Kaylee. And I was just hoping...you'd give me a chance."

The words were so sincere, so honest, that every defensive wall she'd raised came crashing down around her, leaving her exposed and open.

The man was nothing like Derek, who'd only ever let her see strength and power and an unyielding control. *No.* Sawyer was okay with his vulnerabilities. They didn't seem to make him feel weak, didn't make him feel the need to assert anything over someone else. It was like he didn't care if she knew he was as lost and damaged as she was.

"Sawyer..." There was so much she couldn't tell him. So many reasons she should ask him to leave, to leave her alone. But the ache tightening inside of her would never go away if she didn't touch him, if she didn't feel the generous hunger of his lips against hers, the thrilling sensation of his hands reading every curve of her body. So instead of saying anything, instead of casting him out of her life, she scooted to her knees so she could reach his lips, first touching them lightly with her fingers. "You're a good man, Sawyer Hawkins," she whispered. And though she knew he couldn't have her forever, she could give herself to him now. He could have her for this one moment.

His gaze fused with hers, the mesmerizing blue of his eyes smoldering like the center of a flame. His large hands settled on her hips and tugged them until she straddled him.

The swing pitched forward and she wrapped her arms around his neck to keep from losing her balance.

"This isn't why I came here," he informed her hoarsely.

"That's disappointing," she breathed against his neck. The stubble made her lips tingle.

Sawyer sighed in a helplessly delicious way and took her chin in his hand, bringing her lips to meet his, brushing them lightly in teasing preview.

Oh, lordy, lordy, lordy...the man could *kiss*.

He pulled back to look at her, but what good was that? She wanted to feel him against her, solid and safe and warm. So she wrapped her legs all the way around his waist, cinching them tighter until the hard bulge of his desire for her pulsed between her legs. It was blinding the way he made her lungs pound, the way he sent her dizzy heart twirling in circles. His touch brought her somewhere else, made her feel like someone else. Someone whole and unbreakable. The person she'd always wanted to be.

"You feel so good," he murmured, nipping at her neck, sneaking his hands under her shirt and easing them up her rib cage. "God, Ruby you have the most perfect body."

That was sweet, considering his ex-wife looked like a Victoria's Secret model.

"You're not so bad yourself," she gasped, because his hands roamed higher, over her thin bra, his rough skin grazing the points of her nipples, while the soft warmth of his tongue seared her neck.

He laughed against her skin, and she loved to hear him laugh, loved the way it resonated against her, loved the way it erased the evidence of grief from his posture. It was intoxicating, making him laugh. It made her feel like she was giving him something no one else could.

Tracing his lips back to her mouth, he kissed her deeply, hands still stroking the sensitive skin of her nipples, which were already hardened into knots of quivering pleasure.

"Can we," he uttered between kisses, "go in—"

Headlights cut across the dark night, slicing through her vision, and Ruby had to blink her eyes back into focus.

Sawyer looked toward the truck that was humming down the road.

"Uh-oh," he muttered. "Busted." He withdrew his hands from Ruby's skin and her body suddenly felt ice-cold.

Sure enough, the truck bounced into Elsie's side of the driveway, which happened to have a clear view of the front porch.

"Oh, lordy!" What would her boss think of her sitting in Sawyer's lap getting felt up like a sneaky high school girl? Scrambling, she untangled herself from him and jolted to the other side of the bench just as Elsie climbed out of her truck. "Hello, you two!" she greeted them happily. "I'm so glad you're here! How about a cup of tea?"

"Um, sure," Ruby struggled to reply, what with the humiliation crowding her throat.

Sawyer, however, didn't seem to share her awkwardness. He shifted and gathered her close to his side as if it was the most normal thing in the world for her to be sitting on the porch wrapped in his arms. "Evening, Aunt Elsie," he called over. "Tea sounds great." He leaned into Ruby. "We'll finish this another time."

The promise in those words sent a fervent yearning rippling down her stomach until it gathered low enough to make her lady parts throb. Yes. She wanted him. She wanted to make love to him, to share that deeper part of herself she'd never shared with anyone else. Lord knew he was worthy of it.

She wanted to spend the entire night in his arms, feeling his weight next to her, his breath against her skin. But if she did, if she forged that connection with him, she'd only be forced to take it back so she could protect him from the dangers of her past.

She would have to break his heart eventually.

And Sawyer had already lost too much.

CHAPTER FIFTEEN

Nothing like lying awake all night thinking about a woman...

Sawyer patted down his rumpled hair and booked it down the dirt road to the main lodge. He was late for breakfast. Mostly because he hadn't slept much, and since his alarm had gone off, he'd been moving slower than an inebriated suspect. Just about as confused as one, too. Ruby James did that to him. He'd never thought telling her about the baby would change things. He'd only wanted to start dealing with it, like Bryce had said. And he wanted Ruby to know that he had secrets, too.

Then she'd kissed him with those plump lips, and when he'd felt her body against his, it was all over. Probably a good thing Aunt Elsie had interrupted, or he might've rushed things, and the way she'd kissed him said she might've let him. But that would've been a mistake. Something about Ruby was fragile. She was strong, there was no doubt about that, but fear seemed to catch up with her after a while. And if he was gonna do this—put himself out there again—he had to do it right so it didn't go down in flames.

Something told him Ruby wasn't ready to sleep with anyone.

Remember that. Because when he was around her, practical reasoning wasn't exactly his strong suit.

A text dinged from his back pocket, but he ignored it and pushed through the ranch's main door. Bryce was probably texting to get an ETA on his arrival, seeing as how he was supposed to be there a half hour ago.

Just as he was about to turn into the lavish dining room, Aunt Elsie cruised toward him, pushing Thomas in a wheelchair.

Sawyer stopped. "They let you out already?" Hadn't the guy just had surgery?

"Ha," Aunt Elsie huffed. "He didn't give them a choice. But they only discharged him after he agreed to stay in a wheelchair for a few days."

"I don't need a damn chair," Thomas mumbled, his white mustache covering his top lip in old grouch's pout. But a spark of humor still flickered in his brown eyes.

"Least you've got the best nurse money can buy," Sawyer joked, enjoying the blush on Aunt Elsie's cheeks. She was usually the one dishing out the compliments. Every once in a while it was nice to send one her way. It was true, too. She'd taken care of them all for years...

"Can't argue with that," the man said with a wide smile. "This broken leg routine has scored me more baked goods than I've had in years." His grin turned ornery. "Might score me a kiss, too, if I'm lucky."

Sawyer gaped at him. The man must be glutton for punishment, flirting with Aunt Elsie that way.

"Stop, you old coot." She swatted his shoulder and shook her head like a buttoned-up librarian, except her face had flushed and he recognized the shine in her eyes.

"Can't blame a guy for tryin'," Thomas said in his jovial baritone.

Aunt Elsie cleared her throat extra loud. "And what about you, Sawyer, dear?"

"Huh?" Now it was his turn to blush. She hadn't said anything while she'd served them tea last night, but just how much had she seen when she'd pulled into the driveway and caught Ruby in his lap, his hands up her shirt?

"Are you joining us for breakfast?" she asked, easing Thomas toward the dining room.

"Oh." *Whew.* Maybe she hadn't seen anything. "Yeah. I'm right behind you." He followed her across the sitting room and past the stone fireplace that rose up all the way to the vaulted ceiling.

Everyone else was already there. Well, except for Ruby, he couldn't help but notice. He'd been waiting to see her again for about nine hours now.

"Good morning!" Aunt Elsie greeted the kids and wheeled Thomas to the end of the table. Most of them jumped up and ran over to give the man a hug.

"Good to see you!"

"So glad you're okay!"

"When can we sign the cast?"

Sawyer hung back while they took turns greeting the man who'd organized this trip for them. It was obvious Thomas had earned their trust and respect over the years. And today Sawyer hoped he could fill the man's shoes. The swimming lesson was a great start, but they'd have to trust him completely on the high ropes course.

Brooklyn was the first one to notice him. "Sawyer!" She

ran toward him, but then stopped suddenly and looked at the
floor like shyness had taken over.

His heart plummeted to his gut like a stone. What had
happened to her? Why was she here? Why wasn't she at
home with a mom and dad who gave her the kind of life
she deserved? He sauntered over and knelt in front of her.
"Morning, Brookie."

At the sound of the nickname, the girl's chin lifted, and
her smile sparkled in her eyes.

They were innocent eyes, so round and dark it made him
want to protect her forever. "Are you excited for today?"
he asked. "You're gonna love the high ropes course. It's a
rush."

Her eyes got even wider. "Is it scary?"

Probably not nearly as scary as some of the things she'd
been through. "Not at all. Ruby and I will be there the whole
time."

Brooklyn's smile returned. "Where *is* Ruby? I've been
waiting to see her all morning!"

Yeah. He could relate.

"I haven't seen her, but I have a pretty good idea where
she's hiding." He'd heard the pots and pans clanging in the
kitchen when he'd walked in. He led Brooklyn to the table
and pulled out her chair. "I'll go check on her."

It took every ounce of restraint not to sprint through
those kitchen doors. By the time he'd made it across the
room, his heart hammered hard, sending the sting of anticipation through him. God, it'd been a long time since he'd
had that feeling.

He swung open the door and there she was, traipsing
across the kitchen in cropped khaki pants and a tight green
shirt that set off her hair. The rich scent of chocolate only
made the scene more erotic.

Ruby stopped mid-step, a spatula suspended midair. Damn that coy smile on her face. How was he supposed to behave when she looked at him like that—one corner of shapely lips turned up like she had a secret?

He'd give her a secret to smile about...

"Morning, Sawyer," she murmured.

And to think...she could've been saying that in his bed, bare shoulders sticking out from the wrinkled sheets, hair all tangled and sexy from a long night of not sleeping. *Thanks a lot, Aunt Elsie.* How did that woman always know when to interrupt?

"You about ready to hit the ropes course?" he asked so he could get his mind on something else.

Her cheeks glowed pink, making her look so alive. "Of course." She pulled on oven mitts—who would've thought *that* could be a turn-on?—and slid a tray of massive muffins out of the oven.

Sawyer eyed the chocolate mounds of goodness. Looked like she'd added a hearty helping of chocolate chips, too. "Those kids are going to love you." He was in danger, too. Well past the point of danger, actually.

"Hope so." She pulled off the oven mitts and piled the muffins into a wicker basket.

Fascination weighted his jaw, but he cranked it shut. After last night everything she did managed to appear seductive.

Speaking of seductive, might be best if he mentioned that little make-out session they'd had on her porch. Had she thought about it as much him? "About last night..." What could he say? "I hope you don't regret anything."

Her smile softened into shyness.

"I definitely don't regret it." She gathered up the basket of muffins.

He stepped forward, aligning his body with hers. "Then let me take you out sometime. On a real date. Dinner. Wine." And then wherever else that led them...

"You're moving to Denver," she reminded him quietly.

"Which is only four hours away. Not like it's across the country or anything." Sure, it wasn't ideal to do the long-distance thing, but they could still see each other whenever he came back to visit...

"You'll find a whole new life there, Sawyer," Ruby said through a sigh. "Isn't that what you want?"

It had been. His life had seemed pretty shitty a couple of months ago when he'd made the decision. "That doesn't mean I can't hold on to things from my life here." He would hold on to his family. Lily. He would still find a way to be there for them, to stay connected.

Ruby's smile faded as she skirted past him. "We should go. Don't want to keep the kids waiting."

Oh, no she didn't. She wasn't going to run from him again. He stepped in front of her, leaving distance, but also showing her he wouldn't let her off that easy. "When can we go out?"

She took three steps, her hips swaying, until she stood directly in front of him, her lips inches from his. "Let's get through today. Then we'll talk about it."

He forced his shoulders into a shrug. "Fair enough." Damn, it was hard not to push her. But he wouldn't. Instead Sawyer let her lead the way out to the dining room, taking in the view of her backside.

The excited chatter silenced the second they walked in, and Sawyer wasn't sure if it was the chocolate or the way Ruby seemed to light up a room. The loving expression on her face as she greeted the kids left no doubt that she adored them.

"Morning, everyone," she said, that slight country accent twanging. She set the basket on the table.

"Are those *chocolate*?" Javon demanded, helping himself to one of the muffins.

The rest of the kids followed suit, snatching up the muffins until the basket was empty.

"Double chocolate," she informed them with a devious smile. "I added extra chocolate chips."

"Delish!" The kid eyed her, his gaze lowering down her body. "You're pretty delish, too," he said with that boyish smirk of his. Sawyer was tempted to tell Javon to lay off, but he had to admit, the kid had good taste.

Ruby laughed. "And you can have another muffin."

"These are the best!" A full bite muffled Brooklyn's compliment.

"Don't think anyone's ever baked me a muffin before," Neveah said with a smear of chocolate across her chin. "I didn't even know you could make 'em chocolate!"

"I can make *anything* chocolate," Ruby answered with a tempting lift of her eyebrows.

It was the first time since he'd met them that Sawyer had seen them laugh. In less than twenty-four hours, Ruby had completely won them over.

She sat in the chair next to Brooklyn, tipping her head close to the young girl's and saying something that made them both crack up. From across the room Sawyer watched the woman pour out her warmth and generosity on those kids.

And he had never wanted any woman as much as he wanted her right then.

* * *

Ruby gawked up at the platform that had to be looming a good seventy-five feet above her head. It teetered precariously on top of a pole that had stakes poking out all the way up the sides like little hairs.

Shit. All of a sudden she turned asthmatic. Who would've guessed that the high ropes course would be the perfect avenue for ingraining things like trust and teamwork to a bunch of foster kids who stood as frozen and pale as she looked?

Sawyer appeared behind her and cinched the waist strap on her harness. "Ever done a high ropes course?"

Her upper body jerked with each tug. "No. Definitely not." Below her torso, her knees had petrified into stiff, wooden planks. She could hardly ride the chairlift up Aspen Mountain without feeling like she had to throw up. Now he expected her to climb up there with the rest of these kids and jump off the platform to gracefully seize that trapeze like she'd joined some insane circus act? She shimmied away from him and sloped her hands on her hips. Great. Her fingertips were already numb. "When I agreed to help, I didn't realize this was part of the deal."

He laughed like he thought she was joking. "You'll love it."

No. She loved being in the kitchen. On the ground. She loved losing herself in a half hour of kneading bread dough. She slid her hands down the back of her pants to wipe off the sweat. "I'm not big on heights."

Sawyer's neck curved to hold his head higher. Those balmy blue eyes crinkled with humor. "Trust me, Ruby. If you can dunk your head underwater, you can jump off that platform."

"No thanks." Her tone was sharp enough to lop off his outstretched hand. She assessed the godforsaken contraption again. "Is that thing hanging by fishing wire?"

He had the nerve to laugh again. Harder this time. Even though he must have seen how much she was sweating.

"You've got nothing to worry about." He raised his hand and pointed up. "That pulley system is the safest design possible. Bryce has it inspected every year."

"Great."

"Besides that, I'll be the one belaying you." He feigned hurt in a rumple of his lips. "Don't you trust me?"

Yes. She trusted him. But after last night he scared her almost as much as that platform. After he'd left Elsie's house, Ruby decided that she had to put distance between them, to tell him she wasn't interested so he'd stop pursuing her. Then she'd seen him this morning and her body flooded with longing. When he touched her, when he kissed her, reality seemed so far away. He almost made her believe that they were possible.

"I promise I won't let you fall," he murmured, locking her into his hypnotizing gaze.

She avoided his eyes. "It's not you I'm worried about." It was herself. What if she passed out halfway up the pole? What if she missed her grasp on the trapeze and fell before Sawyer had the chance to stop her? Terror inflated her heart until it ached against her ribs. "You know what? I think I'll sit this one out. Let the kids have fun with it."

Brushing a light touch against her shoulder, Sawyer prodded her a couple of steps away from the kids. "They won't do this unless they watch someone else do it first." He smiled, and it was so unfair the way that lovely mouth of his put her under a spell.

"I won't let you fall." That near whisper sent her heart whirling.

"You'll be safe. I promise."

Ha. She was *so* not safe with him. Not when he made her

feel this way. Like she could do anything, be anybody. Like she could let go of every fear.

Except one.

Around them, the shrieks and giggles and quiet gasps gained momentum. Without a promise or a decision, Sawyer winked at her and stepped back to the circle of ogling kids. "Okay, guys. We've already gone over the rules. All you have to do is climb to that platform and jump off to grab the trapeze."

"Hell no!" came from Javon.

Sawyer smiled patiently at all of them before giving the Javon a warning look. "Watch that mouth, buddy." He yanked on the multicolored rope that was woven through some kind of device dangling on his harness. The whole pulley system above their heads jiggled in his grip. "See this rope? I'll be holding on to you the whole time. I won't let anyone fall." He shot Ruby another knee-weakening glance before looking at each kid, apparently trying to beam confidence into their doubting stares.

"How do we *know* you'll be holdin' on? 'Cause I gots people who tell me stuff all the time. And half of it doesn't ever happen." Sweet Neveah stepped into the center of the circle. Though she was short and thin, those round brown eyes dared anyone to argue with her.

Sure enough, Sawyer's arms flew up in surrender. "Okay. Okay. I know this is a little different than what you're used to." He trotted back to Ruby and dangled his arm around her shoulder. *Lordy*. He smelled so good. She inhaled, the mountainous scent of the evergreen trees nearly making her dizzy.

"We'll demonstrate so you can see how easy and safe this is," she vaguely heard him say. "My friend Ruby'll climb up there and show you how it's done."

That got her attention. "What?" Her body shot away from his. She tripped and stumbled until she'd made it to the other side of the circle. Safely out of his grasp. "No. No way."

"If she's not doin' it, I sure as hell ain't gonna try it." Javon backed away. The other kids started to follow.

"Uh-huh."

"This guy's crazy."

Sawyer's mouth tightened into a frown. He focused the glare at her. As if it was her fault they refused. She sculpted her shoulders into an innocent shrug. Hey, they couldn't force them to climb up there if they didn't want to, could they?

"Think about it, guys." He left his post and walked slowly around the circle, pausing to look into each kid's eyes. "Think what it would feel like to stand way up there and look at the view. When else will you get the chance to go for it like this?" He stopped in front of her, a smile hiding in his features. "When else will you have the chance to jump without being afraid to fall?"

She got his hidden meaning. He wanted to free her. But she'd always be afraid as long as Derek was out there…

On either side of Ruby, Brooklyn and Neveah locked their hands onto her arms.

"You can do it, Ruby!" Brooklyn's curls sprung and bounced with each nervous twitch.

"I'll do it if you go first." Neveah ushered her into the center of the circle. Right next to Sawyer. "It's okay to be scared, right?" She stood between them. Between Ruby and a quick, albeit violent, death.

"She won't be scared because she trusts me." Sawyer took her hand to the tune of snickers and whistles.

He didn't even seem to notice the kids elbowing one another and whispering. He tightened his grip on her hand until his confidence filled in the shadows of her doubt.

"That's what this is about. Trust." His eyes locked into hers and asked the question. Did she trust him? Could she trust him? Just for ten minutes. Or an hour. It might take her an hour to climb up to the top of that platform.

The group quieted. Nine pairs of eyes stared at her. Some brown, others blue, green, some with heavy makeup and some that held doubt and disappointment and pain. Her decision would teach them something. What she chose would define this moment for them. For her, too. If she walked away, they would, too.

Shit. "Okay. Fine." Irritation breezed through the words, but she only put it there to hide the raw fear that tried to squeak through.

"Atta girl!" Sawyer patted her ass, and *hello*, that didn't alleviate the wobble in her body.

She tried to smile, but her heart seemed to alternate between palpitations and long pauses. And was her throat swelling shut? Could she be allergic to adrenaline?

"You can do it, Ruby!" Neveah yanked on her arm until she started to trudge toward the pole.

"Hold on a sec." Sawyer swooped in front of her and clicked a silver metal thingie into a loop on the front of her harness. "Now I've got you on belay."

Without meeting his eyes, she sidestepped him. "Great." A blurred film covered her vision as she entered into the shadow of the great platform.

"All right, everyone," Sawyer called. "Let's cheer her on." Behind her the kids started calling out their encouragement.

"Go, Ruby!"

"Don't look down!"

"Be careful!"

Two more steps on solid ground. She took them slowly. As she reached a hand up to grab the first climbing stake, Sawyer caught up to her and leaned close. "You sure you're okay with this? Because if you're not, you can belay me."

She glanced over her shoulder. Brooklyn's hands were clasped at her chest like she was saying a prayer. Neveah jumped up and down. Even Javon and Wyatt watched, eyes wide with anticipation. She owed it to them to do this, to be as brave as they believed she could be.

She secured a hand on Sawyer's shoulder and tried to siphon some of his mountain-man skills. "It's fine. It'll be good for me."

He moved closer, lips brushing against her ear. "I've got you. Okay?" His hand yanked on the rope that wove through both their harnesses.

Ruby felt a lift at her waist, like he could have hoisted her up there himself with the sheer strength of his arms.

"See? I'll be holding on to you the whole time."

"Mmm hmmm," was the only reply she could muster. She didn't want to walk away from him. She wanted to launch herself into his arms and stay there until her heart settled and she could breathe like a normal human being.

But Sawyer withdrew a few steps back and left her with the platform.

Excited squeals pierced the solemn mountain air.

"Is she gonna make it?" Neveah squealed.

"What if she falls?" Javon asked.

"I can hear you." She lifted a foot to the first wooden dowel sticking out of the pole. Reached for the next hand-hold. *Oh, god.* As she hoisted herself up, a sickening rush of blood shot into her extremities. Her legs quivered with the onslaught of adrenaline. Her hands gripped those pegs hard.

One step up. Another. She closed her eyes, feeling her way up the pole. *Don't. Look. Down.*

"That's it! One step at a time."

Her eyes popped open and searched for Sawyer. About twenty feet below, the ground spun in circles. Her knuckles iced over. Sweat melted down her temples. What was she thinking? She couldn't do this. She couldn't—

There was a tug on the rope. A reminder.

I've got you. He stepped into view below, gazing up at her, and just the sight of him was enough to make her want to try. Because maybe if she could conquer this pole, she could eventually overcome her past.

Another tug on the rope surged energy through her limbs. She and Sawyer were connected, and he was guarding her. He wouldn't let her fall.

In robotic fashion she grabbed the handholds and stepped. Handhold. Step. It became a monotonous motion that required no thought. *Up, up, up.* Her heart pulsed in her throat.

"You did it!"

"Climb the ladder!"

She didn't dare look toward their voices. Before she could even focus on how far away the ground was, Ruby pulled herself up the final ladder, gasping and sweating, but her heart soared.

Atop the platform, her legs shook like she was walking on stilts. She peered out over the tops of the trees, and in the distance, Pyramid Peak ruled the valley, a stony citadel.

"Jump, Ruby!"

"You can make it!"

The vista spread out before her echoed their encouragement. She could do this. She could do anything. She was standing on top of a platform! Above the trees! Her feet shuffled to the very edge. She focused on the trapeze bar. It was maybe three feet away. Only three feet. The ground below swirled into a collage of brown and green and gray.

"Want us to do a countdown?" Distance dimmed Sawyer's voice. "Ten...nine...eight...seven...six..."

She held her breath. *Don't think. Don't look. Just...*

"One!"

Her burning muscles launched her body into the air, arms outstretched, hands reaching, straining...

Her fingertips grazed the metal bar. Cold. Too slick.

No!

No, no, no!

Her insides lifted, stomach colliding with her ribs.

Falling. She was falling.

She opened her mouth to scream but a sharp jerk cut her off.

CHAPTER SIXTEEN

Sawyer yanked the rope to brake against Ruby's fall and held on, watching her dangle above him. "Nice one," he called up, still holding her steady.

The kids circled around him.

"Are you okay?" Neveah's shriek shattered the serene mountain air.

"Get her down!" Brooklyn screeched in his ear.

Legs flailing, Ruby swung until she could glare at him. "Yeah. You mind lowering me back to the ground now?"

With a grin, he fed the rope through the belay device. Ruby's body jerked and started into a slow descent.

"Told you I wouldn't let you fall," he said, easing her down.

"You did let me fall!"

"You only fell a foot. Max." He fed some rope more through the figure-eight device on his harness.

Inch by inch she came into focus. Her face was flushed—

excitement or anger? He couldn't tell. The rope caught on his belt and jerked her to a stop again, swaying her body above him. Might as well admire the view. He looked up, appreciating how the harness accentuated her perfect ass.

"Hey!" she yelled. "How long are you planning to keep me up here?"

"Sorry about that. I got distracted." He did his best not to laugh.

"Right. You sure sound sorry," she shot back, her voice still hoarse with fear.

Trying to look repentant, he continued her descent. The pulley system squeaked.

"If that rope snaps, I'll sue!"

"If that rope snapped, I'd catch you," he called up, and when she glared at him, this time he arched his eyebrows into an invitation. He was up for having her in his arms again.

A frustrated groan huffed out of her mouth, but her lips curved as though she had to work hard to fight a smile.

As soon as her feet touched the ground, Ruby stood, then wobbled like her legs were weak.

He steadied a hand against her back. "You did great up there," he murmured close to her ear, just as the kids around them closed in.

"You almost had it." Brooklyn sounded relieved that Ruby wasn't lying on the ground unconscious. "I thought you were gonna get it."

"That's harder than it looks," Ruby said, glancing at Sawyer.

He felt her tremble and realized he was still touching her, that his hand was still splayed across that enticing curve right at her lower back. Her body wasn't all he found enticing, either. "You were amazing up there." As much as he admired her, he had to admit, he'd had his doubts about her making the jump. "I'm so proud of you, Ruby."

Her face colored in a deep flush that made her eyes stand out.

"I wouldn't have done it without you," she said, reaching up to touch his arm.

Whoa. The feel of her fingertips against his skin threw him off balance. What was he supposed to be focusing on again?

The kids started arguing about who was jumping next.

"Ja-von! Ja-von!"

"Hell no!" The kid backed away from the group and ran, the rest of them chasing him with delighted squeals.

"Uh." Sawyer turned back to Ruby, who gazed at him with a smirk, like she could see exactly how much her touch rattled him. No use pretending. He was whipped and he'd prove it to her. Later. Right now, unfortunately, they were surrounded.

"Let me get you unclipped." Slipping in front of her, he started to unclip the carabiners attached to the loop on the front of her harness, but her hands clasped over his and stopped him.

That didn't help his concentration any.

"Thank you," she said. "For making me do that. For keeping me safe."

His arms ached with the desire to pull her against his body again, to properly thank her for reminding him how good it felt to be close to a woman who wanted him, too. Yeah, those sparks were definitely flying again. It'd been a damn long time, too.

But there'd be time to thank her later. The kids didn't need to see him all over her, so he kept his hands fisted safely at his sides. "Trust me now?"

Her eyes dulled and he could almost feel her pull away from him again. "Trusting you has never been the problem."

Before he could ask exactly what the problem was, Brooklyn wedged herself in between them.

"I wanna go next," she demanded. "Now. Before I freak out and change my mind."

"Sure thing." Sawyer finished unclipping Ruby's harness and backed away, but his gaze still belonged to her. *Don't withdraw again,* he tried to tell her silently. Not now. Whatever it was that held her back, he would help her. She just had to give him a chance.

"I'm ready!" Brooklyn reminded him.

Right. Tearing his gaze away from Ruby, he got Brooklyn all hooked up and ready for her jump.

"You're all set," he told her, aware of Ruby watching him. "You've got this."

Brooklyn's dark eyes were round and scared. He walked her to the ladder. "I won't let you fall," he reminded her. But he could see in her wary expression that she didn't trust him. She probably didn't trust anyone.

"What if I can't do it?" Brooklyn froze next to the ladder.

Ruby rushed over and knelt in front of her. "It's scary," she said quietly, so only the three of them could hear. "But it's also the best feeling in the world, Brooklyn."

The woman's smile was different. It radiated a confidence he'd never seen on her face.

"I know what it's like to have people let you down." Tears brightened her eyes. "Trust me, honey. I know. I lived in three foster homes."

The words hit like a punch, sending a sharp pain into his chest. Ruby had been a foster child. Was that why she was so afraid? What had happened to her in those homes? He didn't even want to imagine...

"You lived in a foster home?" Brooklyn gasped.

"Yeah. I did." Ruby stood, still peering down at the girl with those tear-filled eyes that tore at Sawyer.

"They'd always promise to let me stay, but it'd never end up working out and I'd have to move again."

Sawyer was speechless. No wonder she didn't want to get close to him.

"But you know what, Brooklyn?" Ruby swept the girl's long black hair over her shoulder. "Just because you've moved a lot doesn't mean you won't find a family. You deserve a family, sweetie. Someday someone is going to be so lucky to have you as their daughter."

Tears ran down the girl's face, and, damn it, Sawyer had to gnaw on the inside of his lip to fight the sting in his own eyes.

"You're beautiful and smart and strong," Ruby went on. "Especially strong. You can do this. You can climb this ladder and jump. And we'll all be here for you."

The girl wiped her cheeks with the backs of her hands. "Do you really think I'll find a family?"

"I know you will."

The intensity of Ruby's gaze on Brooklyn's hopeful face convinced even Sawyer that she believed it.

A slow smile emerged. "Have you found a family?" Brooklyn asked Ruby.

She glanced at Sawyer, then at the lodge. "I have. I've finally found a family where I fit."

And for once in his life Sawyer was grateful that Aunt Elsie took people in without caring where they came from. Because she'd offered Ruby something she'd never had.

Brooklyn threw her arms around Ruby's neck, and Sawyer had to busy himself with adjusting the belay device so he didn't crash their moment. He wanted to pull Ruby into his arms and tell her she had found a family. With the Walkers. With all of them. But before he could, Brooklyn pulled her shoulders straight and gripped the ladder's handholds. "I'm ready. Let's do this."

Looked like a moment alone with Ruby would have to wait.

* * *

"That was so awesome!" Brooklyn's eyes glowed with the unbridled excitement of a small child. It was a brand of enthusiasm Ruby hadn't seen on the girl's face since she'd met her. She hadn't seen it on any of their faces until the high ropes course. The adventure seemed to make them all come alive.

Including her.

"Better than awesome," agreed Javon, hiking up his low-riding pants, which had almost come down when he'd had his turn to jump off the platform. Each of them had found the courage to fly, and while some took longer than others and had to be coaxed the whole way, they'd found the strength they needed, and it had changed them, just like it'd changed her.

She couldn't seem to erase the smile that had lingered ever since Sawyer had lowered her to the ground. She'd smiled more in the past three hours with these kids than she had in her whole twenty-six years of life, and now the happy ache pinched her cheeks.

Okay, so Sawyer might have something to do with it, too. She'd never seen a man who was so good with kids. The perfect balance of patient, stern, and fun...like he could sense what they needed from him at any given moment. It was something to watch, a man who related to kids that way.

Especially difficult kids who'd had a completely different life from him, most likely. But the differences didn't seem to bother him at all.

"I'm so hungry, I could eat a horse," Sawyer groaned, coming up behind her.

"A barn," Javon corrected.

"A mountain," Brooklyn added, and they all laughed, obviously as giddy as Ruby felt.

"I'll go check on lunch. Why don't we eat out here?" She gestured to the rod-iron patio tables on the edge of the swimming pool. It was a perfect day—the endless blue sky glowing in the brilliance of an early-spring sun. There was enough of a breeze that she'd kept on her fleece, but the fresh chilled air only added to the sense of excitement.

"Sounds perfect," Sawyer said, running his hand down her arm, and suddenly the fleece felt like a fur coat. Lordy, the man had an electrifying touch. One graze of his hand sent her body into overdrive.

He stared down at her as though he knew exactly what she was thinking. Which only made her face burn hotter.

"Be right back," she managed before escaping into the lodge. Once she'd made it safely into the dining room, she ripped down the zipper of her fleece and tore the thing off, dumping it on a table before hurrying through the kitchen's double doors.

"Oh!"

Paige, Avery, and Elsie all stood around the island, snacking on ice cream right out of the carton like they so often did.

"Hi!" she greeted them, that perma-grin etched in deep. Just when she thought the day couldn't get any better, three of her favorite women were all gathered in one room like they were waiting for her.

"Hey, Ruby." Avery had Lily snuggled in her arms. The baby snored softly, her teeny hands clasped under her chin.

"There you are, dear." Elsie rushed over and folded her in a hug, then pulled away and studied her. "How are things going with the kids?"

"Great." She felt like the Cheshire cat.

Paige held a spoonful of ice cream midair. "What's with the silly grin?"

"What d'you mean?" With great effort, Ruby evened out her lips. "I'm just having fun with them, that's all."

"With them?" Paige shot back, her eyebrows raised to the ceiling. "Or with *him*?" Judging from the wide grins around the room, everyone knew which *him* Paige was talking about.

"With the *kids*," she answered quickly, so no one would get suspicious about her developing feelings for Sawyer. "They're amazing. Even after all they've been through, they're funny and brave and compassionate." Which was so much more than she'd been at their age—angry and closed off. What she wouldn't have given to have had a program like this, a place to retreat and be with other foster kids who understood what she was feeling. A place where someone like Elsie would've made meals with love. It could've changed so much for her...

"Well, I saw Sawyer earlier," Elsie murmured, her eyes glistening with a motherly look. "And he sure looked like he was enjoying *your* company."

"Oohhhh," Avery sang.

"Yeah, baby." Paige shoved a spoonful of ice cream into her mouth.

The teasing murmurs heated her face again. "No. Trust me. He's not interested." She had to keep telling herself that, even though he'd been flirting with her all morning, touching her arm or the small of her back, watching her closely. Before they could see the grin, she hurried to the sink and washed her hands so she could transfer the kids' sandwiches from the platter they were on to a picnic basket.

"He sure seems interested to me," Avery cooed, as if saying it to the baby in her arms. "I know Sawyer. He doesn't look at women the way he looks at you. You really got his attention."

Ruby laughed, remembering the way she'd gotten his attention. "That's only because he thought I was a criminal." It slipped out before she thought through the implications.

"What do you mean?"

"Yeah," Paige demanded, her hazel eyes narrowed. "Did he accuse you of something?"

Oops. She hurried to the cutting board and started to slice the whole apples Elsie had set out. She'd heard Brooklyn say she preferred sliced apples...

"Why would Sawyer think you're a criminal?" Avery asked through a laugh, as though that was one of the most ridiculous things she'd ever heard.

Ruby focused on slicing evenly and tried think of a way to keep Bryce's secret intact. "He asked me some questions, that's all." Which wasn't the same as an accusation, but still...

"About what?" Avery demanded, so loudly the baby started to whimper. "Oh, sorry, Lily bean. Shhh, shhh." She swayed her daughter until the cries quieted.

"Um." There was no easy way around that question...

"Does this have anything to do with the background checks Sawyer and Bryce have been discussing?"

The knife fell from her hand. "What?" It came out in a panicked whoosh of air.

"Sawyer was over for dinner last night. Talking to Bryce

about better security measures." Avery shifted Lily so the baby's head leaned on her shoulder. "They said something about doing background checks on employees."

"Background checks?" Like the kind where they looked you up in some computer system? She tried to swallow, but fear clogged her throat.

"That's crazy," Paige said. "It's not like this is a corporation or anything."

"Of course it's crazy," Elsie agreed. "Why on earth would they want to do that?"

"Because of the thefts," Ruby answered, groping for the knife, but her hand couldn't seem to grip it tight enough to make a straight cut. If they planned to do background checks, she'd have to leave. She'd have to leave the only family she'd ever had…

"Thefts?" Avery gasped. "What thefts?"

Uh-oh. Though her hand still trembled, Ruby went back to slicing apples, hoping someone else would answer. No one did.

"Ruby?" Avery peered over at her. "What thefts?"

"Someone broke into the lodge?" Paige asked.

Ruby shared a look with Elsie, but it was too late to backtrack. Bryce may have wanted to keep the thefts a secret, but it seemed that secrets at the Walker Mountain Ranch were getting much harder to keep.

"Um. Well. I guess some money was stolen," she muttered, turning to face Avery and Paige. "And maybe your bracelet."

"Oh my god." Avery seemed to breathing heavily. "Oh. My. God."

"Now, Avery." Elsie scurried to her daughter-in-law's side. "There's nothing to get upset about. Bryce didn't want to worry you, that's all."

"It sounds like whoever did it had a key," Ruby offered. "So it's not like it was just some random person off the street."

"A key?" Avery shrieked. "They have a key to our home?"

Okay, that didn't help.

Baby Lily startled and stretched her arms, hands balled into fists.

Ruby set down the knife and hurried over to take the baby so Avery could digest the news. "Come here, little one." She snuggled the powder-scented sweetheart close against her chest and swayed her until the precious girl's eyelids started to droop again. She hadn't held many babies, and she was struck by the miracle of it. Her heart gasped in surprise at how this tiny beautiful form could hold so much life and love. Closing her eyes, she memorized it, the feeling of that warm weight in her arms. She'd made her peace with never having a child of her own a long time ago, though it still stung, but she wanted to remember that sweet feeling of holding something so precious close to her heart.

While she reveled in baby bliss, Avery paced the kitchen with Paige and Elsie close behind trying to console her.

"I'm sure it's no big deal," Paige insisted in that confident tone of hers. "Bryce probably figures you already have enough on your mind."

"I'm sure he was going to tell you eventually," Ruby added. "But maybe he wanted to figure out who was behind it fir—"

"Hey, ladies," Sawyer said, and Ruby tightened her hold so she didn't drop the baby. When had he come in?

"Wanted to check the ETA for lunch."

Ruby didn't look at him. She couldn't. A mounting sadness swirled into anger. After everything he'd said to her, everything they'd done last night, he wanted to do background checks? How could he have neglected to mention that to her?

"You..." Avery waved her pointer finger at Sawyer, "...are on my list."

He staggered back. "Pardon?"

"I think I have a right to know about thefts in my own home!" Avery strutted over to him like a hen who'd had a feather plucked. "I can't believe you two kept it from me!"

Sawyer shot a disbelieving look in Ruby's direction, a silent *how could you tell her?*

Still cuddling the baby, she shrugged and stretched her lips into a thin look of indifference. This morning she'd told him that she trusted him. She did. She trusted him with her whole heart. But apparently he didn't trust her. Since she'd elected not to tell him anything about her past, he was going to force it out into the open. And she couldn't let that happen.

"Who is it, Sawyer? Who's been sneaking into my house? Stealing things?" Avery's angry voice had turned watery. Her eyes were filled with tears.

Yikes. She'd been a bit hormonal since the birth...

"And *we* already know it wasn't Ruby," Paige huffed. "Unlike some people, we don't go around accusing our *friends* of stealing."

Sawyer's head tipped back in a gesture of understanding. She heard his deep sigh all the way across the room, and while she did feel slightly bad about creating this firestorm he'd walked into, he kind of had it coming.

"I didn't accuse her of anything," he said, looking only at her. "I simply asked some questions."

Ruby shifted the baby in her arms, heat pouring from her face. Her stomach did that traitorous flip it did every time he looked at her that way, all intense and confident, like he knew exactly how he made certain parts of her throb.

"If you won't tell me anything, I'm going to find Bryce," Avery spat. She stalked over to Ruby, taking the baby gently back into her arms.

"That'd probably be best," Sawyer agreed amiably, as though completely unfazed by her anger.

Avery stomped to the door, glaring at him the whole way, then left.

Elsie bustled to the picnic basket that now overflowed with sandwiches. "Paige, dear, why don't you help me serve these to the kids?"

"I'm on it." Her friend gathered up the apple slices and winked at Ruby. Then both women hightailed it out of there before Ruby could beg them to stop. And she would've, too, because she didn't want to be alone with him. Anger lingered, but it had dwindled to a thin veil covering her heartache. How could she walk away and leave the Walker Mountain Ranch behind?

"What happened?" Sawyer crossed the room the same way she'd imagine he did when apprehending a suspect, determined and sure, his eyes locked on his target.

He stopped not more than six inches away.

She peered up at him, at his tender blue eyes, at the stubble shadowing his jaw, at the sturdy structure of his face, and hated the way he made her want him. "How could you say all those things to me last night?" Her throat was as raw as her heart.

"What things? That I'm attracted to you?" He inched closer. "I said it because it's true. This morning I thought maybe the feeling was mutual."

She held her breath, desperate to hold on to the anger so she could stay strong. "You convinced Bryce to do background checks on the employees?" It came out as an accusation. "Why didn't you tell me that?"

"That has nothing to do with you." Even though his voice lowered with sincerity, she backed away from him.

"It has everything to do with me." If he went through with it, she'd have to leave. She couldn't let him unravel the ugly layers of her past. "I told you I didn't take the money. Or the bracelet. I—"

"Ruby." His hands jutted like he wanted to touch her, but for some reason he held back. "We talked about implementing that as a policy to protect Bryce. That's all. We still don't know who's behind the thefts, but I know it wasn't you."

"Then why—?"

With a frustrated grunt, Sawyer leaned down and covered her lips with his.

A surprised squeal slipped out, but Sawyer silenced it by gently caressing her cheeks with his hands, running his tongue along the seam of her lips, melting her surprise into a warm throb of desire. How did he do it? How did he carry her away from reality like this, crossing out every protest that scrolled across her mind. Somehow Sawyer's touch was a remedy against the fears that had branded her heart for so long.

Her mouth opened again, all on its own to let him in because he tasted so delicious, hot and wet and minty. She swept her tongue over his, bracing her hands against his chest when her knees threatened to give.

A hungry grunt resounded in Sawyer's throat. Kissing her deeper, his hands lowered to her rib cage, strong and powerful, feeling their way up her body, and he nudged her against the refrigerator, which was a good thing because it was getting harder to stand.

He kissed his way across her cheek, then down her neck and she let her head fall to the side so he wouldn't stop. *Never. Stop.*

But he did. Instead of kissing his way back up her neck, he traced his lips over to her ear.

"Now you don't have to wonder if I'm suspicious," he whispered, his hot breath making her quiver. "I don't kiss women I don't trust."

A kiss. Is that what that was? Because it felt more like an electric shock, which was still resonating in her toes, by the way. "Okay," was all she could manage.

A smile brought light to his eyes. "Okay," he said.

Then he let her go, turned around, and left her alone in the kitchen.

CHAPTER SEVENTEEN

Sawyer bolted from the kitchen, body enflamed with want. Need. It pulsated through in the steady beat of his heart, which he felt a lot stronger whenever Ruby was close.

God, when he'd walked into the kitchen and saw her holding Lily, cuddling the baby like she was completely comfortable, disbelief had slammed into him. Why couldn't he hold the baby like that? He was her godfather—a blood relative. At first it'd made him angry, to see her doing what he couldn't do so easily. But then, the longer he'd watched her, the more he saw that nurturing instinct in her. The one that lets mothers know exactly how to hold a baby, how to soothe, that lets them anticipate exactly what the baby needs. Then the anger had shifted to fascination, the trampled hope he'd once had for a family piecing itself back together and rising up.

He felt this crazy pull to Ruby, and seeing her with Lily amplified it about a hundred times.

When he'd walked over to her, he'd only meant to kiss her the way she'd kissed him that day on the street—a light brush of the lips, innocent and careful. Whoa, had that backfired on him. At first she'd flinched like she was afraid of him, but then she'd melted into him, opening up, pressing her tongue against his. And her taste...the sweetness of cinnamon. That was the moment he'd given over control, letting himself groan against her. Letting her feel his desire. It flashed through him, white hot and fierce. That's why he had to pull away. They'd gotten lost in that kiss. One more minute and he would've done her right up against Aunt Elsie's refrigerator. Then there'd be hell to pay, especially if he mucked up the perfectly polished stainless steel.

"Sawyer!" Aunt Elsie cruised past him with an empty basket balanced in her hands. Paige was sitting at one of the patio tables hanging out with the kids.

"Is everything all right?" Aunt Elsie asked, her white eyebrows lowered with concern.

"Yeah. Everything's great." His lips still burned. If that kiss told him anything, it was that Ruby had forgiven him for not mentioning the background checks. He wasn't surprised she'd reacted that way. She had every right to be suspicious. She knew he had ulterior motives. He wanted to help her, which meant he had to figure out her secrets. If she'd stop fighting him, he *could* help her.

"You cleared things up with Ruby, then?" His aunt beamed.

"You could say that." He cleared his throat. "She's um... finishing up some things in the kitchen."

"Wonderful. I hope she'll bring down those cookies. I've never seen kids eat like this! It's hardly enough to fill them." She brushed past him and headed into the lodge. "Make sure those sweet kids eat as much as they want, won't you? Some of them look so scrawny. Wouldn't hurt to beef them up."

"I'll take care of it." Not like he'd have to try very hard to convince the kids to eat. The Walker Mountain Ranch kitchen served up the best grub in town. No one ever left a full plate behind. Thinking about the food made him think about Ruby again. Maybe he could convince her that tonight was the perfect night for an adventure on the town. He checked his watch. Waiting all day for a date with Ruby could sure make the minutes crawl by.

In need of a serious distraction he sauntered to the table where Javon and Brooklyn sat. As he approached, Javon hid something underneath the table.

"Whatcha got there?" he asked, trying to get a look.

"My phone." The kid reluctantly held up the latest model of a pretty sweet iPhone. Then he slipped it back into his pocket like he didn't want Sawyer looking at it too closely.

Huh. Javon had a brand-new phone. One of the most expensive phones on the market. His thoughts shifted into detective mode. Because it didn't seem to fit.

Shit. He pulled out a chair, trying to keep his expression easygoing. "Where'd you get that?" he asked, helping himself to the sandwich Aunt Elsie had left for him, even though he suddenly wasn't hungry. Not like he wanted to dwell on the bad feeling that'd put a cloud over the bright sunlight, but the first theft could've easily started the day the kids arrived. No one knew for sure how long Avery's bracelet had been in the kitchen before it was stolen...

"What d'you mean where'd I get it?" Javon demanded. "I bought it, man."

His lips tightened. Where would Javon get the money to buy the latest smartphone?

"Do you have a job?" He hoped it didn't sound like an interrogation. Hell, he didn't even want to ask, but if he didn't, no one else would.

"I got no car, man," Javon said like Sawyer was an idiot. "How'd you expect me to find a job?"

"I used to deliver papers." He shrugged. "I always rode my bike."

"I don't got no bike, either," the kid grumbled. "But I'm saving up for one."

"That's great." He did his best to sound genuine, but he'd heard Javon talk about his foster parents. They didn't have much. And they didn't sound like the kind of people who'd drop a bunch of money on a smartphone, even for themselves. Damn it, why'd he have to be the cop? Sometimes he wondered why he hadn't become a ski bum instead. Would've been so much less complicated. "So how much did it cost?" he asked casually, finishing off an egg salad sandwich on wheat.

Javon wouldn't meet his eyes. "I don't know. Don't remember. Why?"

"I was thinking about getting one. Wondered how much it'd set me back." It wasn't a lie. He'd thought about replacing his phone for a while now.

"It was a couple hundred, I guess." The kid suddenly seemed starving. He shoved a whole apple slice into his mouth.

Sawyer blew out a whistle. "That's a chunk of change. If you don't have a job, where'd you get the money?"

"My real grandma sent it to me," he shot back, his eyes hardened with anger. "You got a problem with that?"

Once again, he'd pushed too hard. He tried to backtrack with a shrug. "No. Of course not. That's great that she sent you money, Javon. Really." He wanted to believe the kid, but suspicion seeped in anyway. As much as he wanted to ignore it, he couldn't let this go. If Javon had stolen from

Bryce, the kid had to be held accountable. How else would he learn? Today it was petty thefts, but tomorrow it could be a felony conviction that'd ruin his life.

Nope. He couldn't let Javon get away with this.

So, like it or not, his investigation had just taken a new turn.

* * *

Ruby wiped the last dinner dish and carefully tucked it away in Elsie's china hutch. Rather than facing Sawyer, she'd spent the afternoon in her safe zone—helping in the kitchen, cleaning up after lunch, and prepping dinner with Elsie while Bryce and Sawyer took the kids on an early-evening hike.

Letting out a slow breath, she leaned into the counter. Yes, she was definitely avoiding a certain officer of the law. What could she say? She'd never been good at figuring out men. How else would she have ended up with a man like Derek? It wasn't like she'd seen any evidence of a healthy relationship growing up. Mama'd had a revolving door of men coming and going, hardly even noticing her or Grady. Most of them came from the bar or the streets where Mama got her supply. Sometimes they'd yell at Mama and get rough. That's why she'd been so drawn to Derek. In those early days he'd never even raised his voice at her.

There'd been a time she thought he'd loved her. A time when she thought she'd loved him. But even Derek's kiss had *never* struck her like Sawyer's, piercing down deep, making her ache in ways she'd never experienced...

"Hey there, Ruby."

She spun and watched Thomas wheel himself into the kitchen.

Instantly she straightened, praying her face wasn't as red hot as it felt. "Thomas." She hurried over to help him maneuver around the island. "Does Elsie know you're wheeling yourself around?"

He chuckled. "Nah, I snuck away from the fire. Thought I'd come up and get the s'mores stuff." After dinner Sawyer had suggested a campfire, complete with stories and songs. And roasted marshmallows, of course. He'd looked just as excited as the kids when he'd come to invite her. She said she had too much work to finish up because what good would it do either of them to continue building the bond they shared? Especially if Sawyer did background checks on all the employees. She'd make sure she was long gone before he could dig into her past.

"Most of those kids down there have never even roasted a marshmallow," Thomas said.

"Well, you're in luck." Ruby slid the tray filled with marshmallows, graham crackers, and chocolate bars off the counter. "I've got everything ready to go. Why don't you hold the tray and I'll push you so you don't get into trouble with Elsie."

Thomas's smile bounced his mustache. "She's a feisty one, that woman."

"She sure is," Ruby agreed, positioning herself behind his chair. Elsie was about the feistiest woman she'd ever met, but she was also compassionate and wise. The mother she'd never had. Everyone's mother, it seemed.

"Does she ever talk about me?" Thomas asked, and Ruby had to lock her jaw tight so an *awww* wouldn't slip out. Thomas was sweet on Elsie…

"You don't have to answer that," he muttered gruffly.

"Oh. Well, actually…" She steered him across the dining room and out the French doors onto the back porch.

"…Elsie did mention something about how good you are with the kids. I believe her exact words were, *he's such a doll*." Okay, maybe she was exaggerating slightly, but she'd noticed Elsie's cheeks tended to get pink whenever she talked about Thomas.

"A doll… ," Thomas mused, as though he had a hard time decoding it.

"I think that means she likes you, Thomas." She eased the chair down the sidewalk. "Maybe you should ask her out. Take her to dinner someplace nice." Normally Elsie played the matchmaker's role, but she seemed to be so busy taking care of everyone else, she'd never pursued a relationship for herself. "I bet she'd love to go on a date with you," Ruby whispered, hoping her voice wouldn't drift down to Elsie. The woman would kill her.

"You think so?" He peered up at her with another side smile. "I guess it wouldn't hurt to ask. Never too old for a second chance at love, I suppose."

A second chance at love. Her heart grasped hope. Could it happen for her? Even with her all her secrets? Maybe.

Hopefully someday.

She pushed Thomas to the outskirts of the bonfire, smiling at the voices and laughter that floated on the night air. Something about the Walker Mountain Ranch made her believe a second chance at love was possible.

"Thomas! There you are!" Elsie rushed over, hands flapping. "Why didn't you tell me you were going somewhere? I would've pushed you—"

"Let me take you to dinner tomorrow night, Elsie," the man interrupted.

Ruby slapped a hand over her mouth.

Shock froze Elsie's face. Ruby had never seen her eyes so wide.

"What on earth has gotten into you?" she demanded.

Holding back her laughter, Ruby drifted closer to the fire so she could give them a moment alone.

Laughter and voices hummed around her, and she felt the warmth of the friendships that had developed between all these wonderful people who had come from such different places.

Her smile grew weighted. The kids only had two more days at the ranch; then they'd go back to their foster homes. Maybe that was another reason she'd hidden herself away all afternoon. She was avoiding that, too. Over the past few days, she'd gotten so attached to them. Especially Brooklyn. The girl was her twenty years ago, except sweeter, not so hardened by her circumstances, yet. Ruby hated to see her go, to see her disappear back into the system, moved from place to place with no one to keep her safe.

God, she'd give anything to change things for them. For all of them.

Shuddering from the thought more than from the brisk night air, she zipped up her fleece all the way to her chin. There was a lull in the laughter, then Sawyer's deep voice carried over to her. He sat on a bench with some of the boys, telling them some story that required a lot of exaggerated arm motions.

Her body warmed from the inside out and she wasn't shivering anymore. He had the best voice, especially when he spoke to kids. It was deep, but full of humor, like he could hardly contain his laughter.

Edging into the crowd, she opted to stand safely behind one of the benches on the opposite side of the fire. After that kiss earlier she couldn't even be near him without infatuation zinging through her, colliding with her nerves, spiraling heat down through her core.

"Hey there," Avery whispered.

Ruby tried to smile at her friend. Little Lily was wrapped up like an Eskimo baby, safely tucked into one of those wrap contraptions while she slept contentedly against Avery's shoulder.

"Hi, sweetie." She touched a finger to Lily's perfect little nose. What was it about baby noses, anyway? So tiny and sweet. She had a hard time looking at that nose without touching it.

Avery never seemed to mind. The woman was happy to share her baby with the world.

Ruby leaned her head closer. "So how are things with you and Bryce?" She hadn't seen Avery all afternoon, either, but she figured she and Bryce must've had a discussion about the thefts, given how she'd stormed out of the kitchen.

A girlish smile flitted on Avery's lips. "We're good."

Envy flashed through her, but it didn't take hold. Everyone dreamed about finding what Bryce and Avery had. They were just one of those couples you could tell were made for each other.

"So I'm assuming, based on your expression, you two made up?" she asked, feeling that ping of jealousy again. Avery never quit talking about the great sex those two had. Even after being married for more than two years. God, it'd been a long time for her. And she wouldn't say the sex in her last relationship had ever been good. Making love to Derek had made her physically ill. She'd avoided it as much as she could get away with.

"We made up." Avery shifted Lily's head to her other shoulder and faced her. "I didn't let him off the hook, though."

Knowing Avery, she wouldn't. She was kind and compassionate, but she didn't let go of things easily.

Still...Ruby thought it was sweet how Bryce always tried to protect her. "I get that he kept something from you, but he didn't want you to worry." Wasn't that a good thing? What would it be like to have someone protect you that way?

"Of course he thought he was protecting me." Avery looked directly at her, the fire's flickering light illuminating her face. "But it's never okay to keep secrets from someone you love."

The words made Ruby's heart pound faster. Avery obviously knew she had her secrets. Everyone had to know. But they'd never asked her about them. None of them—not Elsie or Paige or Avery—had ever demanded to know anything about her past. Though surely they'd wondered.

"Bryce and I are a team," Avery continued, though her tone stepped carefully, like she didn't want the words to hurt. "We fight for each other. That's what a relationship has to be. It doesn't work when you're hiding something."

The words sunk in, heavy and consuming. Would she ever develop that kind of a relationship with someone? Complete openness and honesty? Lordy, with her history, it seemed impossible. She wouldn't even know where to start.

"Ruby..." Avery looked in Sawyer's direction. "I don't know what you've been through, but I do know Sawyer. I know he's the best guy in the world." Glancing at Ruby again, she grinned. "Besides Bryce, course. But they *do* share blood."

"I know." Ruby gazed across the fire. Sawyer sat between Javon and Wyatt, both boys laughing hysterically at whatever he was saying. "He's a great guy." Better than any man she'd ever spent her time with, that was for sure. But Avery had no idea how much she had to overcome. "I can't have a relationship, though. With anyone." It was one thing to kiss the man, but to go on a date with him...to lead him into thinking they could have something real when she knew it wasn't possible? He didn't deserve that.

Avery sighed out a mixture of disappointment and frustration. "Well, if you ever change your mind, just know you don't have to worry about him. He knows how it feels to be betrayed by someone you love. He'd never hurt you."

Ruby closed her eyes. But her past could hurt him.

Lily started to whimper.

"I should get her to bed," Avery said, unraveling the wrap and shushing her daughter softly. "See you tomorrow?"

Ruby stuffed her hands into her pockets. "I'll be here." At least tomorrow she would be.

After that, she didn't know.

CHAPTER EIGHTEEN

In so many ways, it had been the perfect night. Ruby knelt to pick up a chocolate bar wrapper and shoved it into the trash bag she'd found. After Elsie had suggested everyone go inside to watch a movie, the fire had dwindled to a soft orange glow. Instead of going with them, she'd volunteered to stay back and clean up so she could find some space to think through her options.

What if she told Sawyer the truth? The thought pushed her down onto a bench. She slumped and dropped the garbage bag to the ground. He wouldn't let it go. Not someone like Sawyer. He'd sworn to pursue justice at all costs, and if he'd truly come to care about her like he'd said, he wouldn't let Derek get away with how he'd treated her. He'd force her to press charges, to go through a horrible trial...

"Hey."

Ruby sat up straight at the sound of Sawyer's voice and

automatically tried to smooth her hair with her fingers. How long had he been standing behind her, watching her?

"Everything okay? You didn't come in with everyone else." He sat next to her.

"Everything's fine." Except for her heart. It was so tender. One small touch and it would break apart. "I thought I'd clean up. Make sure the fire went down okay." And try to sort out the mess that was her life right now.

Sawyer acknowledged her lie with a nod and leaned back as though settling in for a long conversation.

Her shoulders tensed. How could she have a conversation with him when she had no plan? Should she tell him the truth? Should she leave? Should she beg him not to do the background check? There were no clear answers. Only gaping questions.

"I hope I didn't make you uncomfortable this afternoon." His voice had gotten raspy again, like it had been in the kitchen earlier.

All that sensuous heat he generated inside her built and collected on her face. "Oh. No. I mean, um, it was a surprise, that's for sure."

A slow smile lifted his lips. "That it was."

She resisted the urge to fan herself. Suddenly the minuscule fire felt like an inferno. "But it was good. I mean…amazing. Um…you know, as far as kisses go." Good lord. How did this man jumble up the connection between her mouth and her brain this way?

"Definitely amazing," he agreed, that smile gaining momentum. "So if it happened again sometime, that might be okay?" He bit down on his lip, the slightest bit of hesitancy flickering in his eyes. Shyness?

Lordy, that was appealing. "Um. Well." How could she answer that question? Like Avery said, she couldn't have a relationship with anyone. Not with the secrets she was keeping. Especially not with Sawyer, who'd already been lied to by someone he loved. "I don't know." She avoided his penetrating gaze. "There's so much you don't know about me, Sawyer."

"Then tell me," he said, his sincere eyes threatening to make her crack. "Whatever it is, it might help to talk about it."

That need to know in Sawyer was exactly what made him a good cop. But it was also what made him a threat to her secrets. He wouldn't give up. So she'd have to do it for him.

Looking down, she scuffed her feet in the dirt. "I can't tell you. Not now, anyway. And..." She sucked in air to strengthen her voice. "...we probably shouldn't see each other. Like last night. Or today in the kitchen." God, she couldn't believe she was saying this. The thought of never kissing Sawyer again made her want to cry. "Because you're leaving in three weeks. And I don't know how long I'll be around—"

"What?" His upper body jolted, and he was no longer casual, but sitting straight and rigid. "What d'you mean you don't know how long you'll be around?"

She stared into the fire instead of into his eyes. When his eyes locked on hers all she wanted to do was throw herself at him, pleading with him to make her always feel as safe and wanted as he did when his lips touched hers.

"Does this have anything to do with the background checks?" Gently Sawyer cupped her cheek with his hand and turned her face to his. "Because I can protect you from that, Ruby. If you really don't want to do it, you don't have to. We won't force you."

"You won't?" Surprise weakened her voice to a hoarse whisper.

"No." Sawyer smoothed her hair away from her cheek. "I want to know you. I want to hear your stories—the hard ones, the good ones. But I won't force my way into your life. I won't make you tell me anything you're not ready to share."

Fear loosened its suffocating hold. "Thank you," she breathed, tears gathering. Now she wouldn't have to leave the only place she'd ever belonged.

Seeming to sense her tears, he silently slipped his hand into hers, filling her with the same courage she'd felt when he'd gotten her to dunk her head under the water, when he'd encouraged her to jump off that platform. She wanted to tell him. She wanted him to know her. She wanted that so badly it hurt. It felt like the walls she'd put up were cracking, and while it caused her pain, she could sense freedom, too.

"I didn't realize you were a foster kid," Sawyer said, still holding her hand, brushing his fingers across her knuckles.

She nodded. That was the easiest part of her story to tell. And it's not like that could hurt Sawyer. As long as she was careful she could tell him that much. "My mom went to prison when I was eight. For drugs." It amazed her how easy it was to tell Sawyer something she'd never told anyone except for Derek. Somehow his touch loosened fear's hold on her. "I never even knew who my dad was."

The feel of Sawyer's hand covering hers, heavy and warm and protective, warded off the chill of the night air.

"I hate that you grew up that way," he said. It meant so much more than "sorry."

"It wasn't your typical *Leave It to Beaver* episode," she admitted. "But I adapted. It got easier after they moved me a couple of times. I'd keep my stuff packed and ready, knowing eventually I'd go someplace else." Every time they drove her into the driveway of a new home, her stomach would cramp and she'd wonder if anyone would ever want her.

Those old emotions gripped her throat again. Funny how she thought that never remembering would make that old pain go away. It hadn't. The years hadn't even diluted it.

Sawyer tightened his hold on her. "No kid should have to grow up that way."

Ruby peered up to study him. Most cops she'd known had that wall, that cold indifference when it came to stories like hers. They'd heard so much, *seen* so much. But Sawyer looked at her like he hurt for her.

"It kills me when I look at Neveah and Brooklyn. And Javon," he said, something in his eyes darkening. "Knowing they don't belong to anyone."

"You're great with them." She thought back to the swimming lesson. "With kids, in general." It seemed so unfair that his son had been taken away from him. He would've been such a great dad.

"I love kids."

That didn't surprise her. She'd heard him described by Avery and Elsie as a big kid himself. And she could see that. He had an innocent belief in the good of the world, a quick wit, and a love for laughter...

"Hopefully I'll have some of my own someday."

The air between them grew stale with a long silence. Another reason she had to keep her boundary with him intact. He deserved to be a dad, to someday recover what he'd lost, and kids were the one thing she'd never be able to give him. It didn't torture her like it once had. She'd known since she was fourteen, and she'd dealt with it, but she'd promised herself she'd never marry someone who wanted a family.

"What about you?" Sawyer asked.

"Oh." Cold dread worked its way up her throat. "I don't

know. I haven't really thought about it." Another lie. Add it to the pile.

"You haven't?" He looked surprised. "But you're great with kids. With Lily... and with Brooklyn. You'd be a great mom."

She'd thought she'd made peace with it long ago, but hearing him say it—hearing it come from Sawyer— thrashed her.

"Ruby... what's wrong? Did I say something—?"

Shaking her head, she swiped at her eyes. "No. No. It's just... like you said. It's hard seeing all these kids who'll never have families. I wish I could take them all in. Before they end up on the wrong path." Before Brooklyn fell into an abusive relationship like she had...

"Yeah." He rubbed a hand up and down her arm. "I know what you mean." A sigh slumped his shoulders, and his typical cheerful expression tightened into concern.

Her stomach clenched at the sudden change. Something was off. "What's wrong?"

He hesitated, then faced her. "I have a new theory about the thefts."

The serious look on his face made her fingers fidget. Whatever it was she was pretty sure she wouldn't like it. "Okay. What're you thinking?"

"Javon. I saw him showing off a brand-new iPhone earlier."

"No." Ruby scooted away from him. She shook her head. "Javon wouldn't do that."

Sawyer studied her for a long time without saying anything. Then his eyes shifted like he was torn. "Did your foster parents ever buy you anything like that?" he asked carefully.

Never. She'd never gotten any gifts from the foster parents she'd lived with. There were so many stories of wonderful, warm, and loving foster parents, like Neveah's, who doted on her as though she was the daughter they'd always longed for. But that hadn't been her experience. "There are foster parents out there who treat the kids like their own," she said, because he couldn't believe that Javon would steal from the Walkers.

"Well, sure. That's how I'd treat them." Sawyer paused. "But with the other stuff he was saying, it doesn't add up. And he's only been with these foster parents for a month."

"Maybe they gave it to him as a welcome gift," she said stiffly. Did he even realize how stereotypical he sounded? Yes, the kid dressed like he didn't care what people thought. Yes, he had a rough mouth. But that didn't make him a criminal.

"Look, I know it's not pleasant, but I have to talk to him about it. To all of them, actually."

Ruby shot to her feet, her hammering heart trampling all the feelings she'd had for Sawyer only minutes before. "Do you know what that'll do to him? After this great week, you're going to ruin it all by accusing him of stealing?"

"I won't accuse him of anything," he said firmly. "I only want to ask him about it."

"Like you asked me?" she ground out. "No offense, Sawyer, but you have a tendency to sound suspicious when you ask questions."

He stood, too, towering over her. "The first theft happened after they got here, Ruby. Then it happened again when they came back from the backpacking trip." His jaw tightened around the words. "That can't be a coincidence. Bryce has never had a problem before."

"You can't do this." He was going to ruin the whole week! Every memory those kids had would be tarnished by the accusations. "They already feel like outcasts. What do you think this'll do to them?" She fought to keep her voice calm and even but was quickly losing the battle. "They came here to get away, to feel safe, to escape the reality of their lives." She knew the reality they lived and it was nothing Sawyer Hawkins could even imagine. "But I don't expect you to understand that. Not everyone has such an idyllic childhood," she spat.

"I care about them, too." The anger in his eyes matched hers. "That's why I have to ask. I don't have a choice. If one of them took the money, they have to be held accountable."

"None of them took the money!" Her hands fisted. "Do you hear me? It wasn't them."

"I guess we'll find out tomorrow, won't we?" he asked, and now he was just being a dick.

"*You'll* find out. I won't be around." She wouldn't watch him break their hearts. They thought the world of Sawyer, and now he was turning on them, just like everyone else did. She thought he was different, that he understood where she came from—where those kids came from. But it turned out he was just as judgmental as everyone else.

"Ruby—"

"Good night, Sawyer." She spun and started to walk away, but he clamped a hand onto her forearm, his grip tight, fingers digging into her skin. A shock of fear bolted her feet to the ground.

"Don't walk away. Let's talk about this," he said, and, even though he wasn't yelling at her anymore, her body shook.

"Don't touch me," she rasped.

Instantly he let her go and backed up a step. "Sorry. I didn't mean to scare you."

Trembles rattled her shoulders, the aftershocks spreading

down her arms and legs until it felt like the ground had started to shake. No one was allowed to touch her like that. To force her to do anything. Never again.

"Are you okay?" Sawyer's face had paled. Concern set his jaw. "I would never hurt you." He reached for her, but she flinched back, stumbling.

She wanted to believe that. She wanted to believe a lot of things about him. But right now she couldn't think straight. "I have to go," she gasped, unable to fill her lungs with air.

And before he could stop her, she ran blindly back to the lodge.

CHAPTER NINETEEN

When Sawyer was eight years old, there was a mystery in the Hawkins household that he'd taken it upon himself to solve. One morning, when everyone filed downstairs for one of Mom's gourmet breakfasts, they found a kitchen window broken, unlocked, and open.

Right away Mom had flown into a panic, forcing Dad to call the police. But nothing was missing from the house, so they filed a report, fixed the window, and moved on with life. Everyone except him, of course. The desire to know what had happened burned inside of him and inspired him to launch his own investigation. He started by examining the window, which, judging from how the glass had fallen, had definitely been broken from the outside. But, if it had been an intruder, they would've taken something...Mom's three-carat diamond ring that she always left on the ring stand above the kitchen sink, maybe? It would've been so easy. Someone could've swiped it in two minutes and gotten out of there. But the diamond ring was still there. Which made Sawyer watch his two older sisters carefully.

They'd sure acted shocked, feeding Mom's panic with their dramatic cries.

"Who would break into our house?"

"I don't feel safe here anymore!"

But both of his sisters had moved on from the incident a little too easily, he'd noticed, when not a half hour after the police left, Samantha was giggling on the phone. That moment happened to be his first clue that there hadn't been an intruder at all. After she'd hung up the phone, he'd casually asked her who she'd been speaking to.

Lucky for him it had been Courtney, the only one of her friends to ever even notice he was alive. She spent so much time at their house that he'd developed a little brother relationship with her, too. So after Sam left the room, he called Courtney right back.

Growing up with two sisters had taught him one very important thing about women: they tell each other absolutely every detail about everything that has ever happened to them. It's almost as though they can't think something without voicing it to another female friend, who will then help them dissect it over and over and over, coming to no logical conclusion, but somehow dealing with it in the process.

Courtney had answered the phone right away, and Sawyer, who still sounded like a girl back then, did his best to mimic his sister's voice. "Just wanted to remind you not to tell my parents about last night," he half whispered to cover up the cracks in his voice.

"Are you kidding?" Courtney had squealed. "I'd *never* tell them. I'm just glad they didn't catch you sneaking back in! You'd better remember your key next time you do that."

Case solved. He never ratted out Sam. It was enough

satisfaction to know what had happened, that he'd figured out something when the grown-ups couldn't. That was the minute he knew he'd be a police officer someday. Even back then he'd always exceled at deductive reasoning— taking multiple observations and evidence and facts, whittling them down to form the most logical conclusion.

Now whenever he dealt with a female suspect, he always interviewed the people closest to her. Especially other women. Always.

That's why he'd ended up at Ben and Paige's ranch approximately twenty minutes after Ruby had run away from him. Since that first incident when she'd nailed him in the balls with a rolling pin, he'd been gathering the facts.

Fact: Ruby had panic attacks that obviously resulted from a traumatic experience, most likely with a man, given the way she'd reacted to him a number of times.

Fact: She went to great lengths to keep her past a secret, even to the point of threatening to leave the ranch if he went through with the background check.

Fact: Out of all the Walker Mountain Ranch women, Paige seemed to have a special bond with Ruby. Which made her a key witness in unraveling the woman's mystery.

So Sawyer parked his Tahoe on the side of the Nobles' five-car garage and hopped out, following a cobblestone path to the front door.

Paige's husband, Ben, was made of money—he came from a political dynasty in Texas—but you wouldn't guess it from the looks of their ranch house. It was modest, compared to most of the million-dollar homes in the area. Still a beautiful log-and-slate structure, but definitely on the small side. If he had to guess, he'd say about three thousand square feet. On the other side of the driveway was a guesthouse for Paige's therapy clients. In addition to running a successful cattle operation, the Nobles also ran an equine therapy program, helping people with special needs experience the backcountry on horseback. They were good people. Trustworthy as anyone he'd ever met, and he suspected Ruby thought so, too.

He stepped onto the porch and stood in front of a solid wood door with a mountain scene carved into it. A wildflower wreath hung in the center with a sign that read WELCOME.

Sawyer knocked, wondering if anyone would even be able to hear with that door being so solid.

But a few seconds later the door swung open and Ben's sister, Julia, appeared in her frilly wheelchair, decorated this time with ribbons in the spokes. When she was sixteen her legs had been crushed in a car accident, and she'd never regained the ability to walk. But it hadn't seemed to slow her down any.

"Sawyer!" She greeted him with her trademark spunk. "What a surprise!" Oliver, her trained golden retriever, trotted to the open door, giving him the third degree with his nose.

"Hey, pooch." He lowered to give the dog a good scratch behind the ears. "I'm the one who's surprised." Julia had moved back to Dallas last year after living at the ranch with Ben and Paige for a time. Last winter she'd gotten engaged to her childhood sweetheart at her brother's wedding reception. The memory lured out a grin. That right there was proof that happy endings existed. After the hell she'd been through, Julia and Isaac had found each other again. If she could overcome everything, so could Ruby.

"Isaac and I came for a visit." Julia wheeled herself aside and waved him in. "A *quick* visit," she emphasized, then beamed that bright, fun-loving smile. "Is everything okay? Are you here on official police business?"

"Technically, no." Although he was playing detective tonight. "I need to talk to Paige. Is she around?"

"She sure is." Julia wheeled herself down a slate-tiled hallway, gesturing for him to follow. Oliver pranced beside Julia, obviously convinced that Sawyer was harmless.

"We were just sitting down for dinner, actually. You should join us."

He'd already eaten dinner with the kids, but that had to have been three hours ago now. Besides, you couldn't walk into the Nobles' house and not eat a steak. "Sure. Sounds good."

He followed Julia through the hall, across the expansive sitting room, and into the country kitchen that reminded him of something he'd seen in a European chalet when Kaylee used to make him watch HGTV.

"Sawyer…" Paige was setting a platter of steaks on the custom-made table, which consisted of two antique doors fused together with metal. She set the platter next to the vegetarian grilled eggplant, of course. It was beyond him how she lived on a cattle ranch and still never ate meat.

Her eyes narrowed as she straightened and faced him. "Is everything okay?"

Typical. People saw a cop and they automatically think something terrible has happened. Not that he frequently swung by to visit Paige and Ben or anything. He could see why she'd be surprised.

"Everything's great." After what'd happened with Ruby earlier, his smile felt plastic. Things were not great. Great would be him and Ruby all tangled up on the couch back at his place right now. Instead, he was forced to revert to his detective skills to figure out what kept setting her off.

"Um…" He looked around. Julia was busy setting colorful plates around the dinner table. With the potential threat neutralized, Oliver had given up his post and was sprawled underneath the table.

Might as well get on with the questioning. Not like he cared much if Julia overheard. She was headed back to Dallas soon, anyway. He looked back at Paige. "I wanted to ask you a few questions about a certain baker at the Walker Mountain Ranch."

The woman's eyes lit with an unrestrained excitement. "About Ruby? Of course! Anything! Ask away!" She quickly jogged to a huge china cabinet and took out another place setting, handing it to Julia. "Stay for dinner. That'll give us *plenty* of time to talk."

"I'd love to." Didn't appear he had a choice, anyway.

"We'll be ready in about ten minutes," Paige said. "Hopefully. As long as that husband of mine and his friend come in from the stables." She hurried to the counter and snatched her phone. "I'll text him and tell him we have company."

"I'm not in a hurry." Not like he had a hot date with Ruby or anything. And investigations typically required a hell of a lot of patience. So instead of pressing Paige for answers right away, he sat across from Julia.

"How're the wedding plans coming?" he asked, figuring that's what engaged women loved to talk about.

But Julia waved him off. "We're not really planning. We booked a trip to Tahiti for a destination wedding in the fall." Her dark exotic eyes glistened. God, she looked happier than he'd ever seen her. Even without a real wedding. Or maybe because she didn't have to put on a real wedding.

"How'd your mom take that news?" he asked. He couldn't

resist. Gracie Hunter Noble was a piece of work, the classic southern matriarch.

Julia laughed. "I told her after it was booked. And we didn't get the trip insurance."

"She called Ben sobbing and asked if a marriage was recognized by the church if the wedding wasn't in the United States," Paige chimed in from across the room.

That cracked him up. Knowing Gracie, it was easy to picture.

"She is still coming," Julia said, though she didn't look exactly thrilled. "And so are Ben and Paige. That's the extent of the guest list."

"Sounds perfect." It really did. He and Kaylee had done the whole big wedding thing at the top of Aspen Mountain. Thirty grand and a few years later they were divorced. Seemed like kind of a waste.

"So, Sawyer—"

The door flew open and cut Paige off. Ben sauntered in, followed by his badass ex-Navy buddy Isaac, which got Oliver all riled up. The dog darted over to Isaac, whining and licking his hand.

"Oliver," Julia cooed. "Come." The dog obeyed right away, skulking back to his spot under the table.

"Hey, baby, didn't miss dinner, did I?" Ben captured Paige in a bear hug and dipped her, then kissed her like they were about to fall into bed.

Across the table from Sawyer, Julia rolled her eyes. "And this is exactly why we aren't staying for a week," she complained. "God. It's worse than having two overly hormonal teenagers around."

Sawyer laughed. And averted his eyes.

"You want me to kiss you like that?" Isaac asked his fiancée, already lowering to his knees in front of her chair.

In response Julia mouthed the word "later" with some pretty significant tongue action, and everyone in the room laughed.

The woman glared at Ben and Paige again, but she was smiling. "I'd never make out with you in front of my *brother*." They didn't make out, but Sawyer didn't miss the way Isaac moved a chair closer to his fiancée and held her hand under the table. A warm ray of hope radiated in his chest again.

Ben seemed to get his sister's hint and released Paige. "Sawyer. Hey, man. Good to see you." He walked over and clapped him on the back. "How's the transition going?"

"So far, so good," he said, but it came out flat. He was supposed to be focused on his move to Denver, on starting over, but he hadn't thought about it since the morning he'd encountered Ruby in the kitchen...

"You could always stay, you know." Paige came to the table, too, her cheeks slightly pink and a smitten grin on her face. She sat next to Ben and started to dish out food. "You don't have to move away."

No. He didn't have to, but that's what he'd wanted for so long. "You sound like Aunt Elsie and Avery," he teased.

Her snarky grin made it look like she decided to take that as a compliment. "I just can't imagine anyone choosing Denver over Aspen."

"What'll you be doing in Denver?" Isaac asked.

While he dug into his steak Sawyer politely answered all their questions about his new job, doing his best to sound like he couldn't wait.

When the conversation lulled, Paige targeted him. "So what do you want to know about Ruby?" she asked, grinning and bouncing her eyebrows.

He set down his fork, the steak turning into a rock in his

gut. Ben, Isaac, and Julia looked on with interest, and he guessed it wouldn't hurt to talk in front of them. "Just wondering if you know much about her. What her story is."

The woman's smiled dimmed. "Uh. Well." She seemed to look at Ben for help, but he only shrugged.

"No. Not really. Why?" she finally stuttered out.

Yeah, right. Paige was obviously uncomfortable, which meant she knew a hell of a lot more than she was letting on. It was obvious someone had hurt Ruby. A foster parent? Or someone else? Not knowing tortured him. He pushed away his plate. "We've hung out a few times. But tonight we were arguing about something, and she completely shut down. Freaked out. I don't understand what happened."

Paige shared another look with Ben. Yeah. She definitely knew something.

"The thing is," Sawyer went on before he lost his chance. "It wasn't normal. Her reaction. I went to take her arm so she wouldn't walk away from me, and you would've thought I'd punched her."

Paige's mouth tightened into a frown.

Julia wheeled herself back from the table. "Hey, Isaac and Benny, we need more wine. Let's go pick out some of the good stuff from the cellar."

"We've got good bottles right over there." Ben waved an arm toward the wine rack on the counter.

Julia's sigh condemned him. "Seriously, Ben. Were you raised in a barn? Let's give Paige and Sawyer a minute."

"Oh. Right." A look of understanding dawned. He quickly pushed back from the table and followed Isaac and his sister out the door with Oliver on their heels.

"What do you know?" Sawyer demanded as soon as the door slammed shut. He was done guessing, done stepping around the issues. Because the truth couldn't possibly be any worse than what he was imagining in his head and he couldn't take it anymore.

Paige sighed. "I don't know much. And I'm pretty sure it's not my place to say anything."

She might've said it wasn't her place, but she sure as hell looked like she wanted to tell him. Most likely out of concern for Ruby. All she needed was a little push...

"I like her. A lot." She had to know his motives were good. "But there's this wall. It's like she's hiding something from me. And maybe if I understood it, I'd know how to help her get past it."

The woman seemed to silently weigh her options. Finally she pushed her plate away and leaned over the table. "She hasn't told me anything. Not really. But she hinted that she was in a relationship not long ago. And the guy sounded like bad news."

Anger clouded his vision, shrouding everything in a colorless haze. "What'd he do to her?"

"I'd guess he pushed her around," she said quietly. "But I don't know for sure. It's just... she still seems so afraid of him."

Rage burned through him, tightening his joints, setting his skin on fire. What he really wanted to do was go throw a chair through a window, but he held himself still and forced a peaceful expression. "Thanks. That helps."

"What're you gonna do?" Paige asked as if she could see past the calm façade. She knew him too well.

He'd like to find the son of a bitch and let him pick on someone his own size. But that wouldn't help Ruby. Wouldn't help his cause, either. He couldn't give her a reason to fear him. "I guess I'll have to find a way to undo the damage he did." To convince Ruby she'd be safe with him.

If she'd give him a chance, he'd always keep her safe.

CHAPTER TWENTY

Ruby sat still and silent, gripping the steering wheel so tight her knuckles ached. Though she'd pulled into her driveway ten minutes before, she hadn't been able to unfreeze her muscles enough to walk inside the house. Her skin still smoldered where Sawyer had curled his fingers around her arm. After she'd run from him, Elsie intercepted her in the kitchen, chatting through the events of the day. For a half hour Ruby had managed to pretend her stomach wasn't roiling from the way Sawyer had grabbed her arm like he wanted to wrench her back to him.

That was how it'd always started with Derek. He'd grab her and yank her into range...

The memory sparked again, igniting her body in a blaze of fear.

Sawyer was different. She knew that. But that didn't mean she had any power over the physical escalation of panic she'd been conditioned to feel. It overpowered rational thought, putting her body at war with itself, unleashing adrenaline and a sickening rush of nausea.

Ruby fought her way out of the car, gasping in lungfuls of the chilled night air. The ground felt unsteady beneath her, so she leaned against the car to catch her breath, to set herself right.

It was her fault Sawyer had gotten angry in the first place. He *never* got angry. He had the reputation for being the biggest pushover on the Aspen police force. Every woman in town knew that when Sawyer pulled you over, you only had to turn on the tears and he would let you off with a rather gentle warning. But tonight she'd pushed him. Insulted him.

She hadn't meant to yell, but someone had to speak up for the kids. They didn't deserve to be treated that way, like suspects instead of guests. Her whole life she'd been looked at like trash because of the way Mama had lived, because her clothes were ratty and unwashed. Never once did anyone look past that—past the circumstances she'd been born into to see that she might have something to offer the world. No one except for Ruby James, that was. Her elderly neighbor was the only person who'd given her that glimpse of hope.

One day when she'd been out playing in the yard past ten o'clock, the woman had come out. "Go on inside, girl. Or your mama will worry."

She'd wished Mama would worry. She'd wished she'd even notice. "I don't matter to my mama," she'd said. It was the truth. Nothing had mattered to Mama except her drugs.

Ruby James had marched to the sidewalk where she was sitting on Grady's skateboard. "Your mama might be lost right now, Katie, but that don't change the fact that you matter. Every person matters. Especially the people who have it the hardest. They're most important, you understand me?"

She shook her head no. She didn't understand that at all. She wasn't important to anyone, not really.

Ruby James had knelt down in front of her, the woman's gnarled fingers tipping up her little chin. "You're the one who'll change this world, Katie," she'd said. "You're the one who'll use that hurt in your heart to heal someone else's."

Though her seven-year-old mind couldn't fully comprehend those words, they'd sunk into her, engraved a purpose into her heart.

Now, nineteen years later, here she was hanging out with kids who had backgrounds just like hers, kids who wondered if they mattered.

And Sawyer was about to make them feel like they didn't.

He was determined, and now so was she. She'd find out who was behind the thefts herself. She had no idea how, but she'd show Sawyer that Javon had nothing to do with it.

Resolve rose up and steadied her enough to march up the porch steps. She unlocked the front door and slipped inside, bracing herself for Nellie's exuberant welcome celebration. Though she'd swung by twice during that day to check on the dog and let her out, you would've thought she'd been gone for a decade. Yipping madly the fluffy bundle of joy bounded over to the door, her whole backside wagging with excitement.

"Hey, girl." She knelt and let the dog jump into her arms. Nellie lavished kisses on her face, only proving that a dog could make everything in the world seem better. "Are you hungry?" She stooped to place the dog back on the floor and Nellie jumped around her, crying and leaping for joy.

"Let's get you some food, little sweetie," Ruby said over the noise, then dropped her purse on the couch and went to the kitchen to dish out the canned food the clerk at the drugstore had insisted was the best. "There you go, love." She set the dish on the floor and the dog went at it snarfing and snorting until there wasn't a morsel left.

"Wow. You *were* hungry, weren't you?" She scooped up Nellie again and brought the dog to the backyard, peeking out first to make sure Elsie wasn't home. What would the woman think if she knew Ruby'd gotten a pet without asking? Guilt skittered through her. She'd tell her. Eventually. Or maybe she'd start looking for her own place. Until then she had to make the dog's bathroom time a convert operation.

The windows next door were dark, so she stepped outside and set Nellie on the grass.

The night air was cool, thick with an uncharacteristic humidity. Though the duplex sat in the middle of town, an echoing quietness made it so peaceful. The multitude of stars glimmered overhead, reminding her of the night before, when she and Sawyer had kissed on the porch swing. It played back again like a fairy tale. She never dreamed she'd be wrapped in someone like Sawyer's arms, kissing on a quaint front porch while the stars winked their approval from above. She'd let her past label her as damaged goods, let it steal the hope of a stable, beautiful future. Her eyes closed, sealing her in an empty darkness. Would it? Would her past always taint her future?

It didn't have to.

The realization popped her eyes open. Like Sawyer had said, everyone was damaged. People overcame it all the time. Look at Bryce. His first wife had died. He was an alcoholic. But now he and Avery were so happy, starting a family, living a life he probably hadn't dreamed he would find, either.

Courage flickered. Maybe it was possible. Maybe she could find a way to put the past to rest.

Ruby watched Nellie trot back to her feet. The dog jumped and put her front paws on her leg.

"What do you think, girl?" She knelt in the soft grass, scratching behind Nellie's ears until the dog went limp. "Can I do it? Can I let go so I can move—"

Headlights cut through her vision. On the other side of the house, a car drove slowly down the street.

Her heart stopped for a second before her pulse accelerated. It was time to go inside. Before anyone saw the dog. "Come on, Nellie," she called, smacking her thigh. "Let's go."

Nellie bounded up the porch steps as though going inside was the most exciting thing that had ever happened to her. Ruby grinned. It was definitely therapy to have a dog around.

"You're a sweet one." She plopped onto the couch and the dog jumped right into her lap, nestling down, slumping over so Ruby could pet her belly. "Want to watch *Dogs with Jobs,* Nellie?"

The dog licked her cheek in a hearty *yes*.

Just as Ruby grabbed the remote, the doorbell chimed.

Her hand froze on the dog's back.

Nellie nudged her hand, begging for another scratch, but Ruby slowly stood. No one ever dropped by to see her. Well, except for Sawyer. Had he come to apologize? To finish their argument?

Nell whimpered, then started to yip, but Ruby gently put a hand against the dog's snout. "Shhh." She scooped up Nellie and hurried to her bedroom, closing the dog securely in her walk-in closet. "Hang tight, sweet girl," she called as she went back to answer the door.

Heart clattering, she unlocked the dead bolt and opened it a crack.

Not Sawyer. Definitely not Sawyer. No. It was the mean man from down the street. The owner of her stolen dog...

Ruby exhaled her fear, a protective instinct making her feel taller, stronger. She glared at the man, who looked to be in his mid-sixties with a rim of white hair and a permanent scowl etched into his weathered skin.

"Can I help you?" she asked, making sure to look bored by his sudden appearance.

"I'm looking for my dog," he growled. "Nell. You seen her?"

"Nope." Ruching up her shoulders she opened the door all the way so he could glance around the room. Thank god she'd straightened up and put all of Nellie's toys in the front closet.

Grayish watery eyes narrowed at her. "You sure about that?" he asked as though he knew she was lying.

"Yep." She combated a rush of heat to her face with a shrug. "I'm sure. I mean, I haven't been home much, but I'll keep an eye out." She forced a polite smile, praying the man wouldn't see through it.

He grumbled out his address. "Let me know if you see her."

"Of course," she called as he lumbered down the porch steps and into the darkness. She closed the door, latching it tight again.

Hurrying to the window she watched the man stop in front of her house, looking carefully at her front yard. Then he finally turned and continued on his way.

A yip came from the bedroom. "I'm coming, Nellie." Ruby rushed to the closet and set the dog free. "Everything's okay." She lifted the dog into her arms and planted a kiss on Nellie's forehead. "I promise I'll never let him hurt you," she whispered.

"You're the one who'll use that hurt in your heart to heal someone else's." Miss James's words had never been so real.

Together she and Nellie were healing each other's hearts. And maybe someday the past would no longer matter.

* * *

Ruby slid the muffin tray into the oven and straightened. Wiping her hands on her apron, she glanced at the clock. She had exactly twenty minutes to do a little detective work and search for some evidence before Sawyer confronted the kids during breakfast.

Even though Elsie had offered her the morning off since she'd put in so much time with the kids, she knew getting there before everyone else would have its advantages. It would give her the opportunity to look around in the one place she suspected she might find the real criminal behind the thefts. Since she always woke up at four-thirty anyway, she figured it didn't matter much. She never slept in anymore. She never broke into buildings, either, but Sawyer hadn't exactly given her a choice, now, had he? He'd called her last night and left a message, apologizing for scaring her and also informing her that he was planning to talk to the kids during breakfast. Before he went in for a shift and they left for their horseback-riding excursion with Paige and Shooter. He wanted her to be there, he'd said. But hopefully she could find something to divert Sawyer's attention away from the kids so he wouldn't have to confront them at all.

It's now or never. Pulling the apron over her head, Ruby darted to the back door and hung it on a hook. Glancing outside, she made sure the coast was clear before she dashed down the stairs and across the dew-laden grass until she'd made it to the path that led to the maintenance shed. The air was cold enough to chill her cheeks and hands. Small clouds of steam rose from her mouth. The early-morning haze made the whole thing feel very cloak and dagger, which caused her heart to thump against her ribs. It wouldn't look good if she got caught sneaking around, but if she could find any piece of evidence it would be worth it.

With the day dawning all around her, she hurried past the stables to the large barnlike structure where they kept the extra equipment—rafts and maintenance tools and backpacking equipment. Sure enough, the shed was dark. Actually "shed" wouldn't be the most accurate description. It was more like a sturdy outbuilding, all winterized and insulated, with indoor plumbing, too. At least that was the rumor. She'd never actually had a reason to go into the maintenance shed.

Not that she wouldn't be allowed to, right? She did work at the ranch, after all, and she had a master key.

Glancing around, she crept to a side door and peered in through a dingy window. As far as she knew, the only ones who spent any time in here were the maintenance guys, Yates and Timmons, who were so part-time she'd only seen them once in the past month. And Shooter, who was full-time between maintenance, running the stables, and helping out as a guide when required. Not that she knew him well, either. He'd hit on her a few times before he'd gotten the hint that she wasn't looking for a fling. Once she'd made that clear, he'd ignored her, which was more than fine with her, seeing as how he wasn't exactly her type.

Lifting a hand to the doorknob she tried to open it. Locked. Quickly she dug the master key out of her pocket and fit it into the lock. The old knob creaked and stuck, but finally opened.

With a look over her shoulder, she rushed inside, her flats slipping on the concrete floor, and closed the door behind her, letting her eyes adjust to the dimness.

The place stunk. Horse manure, dust, grime, grease. The scents were so powerful she could almost taste them. A few windows up high let in just enough sunlight for her to see. She passed rows of odd machine parts, some rusted and broken, others whole and shiny. Then she walked past the ATVs and plows and headed for a door at the back. That had to be the office.

It wasn't locked. Heart racing, she pushed through and left it open, not liking how isolated she felt, how vulnerable. A row of lockers hung along the back wall with names on them. Timmons, Yates, Shooter. There was a desk, cluttered with paper and screwdrivers and a few other small tools she didn't recognize. She glanced at her watch. Twelve minutes until her timer went off, until the muffins were done, and until it was a good bet that Shooter would be around. He usually came in around seven, unless he'd been out drinking the night before. But she probably wouldn't be that lucky.

Pulse hammering in her temples, she darted to the lockers and popped open the first one. If someone stole the money, maybe there'd be something. A stash of cash, a receipt for something expensive. She wasn't dumb enough to think they'd be hiding the cash here, but maybe she'd get lucky. Rumor had it that both Yates and Timmons had been in trouble before. A couple of DUIs. Drunk and disorderlies. So they were the most likely place to start.

Quickly she rummaged through the mound of junk in Timmons's locker. A sweatshirt, a belt...*underwear*? She dropped the rumpled plaid boxer shorts hoping she'd never discover whether they were dirty or clean. What...did the guy store his dirty laundry in his work locker? Her hands felt contaminated. Carefully she pillaged through some papers—pay stubs—then a small zippered pouch, which turned out to contain ChapStick and hand lotion. No wonder he didn't want the rest of the boys to see his fruity ChapStick and hand lotion.

That was it, though. No money. No receipts. No evidence of Avery's bracelet.

She was just about to pop open Yates's locker when the barn door burst open. She froze, eyes darting for anything that would give her an excuse for being in the maintenance office when no one else was around.

Footsteps thudded closer.

Screwdriver. She quickly swiped one off the desk and bolted out of the office door, nearly running over Shooter in the process.

"Holy shit, Ruby!" His hands went up. "You scared the hell out of me."

Heat lashed her face but she smiled. "Sorry about that." Fear clawed at the words, tearing them apart. She *so* wasn't cut out for breaking and entering.

"What're you doing in here?" His eyes narrowed and in the dim light the sheer bulk of him made him look the slightest bit dangerous.

"I was looking for this," she managed, holding up the screwdriver, praying he wouldn't see it tremble in her hand. "The mixer broke." The lie made her wince. Elsie always said one lie started an avalanche of untruths. Boy did she know that to be fact.

Shooter half laughed, the lines of suspicion smoothing from his face. "*You're* gonna fix the mixer?" With a martyred sigh, he swiped the screwdriver out of her hand. "What is it with women these days? Never want a man's help with anything, do ya? Too proud to ask for it."

"Ha-ha." She coughed out a fake laugh. "I didn't want to bother you, that's all. I know how busy you are."

"It's no bother." He sauntered a step closer, all swagger and confidence, though he didn't have much to brag about. He was a big guy, well over six feet, and hefty, too. But looks-wise he reminded her of a younger redheaded Jack Black.

"It's my job. I actually like fixing things," he said, bouncing his eyebrows as though that should entice her for some reason. "I can fix all kinds of things—"

"Oh! The muffins!" She'd forgotten. Hopefully they weren't burned by now. She dodged around him and ran for the door.

"I'll stop by the kitchen later," Shooter called after her.

"Great!" she yelled back, then escaped, lungs heaving, sweat itching on her forehead. Lordy, was she in a mess.

She'd better get back up to the kitchen and break that mixer before Shooter found out she'd been lying.

CHAPTER TWENTY-ONE

*W*ell, *shit.* This was a hell of a lot harder than he thought it'd be. From the safety of the sitting room, Sawyer surveyed the kids, who were already sitting around the long table just past the fireplace in the dining room. The next ten minutes would be more painful than a switchblade twisted into his gut.

Ruby's arguments from last night still hazed over his thoughts. Would a confrontation really ruin their entire ten days at the ranch? She'd been where these kids were, so she should know. But what choice did he have?

One of them might've needed the cash. He didn't doubt that. He heard stories all the time about foster kids who were basically on their own, their parents simply pocketing the state's money. But that didn't change the fact that stealing would get them into a hell of a lot of trouble. Sure, a thousand dollars might not be much, but if one of these kids was responsible, they had to learn a lesson now or things would only get worse.

So while the whole thing made him feel like an ass, he trudged into the dining room and sat at the head of the table. "Hey, everyone," he said as if nothing was different. Except he knew everything was about to change.

Thomas nodded a greeting from the other end of the table. They'd discussed his approach on the phone late last night, and while the man hadn't wanted to believe one of the kids would steal from the Walkers, he'd agreed that they should have a discussion.

"What's up, copper?" Javon said, while a few of the other kids smiled and waved. They were busy eating. Aunt Elsie had just filled their plates with some type of egg casserole dish. His plate was full, too, but he wasn't hungry. He pushed it away.

"Where's Ruby?" Brooklyn asked him. Her thick, dark lashes made her eyes so innocent. Another pang of regret gouged him. "Not sure." He should go find her. He needed her here for this. Aunt Elsie said she'd been in earlier, but she must've gone out to run an errand. She'd probably decided to avoid him until he left for Denver. Wouldn't surprise him after last night. He flicked a glance at his watch. He'd have to figure out how to patch things up with her later. Half an hour until he had to head to the station, so he couldn't keep putting this off.

"Hey, gang." He let his voice slip into the official police officer tenor that always seemed to grab people's attention. "We need to talk."

Sure enough, the room quieted, well, minus the throbbing of his heart. God, he hated this.

"Is everything okay?" Neveah asked, her face white with fear. She likely got scared any time an adult approached her with a serious conversation because it usually ended with her being uprooted again.

His shoulders felt like lead, but it was too late to turn back now. To stall, he lifted his mug and sipped the coffee Aunt Elsie had poured for him, but the kids' round, worried eyes forced him to put down the mug and get to the point.

He folded his hands and made himself look at each one of them. "First, I want you to know I'm not accusing anyone of anything."

No one moved. No one seemed to even breathe.

He checked on Thomas. The man seemed to be visually evaluating Javon.

Damn it. He should've waited. Ruby was better at putting the kids at ease than him. Now he just had to get it over with and hope he didn't screw everything up. He cleared the cotton out of his throat. "About a week ago some money went missing from Bryce's office. One of Avery's bracelets was stolen, too." He tried to keep his face relaxed and open, but it was hard to make eye contact with any of them. "Then a few days ago, more money went missing."

The room was silent. Painfully silent. The kind of silence that makes your ears ring.

He couldn't stand it. "Like I said, I'm not—"

"Morning, everyone!" Ruby hurried across the room, her flowy white blouse hanging in a way that enhanced her sexy curves. Then there were those tight jeans…

"Sorry I'm late." Her smile was radiant, captivating. Maybe because now he knew what hid behind it. She'd been hurt to a degree he couldn't even imagine, and yet she still smiled. She still loved these kids. That was apparent by the glow that took over her face whenever she saw them.

"What'd I miss?" She set a basket of muffins on the table and targeted him with a not-so-sweet look.

No one said a word. When her eyes met his Sawyer stared out the windows across the room.

"What's the matter? Why's it so quiet?" she asked slowly, as if she was putting two and two together.

Yeah. There was no way out of this. How was he supposed to know she'd traipse in two minutes after he told them? He would've waited if she would've called him back to tell him she'd be there.

She posted her hands on her hips, her eyes glaring now.

Sawyer sighed. "I was telling them about the thefts. So they can keep their eyes out," he emphasized. Then he looked up and down the table. "Like I said, I'm not accusing anyone of anything, but if you've seen or heard anything, I need to know about it."

Ruby sat stiffly in the chair next to him, her face stony and unreadable.

Silence continued to blanket the room, dense and overpowering. There was no chatting and laughing like there had been when he'd walked in earlier.

"Come on, everyone," Ruby said, smiling softly at the kids seated around the table. Definitely not at him.

"Don't let this ruin your week. We all feel badly for Bryce, but we'll find out who's responsible. You all just enjoy yourselves and don't worry about this."

"Do we have to leave?" Brooklyn blurted, tears already streaming down her cheeks.

The fear in her eyes submerged his heart in a pool of regret. "No." He shook his head, wishing he could convince her that everything would be okay. This wasn't the way he'd intended it to go.

Ruby's face reddened. "Of course you don't have to

leave, honey. No one has to leave. We know none of you had anything to do with this."

What? Sawyer shot her his own stony look. Didn't she see that it had to be one of them? It had to be. What other explanation was there?

Though Brooklyn nodded and picked up her fork, her lips sagged like her heart was broken.

Damn it. He rifled a hand through his hair. He should've led with telling them they wouldn't be in trouble if they fessed up.

"Sawyer," Ruby muttered through her locked jaw. "Can I have a word with you in the kitchen?"

"Sure." He stood and followed her, bracing himself for another argument. This time he wouldn't touch her. He wouldn't make her feel threatened at all.

Once the kitchen door swung closed, Ruby spun. "I thought you would wait for me."

He leaned against the counter, forcing himself to give her space, even though he wanted to crush her body against his and make her see that he could love her. He could show her how it was supposed to be, how a man was supposed to love a woman. How he was supposed to protect her. How they were supposed to protect each other...

"You should've waited." Ruby's body was stiff, unyielding. Her anger almost made him smile. It was that strength coming through. Whoever she'd been when she'd gotten herself stuck in that bad relationship, she had become a completely different person. One who stood up for others. One who stood up for herself. Everything in her posture right now told him she would fight back. She would fight anyone who threatened those kids.

Damn he liked to see her fight. "I waited as long as I could, but you didn't show up."

Color flared on her cheeks. "I had some things to finish."

"Well, I wanted to get it over with." He checked every word before it came out to make sure it wouldn't be too strong. "Before they go riding and I go to work."

"What makes you so sure it's one of them?" she demanded, stalking over to him, hands pinned to her hips.

Her stance was all fight, but he wouldn't retaliate. Not this time. Ruby needed tenderness, not force. So he laid a hand on her arm, rubbing it up and down to remind her they were on the same side. "I'm open to other possibilities. But who else could it be?" The question was direct but also careful, because tenderness didn't mean he had to agree with her on everything.

"I wish I knew." Defeat resounded in the words. Sighing, she leaned against the counter next to him, so close her shoulder brushed his. She didn't want to fight him this time. And she didn't want to run from him, either.

Even with everything that had happened in the dining room, some of the weight slid off his shoulders because Ruby was standing next to him, touching him. She was letting him see her internal battle. Which meant... she wasn't afraid of him. Even after last night.

He shifted to face her.

She stared at the floor.

"Hey." His fingers grazed the soft skin on the underside of her wrist.

Some of the anger melted out of her eyes.

"I didn't mean to worry the kids. I'm only trying to help Bryce and Avery, Ruby." He slid his fingers down her palm until they found hers. "They can't keep taking hits like this. They do a lot for the community, but they won't survive if they don't have someone looking out for them."

"I know." She peered up at him with a small smile.

"Don't worry about it. I'll talk to them while you're at work. Smooth things over. They'll have a great day of riding and forget all about it."

"So you're not mad at me?" He inched closer to her, hunger growing inside of him. "Even about last night? Because I'd never hurt you. I didn't want you to walk away from me. That's all."

A shadow of a smile crossed her face. God, those lips. Those beautiful lips. "I know," she said again, her voice low.

His eyes were lost in hers. That hunger grew. He suddenly felt empty, like she was the only thing that could fill him. "We'll make sure the kids still have a great time. Trust me, now that this is out of the way, we can move on," he murmured, this time tracing his finger down the delicate line of her jaw.

"I trust you," she whispered, leaning into him.

And that did it. He couldn't be apart from her anymore. He couldn't behave...not with her chest against his, her lips so close...

Sawyer covered her mouth with his and Ruby threaded her hands into his hair, pressing her body into his, her lips working him over with the same desperation that flowed through him.

He moaned against her skin, powerless to keep his desire for her to himself. He'd had a taste of her, but it wasn't enough. Every time he touched her, every time he kissed her, the intensity escalated, and now the need for more drove into him hard and fast, knocking him over the cliff of restraint. "I need to see you tonight," he growled. "Away from everyone else." Away from prying aunts and hyperactive kids, even though they were great and all.

"Yes." She panted against his mouth, gripping his shirt in her fists and tugging him closer, as though she had been caught in the same current he was. It was swift and breath-taking, and he knew they were both going down.

"My place or yours?" he managed to ask before her tongue slipped into his mouth and sent another hot rush of blood south.

"Yours." Ruby gasped, clawing at his back like she wanted to climb up his body and wrap her legs around him the way she had on the porch swing that night.

Didn't have to tell him twice. Lifting her into his arms, Sawyer kissed her as deep and hard as he'd wanted to for days, letting his lips and tongue and the way his hands held her ass say the things neither one of them had found the courage to say...

"Damsels in distress take heart—holy shit."

Sawyer froze. Shooter? He blinked the world back into focus and sure enough, the Walker Mountain Ranch guide stood in the doorway.

Ruby untangled herself from him, feet hitting the floor before she stumbled backward. Her face glowed as red as the stained-glass rose that hung in the kitchen window.

"Did I interrupt something?" Shooter asked with a grin that said he knew exactly what he'd interrupted.

"No," Ruby muttered, smoothing her hair with one hand while she steadied the other against the counter.

Sawyer begged to differ.

His body really begged to differ. Even though she now stood a good ten feet away, certain parts of him were still smoldering.

"The broken mixer is right over here," she croaked, directing Shooter to the opposite side of the room.

Watching her hips sway like that didn't help to calm the blood flow. And now he had to go to work all day. Damn. He should've called in sick.

Shooter lumbered behind her. "Now I get why you won't go out with me. And to think, I actually thought you were just shy."

She was shy. In fact, right now she looked like she wanted to crawl into one of the cabinets and hide.

"We were only talking," Sawyer said in a way that challenged Shooter to argue.

"Oh, that's what the kids are calling it these days," he mocked, fiddling with the mixer.

A ding sounded from Aunt Elsie's cuckoo clock. *Great.* He was late for work. "I've gotta go." Shoving past Shooter, Sawyer caught Ruby's hand in his and towed her out to the porch so they could have one more minute alone. Before tonight, that was.

"I'll make sure he doesn't say anything to anyone." God knew Sawyer had bailed that guy out of more misdemeanors than he cared to admit.

Peering up at him with a smile, Ruby rested her palm against his chest as though confiding herself in him. "Thanks." The passion still glowing on her face reeled him in for another kiss. This time he kept it slow, savoring her so he could get through the day.

When he pulled back, Ruby's eyes glistened.

"Promise me we'll finish this later," he said, not caring if it sounded like he was begging. He had no problem admitting that she made him desperate.

"Call me after you get off work," she teased, but there was a promise in her smile.

CHAPTER TWENTY-TWO

Damn, he was gonna miss this place. Sawyer took his time walking up the sidewalk to the Aspen City Building. As far as buildings go, it was a cool place—a historic brick structure with long arched windows, pointed eaves, and a domed clock tower that always ticked a few minutes behind the actual time. The manicured lawns and gardens made it look like a grand old courthouse, and even with the defective air conditioner, it'd been a great place to work.

Once upon a time he and Bryce used to pull pranks here. Once, after they'd been out drinking in high school, they'd gone and found a Porta-Potty a couple of blocks away. They'd carried the damn thing all the way here and set it right on the stone porch so it blocked the doors. To this day no one knew it was them. Though the police questioned a good number of the seniors, they'd never fessed up. It was one of a thousand memories he'd be walking away from.

He paused on the step, stuck in that thought. Things in Denver would be different, there was no doubt about that. He'd most likely work in a more corporate environment. Wouldn't be as laid-back as it was here, that was for damn sure. And he wouldn't know a single soul. At the time that had been the most appealing thing about the new job, but what about Ruby? What about that kiss? That had felt more like a *we'll see where this thing is going* kiss. It went deeper, carried weight. Especially after what Paige had told him about her past. He'd never kissed a woman without it meaning anything. And something told him, after what she'd been through, she wouldn't have kissed him that way— frantic and passionate—if it didn't mean anything to her.

He wanted her. He wanted her like he never wanted anyone. But how could he fix things for her? How could he erase her past so she didn't live in fear?

Damn, his head was a mess. When Chief had asked him to pick up another shift, it'd been a no-brainer. He needed something to keep him busy, especially since the kids would be gone all day. All the thinking about Ruby and her sorry-excuse-for-a-man ex was making him crazy.

He'd seen victims of domestic violence. Women who'd been battered. Those were always the toughest calls for him. Those were the only moments when police brutality felt like a good option. Having three women in his house growing up, respect had been engrained into who he was. Didn't matter what she did, hitting a woman was out of the question.

Once, when he was ten years old, he'd been so mad at his sister that he'd hit her in the face with his fist. Only happened once. She'd gone down like a deflating balloon, and Dad had taken him by the collar. Kneeling on one knee, he'd jerked Sawyer's face right up to his.

"Any man who hits a woman is weak, son. Do you understand me? You ever hit a woman again, I'll hit you."

Calling Sam a woman was a stretch, he'd thought, but
he didn't dare say it out loud. Dad had never gotten in his
face like that. He'd never grabbed him so rough. That's how
Sawyer knew he meant it.

His gut roiled to imagine how bad it must've gotten for
Ruby to run away. He couldn't think about it anymore.

Resting a hand on the wrought-iron banister, he trudged
the rest of the way up the stone steps and pushed through the
door, plowing down the hall toward the station with his head
down. Maybe he should do some detective work...look
the guy up. If she'd ever filed charges, there'd be records.
Sawyer had a lot of resources. Maybe he wouldn't be that
hard to find.

He moved faster, following his worn path to the station's entrance, but before he push through the door, it
flew open.

"Surprise!"

"Holy—" Sawyer staggered back right as about twenty
of his friends and colleagues stampeded him.

Steamers crisscrossed over his head. Colorful balloons
dangled over the station's reception area. A banner strung
across the wall read GOOD LUCK, SAWYER!

"Wow." He took in the scene as people paraded past
him, whacking him on the shoulder, holding up their frosted
donuts in a toast.

"We're gonna miss you, man." Clay Patterson, the school
resource officer and police force clown, leaned in and gave
him a bear hug, lifting Sawyer off his feet.

Everyone standing around them laughed as Sawyer
fought his way back to the ground.

"Here." Vicki Meeberg, the receptionist, shoved a chocolate donut into his hand. "You eat as many of these as Clay does, and he won't be able to do that to you anymore."

The woman had a point. Sawyer accepted the chocolate-glazed offering and bit off a hearty chunk.

"Thanks, Vicki," he said, not caring that his mouth was full. Everyone knew she planned all the office celebrations. She'd been around forever and took it upon herself to make sure anyone who left got sent off properly.

"Surprised?' she asked hopefully.

"Yeah. I had no idea." He should have anticipated it when Chief called and asked him to come in early. But his mind had been occupied by Ruby. The woman seemed to pop into his brain all the time—when he was trying to sleep, when he was eating, when he was lying alone in that king-size bed in the cabin.

Especially when he was alone in the king-size bed...

"Oh, I almost forgot." Vicki rummaged in her pocket and handed him a piece of paper. "Some old man has been calling for you. Says his dog was stolen. He said he's talked to you before?"

Sawyer studied the paper. Sure enough, the scrawled address said 4th Street. It had be to the same man who'd kicked his dog in front of Ruby. "Yeah. There was an incident a few days ago." He didn't expand. It hadn't been official police business and yet somehow the man seemed to know who he was.

"Well, I told him you'd check it out today." Vicki rolled her eyes. "He called three times. I had to get him off my back."

"No problem." He slipped the paper into his pocket. "I'll head over there and check it out this afternoon."

It would actually work out perfectly. Instead of calling Ruby he could just swing by and pick her up. Maybe have her pack an overnight bag...

He held back a groan. Thoughts like that were gonna make this day last forever. So instead of thinking about what sort of lacy items Ruby might pack in an overnight bag, he headed for the coffee bar.

Mike Ferris, one of the new detectives, stood nearby sipping from a Starbucks cup. "So, Hawkins, steppin' into the big time, huh?"

"I guess." Even though Denver was no New York or L.A., it definitely had a higher crime rate than Aspen. As long as he could remember, crime stats around here had been pretty low. Worst thing they dealt with were the drugs, assaults, an occasional accident on the highway, but mostly it was the black bears lumbering into town and helping themselves to the trash. There were minimal thefts, given the top-of-the-line security measures most people used to protect their mansions, and he'd never dealt with a murder during his time on the force.

"I just came from Dallas," Ferris said. "Worked on homicide. Happy to get outta the rat race, you know? Ready for something slower paced."

Vicki patted Sawyer's shoulder. "Yeah, but Denver'll be great." He'd known her long enough to detect the forced positive ring in that tone. "I'm sure it's not nearly as dreadful as Dallas."

"Right," Sawyer agreed. Denver was a great city—good nightlife, trendy neighborhoods. But even as he smiled, he knew Denver was no Aspen, with the expanse of open space and the friendly small-town atmosphere and the opportunity to ski every single day from November through April...

"You'll love it there," Vicki insisted, but her eyes reddened. "If you'll excuse me for a minute..." She ducked her head and scurried away, heading for the box of tissues on her desk. Not that he was special or anything. She always got choked up when anyone left the force.

Ferris gave a shake of his head and shrug that clearly said, *what the hell is wrong with her?*

"She thinks of this as her family," Sawyer explained. And there were times it really did feel more like a family than a police force. Like when Nicky Alverez was diagnosed with cancer last year and they threw together a fundraiser fair complete with rides and a petting zoo in the park. Or when Vicki herself unexpectedly lost her husband three years ago to a heart attack, and everyone on the force took turns making dinner (or buying something that actually tasted good, like Sawyer had) and going over to eat with her every night for a month so she didn't have to eat alone.

"See?" Ferris clapped him on the back. "That's why I came here. It's stuff like this party that makes this job bearable. Havin' a whole bunch of people who've got your back."

Sawyer looked around the room. All of them had had his back at one time or another. Hell, when Kaylee had cheated on him, most of these guys had taken turns showing up at his door to take him out for a beer...

"So when's the big move, anyway?" Ferris asked.

The question released a buzz of panic. What was he doing? What the hell was he doing?

The answer wasn't pretty. Avery was right. He was running...from Kaylee. He didn't want to run into her at the grocery store anymore. Or on the ski slopes. Or walking around town. Because every time he saw her, he remembered what he'd lost. He couldn't even stand to look at her.

"Yo, Hawkins. You okay? You look like you just saw Patterson cram that whole box of donuts into his big trap."

"Yeah. I'm fine," he said, his chest tightening. "I just... need a minute." Air. He needed air. No matter how fast he walked, though—down the hall, out the building's double doors—he couldn't outrun the truth. He wasn't going to Denver to pursue a new life. He was running away from his old one.

The sun was blinding and bright, but the air filled his lungs and evened out his pulse.

"Hawkins? Everything okay?" Chief stood on the stone steps, shielding his eyes from the sun. "You're not supposed to skip out on your own party. Vicki'll track you down and have you hanged."

He spun. "Not skipping out." He couldn't. He knew he had to go back in there and show her how much he appreciated this. "I needed a minute." Clarity. Air.

Chief ambled down the steps and stood across from him. "So you've got another few weeks, huh?"

Suddenly a few weeks felt like nothing. "Yes, sir."

"And you're still dead set on leaving?" the man asked, clasping his hands behind his back in an authoritative stance Sawyer had seen his own father assume on more than one occasion.

"I have to go." He had a job lined up. An apartment lease. Everything was packed, except for some of his clothes.

"That's a shame," Chief muttered, chomping on his mustache. "Thing is, Hawkins, Assistant Chief Gerke just gave her notice. She's moving to California. Wants to be closer to her family or something." He rolled his eyes like he couldn't imagine anyone wanting to live close to their family. But Sawyer got it. He was having a hard time imagining what it would be like to live four hours away.

"I've got two weeks to find a replacement." The man turned and started back up the steps. "You'd be damn good at the job. Just wanted to put that out there." Without another word, he slipped back inside.

* * *

"Ruby, there you are!" Elsie stuck her head through the door of the kitchen's tiny office.

Ruby immediately shut the laptop. Didn't need anyone to see her doing background research on Yates and Timmons. As crazy as she knew it was, they were the only suspects, the only other people she could fathom who would steal from Bryce and Avery. Except she hadn't found anything that said either one of them were thieves. In fact, aside from the drinking issues, they seemed like pretty good guys, judging from their Facebook profiles.

"Avery and I are having tea on the patio," Elsie said. "Care to join us?"

"That sounds perfect." Ruby stood and worked the kinks out of her back. After that encounter with Sawyer earlier, the afternoon had been crawling by. Every time she thought of seeing him that night—of picking up where they left off—her stomach started doing cartwheels. Somehow his passionate touch freed her to be the person she wanted to be, and she'd completely lost the will to battle her emotions. Sawyer would only be around a couple more weeks, and then he'd move away. He'd move on with his life. So what was the harm in spending the night with him? At least she'd have good memories. Maybe they'd be enough to erase the bad ones.

Anticipation swirled through her again, but a quick glance at the clock stamped it down.

This day was taking forever.

Tea with the girls is exactly what she needed right now. She followed Elsie into the kitchen and picked up the silver tray the woman had prepared.

Elsie hummed lightly while she slipped on a light jacket.

"What're you humming?" Ruby asked. It sure sounded like a love song.

"Oh. It's an old song. You probably wouldn't know it." The woman's fair skin deepened a few shades of red.

"Try me." Before she'd passed away, her grandma had given Ruby all her old record albums. The woman had been a sucker for a romantic song.

Elsie didn't answer but continued humming.

"'At Last'!" Ruby blurted. "Etta James."

Elsie didn't turn around. She simply led Ruby through the dining room and outside to the back patio.

"That's quite the romantic song," Ruby mused while she set down the tray.

"What is?" asked Avery.

Ruby sang the first lines, making sure to draw out the syllables long enough to ignite Elsie's face with color again.

"She's been humming it all morning," she added, pressing a thoughtful finger against her chin. "I wonder why. How do you get a song like that stuck in your head...?"

She and Avery both looked at Elsie expectantly.

The woman brushed them aside with a wave of her hand. "Thomas and I were listening to some old songs," she said briskly. "Lord knows they're a million times better than the rubbish that's out there today."

"Were you listening to them before or after he took you out for coffee?" Ruby teased. Mysteriously, Thomas and Elsie had both disappeared after the kids had left for their riding adventure. When Ruby had called her cell phone, the woman sheepishly admitted that she was at the coffee shop with Thomas.

"Mom!" Avery slapped a hand over her mouth. "You didn't tell me you were going on a date with Thomas!"

"It wasn't a date," she insisted, pouring tea into three mugs like it took every ounce of focus she had to spare.

"But you *did* go out to coffee with him?" Ruby prompted, her heart overflowing for the woman. If anyone in the world deserved to find love, it was Elsie Walker. Seeing as how she was one of the only people who seemed to know how to love someone else, it only seemed right.

"We went to get a cup of coffee," she admitted. "As *friends*. That's all. Thomas is a dear friend of mine. And so was his lovely wife." But Ruby was sure that gleam in her eyes had brightened since yesterday.

"Seems to me Mom's not the only one who has a reason to hum." Avery's head tilted toward Ruby. "I ran into Shooter earlier."

Wow. It sure didn't take long for word to get around this place.

Elsie looked back and forth between them. "What did I miss?"

"It seems that Ruby and Sawyer were making out in the kitchen this morning," Avery said through a sly grin.

Now it was her turn to blush. Not so much from embarrassment, either, but because anytime she heard the words "Sawyer" and "kiss" her body flamed. There were so many reasons she should be guarding her heart and pushing that man away—out of her life—but instead, whenever he came within two feet of her, practical reasoning threw caution to the wind and literally blew her right into his arms.

Promise me we'll finish this later.

She'd never wanted to finish something so bad in her whole life.

"Shooter walked in on them," Avery informed Elsie. "Said it looked pretty hot and heavy."

Ruby resisted the urge to fan herself. That would be an accurate description.

"That's terribly romantic," Elsie murmured. "I've always thought the kitchen was the best place to make love."

Ruby choked on a swig of tea. Since when did Elsie make love! And in the kitchen? Lordy! Remind her to wipe down the counters later...

"You two!" Avery's head fell back with a dramatic pout. "You're making me jealous. I'm not getting *any* right now. It's like Bryce is too afraid to touch me. He's afraid he'll hurt me."

"Well, you did just give birth," Ruby reminded her. "Wasn't your labor like twenty hours or something?"

"Yeah, yeah, yeah. Can't forget that. Trust me." Avery leaned closer. "That's why I want details, honey. All the juicy ones. Fill me in. Let me live vicariously."

"Well..." She replayed the kiss in her head, and even though her body clenched with anticipation like it had when Sawyer's hand slid up her ribs, she didn't know how to describe it. How could you describe perfection? "He...kissed me." She actually wished there was more to tell. "And he's really good at it." Really really really really good, her lady parts reminded her with an affectionate squeeze. It was good to have them back. They'd pretty much been silent until Sawyer had waltzed into her life.

"So are you two together? Dating?" Avery's palms tilted toward the sky. "I mean, seriously. How many times have you kissed now?"

More than she knew about, but Ruby opted to keep that to herself. "It's complicated." She should keep reminding herself of that fact. "He's moving away." A sudden sadness gripped her throat. In a couple more weeks Sawyer would be gone. Once that had brought relief, but now it made her heart ache. Screw her secrets, all the reasons she couldn't have Sawyer. None of that changed the fact that she didn't want him to leave.

None of them did. That was obvious from the sullen silence that took over. The three of them sipped their tea, eventually finding more to talk about—Lily's new habit of blowing raspberries and summer bookings at the ranch. After the tea was gone, Ruby stood and carried the tray back into the kitchen, finding that Elsie's song had stuck with her.

At last…my love has come along…my lonely days are over…

Humming it to herself, she knew she'd give anything— even all her secrets—to be able to say that someday.

CHAPTER TWENTY-THREE

At exactly 4:59 p.m. Sawyer booked it out of the station and headed for his Tahoe. It'd been hard to focus all day. Luckily it was a typical shift in small-town Aspen. He'd gone out on patrol but had to give only a few warnings. Not like his quota mattered when he was planning to leave anyway.

Except he didn't have to leave. He could stay. He could take the job.

As he'd driven around town all afternoon, he'd actually noticed the things he didn't normally pay attention to— things he took for granted having grown up basically in a Garden of Eden. Things like the way the new green grass glowed on the carved slopes of Aspen Mountain. Like the friendly cobblestone walkways and small cafés that gave people the chance to connect and build community.

When he thought of leaving, of losing all of that, his ribs cranked tight.

He slid into the SUV and shoved the keys into the ignition but didn't release the emergency break. Instead he let his head rest against the steering wheel.

The party had reminded him how much he was a part of this community. How much this community was a part of him. At the time leaving seemed like the only way out of his grief, but that wasn't true. Much as he hated admitting Bryce was right about anything, it seemed his cousin had gained a fair amount of wisdom after living through a tragedy that would've broken most men.

You'll never deal with it if you keep it to yourself. He'd taken the first step by telling Bryce. But he'd never deal with it if he didn't face it head-on, either.

It was time. Instead of fearing he'd run into Kaylee randomly, it was time for him to go and seek her out. To put the past to rest for good. If he couldn't take that step, he couldn't stay in Aspen.

It was time.

Firing up the Tahoe he eased onto the road and drove straight to the place he'd avoided for the past year. After he'd stopped to see Kaylee, he'd go by Grayson Collins's house, then straight over to Ruby's.

That thought was enough to make him ignore the five speed limit signs he passed on his way to Awakenings Coffee House.

The green-and-white-striped awning stretched cheerfully over the sidewalk. Before Kaylee had gotten a job there—after she quit at the ranch—he'd gone for coffee nearly every morning, preferring the local hangout over Starbucks. But after she left him he couldn't stand to even drive by it, knowing he might see her. Maybe it was guilt or maybe anger or maybe grief. Whatever it was, he'd deal with it today.

How could he expect Ruby to confront her past when he wouldn't confront his?

Before he could overthink anything, Sawyer got out of the car and cruised through the glass door. A cheerful ding sounded overhead, but everything seemed dark. They'd remodeled since he'd been in. Instead of colorful walls decorated with whimsical art, everything was sleek and earth-toned. Leather. Dark wood. Drab modern paintings. The place was pretty empty. Only a couple of customers sat at a high bar table near the window.

"Sawyer." Kaylee froze at the espresso machine. She didn't say anything else, not "hi" or "leave." She didn't seem to be able to speak at all. He never came to see her. He'd gone out of his way to avoid her ever since he'd caught her in bed with Jace. She must've known he wasn't there for one of her superficial chats.

He marched over to the counter where she stood and braced his hands against the surface. "Hey."

She mostly looked the same as she did every time he ran into her. Shiny dark hair cut in a stylish bob. Tight, expensive clothes that fit her petite frame snugly. A lot of makeup. But she also looked tired. There were lines around her eyes that hadn't been there before.

"What do you want?" The same wariness in her eyes leaked through to her words.

For the first time looking at her didn't make him mad. Or resentful. It didn't make him feel anything, really. "I guess I came to tell you I'm sorry."

She set down the rag she'd been using to clean the machine. "What?"

"I'm sorry I failed you. I'm sorry I couldn't be what you needed." But it was time to let go of the regret. And even the release of those words made him lighter, the same way it had when he'd told Bryce about the baby.

She looked at him the way she used to right before

she'd yell. "I don't want you back. Got that? I don't need you."

He almost laughed. She didn't need anyone. Maybe that was her biggest problem.

That was the difference with him and Ruby. He needed her. And she needed him. "I didn't come here to get you back," he said, knowing the threatening smile would send her into a rage. So he kept it hidden inside. "I'm moving on. And I wanted to make sure you knew that I own it. I know I screwed up with you. I said some shitty things. And I'm sorry."

Tears slipped down her cheeks. She swiped at them like they made her angry. "It wasn't your fault."

"Maybe not all of it. But a lot of it." And he'd like to think he wouldn't make the same mistakes again.

Kaylee sniffled. "When the baby died, I felt guilty. Like I'd ruined your life."

He looked into her eyes. God, if only he could take back the things he'd said so she didn't have to live with guilt. "You didn't cause it," he said. "I know that. The miscarriage just happened. You couldn't have done anything differently." He hoped she believed it. The day he'd said those things to her was the day he'd learned the power of words, that they could never be taken back.

"I didn't want him like you did, Sawyer." Kaylee closed her eyes. When she opened them, they were red. "The thought of having a baby scared the hell out of me. But you...you were so excited. And then the miscarriage happened. You took it hard. I couldn't watch you hurt like that."

"So you left." It wasn't an accusation. He'd simply never realized that. She'd left because she didn't want to watch him hurt. But that's what people were supposed to do in a relationship. They were supposed to be there. That's what made the hurt bearable.

"You expect so much," Kaylee muttered, staring at the granite countertop. "I couldn't give you all of me. I don't know how to give that to anyone."

He hoped she'd figure it out when she found the right person. That was the only way to have a real relationship with anyone. To be open. Self-sacrificing. That's what Bryce and Avery had. What Dad and Mom had. They'd fought hard for it, for each other. And Kaylee would never fight for anyone because it was too hard. It cost too much.

"If it makes you feel better, Jace and I broke up," she said indifferently. The tears had dried as quickly as they'd started. "I'm not good with commitment, Sawyer. You had to know that."

"I didn't." There was so much he hadn't known about her. So much he hadn't known about relationships in general. His parents had made it look easy. They'd argue, sometimes raise their voices, but their respect—their devotion to each other—always won out, no matter how ugly the battle got. It took two to make something like that happen, though. Two people who would fight for it every day of their lives.

He straightened, prepared to walk away from her, from the regret, from the grief. "I hope you find what you're looking for."

Because he was starting to think that he finally had.

* * *

When Sawyer pulled up in front of Grayson Collins's house the man was waiting on the curb. When he left the coffee shop, Sawyer had called him to make sure he was home, and now, a few minutes later, the man stomped over to his car.

Sighing, Sawyer pushed open the door and got out. Like he'd told Collins on the phone, the fact that his dog had gone missing didn't mean someone had stolen it. Dogs ran away all the time. Sad as it was, sometimes around here a coyote or a mountain lion swiped them, though there hadn't been any reported sightings in the area. He'd told him that, too, but the man wouldn't let it go.

"Nell's been missing two days now," Collins growled, like it was Sawyer's fault.

Maybe it you were a nicer person, the dog wouldn't have taken off. Not that he was allowed to offer his personal opinion or anything. He'd do his best to keep it professional, even though Collins deserved a swift kick. "We can file a report," Sawyer said, reaching back into the car for his clipboard. "I'll have you fill out the paperwork—"

"We don't need paperwork." Collins shuffled to the edge of the sidewalk, staring down the street. "That girl took Nell. I know she did. She has my dog at her house."

Sawyer gazed toward the duplex Ruby shared with Aunt Elsie. "I'm sorry. Which girl?" he asked, playing dumb.

"Your friend. She stole my dog."

"Did you see her take the dog?" The fuse on Sawyer's temper was lit. Ruby wouldn't steal someone's pet, for god's sake.

"I didn't see her. But you were here the last time. You saw how she acted."

He couldn't deny Ruby had been upset, but she wasn't stupid. "She didn't take your dog, sir. Like you said, she's a friend of mine. And I'd know if she had a dog at her place." Wouldn't he? Surely she'd mention something. Or he would've seen it. He'd shown up there the other night…

"Then she hid it somewhere," Collins yelled. "Where else would she be? Nell doesn't run."

Sawyer leaned against the car, surveying the quiet street. "Have you seen any animals in the area?"

"No," the man snapped.

"What about your fence? Could the dog have slipped out somehow?"

"Nell. Doesn't. Run."

For the life of him, Sawyer couldn't figure out why. If he were this man's dog, he would've run away a long time ago.

"Does the dog have a collar? Any identification?"

"Of course." Collins held out a paper. "Here's her registration. She's a damn champion. Worth a hell of a lot of money and I want her back."

Just to humor the man, Sawyer scanned the paper. "Well, I'll file a report. In the meantime, I'd suggest you post signs around the neighborhood—"

"You're not even going to ask that girl?" Collins interrupted.

"I see Ruby all the time." He fought to keep his jaw soft. That was an exaggeration, but Ruby didn't have time for a dog. She'd been at the lodge nonstop. "She doesn't have your dog."

"I went to her door the other night. She was acting suspicious."

You've got to be kidding. He didn't like the thought of this man stalking Ruby at her house. Not at all. "What do you mean suspicious?"

"She was in a hurry to get rid of me."

Again…couldn't blame her. Especially given her history. It probably freaked her out to have an angry man show up on her doorstep. He should talk to her about not answering the door. Never could be too careful.

The man's lips curled in a scowl. "The dog is there. I know the dog is there."

Obviously this man wasn't going to let it go. The only way to get him off Ruby's back would be to go over there right now while Collins watched. Sawyer looked down the street again. Ruby's car was in the driveway, and he'd planned on going over anyway. It'd just be a little earlier than he thought. He shrugged. "I'll stop by and check in with her."

Then he'd take her over to his place and make her a dinner she'd never forget.

CHAPTER TWENTY-FOUR

Nellie!" Ruby leapt to grab the dog just as she bounded out of the bathtub. Water and suds sprayed everywhere. "Come back here!"

Yipping with gusto, the dog tore circles around the white subway tile in the bathroom, paws slipping, dark eyes flashing with glee.

Despite the fact that she was sopping wet, Ruby laughed. "Crazy dog." Who would've thought giving a dog a bath could be a better workout than hiking up a mountain?

"C'mere, Nellie," she cooed in the sweet tone the dog could never resist. Kneeling, she held out her hands. She'd learned that talking to Nellie in a stern voice only sent the dog running for cover, usually underneath the dining-room table. Like she was afraid Ruby might hurt her. But when she called Nellie happily, the dog stopped in her tracks and ran right over, tail wagging with excitement. "Come on,

Nellie. You know you want to come over here. I'll scratch your belly..."

Sure enough, the dog leapt into her arms, licking her face.

"There, now. We have to finish your bath." Ruby hauled her back to the bathtub and gently placed her in what was left of the sudsy water.

Nell mournfully looked up from under those long doggie eyelashes of hers.

"Don't look at me like that." Shaking her head, Ruby went back to scrubbing. "I'm not the one who got into the trash." When she'd gotten home from work, she'd found the maple syrup container torn apart and the remnants stuck in Nell's soft fur. That would be her fault. She should've known better than to leave the trash can out in the open.

"We're almost done. Trust me. I'm trying to make this as painless as possible." The sight of her soaked shirt mocked her. Painless for Nellie, anyway. "I know the syrup smelled good and all, but next time can you try to avoid temptation? That way I'll never have to give you another ba—"

The doorbell's chimes cut her off.

Her hands froze around Nell's healthy middle. A breath lodged in her lungs. What was with all the random visitors on her porch? First Sawyer, then the man from down the street...now who?

The doorbell chimed again.

Damn it. Not like she could find out from the bathroom.

Whoever stood on her porch right now had to know she was here. Her car was parked right out front.

"Okay," she said firmly, to steady herself. "You stay here, sweet girl." She lifted Nell out of the tub and rubbed her off with a towel, then slipped out the bathroom door, closing it firmly behind her. On the way to the living room, she caught a glimpse of herself in the mirror. Her white shirt was now as sheer as a drapery panel and twisted like she'd just rolled out of bed. Her hair, which had been neatly knotted on top of her head twenty minutes ago, was frayed and wild. "Perfect." She tried to smooth it back.

The doorbell rang again, this time accompanied by a knock. "Hello?" The deep, muffled voice lurched her heart into her throat.

Sawyer?

"Ruby? Are you there?" He knocked again.

Shit. Inspecting herself in the mirror again, she frantically tried to straighten herself out. What was he doing here? At her house? He was supposed to *call* her.

Lordy, her heart was spinning in joyful circles, but her stomach clenched with nerves.

A shadow crossed in front of the draped window. Now he was looking in her windows. Oh, for god's sake!

Even though she looked like hell, she stalked to the door and tore it open. "What're you *doing* here?"

He looked her over, seeming to study her wet shirt longer than the rest of her. "What are *you* doing?" he finally asked.

She looked down. Oopsie, the outline of her bra seemed to be pretty visible there. She crossed her arms to hide the goods and raised her head.

Hell-*ooo*. In all the commotion, she seemed to have missed that Sawyer was decked out in his uniform. The crisp blue button-down shirt pulled taut around his broad shoulders. Short sleeves seemed tight around his biceps. His hair was combed and he wore aviator shades.

"You look like you went for a swim," he said, leaning a shoulder into the doorframe, and for some reason, that casual pose upped his sexy factor by about five hundred percent. He looked at her, waiting for an answer.

"I was...um..." *bathing a dog. That I'm harboring as a refugee. Nope.* Couldn't tell him the truth. "Cleaning." Her arms tightened around her chest.

"Cleaning." His gaze lowered to her shirt again, and even though Sawyer's presence here was a big problem, what with Nell still trapped in the bathroom and everything, her face flushed at the way he looked her up and down.

"How'd you get all wet?"

"I spilled a bucket of water," she said, as though that sort of thing happened to her every day.

"Do you...want to go change?" he asked slowly, like he couldn't figure out why she hadn't already thought of that.

And, yes. Of course she should've thought of that. She should've thought to pull on a new shirt before broadcasting the fact that she preferred lace undergarments. "Actually, yeah. I should change."

"I'll wait." Sawyer moved to step inside, but she blocked him, thrusting herself a little too close to his macho, uniformed body.

"Um." She backtracked. "Do you think you could wait on the porch?"

"Why?" He whipped off his shades, tucking them in the collar of his shirt, and his beautiful blue eyes creased in the corners, making him look every bit the skeptical cop. Sure enough, his eyes started a visual inspection of the living room over her shoulder. "Ruby...why won't you let me come in?"

She recognized that look. It was blatant suspicion, the same way he'd looked at her that first morning they'd talked in the kitchen.

Sighing, she glanced over her shoulder. All of the dog toys were cleaned up, stowed away in the crate she kept in her bedroom. So really, what was the harm of him sitting on the couch to wait two minutes while she put on a new shirt? "Sorry." She stepped aside and opened the door wider so he could come in. "I just haven't cleaned out here, yet. I've been…mopping the bathroom floor." She'd definitely be mopping it later.

"Looks pretty clean to me." His eyes had gone back to their normal puppy-dog shape. They were so striking, those eyes. Downright dangerous.

Before his eyes could reel her into him, against that solid, protective wall of a chest, she bolted for the bedroom. "I'll be right back," she said, darting down the short hallway to the safety of her bedroom. She shut the door and locked it. Like he'd really barge in while he thought she was changing.

Great, heaving breaths collected in her lungs as she hurried about, ripping off the wet blouse and pulling on a red peasant tunic instead. *No.* She took it off. It made her look too frumpy. Instead she hurried to the closet and selected a long-sleeved green t-shirt with a lace overlay across the shoulders. Casual but nice fitting.

Scratching sounded at the master bathroom door. *Nell!* Ruby jogged across the room and opened the door, scooping up the dog and lavishing kisses on her head. "You have to be very quiet, sweetie," she whispered. "No one can know you're here." Especially not Officer Hawkins. She hurried to the crate that held all the dog supplies and dug out a chewy stick. Then she gently set Nellie in her bed. "You stay," she said, backing away. The dog gnawed happily on the treat and didn't even attempt to get up. "Good girl," Ruby whispered as she lurched back to the mirror. *Whoa.* She had to do something about that frizzy hair. Carefully she managed to untangle the rubber band, then combed her fingers through until it lay soft and wavy around her shoulders.

Well, it wasn't great, but it would have to do. "I'll be back, girl." She blew a kiss to Nellie and slipped back out into the living room, a calm smile hiding the roar of chaos inside of her.

Sawyer stood by the bookshelf near the window, studying the various titles she'd collected. Romance, mystery, fantasy...anything that used to promise an escape into a different world where justice always won. In all those stories the characters overcame the odds and found what they'd been searching for. Standing there staring at Sawyer, heart melting in her chest, it felt like she had, too. Except she couldn't have him. Not forever.

Sadness clogged her throat, but she tried to clear it away. "Sorry about that." A sheen of perspiration seemed to coat her skin, but she could only smell the watermelon-scented shampoo she'd been using on Nellie, thank the Lord.

Sawyer turned and seemed to admire her. "No problem."

"Um." Anytime he stared at her like that it robbed her of the ability to move. She stood in the middle of the room feeling awkward and harried under his examination. "I wasn't expecting to see you until later." She'd practically been counting the seconds all day. "So...are you here on official business?" Or had he just worn his uniform to make her lust after him? Because it was definitely working.

"Just finishing up my shift." He lowered himself into the wingback chair next to the couch. "Your neighbor called in. Said someone had stolen his dog."

"Really?" she gasped. *Stolen?* That was bit strong, wasn't it? She hadn't *stolen* anything. She simply hadn't forced Nellie to go back to a bad home. Despite the logical justification, a tremor weakened her legs. "How awful."

"Yeah." Sawyer leaned forward slightly, resting his elbows on his knees. "It happens to be the same dog you saw the other day. When you called me."

"Huh." Her shoulders tensed, but she forced them into a shrug. "I guess I can't really blame the dog for running away." A heart could only take so much abuse, after all.

"I'm guessing that's what happened. But he's convinced someone took her."

A strangled laugh slipped out. Strangled because she was pretty sure her throat had started to shrink. "That's crazy." Hopefully he couldn't tell how hollow her voice sounded.

"Yeah. The guy's kind of a nutcase." But there was still a question in Sawyer's eyes. "I promised I'd look into it. So you know nothing about the dog's disappearance?"

"No." Technically that wasn't a lie. She didn't know *how* Nellie escaped. She didn't see her get out. She'd only taken Nellie home *after* she'd gotten out. Like Sawyer said that day she'd called him, there was nothing he could do to protect the dog. That's why she had to figure it out herself. She'd made a promise to Nellie.

Before he could see the nervous twitch that ticked in her shoulders, she lightened the mood with a smirk. "Want me to get a chair so you can sit me down and interrogate me again? Maybe a spotlight, too?"

"That won't be necessary." His lips hinted at that sexy quirked smile, like he was holding it back. But he looked tired, too. Or maybe withdrawn?

"Long day at the office?" she asked, still standing in the center of the room, frozen by the knowledge that Nellie was right next door. The treat would keep her busy for a while, but what if she scratched? Or yipped?

"Kind of." A sigh pushed his back against the chair. "But my shift is over now. You still up for hanging out?"

"Sure," she answered quickly. But they definitely couldn't

sit right outside of her bedroom door. "How about a drink?" She drifted to the kitchen door and held it open. Maybe after a quick drink, she could convince him that they should go over to his place for dinner. "I don't have much." She wasn't a big drinker. "But Paige brought over beer a few weeks ago." Lord knew she wouldn't be drinking them...

"Sounds perfect." Sawyer pushed off the couch, and something was different about him. Off. He kept his distance from her. Though he watched her carefully, he seemed cautious, somehow.

"Bet you'll be glad to move on from small-town politics, huh?" she asked, trying to make conversation.

"I don't know." The words drifted without his usual conviction to anchor them.

She studied him. Why was he so withdrawn? Usually that was *her* M.O. Turning away, she dug a beer out of the fridge and handed it to him. "Are you okay? Did something happen?" Who knew what he had to deal with every day, being a cop and all.

"Today was interesting." He popped off the bottle cap and took a swig.

She watched him, trapped inside of a fierce craving to let herself melt into him. He was just so damn beautiful, his long tanned neck, now clean-shaven, his sturdy jaw, so rugged and defined. Whenever she happened to be near him, he consumed her concentration. Even when he was only taking a drink.

He set down the bottle, watching her watch him. "They had a send-off party for me at the station."

Even though his eyes held so much solemnity, she couldn't help but smile. That was a small town for you. Everyone got a going-away party. "I'm sure they'll miss you."

"Will you miss me?" The question came from some low,

deep place. She'd never heard his voice sound quite like that, except for maybe this morning in the kitchen when he'd told her he needed to be alone with her tonight.

The craving seemed to expand inside of her, overpowering thoughts and reason, sending her heart into a titillating purr. "Yes." Her feet felt like they'd been glued to the floor. "Yes. I will definitely miss you, Sawyer." Each honest word grew her courage until a complete fearlessness took over and she could slowly walk toward him. She needed him to know how badly she wanted him. She might not be able to share the truth with him, but that much he deserved to know.

He forgot about his beer, apparently, because she blinked and he stood right there, close enough to kiss her. "Maybe I don't have to leave," he uttered, that low vibration in his tone tingling through her. "Maybe I'll stay."

The longing he kindled inside of her both burned and froze her. "You can't stay for me," she whispered. Especially when she had nothing to give him.

"I wouldn't." His face lowered to hers, but he didn't kiss her. He only gazed into her for an endless moment. "I would stay for me." His lips grazed hers and she wanted to hold him there, to pause this second so she could memorize how it felt, how his kiss and his hands on her hips made her body molten.

"I'm not sure I want to go somewhere you won't be," he murmured, the last of the words drowning in another seductive kiss.

Desperation surged through her as she kissed him back, and she fisted his shirt, pulling him in closer, tighter. *Stay,* she silently begged, but that was so selfish. He deserved to go, he deserved to find the life he'd always wanted. Instead of answering, instead of risking too much truth coming out of her mouth, she kissed him in a way she'd remember forever, losing herself in the taste of him, in the stunning rhythm of his mouth moving over hers.

"God, it's hard for me to keep my hands off you," he sighed, his skilled lips working their way down her neck.

Her head tipped to the side. "What makes you think you have to keep your hands off me?"

He pulled back. "I want to be careful with you, Ruby," he said, as though he had to remind himself.

But she was so damn tired of being careful. This man made her want to be brave again. He'd made her brave, little by little. In the pool. On that ropes course. He made her believe she didn't have to be the woman who'd let a man hurt her.

"Sawyer..." She raised her hands to his face and guided his warm, delicious mouth back to hers. "Don't be careful," she whispered pushing him against the counter. Because she'd finally let down her guard and she wanted this night with him.

No matter what it cost her.

Smiling an invitation she ran her hands up that crisp, starched shirt of his, tugging it loose from his pants while she kissed her way up his neck.

He uttered a helpless grunt, then his hand palmed the back of her head, and this time the kiss wasn't gentle. It was sensual and deep...consuming. His breath was hot in her mouth, his tongue soft and swift, tracing her lips, claiming her entire body.

His hands slipped low to her hips, then under her shirt, gliding up her skin.

Choppy breaths stuttered out of her, along with a whimper. God, she wanted him to take her somewhere else. Somewhere they were both free...

As he raised her shirt up, she wriggled out of it and let it fall to the floor.

"You're beautiful." His finger traced from her collarbone down to the valley between her breasts, and thank goodness she'd worn the white lacy bra.

Sawyer's lips pressed into her neck and he kissed his way down, the shadow of scruff scraping her skin. He somehow unclasped her bra and slipped it off her shoulders.

Oh, lordy. That mouth. Those lips. That tongue. He covered every inch of her chest quite thoroughly, until the heat pulsing between her legs seemed to fill all of her.

She fumbled with the fastener on his work pants and it popped open. Easy access, those official officer pants...

Her fingertips descended his muscled lower abdomen until her hand slipped beyond the elastic of his boxer briefs, and when she caressed him, he shuddered against her.

"Ruby...oh, god." His lips nuzzled her neck. "Tell me to stay."

"What?" She pulled her hands to her sides, trying to breathe, trying to steady herself, but that was impossible. The foundation of her whole façade was shaking, crumbling. "What, Sawyer?"

"Give me a reason to stay," he said, running his thumb down her cheek.

Her heart thumped wildly in her ears. Lordy. Oh, lordy, she couldn't do this to him. Crossing her arms over her bare chest, she stepped back. "I can't." Her head shook. "I can't give you a reason to stay." He *shouldn't* stay. No matter how badly she wanted to, she couldn't make him any promises. She couldn't plan for a future with anyone...

"You have to go," she said through a smile that made her hurt. "This is the opportunity of a lifetime for you. For your career." And she wouldn't take that away from him.

"I'd stay," he said, tugging her back to him. "If I had a reason." His hands cupped her jaw and he pulled her into another kiss, but a crushing weight squeezed her heart. He deserved more than this. "Sawyer. Wait. We have to stop."

His hands let her go, sliding slowly down her abdomen before resting on her hips.

"I'm sorry," she croaked. "This can't happen. Not right now." There were too many lies. She was hiding a missing dog in her bedroom. He didn't even know her real name. She couldn't sleep with him. Not like this.

"It can't?" He almost sounded like he'd been hit in the balls with a rolling pin again.

She cupped her hands on his jaw, looking in his eyes so he could see how badly she wanted him. But... "It's too fast, that's all. We hardly know each other." Well, that wasn't exactly true. She knew most everything about him. He just knew nothing about her.

A sigh lowered his head until his forehead rested lovingly against hers. "I wish you'd talk to me." He brushed a light kiss on her lips. "I wish you'd tell me what you're running from."

He made it sound so simple, but how could she risk her past ruining his future? "I think you should go." She ground her jaw against the threatening tears. "I'm sorry."

But he shook his head. "You have nothing to apologize for, Ruby," he said, the words weighted with a familiar sadness.

If only that were true.

CHAPTER TWENTY-FIVE

"Y ou want me to do *what*?" Ruby peered over the edge of the zipline's wooden platform. The rocky ground had to be a good twenty feet below her. Then again, it was kind of hard to tell, seeing as how she'd suddenly gotten dizzy.

"You have to go first so you can be there to help the kids when they come down," Sawyer explained patiently, with that same blank look in his eyes that'd been there all afternoon.

How did he remain so indifferent when she thought about last night's little tryst every time she happened to glance at his shorts?

"It's not as terrifying as it looks. I swear." Even his voice had that distant ring, like he hardly knew her.

Ouch. Though she supposed she deserved it. It was better this way. It was better if she pulled away so he would leave Aspen.

"You'll be fine, Ruby." He knelt in front of her and slipped his fingers underneath the harness straps that cinched against her upper thighs.

Hello!

"Does it feel tight enough?" he asked, giving the straps a good yank.

"Um. Yes," she squeaked. The harness wasn't the only thing feeling tight. It was like the more she pushed the man away, the more her body ached for him. After he left her kitchen last night, she'd had to hide her cell phone in the couch cushions so it wouldn't be easy for her to call him and ask him to come back over so she could tell him everything and they could finish what they'd started.

Sawyer stood and backed away from her, that expansive chest of his tenser than normal.

The kids were all edged against the platform's railing as though they feared the height as much as she did. She looked up at the heavy cable that was strung from the tree next to her all the way down to another wooden platform about halfway down the mountain.

"When you get down there, go ahead and unhook your harness clip from the cable and I'll send Brooklyn down next."

The girl squeaked and clutched her fists under her mouth. "It's so far! I don't think I can do it!"

"Sure you can," Sawyer insisted, kneeling in front of her. Ever since the confrontation at breakfast yesterday, he'd been unbelievably sweet to all the kids. But especially to Brooklyn. He'd carried her backpack all the way to the zipline for her. He'd made sure she was always included, first in line…

Now Sawyer was on his knees peering up into the girl's face like a defenseless daddy. "I won't let anything happen to you, Brookie. I promise. You'll be safe."

The girl's face erupted into the biggest smile Ruby had ever seen. Brooklyn threw her arms around Sawyer's neck, seemingly forgiving him for upsetting her yesterday.

It was enough to make Ruby's uterus ache. Yet another reason she had to let him go. She couldn't carry a baby, and Sawyer deserved to have kids.

As he hugged Brooklyn back, his gaze caught Ruby's, and that distance that'd been there earlier faded. Something unfathomably deep passed between them, but she looked away as though she didn't feel that hard tug in her heart.

"You ready for this?" he asked her, moving his hand toward her like he wanted to rest it on her arm. Instead it stopped awkwardly inches away.

Blood pumped hard through her heart, warm and thick. "Yes." When his eyes were on hers, she could be ready for anything. Any. Thing.

A small smile made him look like a sexy renegade as he went to work clipping her up to the device thingie attached to the cable. "It'll be fast," he told her. "Make sure you hold on and wait to unclip until the stopper catches."

"Mmmm-kay," she murmured, still intoxicated by his closeness, his ruggedness, his pure manliness. By the memory of his mouth against her skin...

"Be careful!" Brooklyn threw her arms around Ruby's waist. "Please don't die!"

"She'll be fine." Sawyer's great big masculine hand swallowed Brooklyn's. "Let's give her a countdown," he said in a way that seemed to evaporate the girl's fear. "Ready?" His brows shot up.

"Ready!" Brooklyn squealed, gripping his hand tight. Everyone else gathered around.

"Five...four..."

"Wait!" Ruby gripped the cable in front of her with her

glove-clad hands. "Can't we count down from twenty? Or thirty?" *Or three thousand?*

"Two!" Sawyer shouted, inching closer to her. "One!" He gave her shoulder a tight squeeze, then nudged her off the platform and her feet were groundless.

Wind whipped her hair into her face, her eyes. "I can't see!" she screamed. But did the sound escape her lips? Because she couldn't breathe. The world zoomed past her, the trees and rocks and dirt a blurred haze.

Hold on! Hold on! She tightened her grip and forced herself to lift her head. Even though it was fast and terrifying and so out of control, it was beautiful. The world was beautiful. She could see all the way down the valley, to the town. The colors seemed more luminous—the dark green trees glowing, the glistening blue sky bubbling above her as if it had turned liquid.

Her eyes burned and watered with the wind. Or was it tears? Because the world was below her and she was free of it. Free of everything.

Slam! The momentum stopped instantaneously. She looked around to make sure she hadn't slammed into a brick wall. Turned out she hadn't. The stopper had simply caught her and now she was dangling over another wooden platform.

"Woo hoo!"

Behind her, on the upper platform, all the kids cheered. And Sawyer. Louder than any of them.

After unclipping herself and teetering around the platform on her wooden legs, she waved at them. "It's so fun!" she yelled.

She watched Sawyer clip in Brooklyn, then raised both thumbs into the air as the girl stepped to the edge of the platform. Hope bloomed in her heart. Sawyer's little chat with the kids yesterday may have dampened the mood, but it hadn't ruined anything for them. These past ten days would still be some of the best memories these kids had. And good, positive, wonderful memories were the one thing no one else could ever take away from them.

Tears clouded her eyes as she watched Brooklyn sail toward her, screeching with delight. She stepped back, ready to receive the girl into her arms.

When she came to a stop, Brooklyn was laughing and crying. "That was so amazing," she sniffled. "So, so, so amazing."

"You were brave," Ruby said, unclipping her harness. "I'm proud of you, Brooklyn."

The girl beamed, making her eyes as bright as the sun. Or maybe even brighter. She hugged Ruby tight. "I never want to leave. Never." Her little voice was muffled against Ruby's sleeve. "Can't I stay here? With you and Sawyer? You could adopt me..."

"Oh, honey." Her heart bled. "You don't know how much I want that." But she was living a lie. She couldn't adopt a child with a fake identity...

"I don't want to go back to my foster house. They don't love me." She sniffled. "They don't want me."

"I'm sure that's not true." But the words were rotten in her mouth. Because she knew how it felt to wonder if the people you lived with really cared—if they *wanted* you there or if they were only putting a roof over your head for the money it brought in.

No child should ever have to wonder about something like that.

Taking the girl's hand, she led her to the edge of the platform, right next to the rail so the others would have plenty of room to land. "I'll tell you what," she said softly. "I'll give you my email and phone number, and you can call me anytime you need someone to talk to. Okay?"

The girl nodded slowly, her eyes round and sad.

"Anytime. I don't care if it's two o'clock in the morning. I'll always answer the phone when I see your number."

"Okay," Brooklyn said, smiling a little. "I guess that's good."

"And I'll talk to your foster parents about visiting sometimes," she added, because she knew how much this girl needed someone in her life. Someone who'd be there even when she had to move again.

"You promise?" Brooklyn gasped. "You'll visit me?"

"I'll do everything in my power to make that happen." Even if she had to get on her knees and beg the girl's foster parents.

She'd find a way to make it happen.

* * *

Sawyer climbed down the platform's ladder and dropped to the ground. He was sweaty, dusty, tired, and his hands ached from fastening and unfastening carabiners all day, but the ecstatic looks on the kids' faces made every second worth it.

And then there was *her*.

He watched Ruby walk past and he had to lock his jaw so it wouldn't hang open. After last night he knew the perfection of those curves, the sweet taste of her skin. He knew, and now he couldn't touch her—couldn't hardly look at her without that jolt of need softening his knees.

But she'd told him to go. *I can't give you a reason to stay.* Maybe she couldn't find the words, but her actions betrayed her—the way she clung to him, the way she smiled at him, the way she wrapped herself into him. Her body sure seemed to want him around. So maybe she'd said she didn't want him to stay, but he wasn't sure he believed her.

He wasn't sure he wanted to walk away from her, either. Ruby had a tenderhearted depth that drew him in, and knowing she had been mistreated made him want to stay and protect her.

Every time he watched her sail down that cable, red glistening hair whipping in the wind and sun, an open-mouthed smile beaming from her face, he'd been mesmerized. He loved seeing her let go. Loved seeing her soar above the trees like she was carefree and light, unburdened by the things that haunted her. God, he wished she'd let him help her. He didn't want to force her. He wanted her to trust him enough to tell him everything.

And despite the fact that she'd kicked him out last night, they were getting closer. No matter what she said, no matter how many times she threw him out, he wouldn't stop trying.

The kids were all preoccupied with trying to chase a monarch butterfly that had fluttered into the midst of their circle, which gave him the perfect opportunity to tromp over to where Ruby bent, attempting to remove her harness.

"Need some help?" he asked, gazing down at her mile-long legs.

"Oh." Her head snapped up. Didn't take long for a blush to engulf that fair skin of hers.

The same heat flowed through him.

"No, thanks." She finished loosening the straps, then stood, stepping out of the harness the way she might step out of a lacy thong.

An internal groan echoed, but he raised his eyes to hers to keep himself in check. She'd made it clear that she wasn't ready for anything more physical than a kiss, and he had to respect that.

But he didn't have to like it.

"Nice job out there today," he said when he realized he'd been awkwardly quiet for too long.

That shy smile settled into her cheeks. "Thanks. It was pretty amazing." A thrill flickered in her eyes. "So fast. And high. I can see why people love adrenaline so much." Her skin was still flushed, making her look alive and warm.

The temptation to touch her almost overpowered him.

"You were great with the kids, too." He shuffled a step closer. Not too close. Not too far? "They love you," he said, then added, "and I can see why."

Not only because she was fun but also because she was compassionate. Both careful and wise. It was obvious she lived deeply, lived in a way he'd feared to live since he'd lost his son. Somehow Ruby had taken the terrible things that had happened to her and let them teach her how to live.

"The kids are incredible," she finally replied, looking over at the group, who were now engaged in some kind of hip-hop dance-off. She smiled, but her eyes were far away and misty. "I wouldn't mind taking them all home." With a shake of her head she looked embarrassed. "I mean. That's ridiculous, but if I could give them a home, I would. I'd give them..." The words trailed off and he read between the lines. She'd give them a home like she'd never had.

"You'll make a great mom someday." The words flew out past his internal filter.

A sigh rushed from her lips and she turned away from him as though she didn't want him to see her face.

What had he said? Before he could ask, Brooklyn ran up between them.

"Ruby...Javon said there's no way you're gonna visit me," the girl cried, aiming an accusatory glare at Javon, who held up his hands.

"What?" he demanded. "That's impossible. You people can't just drop in and visit us whenever you want. There's rules about that kind of thing."

Sawyer's mouth dropped. "Visit you?" he asked, just to make sure he'd heard right.

Brooklyn's head bobbed in an emphatic nod. "Ruby promised she'd visit me! And she's gonna give me her phone number so I can call her whenever I want!"

"Wow." He tried to infuse it with some enthusiasm, but concern worked its way through. Avoiding Ruby's eyes, he stacked up the harnesses and plopped the box in Javon's hands. "Hey, why don't you guys head back to the lodge and warn Elsie we're on our way for dinner? Leave the harnesses on the deck."

"Come on!" Brooklyn snatched Ruby's hand, but Sawyer tugged her away and nudged the girl toward Neveah instead.

"We'll be right behind you," he said.

Javon whistled low. "I think they need some *alone* time." He snickered while the rest of the kids made kissing sounds.

"Yeah, let's give them some time alone," Neveah sang, sweeping an arm around Brooklyn and leading her up the hill.

Sawyer cleared his throat. "So apparently we're not as subtle as I thought."

If her narrowed eyes were any indication, it didn't look as though Ruby wanted to talk about him and her. He could already see her defenses rising.

She posted her hands on her hips. "Don't lecture me about supporting these kids, Sawyer," she said before he could speak.

"I won't lecture you, but…" He tried to come up with a gentle way to say it. Except most of his training had revolved around being blunt. Maybe he should try a hostage negotiation class sometime.

A tilt of her head prompted him.

He relented with a sigh. "I think you should be careful, that's all."

She flinched. "Careful?"

"About making her promises. You don't know if her foster parents will allow you to talk to her on the phone, let alone see her again."

Her body went stiff. "It's none of your business."

She had a point, but she was emotional, not thinking clearly. He raised a hand to quiet the anger in her eyes, but she backed away from him.

"I know you want to change things for her, but it's not as simple as handing her your phone number." Chances were the girl's foster parents wouldn't allow it. Then Brooklyn would only be disappointed again.

"You think I don't know that?" Ruby seethed. "I know it's not simple. I know that better than anyone. Certainly better than you."

"I know you see yourself in her, but—"

"Don't." Her head shook. And that was no blush on her face. It was pure anger. "Don't say that. You don't know anything about me."

"That's because you won't let me." He stomped over, anger filling him until it felt like it would brim over. Because someone else had hurt her, someone else had wounded her so deep that he couldn't undo the damage. "I *want* to know you. I want *you*." Didn't she know that? Hadn't he made that clear? This wasn't about getting her into bed...

"If you knew, you wouldn't want me," she whispered.

"If I knew what?" he demanded. God, she was so confusing. Why did she think it would matter to him that someone else had hurt her? That wasn't her fault...

She simply shook her head, her shimmery green eyes brimming with tears. "There's so much you don't know."

Risking another chance for her to push him away, he pulled her close. "Then tell me. I can handle it, Ruby." After she gave him details about the son of a bitch who'd beat her up, he might have to go tear down a tree or wrestle a damn bear, but he wanted to know. He wanted to know why she shuddered when he got too close. He wanted all the facts so he knew how to prove himself to her.

She wrenched free of his grip. "I can't. I want to but I can't."

Yes, she could! That was bullshit. Frustration swelled and, damn it, he didn't care about protecting Paige's confession anymore. "It's not your fault." Why couldn't she see that? "You didn't deserve it. No one deserves to be abused by someone who's supposed to love them."

Ruby stumbled backward, her eyes now as red as her face. "How do you know?"

"I don't know." He wanted to follow her, to touch her, to calm her, but he stood his ground. "Not much anyway."

"Have you been checking up on me?" She didn't give him a chance to answer. "You said you wouldn't. You said you didn't have to do a background check."

Damn it. They were back to that. Now he didn't have a choice. He'd have to out Paige so Ruby wouldn't think he'd lied to her. "I didn't do a background check. I asked Paige."

She stared at the ground in disbelief. "Paige told you...?"

"She didn't tell me much. She only said she suspected that your ex hurt you." And did Ruby really blame her for saying something? "Your friends care about you. *I* care about you." Everything he'd seen from Ruby over the past couple of days had told him she was loyal and softhearted.

More authentic than anyone he'd ever met. Even with her secrets. She was worth fighting for. He simply had to learn how to win her over.

She completely ignored his confession and turned away again. "I can't believe this."

His feet itched to chase her but he knew enough to stay put. "She wants to help you. So do I."

"I don't need your help," Ruby muttered, though the tears streaking down her cheeks made her look very much like a woman who needed to be rescued. "I don't want your help, Sawyer. With anything." It was obvious that she was trying to be strong, but it would've been a lot more convincing if the words hadn't been a whimper. "Leave me alone," she muttered, her voice breaking. Then she tromped away and headed up the hill toward the lodge.

This time, he let her go.

CHAPTER TWENTY-SIX

She had to leave.

Ruby tore three suitcases out of her closet and tossed them onto the bed.

Right at her feet, Nellie chomped on her squeak toy like she was nervous.

Squeak, squeak, squeak.

"You're gonna kill that thing, sweetie." Sitting on the edge of the bed, she lifted the dog into her lap, running her hand over that soft fur until Nellie rested her head on Ruby's leg.

"Everything'll be fine," she murmured. Once they got out of here. She couldn't stay. Not when Sawyer knew the truth. It was only a matter of time until he brought everything to the light, and she couldn't let him do that. Derek was dangerous. Violent. The most skilled liar she'd ever seen. And she would not stay and watch Sawyer go up against him. She would not ruin his plans to move to Denver. She would not let him give up anything for her.

She glanced at the overflowing closet and then back at the suitcases on the bed. When she'd come to Aspen those three suitcases had held all her personal belongings. She had known she wouldn't have much time to pack when Derek had left for his shift that day. There hadn't been much that belonged to her, anyway. But now, in one year, she'd accumulated so much more. Memories of the first happy place she'd been her whole life, and she didn't want to leave them behind.

Sighing, she scooted Nellie off her lap. "We're gonna need some boxes."

According to the clock, it was well past midnight. Somehow she'd made it through dinner with the kids, then helped Elsie clean up. Sawyer was noticeably absent the entire evening, and she didn't blame him. She hadn't gone looking for him, either. It was in his best interest to stay away from her. She'd toyed with him, though she hadn't meant to. And now she had to get away before she did any more damage.

"I'll be back in a little while, Nellie." She stood and found a chewy stick for the dog, tossing it on her bed. "You sit tight, sugar. With any luck, we'll be able to drive out of here first thing in the morning." But that meant she'd have to get enough boxes to pack everything up.

Luckily Elsie kept a stash in the ranch kitchen's storage room.

The drive felt lonely. It was so dark. No one was out on the roads. Even the stars hid under a thick blanket of clouds. As she pulled off onto the Walker Mountain Ranch's driveway, her eyes teared up.

She'd miss this place. There was no way she'd ever find what she'd found here, but in some ways she'd known she wouldn't be able to stay forever. That didn't happen for peo-

ple like her. The Walker Mountain Ranch had been exactly
what she'd needed last year. Now it was time for her to
move on.

Inhaling deeply, she sought the strength she'd need to
walk away. That would be best for Sawyer. That's what she
had to focus on. This was how she could protect him. This
was the only way she could protect them all.

Ruby parked the car in front of the office and got out. She
zipped up her fleece against the cold night air. Small clouds
puffed from her mouth. Glancing around to make sure the
place was deserted, she tromped toward the lodge. The clouds
above her looked as heavy as her shoulders felt.

She hated to leave the kids without saying good-bye. Espe-
cially Brooklyn. But Sawyer was right. She couldn't make
Brooklyn any promises. She wasn't even living her own life.
She was living Ruby James's life. Not Kate McPherson's.
How could someone who was hiding from her past—from the
world—ever make a difference in a child's life?

She couldn't. She couldn't even do anything for herself.
How could she expect to do anything for Brooklyn?

Instead of heading around the back of the lodge to the
kitchen door, she crept across the porch and unlocked the
main door. Checking over her shoulder, she slipped inside the entryway and flicked on the overhead lights. The
room breathed its welcome through the homey touches
that Bryce and Avery had so carefully selected. The large
framed pictures of the staff and guests building happy
memories that were changed out every year. The potted
dwarf pine trees clustered in the corners. She drifted past
the famous coatracks that looked like leafless trees and
ambled into the great room. The fireplace towered in the
center, the colorful rock making it look like a beautiful
wall of stone.

She'd sat on that hearth so many times throughout the long winter, sipping hot chocolate and peppermint schnapps with the girls, listening to Elsie and Bryce tell stories about the lodge's earliest days as the evening stretched into night. Those moments had made her feel like she was part of their family, part of something larger and more profound. Her whole life she'd dreamed of having those deep connections, and she'd found them at the Walker Mountain Ranch.

A sense of grief swallowed her heart, making it limp and lifeless in her chest.

Her gaze fell to the rustic picture that hung on the wall next to her. It was an old pallet Avery had found in the shed. She'd sanded it and then painted a mountain scene across the bottom. The words she'd stenciled along the top gripped Ruby in a way they never had before. *Every heart comes alive in the mountains.*

That had been true for her. Although it wasn't only the mountains that revived her. When she'd come here, she'd been a shell of a person and everyone had embraced her, Paige and Avery and Elsie. Sawyer. They'd filled her up again. They'd helped her find her strength. And now she'd have to use that gift they'd given her to embrace a new life. They'd been so generous to her, she'd been able to save money. She could go to California now. She could—

"What're you doing?"

Her same heart, the one that had felt cold and empty only seconds before, leapt to life again, aching, beating too hard at the sound of Sawyer's voice behind her. She didn't turn. Couldn't. How would she face him? How could she tell him she was running away from him?

"Ruby . . . what're you doing in here?" he asked again, the words three parts fear and one part accusation. "It's the middle of the night."

She forced herself to turn around.

Sawyer stood under the antler chandelier. He was dressed in sweats but no shirt. Hair mussed like he'd just rolled out of bed and run right over here.

"What're *you* doing here?" She sent his own question back to him so she wouldn't have to answer it.

"I couldn't sleep so I got up and went into the kitchen. Then I looked out the window and saw the light on, and I thought—"

He'd thought he would find out who was behind the thefts. That's why he'd come so fast.

Heat gathered on her face. "I know how this looks."

The mouth that had been so soft and generous with hers pulled tight. "Why are you sneaking around?"

She could tell him that she'd lost something. Or that she'd forgotten to finish something in the kitchen so she had to come back. But she was so damn tired of lying to him. She sighed out the sadness that clouded her lungs, hoping he wouldn't come closer, because if he did—if he touched her—she knew she wouldn't be able to go through with this. "I came to get some boxes," she said, shocked at how indifferent she could make herself sound.

"Boxes," he repeated, taking long strides as though he wanted to look into her eyes for proof.

"From the storage room. Elsie keeps extras in there."

"Why do you need boxes?" he asked, but he already knew. She could tell from the way his shoulders tensed. Like he was bracing himself.

"I have to go." Tears bathed her eyes in warmth, but she wouldn't let them fall. She'd be strong the way he taught her. She'd do what was best for everyone. "I'm sorry, Sawyer. But I have to." And that was all she could say. If she opened her mouth to speak one more syllable, she would shatter.

"When will it stop?" Sawyer didn't seem to sense her fragility. He stormed over to her.

"What?" she squeaked, shrinking back so he wouldn't touch her. If he pulled her into his arms she wouldn't be able to walk away.

"If you run from here and go someplace else, you'll have to run again," he said, passion flaring in his blue eyes. "That's not a life, Ruby."

She stumbled back. Distance. She needed distance and clarity. "I can't stay." Fire roared up her throat. He didn't understand the danger. "If anything happened to any of you, I'd never forgive myself. Never."

"You deserve more than this." He swallowed the distance between them with two easy steps and she had nowhere else to run. "You deserve a place. A family." His hands clasped hers and he towed her in closer. "You deserve to be loved."

His touch completely disarmed her, quieting the chaos, softening her knees in that lovely, lazy way.

"Whatever it is—*who*ever it is—I'm not afraid," Sawyer insisted, his thumbs grazing over her knuckles in a soothing caress. "Which means you don't have to be afraid, either. You're not on your own anymore, Ruby. You don't have to face anything alone."

She searched his fathomless blue eyes. They held so much. No one had ever said something like that to her. She'd always been alone. Never more alone than when she was with Derek. But Sawyer meant it. She saw the emotion in his eyes, heard the catch in his voice, the sound of faithful sincerity. So authentic. Maybe it was because of all he'd lost. "Kaylee had everything in you," she whispered, resting her palm on his cheek. "And she let you go. I'm so sorry."

"I'm not." The words scraped with a rough edge. "If she hadn't let me go, I wouldn't be standing here. With you."

A breath hitched, stinging her body with anticipation as he lowered his face to hers.

His gentle eyes held her gaze. "Can I kiss you, Ruby? *Really* kiss you?"

She knew why he was asking. Because she pulled away and ran from him so easily. But not this time. This time she would stay. She would let her heart pound until it felt like it would burst. She would let his touch take her places she'd likely never been. "Yes." She bit her lip and drew out the word, savoring it. *Yes.* That simple word shoved everything else aside—her pretend name, her bruised memories, the dog she'd hidden away at home, the lies she'd told.

His half smile bloomed into a grin and he closed his lips over hers, enveloping all of her in a soft, lovely warmth. It was gentle, careful, and precise, as he had always been with her. Fully in control. But she wasn't. The feel of his lips pressed into hers, of the stubble that scuffed her cheek, ignited every cell until they glittered with heated light. His hands slid up her back, caressing her again, the pure pleasure of it contorting her body. His chest rose against hers and his hands cradled her cheeks, his lips gently prying hers open until his tongue slid into her mouth and shut out everything else.

All she could think about was being in his arms, against his solid form, safe and wanted.

He pulled away. "Come back to my cabin..."

She knew what he was asking. He wanted her to trust him with her secrets, maybe even more than he wanted her body. And it was time. Yes, it was time.

"Let's go," she whispered, nodding before she lost the courage. "Of course I'll come with you." After everything he'd given her, all he'd done for her, he deserved to know why she hid.

She only hoped he didn't change his mind about her when he knew the truth.

* * *

Before he'd gotten married, Sawyer's mom had given him only one piece of advice. *Learn how to listen,* she'd said. *Learn how to listen first without speaking and you'll have a good marriage.*

He hadn't taken her advice. Maybe if he had, he and Kaylee would've known each other better, maybe they would've developed the intimacy he already felt with Ruby.

But listening was hard when there were things you didn't want to hear. Or that you were afraid to hear. Listening was hard when silence pounded against your eardrums. With Kaylee he'd always tried to fill it, but now, sitting next to Ruby on the soft leather couch, he choked back words that tempted him to speak—*you don't have to tell me anything except for the bastard's name and I'll take care of the rest*— and let the silence give her the space she needed. Because he knew she needed to tell him. After he'd told Bryce about losing the baby, he'd felt this enormous burden lift. He hadn't even realized how much the weight of it had been crushing him. Now he wondered how he'd even carried it so long alone. Since telling Bryce, things had changed. While he still felt the loss, it seemed more like a healing wound than a cross he had to carry through life.

He was tempted to tell Ruby that—how freeing it is to share your pain with someone—but again, that wouldn't be listening. She didn't need any lectures. Right now she only needed someone to listen. So as hard as it was, he embraced the silence and sipped the coffee he'd brewed to give them both a second wind.

Ruby sipped hers, too. She hadn't said anything since they'd sat down, and while it felt like a damn eternity, it probably hadn't been more than five minutes. Five long, silent minutes. She sat straight, her body pulled taut as though she wanted to be ready to run. Her hands were frozen around the mug, her knuckles white. God, he couldn't stand it, the blank look in her eyes, the paleness that drained the life from her face. She'd gone back to that place, he could see it. She was relieving every horrifying moment.

He leaned over and took away her mug, set it on the coffee table. Then he held her hand, threading their fingers together, hoping it was enough to bring her back.

She blinked but didn't look at him. "I was going to leave because..." A swallow seemed to stick in her throat. "...I can't risk him finding me," she whispered. "Then he would find you. And Elsie. And Bryce and Avery." Her hand trembled against his. "I can't let anything happen to you, Sawyer. You don't know what he's capable of."

Anger flowed in, rising into a seething hatred. The son of bitch was still controlling her. He'd traumatized her into thinking he should have a place in her life forever...

Sawyer kept his eyes focused on Ruby's broken face so he wouldn't let the rage overpower him. She needed him to keep his shit together, no matter how much he wanted to launch himself off the couch and tear that man apart with his own hands. "Who is he?" he asked, binding the words in a fragile restraint.

"That's why I wanted to leave." Ruby's head cranked slowly until she gazed at him. "Because you can't fix it. And I knew you'd want to try." Huge tears bubbled out of her eyes, but she didn't wipe them away. "I don't want it fixed for me. I don't want to go back. I don't want to remember. I only want to move on."

But she did remember. That man had victimized her. He closed his eyes, inhaling and exhaling until his pulse stabilized. *Focus on Ruby.* Only on Ruby. He could deal with the monster later. "How long were you with him?" he asked, wrapping his arms around her, pulling her against him, holding her so she would feel safe and protected.

The back of her head rested against his chest. "Um. It was a couple of years." Anguish suffocated the words. "We were engaged."

He tightened his arms around her as if that would help hold her together. God, he wished it would. He wished he could put back all her broken pieces...

"He was great. At first," she went on. "I had no family. Only a few friends, who were pretty bad news."

And he took advantage of that. Men like that knew; they could spot vulnerability fifty miles away. Sawyer inhaled against her hair, breathing in the faint scent of coconut. He held on to that fragrance because it kept him there, with her. Instead of letting him plot and strategize that sorry-ass-excuse-for-a-man's demise.

"I met him at the bar where I was a waitress." Her voice had gained strength, a note of indifference, like she was trying to distance herself from it all. "We started dating and he did everything right. He treated me like a queen. Then we got engaged and I moved in with him." Her hand slipped into his. It had started trembling again, as though she'd suddenly gotten cold. "That's when everything changed. The first time he hit me, I thought it was an accident. He begged me to forgive him and swore it would never happen again."

The hatred prowled again, stalking the outskirts of his thoughts, tempting him to say something, tempting him to make threats against the man who'd cut her so deeply. Instead Sawyer stroked her hair, focusing on the softness, on the feel of her in his arms. "But it did happen again," he prompted.

She nodded against his shoulder. "It got worse. The littlest things would set him off, and I...didn't know what to do. A couple of times I called the police, but he was a—"

The words died out suddenly.

He sat up, gently turning her face to his. "He was a what?"

Her eyes strayed. "He was...um...well-liked. People in the community knew him, so he always smoothed it over. No one really believed me."

"God, Ruby." *God*. The anger boiled in his gut now, hot and fierce, threatening to spill over. He kissed the top of her head. As long as he was touching her, he could fight the drive to make her ex suffer as badly as she had.

"The last time he came after me, he said he'd kill me if I told anyone." She leaned against his chest again, as though she was so exhausted that she couldn't hold herself up anymore. "He said he knew how to make it look like an accident."

Which meant it was about power. The guy got off on being in control. He wasn't even worth the rage. Not worth that effort. Sawyer had learned to fight with the law, and he knew justice was the ultimate punishment. The only punishment that mattered. That's how he'd ruin this man. He'd hold him accountable. Someday. When the time was right, he would find him and make sure he saw the inside of a prison cell.

"That's when I ran," Ruby murmured. "I packed up all my stuff when he was at work and I just started driving."

He bent and lowered his lips next to her ear. "I'm so glad you did." Glad. That wasn't nearly enough to describe it. Relieved. Happy, too, because she'd ended up here. With him. She'd ended up with all of them. And they needed her as much as she needed them.

She peered at him over her shoulder. "I know you're not him. But sometimes...physically...it's hard to forget the way he hurt me."

He wouldn't forget it, either. She might not let him track the bastard down tomorrow. But he would. Eventually. And he'd make him pay.

"Don't leave, Ruby." He straightened and brought her fingers to his lips, kissing her, begging her. "You belong here. At the Walker Mountain Ranch. With your family." With him.

He'd expected that sweet smile of hers in response, but instead she pulled her hand from his and scooted to the opposite side of the couch.

The distance left him cold. Had he misread things?

"There's something else you should know." Her shoulders steeled, as though she was bracing herself again. "I can't have children. It's not possible."

His stomach clenched, emptying him from the hope he'd felt. Because that's how her eyes looked. Empty and hopeless.

"When I was fourteen, I had an ovarian cyst." Her voice wavered, but there were no tears in her eyes, which somehow made it worse. Like she'd accepted her fate to be completely alone in the world for the rest of her life...

"My foster parents at the time didn't believe me. They thought I was trying to get attention, so they never took me to the doctor."

All the anger he'd held off before swarmed him. "That's neglect." How could someone do that? How could a parent keep a helpless child from getting the care they needed?

She shrugged like he didn't know the half of it. "The cyst

ruptured, and they finally brought me to the hospital. But there were complications." The words didn't waver at all, but tears slipped down her cheeks. Just a couple, then she whipped a Kleenex out of the box on the coffee table and blotted her eyes like she wanted to be done grieving. "Turns out I have endometriosis."

A shard of her grief splintered into him. She said it like that meant she'd been damaged, like she thought it excluded her from ever being loved. "I don't care." Sawyer followed her to the other side of the couch, lifted her chin, and stroked her face. "That doesn't matter to me," he murmured, pinning her eyes with his so she'd know it was the truth. "There are other ways to have kids, Ruby." Hell, his cousin Chase had married his partner, Robert, two months ago and they'd already found a surrogate. And his buddy at the station just adopted twin girls from Haiti.

"But I can't have a baby," she repeated, her voice hoarse with pain. "Not your baby." Her face hardened with the same resolve he'd seen in the pool, on the ropes course, when he'd accused the kids of stealing. And that right there was what made her so remarkable. When she believed she knew what was best, she didn't give up. She fought hard. But she was wrong this time. His life would be better with her in it, he already knew that. And there was no way in hell she'd convince him otherwise.

"You deserve a baby, Sawyer. I could never give that to you," she said, her strength breathing through.

But she didn't have to be so strong and she didn't have to carry that alone. He studied her, seeing all the things he loved most—her compassion, her courage and vulnerability, her conviction. The feelings he had for her gathered like a warm ray of the mountain sun in his chest and brought a smile to his face. "It doesn't have to be a baby. I only wanted a family." And she knew better than anyone what that meant, what a family should be, because she'd always dreamed of having one of her own. He knew she'd never take it for granted.

Her jaw pulled tight, trying to ward off the tears, it seemed, but she failed. They fell faster, bringing with them soft sobs that made him hurt. But they were necessary, too, those sobs. She had to let the grief flow out so she could make room for joy. He knew.

That's why he held her tight, pulling her down to lie with him on the couch, murmuring over her, stroking her skin, telling her it was okay. Everything was okay. He didn't know much, but he knew everything would be okay as long as he had her with him.

That was the last thing he whispered before she fell asleep.

CHAPTER TWENTY-SEVEN

There hadn't been a day in her life when Ruby didn't want the sun to come up. Until today. But it had anyway. For the past hour—since she'd seen the very beginnings of light smudge the sky pink, she'd remained still, more still than she'd ever been in her life.

Sawyer spooned her on the couch, his chest a solid, protective wall against her back. His rhythmic breathing had lulled her body into peace and hope and more love than she'd felt for anyone, ever. After everything she'd shared with him last night, the world looked different. It wasn't only the way that the early-morning sun rays peeked through the window, illuminating everything in their soft light. It was the fact that, maybe for the first time in her life, she felt safe. And she didn't want that feeling to end. So she'd lain against him, unmoving, staring out the window on the opposite wall watching light chase away the darkness.

Her careful stillness didn't matter, though, because Sawyer

stirred, then slipped his arms around her. "What time is it?" he asked, the words almost a whisper in her ear.

And she knew she had to answer, no matter how badly she didn't want to. "Six-thirty."

"Did you sleep?" he asked, his fingers playing with her hair.

Her eyes closed, but happy tears still gathered. "Yes." She'd slept off and on, but then she'd wanted to keep herself awake so she could feel him next to her, wrapped around her.

It couldn't last forever, though. Not when they both had other responsibilities. Ruby sat up. It was like tearing herself away from the warmest, coziest blanket she'd ever snuggled with. "You have to work today."

"Yes." He groaned as though that was the worst news he'd ever heard. "I have to be at the station by eight." He pulled himself to a sitting position, dark hair all bedraggled and adorable, t-shirt twisted and wrinkled, and it was so intimate and lovely waking up with him this way. She wanted to break the clock that hung on the opposite wall and wrap herself back into him forever.

A small, knowing smile quirked his mouth. He'd read her mind. "Good morning, Ruby," he murmured, lowering his face to hers. "You're beautiful in the morning, by the way."

She doubted it—already she could feel her frizzy hair tickle her face, but this moment was so beautiful that she chose to ignore her serious case of bedhead. "Morning, Sawyer," she managed, heart gasping with sweet desperation.

Holding her cheek against his palm, he kissed her softly, almost innocently, but the delicious pressure of his lips against hers made her face feverish.

"I'll go take a shower, then I'll make you breakfast," he said, rising from the couch as though he was suddenly in a hurry to get away from her.

"Breakfast," she repeated, admiring his startling physique. And wondering if his haste had something to do with the way his jeans strained at his crotch. He was being careful with her again.

"I don't cook much, but I make the best pancakes." His chin dipped slightly and his eyes raised as though he was tempting her. "Trust me. They're mind-blowing."

They very well might've been, but it wasn't exactly pancakes that she wanted blowing her mind at the moment. "I can't wait," she said, lifting her lips and brows into her own tempting expression. Because she didn't plan on being careful with Sawyer. Not anymore. Last night he'd taken her very heart in his hands, proving he would guard it and protect it in a way no one else ever had. She'd told him things she'd never told anyone else, and even though she hadn't disclosed everything, his sheer compassion, the way he'd held her and let her cry, had rooted their connection so deeply inside of her.

She'd never *wanted* to make love to a man before. After seeing Mama fall into bed with all the losers in her life, Ruby had guarded herself closely. Until Derek. And the thought of making love to him used to make her physically sick. When he'd start throwing out hints, she'd have to escape to the bathroom and throw up before he cornered her and took what he wanted.

Over time she'd learned how to disconnect, so that he only had her body. Sex had been empty and terrifying. But after last night she yearned for Sawyer. She needed to be with him. She needed to lose herself in the passion that had already flared with that light brush of his lips against hers. It had inflamed all of her, both body and heart, and made her writhe with a frantic longing she'd never experienced.

"Give me ten minutes," he said, already turning away from her.

"Ten minutes," she repeated, letting him think he would leave her behind. But she'd only give him two, just long enough to get himself undressed, then she'd follow him and offer herself over, knowing that, for the first time in her life, it would be real. All of her. Heart, mind, body, soul. Everything.

Seconds seemed to slow as she watched the clock's long arm strut past blurred numbers. God, it must the slowest clock in the world. Maybe it was broken. She forced herself to remain on the couch, though an aching desire simmered low and deep. Already her breasts were tingling, the softness between her thighs throbbing. For Sawyer. For the way she knew he could love her...

Forty-five seconds and she couldn't sit still. Not anymore. A daze settled on her as she quietly made her way down the hall, into the master bedroom. Evidence of Sawyer was spread around the room—tennis shoes on the floor, a stack of books on the bedside table—but it wasn't messy, only lived in.

The sound of the shower beyond the bathroom door lured her closer. Steam curled through the opening.

She was sure her heart would float away as she pushed through and stepped inside.

The door creaked behind her.

Sawyer had already made it into the shower. She could see only the outline of his muscular body standing underneath the spray, but even that was enough to dissolve her knees.

Bracing a hand against the wall, she crept closer. "Sawyer?"

His body froze. Then he wiped a hand against the glass, clearing away the fog.

She smiled, hoping it looked seductive and not terrified. "Do you want some company?" Her throat had gone hoarse. But it wasn't shyness. It was the force of her love for him weakening everything else. Even her ability to speak.

The glass door swung open and he stepped into view.

Wow. *Wow.* He was beautiful, all hard muscle and firm skin. Dark hair sprinkled the right places on his defined chest. Her gaze lowered, following the dark trail past his hip bones and down to his erection, which was still flexed and straining.

Happy to see he hadn't taken care of that, yet.

Seeing that he desired her the same way she wanted him brought that warm surge of pleasure tingling through her again. Her breasts felt full and warm, ready for his touch, *aching* for his touch…

Sawyer stayed where he was, droplets of water coursing down his wet body. "Only if you're ready, Ruby," he said low and quiet. "Only if you want to."

"I wouldn't be standing here if I didn't want this, Sawyer. If I didn't want you." But words were not enough to express how much she wanted him, so she pulled her t-shirt over her head and dropped it, letting it puddle on the floor beside her. Her heart whooshed with an onslaught of blood that tempted her to hurry, but she moved slowly, spurred on by the mesmerized way Sawyer watched her, his eyes roaming her body, his broad shoulders rising and falling with heavy breaths.

Slowly she unbuttoned her jeans, then seductively slid

them down, keeping her gaze fused with Sawyer's as she wiggled her hips.

His eyes seemed darker, heavy. "You have no idea what you're doing to me," he uttered in a way that made her want to do so much more.

Without speaking, she hooked her fingers through her white lace underwear and peeled them down until they slid to the floor. Then she stepped out of them, flinging them to the side with her foot. Arching her back in a way that made Sawyer suck in a breath, she unclipped her bra and tugged the straps off her shoulders, saving the cups that covered her for last.

Sawyer said nothing, but his hooded eyes pleaded with her to hurry, to reveal everything and abandon herself into his arms.

Hurry. Yes. She was torturing herself as much as she was torturing him. Unable to prolong the torment, she let the bra fall away from her body.

"Finally," Sawyer gasped, reaching out his hand.

She took it and let him pull her into the shower.

Hot water sprayed down on her, enhancing the sensations that already danced across her body.

"I love your curves," he uttered helplessly, smoothing his hands across the arc of her lower abdomen while he kissed her shoulder, then her neck, then her nipple...

Each light touch of his lips on her skin left behind a tantalizing heat, engraving both her body and her heart.

He stepped back, his hungry eyes following the contours of her body, fixated first on her breasts, then on her hips like he wanted to savor the details.

Except she'd already been waiting too long. The sensations that had been torturing her since she'd woken up only intensified, infusing her with a passionate desperation.

"Come here," she murmured, clasping both of his hands in hers and towing him closer. Pressing her body against his, she kissed him, not soft and light like she had before, but hungry and frantic, gasping into his mouth. Water showered down on them, steam clouding the air. And it was so hot. So damn hot the way his tongue caressed hers, the way their bodies fused together. His erection pressed into her stomach and made her nipples quiver against his chest.

"I don't think I've ever been this hard," Sawyer growled. He gathered her hair in his hands and kissed his way down her neck, over her breasts, sucking and nipping, devouring her skin with the same urgency that coursed through her.

Elation hurtled into her lungs, pumping them faster, making them feel like they would burst open. "It's never felt like this," she breathed, somehow finding enough air. "I didn't even know…" It could feel this way. Every sense heightened and engaged, so exhilarating it was almost overwhelming.

"I'm gonna make you feel everything," Sawyer panted, kissing his way down her neck, her sternum. Taking her backside in his hands, he lowered to his knees and tasted his way down her stomach, then lower, swirling his tongue against her inner thigh.

Now she couldn't draw in a breath. There wasn't enough air for how fast her lungs worked.

Sawyer spread her legs with his hand, grazing the folds of her skin, sending an electrical current all through her.

"Lordy," she hissed, and he laughed, the vibration of his voice working its way over her, into her. Then his tongue. Oh, sweet mercy, his tongue. It dipped into her, soft and hot, riveting every cell in her body with breathless anticipation. Bracing her hands against the tiled wall, she clenched herself tight as his tongue moved over her, slicing through her swollen flesh, because even though it was ecstasy, it wasn't enough. "Sawyer…" His name ended in a moan on her lips. The tantalizing thrill spread higher, almost taking her over, but she fought. She wanted to look in his eyes as she let herself go. She wanted to see him let go, too.

Sawyer pulled back and grinned up at her. "Let it take you," he instructed her. "There'll be time for more later."

"But…" She couldn't get anything else out except for another helpless moan because he wouldn't let her. That's what Sawyer did. He took away her instinct to fight, melting it into an irresistible urge to give in to him. So she did. She slumped and let her hands hold her weight, focusing only on the titillating sensations that gathered inside of her to create a tight ball of pleasure that rose higher and higher until it exploded, sending up sparks to blind her. The force of it softened her bones, and just when she thought she wouldn't be able to hold herself up, Sawyer was on his feet, catching her in his arms.

"Easy," he murmured against her cheek.

She draped herself over him, still unable to balance herself. "My god, I can't even stand up," she announced, in case he couldn't tell.

"You don't have to stand," he said through a grin that promised the fun wasn't over yet.

That grin was all it took to start the throbbing again.

"We're just getting started, Ruby," he murmured all sexy and low. And, yep, she could go for another round.

His arms threaded around her and lifted her. Bracing her back against the wall, he pushed that impressive erection into her, staring into her eyes with a passionate devotion that she would never forget. His wet lips closed over hers as he withdrew and thrust back into her, filling all of her, grazing some uncharted spot that pried a cry from her lips. He did it again, slower this time, seeming to enjoy watching her come apart in his arms. "Faster. Please," was all she could get out between the hard thumping of her heart and the blinding rush in her body. She wanted him to take her over the edge, to mesh their hearts together, to feel the heat and power of him as he came in her arms.

"I like taking my time with you," he grunted against her hair, but his breaths were ragged, giving him away. He couldn't stay like that forever, just like she couldn't. She was too close. The feeling of him inside of her, giving himself over to her just as she gave herself over to him, nudged her closer and closer to the edge of ecstasy. They were both on the verge of that same explosion she'd just survived, the outpouring of unimaginable pleasure but also unimaginable depth that would take their connection further.

"Thank you, Sawyer," she murmured, kissing her way across his jaw to his ear. "Thank you for showing me what it means to be cherished."

"You deserve to be loved," he said again, his eyes intent in hers. Still holding her tight against him, Sawyer spun away from the wall, plunging deeper, until every muscle in her pulled taut with anticipation, until she was clinging to him like he was life. "I can't hold on much longer," she panted. She didn't want to. She wanted to let go, wanted him to let go.

"I've never wanted anyone as much as I want you right now," he said, kissing her forehead, burying himself deeper inside of her than she thought possible.

And she couldn't hold it back anymore. The force of the orgasm seized her abdomen, echoing through in her euphoric trembles. His body rocked and swayed as he moaned her name, but his arms held her strong and tight, which was good because she was spent, draped over his upper body like a rag doll, body still reveling in the aftershocks. The water ran down her back, warm and tranquilizing.

"Damn, I wish I didn't have to go to work." Sawyer's chest heaved against hers, exuding the same exertion that had drained her. He carefully set her feet back on the floor and kissed her forehead, her nose, and her lips with a tenderness that prompted happy tears. She'd never belonged to anyone, not this way. Not all of her. She'd never given all of herself to anyone.

Sawyer gathered her into his arms, holding her like he'd held her all night. "Can I make you some breakfast?"

She quirked her lips at him. Just like a man to think about food right after sex. "I'm pretty sure your pancakes won't blow my mind the same way this did." She latched her hands behind his neck and gazed up at him, still under the spell of her body and heart harmonizing with his. "I don't know if I'll be able to walk to the kitchen," she said honestly.

He laughed and swept her into his arms, flicking off the faucet, stepping out of the shower, and somehow snatching a towel off the hook. "You don't have to walk." He carried her into the bedroom and gently set her on the mattress. "I can bring you breakfast in bed."

She propped herself up on her elbows while he conducted a visual inspection of her body.

"What I have in mind has nothing to do with breakfast." She glanced at the clock. "Far as I can tell, we have exactly forty-five minutes before you have to be at work." Her voice purred as it never had before, and her blood had already thickened into honey again. "I think we should make the most of it."

"You have the best ideas," Sawyer uttered in that alluring gravelly tone. Then he sank to the bed and pulled her body over his.

Heart humming in a new rhythm, she lost herself in the feel of his warm skin against hers, in the way his lips erased every thought.

He'd introduced her to this new world of sensual intimacy, and now she never wanted to leave it.

CHAPTER TWENTY-EIGHT

Maybe I could call in sick," Sawyer suggested, dragging his feet in front of the door.

Ruby took the opportunity to admire him in his uniform again, all strong and crisp and noble.

"Officer Hawkins," she teased. "The community needs you out there. There's no playing hooky so we can stay in bed all day."

"Who said anything about bed?" he asked, coming at her. "I was thinking the table...couch...kitchen counter..." His hands captured her waist and he pushed her back against the wall, kissing her until her fists had rumpled his pressed shirt.

Lordy, was she glad he wasn't treating her like a fragile artifact anymore. Stepping away from him, she smoothed his shirt. "I'll see you in nine hours."

His lips pouted. "That's a long time."

Tell her about it. But she opened the front door and

walked out onto the porch anyway, since it was obvious he wasn't going to be first. "You have to go to work," she reminded him.

Besides that, she had to get home to poor Nellie. She couldn't bear the thought of the dog being lonely, wondering if she'd been abandoned.

"Fine." Sawyer shuffled reluctantly onto the porch behind her, sliding his arms around her, pulling her against the solid wall of his chest. She leaned her head back and closed her eyes, only for a second, letting the feel of his strength and tenderness soak into her body.

A car engine startled her eyes back open. She recognized Paige's silver truck right away. Sure enough, it stopped right in front of the cabin. The window rolled down.

"Well, well, well," Paige called. "What do we have here?"

Uh-oh. Busted.

Quickly, Ruby wriggled away from Sawyer and planted one last kiss on his lips. "Work, buddy. Now." She gave his ass a hearty slap. "You're already late."

"I'll see you later?" he asked, then kissed her before she could answer right away.

Her face felt neon, seeing as how Paige was right down on the road, watching everything. "Yes," she promised. There was a going away party for the kids later that evening. And, while the thought of saying good-bye to them hurt, she wouldn't miss it. Not for anything. "I'll see you at the party."

"Maybe after the party, we could get takeout?" he asked hopefully. "And go back to my place?"

Despite the surge in her body, she simply shrugged. "Maybe."

"I'm happy to make it worth your while." One side of

his mouth turned up in a grin, and she knew he'd make good on that promise. He'd made everything worth her while four times this morning. The aftereffects still shivered through her.

"Trust me. It'll be the best takeout experience you've ever had."

She laughed and followed him down the steps, knowing there was no way to avoid a conversation with Paige.

"I'll be thinking about it all day," he promised.

Shaking her head at him, she waved. "'Bye Sawyer. See you tonight."

With a silly grin on his face, he trotted to his SUV while she headed over to Paige's idling truck, ready to face the music.

"So…" Paige's arms were already draped over the open window. "It's eight o'clock in the morning. You're standing on Sawyer's porch. *Kissing* him. On your day off." She tapped her finger against her chin as though considering all the facts.

"What're *you* doing here?" Ruby asked, giving a change of subject her best shot. She wasn't exactly ready for the world to know about her and Sawyer.

"Helping out on the rock climb with the kids." Paige stabbed a finger into Ruby's collarbone. "What were *you* doing in *there*?" She pointed at Sawyer's cabin with a smug grin.

"We were…discussing some things." That's how it'd all started, anyway.

"Your shirt is on backward," her friend informed her.

She looked down. Sure enough…

Her cheeks tingled too much to battle the sheepish smile. What could she say? She'd probably be smiling all day. For a year…

"Holy Mona Lisa!" Paige slapped the steering wheel. "I knew it!" She leaned out farther and lowered her voice, thank the lord. "Did you tell him everything? About your ex?"

She should've. She knew that. Eventually she'd have to tell him she was Kate McPherson, but he'd been so angry when she was talking about Derek. Though he'd tried to hide it from her, he looked like he could kill someone. His face had turned to stone. His eyes had been narrow and dangerous. "I didn't tell him everything. I'm afraid of what he'd do."

Her friend's face sobered. "Yeah. Sawyer wouldn't tolerate that kind of thing. And he can definitely be a badass when he wants to be."

"Exactly. And I don't want him to find my ex." It wouldn't be that hard. Sawyer knew where she'd lived. Derek was a cop. She had not doubt that Sawyer would be able to track him down.

"You have to tell him everything eventually," Paige said quietly, like she hated to relay bad news.

"I know. I will." After some time had passed. After his anger had faded and she could be sure he wouldn't try to hunt Derek down.

"You can always change your name if you don't want the guy to find you," Paige said thoughtfully. "I know people who've done it. Had a friend who smoked a lot of weed back in college. She changed her name to Mary Jane."

Ruby laughed. Paige was always good for a laugh. "That definitely wouldn't fit me." But maybe she'd look into legally changing her name eventually. She was kind of attached to Ruby now. It seemed to fit her better.

"I'm texting Avery," Paige informed her, digging her phone out of a small backpack. "We're having a girls' night tomorrow. Got it?" In her trademark frenzy, she didn't give

Ruby a chance to disagree. "Because I want to know exactly how that shirt ended up backward." Paige sent the text with dramatic stab of her pointer finger and tossed her phone aside. "But right now, I've got to get down to the climb site and set up."

"Got it." A girls' night sounded great. She actually wouldn't mind reliving the morning of passion with Sawyer. Not that she'd give *all* the details away. But she'd definitely be reliving it for a long time.

"Oh, and, Ruby…" Paige slipped the truck into gear, her eyes serious again. "Just make sure you tell him everything soon. Okay? Before things get too serious. Kaylee lied her ass off for a long time. He won't take it well if he finds out you didn't tell him."

"I know." She'd tell him as soon as it was safe. But for now she would keep things this way.

As long as he didn't make an issue out of finding Derek she could stay in Aspen. She just had to convince Sawyer that finding her ex wasn't worth the fight.

* * *

"Well, someone's sure been chipper today," Vicki commented from behind her desk.

"I have no idea what you mean," Sawyer insisted, filing the last of his paperwork. Okay, so maybe he was grinning like a shot fox. Whistling, too. He couldn't help it. For only getting two hours of sleep, he sure had a lot of energy, thanks to Ruby. He had a hard time wiping that just-got-laid grin off of his face.

A wave of heat rolled through him. God, that woman. She'd given him a hell of a lot to think about today. The shower. The bedroom. The best couple of hours of his life.

And he'd get to see her in…he glanced at the clock… approximately twenty minutes. Not that there'd be time to re-create what had happened this morning. No, this little meeting was all business. Knowing that the kids were heading home tomorrow morning, he figured they had one more shot to bring up the thefts, and he wanted to do it before the party. No sense in bringing down the mood when the kids were supposed to be enjoying their last night at the ranch.

So he'd called Thomas and Ruby and asked if he could swing by after lunch. He'd been surprised that Ruby was open to the idea, though she'd made him promise to keep it short and sweet. They didn't have much of a window with the kids packing up and everything. Which meant he'd better get over there.

"I'm headed out, Vicki." He snatched his keys off his desk.

"See ya, Hawkins," she called. But then her eyes narrowed. "By the by, have you made any decisions about sticking around?"

The shock must've shown on his face because she laughed. "No such thing as secrets around here, doll."

"No, I guess not." Especially when she bribed Chief with a latte every morning.

"So?" she prompted, palms tilted. "I won't tell anyone. I swear."

He busted out a laugh. There was a lie if he'd ever heard one. He knew exactly why there were no secrets around this place. Before anyone else could hear her yapping, he walked over to her desk. "When I figure it out, you'll be the first to know," he lied. That honor would belong only to Ruby. And he'd tell her soon. Not like the decision felt that difficult.

After he'd seen Kaylee, he realized he didn't have to

leave. Didn't matter where he went, the grief would follow. That's what he needed to work on. And he knew it'd be a process, but he also knew he wouldn't have to go through it alone.

Vicki frowned. "Fine. Just give me enough time to plan your welcome back party, will you?" she sassed.

"You got it," he said, heading for the door before she could read anything into the look on his face and use her women's intuition to figure it out on her own. He didn't need any rumors flying until he'd made things official. He still had to politely inform the Denver precinct that he wouldn't be coming. And then there was the whole business of finding a place to live. He couldn't mooch off his cousin forever.

But there'd be time to figure all of that out later.

As he trotted across the parking lot, he shifted his thoughts to the kids. The short drive over didn't give him time to script out exactly what he wanted to say, but it didn't matter. This time he wouldn't rehearse. He'd simply speak from his heart and leave the rest up to them. That's what Ruby had advised him to do and he knew she was right. So wise, that woman.

On the phone she'd admitted that it was strange the thefts had started after the kids had arrived at the ranch. Between that fact and a hunch that wouldn't leave him alone, he was pretty sure one of the kids had stolen the money. He'd place his bets on Javon.

If this meeting went well, hopefully they'd find out soon.

He parked the Tahoe outside the lodge and hurried across the parking lot.

Ruby met him near the front doors. The sight of her in those cut-off shorts and a fitted V-neck stalled him. God, she was stunning.

"Good day on the job?" she asked, pulling him in with that small, secretive smile. And yes, they did share a couple of secrets.

Grateful no one else was around, he pulled her into his arms. "I've been thinking about you all morning."

She smoothed her hands over his uniform shirt, eyes dancing. "I've been a bit distracted myself."

She knew exactly what to say to get him going. "When can we be alone again?" he asked, flashing back to earlier that morning.

"Hmmm…" Her folded lips teased him. "I'm busy tomorrow night. What about Friday?"

"I don't know if I can wait that long."

She relented with a lengthy sigh. "I might be able to make tonight work." She tugged on his shirt. "As long as you wear this."

"You've got it." He lowered his mouth to hers, tasting the sweetness of her lips. Only for a second…

She eased her head back with an apologetic smile. "We'd better get in there. They're waiting for us."

"Right. Yes." Somehow he had to concentrate, even with the heat that woman generated inside of him.

A soft smile plumping her lips, she took his hand and led him through the doors and into the sitting room where everyone had already gathered.

They sat around the coffee table playing an intense game of Uno.

"Hey, gang," he called over the squeals and arguments.

Some of the noise quieted.

"Sawyer!" Brooklyn popped off the couch and ran over, throwing herself against him in a fierce hug.

"Uff," he grunted, exaggerating a stagger until she started to giggle.

"Sit by me," she begged, leading him to the couch. He sat down, and this time he didn't dread what was coming. He cared about them. They had to know that. If they didn't, he'd make sure they knew it today.

"What's up, Hawkins." Javon high-fived him across the coffee table.

"Why are you wearing your uniform?" Neveah was the only one who looked him over with blatant skepticism.

"Just got off my shift," he said casually. "Thought I'd stop by before the party tonight."

"And we wanted to have another chat," Ruby added, nodding him along. She'd told him on the phone that she'd volunteered to help the girls pack up their things and she wanted to have it done before the party.

"A chat about what?" Brooklyn asked, peering up at him with those round, angelic eyes.

"Well…" Sawyer glanced at Ruby, who stood behind Javon's chair. She smiled, staring back at him with confidence.

"We still haven't found the money that went missing," he said carefully. "Or Avery's bracelet."

Silence fell. He felt Brooklyn's shoulder tense against his arm.

"I'm not here to accuse anyone," he said quickly. "I only wanted to say that I know each of you now, and…" Damn, he hadn't counted on getting a little choked up. Though he was tempted to, he didn't clear the emotion out of his throat. They needed to hear it. They needed to know that they mattered to him. "You guys are amazing. Each one of you is smart and kind and strong."

Tears slipped down Ruby's cheeks. He blinked hard so he wouldn't give in to the same fate. Emotion was one thing, but crying? He couldn't do that. Especially not in his uniform. "I know you've had it rough. You've had to overcome so much." More than any child should have to. "And I know that sometimes, when you're afraid or not sure what'll happen in the future, it's easy to make a bad choice."

"Have you ever made a bad choice?" Brooklyn asked.

He coughed out a laugh. "I've made a lot of bad choices." Though he wouldn't expand on his wild high school days. Didn't want to give the kids any good ideas.

"Even though you're a cop?" Neveah demanded.

"Even though I'm a cop," he confirmed. "We all make mistakes. Making a bad choice doesn't make you a bad person." He snuck a glance at Javon, who'd looked down to stare at his hands. "All that matters is what you do to make it right." He glanced around the circle at them, careful not to keep his eyes on one face for too long. "We're here for you. All of us, me and Thomas and Ruby and Bryce."

"You can talk to us about anything," Ruby added. "You never have to be afraid."

Sawyer shot her a grateful smile. "We'll help you figure stuff out. That's what we're here for."

It was still quiet, but he was relieved to see that none of the kids looked terrified this time. Contemplative, maybe even grateful, but not fearful.

"That's all we wanted to say. We won't bring it up again," he said, ready to lighten the mood and help them enjoy their last few hours at the ranch. "Now who's brave enough to take me on in a game of Uno?"

"Brave enough?" Javon scoffed as he snatched the cards and shuffled the deck. "I'll take you, bro. I'm the reigning champion."

Sawyer loosened the collar of his uniform. "Not for long."

CHAPTER TWENTY-NINE

Perfection. *This is sheer perfection.* Ruby's heart silenced in awe at the beautiful scene below where she stood on the ranch's upper patio. She didn't want to look away. She didn't want to even breathe, to risk altering that image of the kids playing in the pool shielded on one side by massive mountains that were carpeted with green meadows and studded with pine trees. Above them, the blue sky shimmered like silk and sunrays sparkled on the pool's turquoise water.

Despite the cool temperature, the kids splashed and laughed. It was the laughter that got to her most. The music of pure, innocent happiness. She'd so longed for them to have happiness, and here they were storing it up so they could take it with them when they left.

Thomas and Elsie sat side-by-side on a bench near the water. Closer than two people who were mere friends, she observed, though she would keep it to herself. Even with all the secrets Ruby'd brought with her to the ranch, Elsie had never once pushed her to share anything she didn't want to, and the woman definitely wasn't ready to talk about Thomas.

Bryce and Avery sat on the other edge of the pool, the sweetest picture of a perfect family. Bryce held the baby up, dangling her tiny toes into the water, while Avery laughed and clutched his arm.

The door to the pool house opened and Sawyer emerged wearing dark board shorts and a T-shirt. Even from the distance, his body looked tall, muscled, and tanned, almost celestial the way that sinking sun backlit his form. She knew that body now. Knew every inch of skin beneath those shorts intimately. Her heart dove straight for her stomach. Lordy, how would she even be able to walk down there with her legs wobbling like this?

Sawyer's aviators were on, catching a blinding glint from the sun. Next to the pool, he pulled off his shirt and sunglasses and tossed them on a nearby table.

Grinning, Sawyer backed up, ran hard, and catapulted himself into the air. "Cannonball!" he yelled, making the kids scream and scatter, but not in time. The massive splash still swamped them all.

Laughter rose again, and she joined them, still on the outskirts, but not minding at all because it was so fun to watch them. Except that's when Sawyer caught her. He seemed to search the area with those watchful eyes of his, and now his gaze homed in on her.

Yes, her legs—and other body parts—still trembled at the sight of him, but somehow she managed to hurry down the stairs.

Sawyer hoisted himself out of the pool and stood there

dripping. "You're late," he said, eyeballing the sheer cover-up she'd borrowed along with Paige's swimsuit.

"At least I came," she countered. She almost didn't, seeing as how swimming wasn't exactly one of her favorite activities.

Sawyer only grinned.

The kids lined up along the pool's edge, most of them holding on to the side, peering up her. There was Javon and Wyatt, Neveah... "Where's Brooklyn?" she asked.

Neveah shrugged. "She said she'll be out soon. I think she wanted to finish the book she was reading."

The book Ruby'd given her. *The Secret Garden.* She still had the tattered paperback that had kept her company through all of her foster homes. Something told her Brooklyn would rather escape into another world than face the impending good-bye. The girl had already cried twice while Ruby had helped her pack up her things. Her weighted heart sank. She'd give her a few minutes, then go in and find her. Somehow they all had to find a way to enjoy this night.

"What's in the basket?" Sawyer asked, trying to take a peek.

"I brought dinner." Ruby moved the picnic basket out of his reach. It was full of sandwiches and homemade sweet potato chips and sliced fruit. She'd offered to bring dinner for everyone since Elsie seemed to be so busy taking care of Thomas.

Speaking of, she noticed Elsie had scooted farther away from him on the bench, as though she wanted to keep up appearances that there was distance between them. Too bad Thomas's lovesick gaze gave them away.

"Thank you for bringing dinner, dear," the woman called. "You set it down, and have some fun. I'll get everything organized."

Before she could object, Sawyer slipped the basket out of her hands and set it on the table. His hand clasped onto hers. "If I were you, I'd lose the dress thing before it gets wet." Mischief glinted in his eyes.

But she didn't take it off.

The kids went back to laughing and playing.

Not Sawyer. He was staring at her like he couldn't wait for her to strip down to her bikini.

"I'm not planning to swim," she informed him. It was more fun watching the kids enjoy the water. Especially since most of them hadn't known how to swim before coming to the ranch.

"You have to get in. Show off your new skills." He didn't let go of her hand.

She gave him a look that clearly asked for patience. Or so she hoped. "I'll get in soon," she promised. Right now, the kids were obviously getting restless for him to do another cannonball.

"Okay." He let go of her hand and did not disappoint. This time the splash soaked her, too.

"Watch it, man." Bryce passed Lily to Avery. "You almost got my little girl." He slipped into the water and started a juvenile wrestling match with Sawyer, hooking his arm around Sawyer's neck and pulling him under the water like they were ten-year-old brothers.

Laughing, Ruby stole Bryce's spot next to Avery. She pulled off her cover-up and tossed it over the chair behind her, noticing that Sawyer had paused in his pursuit of Bryce. His gaze was blatant and hungry, and she knew exactly what he was thinking. She felt it, too. That need to be with him again...

"Gotcha!" Bryce slammed into him and they both went underwater. Avery shot her a perceptive look.

"That's what you get for checking out a girl when you're supposed to be playing a game," Javon yelled, taking his own shot at Sawyer. But Sawyer caught the kid and tossed him high into the air.

Laughing, Javon splashed into the water.

"So I heard about last night," Avery said casually.

Ruby didn't ask how she knew. Surely she'd run into Paige at some point today. "I have no idea what you're talking about." She didn't dare turn to look into her friend's eyes.

"I'm talking about you and Sawyer." She laid Lily on her lap. The baby's eyes were wide open like she was fascinated by all the chaos around her. "He hasn't stopped checking you out since you walked down here."

She could relate. She hadn't stopped checking him out, either.

"So is it serious?"

"It's complicated." She sighed. "Wonderful, but complicated." There was still the issue of her name. And Nellie. What would Sawyer do if he found out about Nellie?

"Relationships usually are complicated," Avery reminded her.

She turned to her friend, a breath of courage fueling honesty. "I have a lot of secrets. Things you don't know about me." She had told Sawyer some of them, but it was time to start letting other people in, too.

"We all have secrets, Ruby," Avery said quietly. "Even Sawyer. He's not perfect. Trust me. He has issues."

She doubted that. Sure, maybe he was a little suspicious, but that was to be expected for a cop. "No. These are big. Things that would change the way Sawyer saw me." What would he think if he knew she was using the identity of her dead neighbor, which was against the law? What would he think if he knew she'd lied about the dog? "I have a lot to figure out."

"You don't have to do it alone," Avery said. "There're so many people who love you. We're all here for you."

It was the same message Sawyer had relayed to the kids just a few hours before. She hoped it had warmed their hearts the way it did hers. "Thank you. Really, Avery. You all have changed my life." It was amazing how much love could do for someone. And it was so simple to offer your heart to someone else, to see the best in them and help them find it.

Speaking of . . . "I think I'll go in and see if I can find Brooklyn." She shouldn't be missing the party. She'd likely regret it after she got home.

"Of course. I was wondering about her," Avery said, shifting the baby to her shoulder. "And we're so happy you're here with us, Ruby. Can't imagine the Walker Mountain Ranch without you."

She received the words like a gift, tearing up at her friend's sincerity as she snuck away from the party. Instead of going through the patio doors, she followed the path to the kitchen door. She should grab more napkins, anyway. She tended to make her brownies and cookies extra gooey.

A smile dawned as she tromped up the steps to her favorite room, the place she'd found herself. A place that had become so much a part of her. She opened the door and stopped cold.

Brooklyn stood near the island, a diamond bracelet dangling from her fisted hand.

The warmth and happiness turned into a cold weight on her heart. "Brookie," she whispered.

The girl's face crumpled with a sob. "I'm sorry," she

whimpered. "I'm so, so sorry." She set the bracelet on the countertop, hid her face in her hands, and cried.

Brooklyn. Ruby stood there blinking. How could it be Brooklyn when she was sure it had been Javon? Good god, the girl was only eight years old.

Those heart-wrenching gasps chipped away the shock and suddenly she was moving, running to the girl and wrapping her arms around her. "Okay. It's okay."

"No it's not." Brooklyn sniffled. "It's not. I took the money, too." She dug a wad of bills out of her pocket and threw it on the counter. "It was me. I stole from Bryce and Avery."

Her heart was sinking deeper and deeper into the girl's despair. "Sweetie." She pressed a kiss into that wonderful curly hair. "You made a mistake. That's all."

"I'm so bad," Brooklyn cried. "No wonder no one wants me."

Ruby tightened her throat so she wouldn't sob, too. She remembered that same lie rearing its ugly head in her life. She remembered how it'd fueled her to make it true. For so long she'd believed it. She'd seen herself as unworthy. It was only recently that she'd begun to see the truth.

"You're not bad, Brooklyn," she said firmly. "And it's not true that nobody wants you. I want you." Holding the girl at an arm's length, she looked her straight into her eyes. "I would make you my daughter, if I could." If she'd straightened out all her lies—if she'd had the courage to use her real name...

"You would?" The girl's sobs eased into hiccups. "You would adopt me?"

"If I could," she repeated. "Nothing in the world would make me happier." Nothing. The truth of it filled her with a sudden urgency. Maybe she could. Maybe she could straighten out her life and become a foster mom. Then she could legally adopt her…

"Everything okay in here?" Sawyer stood in the open doorway as though he was unsure if he should come in.

Ruby gazed at him and her eyes must've screamed for help because he rushed over. "What is it? What's wrong, Brookie?" he asked, kneeling in front of her.

The sobs started again, nearly choking the poor girl.

Sawyer peered up at Ruby, fear making his face look pale.

"She took the money," Ruby said quietly. "And the bracelet. She was putting them back when I came in."

A sigh punched out of his mouth and his shoulders sagged with the same sadness that weighted her. He rested his hand on the girl's back. "Everything'll be all right," he murmured, and his gentleness seemed to calm her. "I promise you, Brookie. It will be all right."

"I'm so bad," she whimpered again, latching her arms on to him, as if she was convinced he had the power to rescue her.

"No." Sawyer held her tight. "You made a bad choice, but you were giving everything back," he reminded her gently. "You were doing the right thing, Brooklyn. A bad person doesn't do the right thing."

She pulled away, gasping and hiccupping again. "I only took it so I could go find my mom. I wanted to run away. Because maybe she would want me now."

Sadness clawed its way up Ruby's throat. She knew that desperation, that intrinsic need to be accepted by the one person who is supposed to love you the most…

"You can't run away, Brookie," Sawyer said in the same voice that disarmed Ruby. "You can't because there are so many people who love you."

The girl's head fell forward and came to rest on his shoulder as she started to weep again.

"All right," he murmured over her. And it was so sweet the way he hugged her and smoothed her hair that Ruby couldn't hold it together anymore. She gripped a hand over her mouth so she wouldn't sob, too.

Sawyer glanced up at her. "Can you go find Thomas?" he whispered.

Wiping away her tears, she nodded, then hurried down to the pool area. The group had abandoned the water and was scattered around the tables, eating and chatting and laughing. Thomas had parked his wheelchair next to Elsie at a nearby table.

Hurrying over, Ruby kept her head down so no one would see her tears.

"Ruby!" Elsie pulled out the chair next to her. "Have a seat, dear girl. You work too hard."

She manufactured a smile. "Thanks, Elsie, but actually I need to speak with Thomas for a minute."

"Oh." The woman's cheerful expression turned solemn, as if she somehow knew what had happened. "Of course."

Thomas had already started wheeling himself toward her. "Everything all right?" he asked in a low tone.

"It will be." She turned away from the party and followed him up the hill. Outside of the lodge, she scooted in front of him to open the patio doors. "When I came up earlier, I found Brooklyn in the kitchen. She was putting the bracelet back."

She expected him to look shocked, to ask questions, but he only heaved a sad sigh. "I wondered."

She gawked at him. "You suspected Brooklyn?" The sweet girl was the last one of the kids she would've suspected.

"Her last foster home was a nightmare," he said gruffly. "They didn't feed her enough. So she started stealing. Learned how to take what she needed so she could care for herself."

Nausea crowded her stomach. She gripped the door's handle for support. "That's awful." God, that was shameful. How could anyone not love Brookie?

"Where is she?" Thomas asked.

"In the kitchen." The chaos in her stomach made it hard to talk. She could throw up right now...

Instead she fisted her hands. Brookie needed her. So she opened the door for Thomas and followed him into the kitchen.

Sawyer still had Brooklyn sheltered in his arms. She wasn't crying anymore, but her head still rested on his shoulder. Her eyes were blank and tired.

Thomas wheeled over, such compassion on his weathered face. "I'm so proud of you, Brookie." He tugged on her chin until she raised her head and looked at him. "That took so much courage, putting everything back," he said, and his gruff voice had turned tender. "You're such a good girl."

What might've been a platitude for most children made Brooklyn's eyes light with joy.

It glittered inside of Ruby, too. Both hope and joy. Because Brooklyn's life could change, too, just like hers had.

Sawyer took a knee again, so that he was the same height as her. "What do you think is the best way to make this right?" he asked Brooklyn, putting the outcome in her hands.

She thought, lips bunched, eyes searching the room. "I need to tell Bryce and Avery I'm sorry." Sincerity whispered through the words.

Thomas patted her shoulder. "That's a great idea. I'll take you down to see them right now." He leaned closer to the girl, waiting until she gazed into his eyes. "But then it'll all be over. You won't have to worry about it anymore, honey," he said, lifting the burden off her.

Off Ruby, too. What a good man. What a good, kind man. He deserved Elsie as much as she deserved him.

"Okay." Brooklyn's hands scrubbed her eyes and she inhaled deeply, as though trying to be brave. "Yeah, I want to tell them I'm sorry."

Sawyer turned to Thomas. "Maybe she could make it up to them, too."

Ruby studied his hopeful face. "How?"

Brooklyn gazed up at him like he was pure sunlight. And he was—a beautiful soul who'd brought light and hope into her world.

"Yeah. How?" Brooklyn asked.

"Well, I know they need a lot of help around the ranch," Sawyer said. "Maybe you could come out on the weekends sometimes and work with the horses."

Tears filled Ruby's eyes at the way Brooklyn grasped on to that offering.

"Really?" she gasped. "You think I could come back?"

Thomas looked thoughtful. "Definitely a possibility," he said. "I'll talk to Greg and Diane, but I'd venture to guess that your new foster parents would think it was a very good idea."

Yes. It was a very good idea. The best. And Ruby knew exactly why Sawyer had suggested it. So they could stay in touch with her, so they could keep an eye on her and give her a place to belong just like they'd done for Ruby.

A rush of love for him pushed her to his side.

He draped an arm around her as they watched Thomas give Brooklyn a ride in his chair at breakneck speed out the door.

"She's gonna be all right," Sawyer murmured, turning to face her, looking down at her with those enchanting eyes.

"I know she is." Because love could heal any heart. It didn't matter how broken it was. That's what Sawyer had taught her.

His hands slipped to her waist. They were so large they almost made her feel petite.

"Come home with me tonight," he whispered, eyes softened with a look of desire.

Peering up at him, she crawled her fingers up his chest. "I can't." Tonight she had to force herself back into her past so she could determine how to put it to rest for good. "I have to take care of some things at home."

"Don't tell me you're cleaning again," he whined. "Because I can promise you...staying with me tonight would be a hell of a lot more fun."

"No." She smiled at him. "I just still haven't unpacked my bags." Was it only last night that she'd planned to run away from him?

"Right." A shadow of fear crossed his face. "You're not planning to leave without saying good-bye?"

"No." She wouldn't leave. Not forever, anyway. "I just want to get everything situated again before work in the morning." She pressed to her tiptoes and kissed him, holding her lips against his, soaking in his goodness. "Tomorrow night," she whispered against his lips. She would cancel on Paige and Avery. "I promise. I'll go to the store and we can make a quiet dinner at your place."

"Make dinner. I like it." He bounced his eyebrows as

though he was picturing her wearing one of those frilly aprons she had . . . and nothing else.

"Tomorrow," she confirmed. Hopefully by then she would know how to fix the lies that covered her past so she could start walking toward a future with Sawyer.

CHAPTER THIRTY

So you're telling me the bastard beat her up?" Bryce stared at him in disbelief.

"Yeah," Sawyer answered, lining up for a killer shot into the right corner pocket. *Thunk.* He tapped the ball and sunk it. They were down in Bryce's man cave basement, playing pool and smoking cigars, don't tell Avery. "And he was a re-peat offender." God, he didn't even want to know how many times that man had laid a hand on Ruby. Sawyer hadn't meant to say anything to Bryce, but seeing as how Ruby consumed his thoughts these days, there wasn't much else he wanted to talk about.

"Damn." Bryce shook his head and leaned down, eyeing the table for his next move.

"I'm ready to track him down and send his ass to prison, but she wouldn't give up his name."

"He wouldn't be that hard to find." *Thunk.* Bryce hit the solid five too hard and missed the corner pocket by a mile.

Sawyer took a drag of his cigar, welcoming the buzz, seeing as how he didn't do beer around Bryce. "I've thought about that." He knew Ruby was from North Carolina. And the name Ruby James couldn't be that common. He could easily type her name into the computer and see what popped up. Then again, he'd promised her there'd be no background checks...

"I've got the iPad down here." Bryce leaned his pool cue against the table and puffed on his cigar. "Maybe we should do some detective work."

"Sure. Why not?" He didn't have to *do* anything with the information they found. But at least he'd know who the guy was, where to find him when the time came. Because any man who abused a woman that way had to be held accountable.

He followed Bryce to the wet bar area, which Avery kept stocked with soda and nonalcoholic beer.

His cousin handed him the iPad. "Here. You can find anything or anyone on Google."

Sawyer slid onto a stool and fired it up. He typed *Ruby James, North Carolina* into the search bar. Some singer popped up. That wasn't her. He scrolled through various Facebook profiles, which he'd be willing to bet she'd never had, considering she'd been hiding from this asshole.

"See anything?" Bryce looked over his shoulder.

There was a lot to see, but none it seemed to be related to Ruby.

"What's that?" His cousin pointed at the screen.

Sawyer squinted. An obituary from the archives of a small newspaper. For Ruby James from Cherryville, North Carolina. He clicked on it and scanned the words.

"It's not her." Because this Ruby James had died well

over a year ago at the age of eighty. He read the rest of the article.

In the absence of any children of her own, Ms. James left her estate to Kate McPherson, a young girl who lived next door to Ms. James years ago. Ms. James's attorneys are trying to locate Ms. McPherson so they can settle the estate. Ms. McPherson was taken away from her mother and put into the foster system at the age of 8 and would now be 26 years old. If you have any information…

"Holy shit." Bryce seemed to be reading over his shoulder. "You said Ruby was in the foster system."

Sawyer blinked at the words, trying to bring them back into focus. Kate McPherson.

Kate.

"How old was she when she went in?" Bryce asked, clearly clueless to his current state of chaos.

Ruby lied to him. She wasn't Ruby. She was Kate. He stared at the small scratched picture of the girl they'd been searching for. Looked like a school portrait. Hard to tell what color her hair was, but the girl had the same full cheeks and large eyes as Ruby.

Kate.

As Kate. How could Ruby be Kate McPherson?

He closed out of the news article and typed *Kate McPherson, Cherryville, North Carolina* into the search bar.

A newspaper article popped up. An engagement announcement. With a picture of Ruby. Kate. He shook his head, confused as hell because she looked the same. Gorgeous red hair. Those stunning green eyes…

Derek Alders and Kate McPherson are engaged to be married…

Kate McPherson. This whole time she'd been pretending to be someone else. With him. With Elsie and Bryce. The shock of it darkened into anger, casting a shadow over everything they'd shared. Jesus, didn't she know identity theft was a felony? She could go to prison. And the Walkers could be accused of harboring a felon...

"Well..." Bryce took a long drag on his cigar. "Looks like you found the fucker."

"Why didn't she tell me?" That she'd stolen her old neighbor's identity? Or at least that Ruby wasn't her real name? He'd slept with the woman and he didn't even know her real name...

"Don't take this the wrong way, but I probably wouldn't tell a cop if I was using a fake identity, either." Bryce leaned against the bar. "I wouldn't take it personally, though. Her ex obviously scared the hell out of her. Maybe she didn't think she had a choice."

Maybe not at first. But what about last night? She could've told him. If she trusted him like she said she did, she would've told him.

He'd thought she told him everything. How could he have been so stupid? He should've recognized it. He was a cop.

"What're you gonna do?" his cousin asked, stubbing out his cigar in the ashtray.

Sawyer set down the iPad and stubbed out his cigar, too. "I'm going over there. To talk to her."

He had to see her. Even though he didn't know what to say.

* * *

Even with the windows down, the facts he'd learned about Ruby smoldered inside of him, creating a firestorm of anger. Technically, he should arrest her. He'd sworn to uphold the law.

His fists pounded the steering wheel. *Damn it!* How could she have put him in this position? She obviously knew it was against the law to steal someone else's identity, even if that person was dead. That's why she hadn't told him. She'd purposely withheld that little fact.

And that one fact could bring her down.

Fuck. What the hell was he supposed to do? The feelings he'd developed for her went so deep, tangling with the obligations he had to his badge. She'd lied. And somehow it seemed worse than lying about sleeping around. She'd lied about who she was. She'd kept him from knowing the real her.

Even when he was making love to her in the shower.

The tires skidded as he hit the brakes in front of her house. He could sit there for a few minutes and try to get himself together so he didn't go in on the offensive, but no amount of time would subdue the sense of betrayal. He had to see her face. Look in her eyes and ask why.

Lights glowed from the windows of Ruby's duplex, making the place look warm and cozy. A flash of longing cut through the madness and for an instant he wished he was there to visit, to sit on the front porch with her wrapped in his arms. But no. No. He shoved it off. He couldn't let it go. He couldn't go on pretending he didn't know the truth.

To him, truth was everything. Especially after what he'd gone through with Kaylee.

The anger recharged, sending him swiftly up the porch steps. He pounded on the door.

There was some kind of commotion inside. Thudding and shuffling, and he could've sworn he heard her talking. Or was it the television?

His boot tapped as he waited. Took a long time before the door finally swung open and Ruby stood in front of him.

Once his eyes fell on her, he had to look away. The sight of those black leggings and fitted t-shirt was too much. She'd piled her hair on top of her head, leaving loose tendrils to spill down over her shoulders. She looked so happy and comfortable that the reality of what he was about to do turned his body to stone.

"Sawyer." Her sweet smile gouged him. "What are you doing here?" she asked, stepping out onto the porch and closing the door behind her.

He kept his distance from her. Couldn't let himself indulge with a steady look in her eyes. "Why didn't you tell me the truth?"

She staggered back a step. "Wh...what?"

She'd heard him. He knew because her face flushed with panic.

Another gust of anger blew right through him. "The truth, Ruby. Why didn't you tell me the truth?"

"I'm sorry." Her back slumped against the door, slouching her shoulders. "I'm so sorry, Sawyer."

"I don't want an apology." God, didn't she realize an apology couldn't change anything? "I want to know why." He'd given her every opportunity to tell him. He'd told her he'd do whatever he could to help her. And she'd still lied to him.

A sudden force stood her upright. Those green eyes flashed. "I would've told you, but you said you couldn't help. You said there was nothing you could do."

"When did I ever say that?" he demanded, and yes his tone was getting away from him. But what the hell? All he'd done was offer to help her. He'd done his best to make her feel safe and protected. But he couldn't help her if she wasn't honest with him.

"When I called you that day," she shot back. "I told you

the man was hurting Nellie." She waved a finger in his face. "You said there was nothing you could do."

Her words turned his mind in circles. It took him longer than it should've to unravel their meaning. "Oh my god." He braced a hand against the porch railing, gripping it so hard he was shocked it didn't splinter. "You stole the dog."

"He was hurting her," she yelled. "And I didn't *steal* her. Nellie practically came right up to my door."

Shit. So she wasn't just an identity thief, she was also an animal thief. Raking his hand through his hair, he exhaled to stabilize his revving pulse. He shouldn't be shocked. She'd been through a hell of a lot with her ex, he got that. But he'd asked her about the dog. And she'd lied to his face.

Not to mention…she'd committed another class-three felony. He could arrest her right now. Technically, he *should* arrest her right now…

"I'm sorry," she said again, and now her face and eyes were soft. "I didn't mean to lie to you, Sawyer."

Well, she may not have meant to, but she had. Repeatedly. And it wasn't like the lies only hurt him. They could hurt her; they could ruin her life. His throat tingled, threatening to yell, but he swallowed hard before he spoke. "I came here because I found out you're not Ruby James. You're Kate McPherson."

Her gaze plummeted to the ground, eyes gaping at nothing. Her shoulders seemed to sag, too, almost like she was cowering. "How…how did you find out?"

The fear in her posture drew him closer. She'd been scarred. It might not be visible, but he had to remember that. "I Googled Ruby James," he said, guarding his tone. "So I could find your sorry-ass ex. So I could figure out how to go after him."

Her head hung. She still wouldn't look up. "I asked you not to."

"Why?" The heated question flew out of him before he could check it. "So you could keep lying to me?"

She staggered, her back colliding with the door again. Her legs seemed to give and she slowly deflated to the concrete.

Seeing her huddled on the ground like that—like a lost and terrified girl—dropped him to his knees. He inched forward. "Ruby..." He touched her cheek. "Talk to me."

Her head shook and those tendrils of hair covered her face. She kept her eyes focused downward, as though she was afraid to look at him. "I was scared." He couldn't see the tears, but he heard them in her voice.

"I didn't know how else to get away," she whispered. "He threatened to kill me and make it look like an accident. And..." Her breathing grew labored. "He could've, Sawyer. He knew how. He was a cop."

The cold from the concrete seeped into him, icing over his self-righteous indignation. That piece—that missing fact—clicked into place and brought the picture into focus.

Her ex was a cop. The man who'd turned her into a victim was the worst kind of cop. One who abused his power. No wonder she'd hidden. No wonder she hadn't told him.

She was crying now, fat tears and soft sobs that punctured his heart and made him see her—Ruby. She was Ruby James, the same girl he'd fallen for. A name meant nothing. He knew her.

"C'mere." He gathered her against him and lifted her into his arms. "We'll figure this out." He rose to his feet and carried her into the house, carefully lowering her to the couch.

For the first time in too long, she peeked into his eyes. "I wanted to tell you everything, but—"

"It's okay." He smoothed a hand down her silky hair. "I

understand why you didn't feel like you could." She didn't need to explain. It didn't matter what had happened before. All that mattered was that they figure out how to deal with this, how to protect her from the potential consequences. He paced a minute, trying to figure out where to start. First, he had to find out how deep she was in. "Have you filled out any legal documents as Ruby James?"

She shook her head. "No. Nothing."

Relief blew through him, scattering his concerns. "That's good." That meant he could still fix it before she'd have to face any legal consequences. "Now about the dog…"

Before he could sit down with her, a scratching sound scraped the bedroom door.

"Can you let Nellie out?" Ruby asked, pulling her knees into her chest like she was too weak to walk.

Nellie. She'd already given the dog a nickname, and unless he missed his guess the two had bonded. Which was going to make his job hell here in a little while. Dreading what he would have to do, he opened the door.

The dog bounded out of the room, tearing in two circles before launching itself onto the couch and into Ruby's lap, whining and licking her face.

Ruby hugged Nell tight. "Hi, sweetie," she murmured. "Everything's okay."

Sighing, Sawyer dropped to the couch next to her. It was obvious that they were crazy about each other, but he had to protect her. If someone else found out…he couldn't even go there. She obviously didn't realize what could happen. "You can't keep her, Ruby," he said as gently as he could. "You could get in huge trouble." At least he'd been the one to find her out…

Her face crumpled again. "I only wanted to protect her," she cried.

The way she'd never been protected. She didn't have to say it.

The dog stretched in her lap, scratching her small paws against Ruby's chest so she could lick her cheek.

Damn it. Sawyer looked away. This was gonna suck.

"She's so happy here." Ruby sniffled, gazing down at the dog the way she'd looked at Brooklyn earlier in the kitchen. Like she would offer up her own happiness to secure the dog's. "She doesn't even cower anymore."

"Of course she doesn't," he said, rubbing his hand against her thigh. "She has you." And Ruby had the kindest heart he'd ever encountered. But a judge wouldn't care about her heart. "Ruby, honey." He lifted her chin and forced her to look at him. "I *have* to take the dog. Tonight. Now." He couldn't let her risk five more minutes because Collins somehow knew she had Nell and it was only a matter of time until he proved it.

The color drained from her face, making her look like she was about to be sick. "He'll hurt her." She doubled over, cradling the dog in her arms. "Please don't take her. You can't take her away from me," she said, her voice wobbling with a fresh round of tears.

Nell whimpered, obviously concerned that something was terribly wrong.

And she'd be right. No one should ever hurt an animal, but Ruby also couldn't hide the dog forever. Eventually the truth would come out, and that would be much worse for her.

He scooted closer to her, rested his hand on her back. "I'll take her to the pound. We'll have a vet check for evidence of abuse," he promised, his voice soft, because damn it, she looked so fragile, like he was breaking her heart in half.

Her teary eyes met his. "Promise?"

"I promise," he said, gently taking Nell into his arms. Before it got any harder for him to do this, he stood.

She pulled herself to her feet and rubbed the tears off her face like she was trying to be strong.

But didn't she know? She already was strong. He saw it in her. A deep strength that not many people could claim. Securing the dog in one arm, he touched her cheek, running his thumb across her silky skin. "You deserve more than this, Ruby. You shouldn't have to live in fear. You shouldn't have to hide. It's robbing you from ever having a life. You'll never have anything real."

"I didn't mean to hide it from you," she whispered. "I didn't know what else to do."

He traced his fingers down her neck and swept her hair over her shoulder. "Let people help you. You don't have to confront anything alone." She had to know he wasn't only talking about the dog. Her ex still had her in his prison. He couldn't hit her anymore, but she still lived in fear.

The dog squirmed and whimpered like it was trying to get back to Ruby. As if he didn't already feel like shit.

"It's okay," Ruby murmured, leaning in to kiss Nell's nose. "You have to go with Sawyer. He'll take good care of you, sweetie." Her voice broke again. "Do you think I can have her back?"

Those tears. God, they killed him. But he had to be honest with her. "I don't know. I'll do my best to make that happen."

Sobbing into her hand, Ruby hurried to the front door and opened it like she wanted to get it over with.

He did, too, but on his way out, he paused. "You're so much braver than you think you are, Kate."

She visibly flinched the second that foreign name left his lips.

He did, too. *Kate.* That name didn't seem to fit her. She was Ruby to him. Even though he hadn't known her real name, he'd seen her heart... with the kids, in those intimate moments they'd spent in his cabin. The name changed nothing. He leaned forward and pressed a long kiss against her forehead. "Don't hide anymore," he murmured. "You deserve a happy life." And she'd only find it in freedom.

He kissed her once more, resting his lips against hers, stroking her cheeks with his fingers. Then, before he lost the strength to, he tucked the dog into his coat and left.

CHAPTER THIRTY-ONE

Ruby stood frozen in the center of the living room. The sound of her real name on Sawyer's lips still resounded through her. She hated it. Hated how it thrust her back into the past. Kate was weak and scared, and for the first time in her life, Ruby felt strong.

Don't hide anymore.

Sawyer was right. She'd been hiding far too long, and it was costing her too much. She'd lost Nellie, and she'd likely lost Sawyer because she hadn't been honest with him. And what kind of example was she setting for Brooklyn?

Anger rose up, charging her with the same power she'd felt when she'd zinged down that zipline—adrenaline and fight. She was done hiding. She'd been hiding her whole damn life. It was time to fight, and she knew exactly how she would do it.

The strength of her will bled into her body, fortifying her, making her feel stable and capable. She stomped into the bedroom, pulled a suitcase out of the closet, and started to rip open drawers, blindly throwing in enough clothes to last her a while. It was the same suitcase she'd packed when she left Derek, except then she had been quiet, tiptoeing, afraid he'd come home early and throw her against the wall when he saw what she was up to.

But she didn't want to be afraid of him anymore.

If Sawyer had taught her anything these past weeks, it was that she didn't have to be afraid. She'd learned how to swim. She'd jumped off a platform. She'd zinged down the zipline above the trees. He'd made her stronger. He'd guarded her and protected her with his tenderness, making her believe in love. Being with him had given her a vision of a future she never thought she could have. But it was right there in front of her, waiting for her to confront the past so she could embrace a new life.

If she ever wanted to have a life, she had to go back and confront Derek. She had to release herself from the power he had over her. It was time.

After stuffing down the jeans and sweatshirts and socks, she zipped up the suitcase, then withdrew the envelope of money she kept under the mattress. Using a fake name had meant she couldn't open a bank account, so everything had been cash. She flicked through the bills. Eleven thousand dollars. She'd done her best to save over the past year, and with the generous amount Elsie paid her, now she could fly back to North Carolina and stay as long as it took to make sure Derek never hurt anyone again.

That vision—the one of him holed up in a jail cell—crowded out everything. It was all she could see.

Stuffing the money into her purse, she marched to the antique writing desk Elsie and she had found at a yard sale last summer. She sat and withdrew three pieces of paper.

The tears flowed again as she wrote a note to the Walkers, thanking them for everything they'd done. Telling them she planned to come back as soon as things were settled. *If Sawyer finds a way for me to keep Nellie, please take care of her until I come back,* she wrote in the P.S. Because by the time she returned to Aspen, Sawyer would likely be settled in Denver. Sadness gaped inside of her, threatening to pull her into its darkness. But she warded it off by remembering how it felt to be in his arms. Even if she never found herself there again, she was grateful for what they'd shared.

Before the tears started falling again, she wrote a note to Brooklyn, apologizing for not saying good-bye but promising her that she would find her again someday. That she would keep in touch and watch out for her the way no one had ever watched out for Ruby. She didn't care what she had to do to make it happen. She'd pay any amount of money to stay in the girl's life.

Her hand trembled as she addressed the third letter to Sawyer. *I love you,* she wrote, and that was enough. It said everything she wanted him to know.

Drying her eyes, she sealed the letters in envelopes and left them on the desk. Then she hauled her suitcase out to the car and loaded it up.

Climbing the steps to the porch, she went into the house one more time.

It was so lovely, her little house. Bright and cheerful, old but charming. A perfect place to begin again. Slowly she walked through every room, leaving all the lights on.

Because she would be back. Once she'd put the past to rest, this is where she wanted her real life to start.

* * *

"Whoa, Nell. Settle down there, Trigger." Sawyer tried to calm the dog with one hand while steering with the other. He'd spent all night dealing with Nell. First at the city pound, where he'd called in a very pissed-off vet. Although once he'd assured the man of the healthy compensation he'd receive, the vet had done a thorough examination, complete with X-rays. Apparently the dog had suffered multiple fractures to the ribs over time, which had obviously never been treated properly given how poorly they'd healed.

In the vet's professional opinion, the dog had sustained substantial abuse. Which meant Sawyer'd had the pleasure of showing up at Grayson Collins's house just before dawn to let him know he was facing animal cruelty charges. It'd be a lie to say he hadn't enjoyed slapping cuffs on the guy's wrists. On the way to the station, Collins informed Sawyer that he didn't want the dog anyway. Apparently he wasn't as attached as he'd made everyone think.

Not like Ruby had been.

The memory of her brokenhearted expression gave him a good jab. He'd stopped at her house after Collins had been booked, but she wasn't home. That's when Nell had gone bonkers, launching herself against the door like she wanted to break it down and get back to Ruby.

"We'll meet her at the ranch," he said to Nell, who continued to yip and bounce in the seat next to him. They were all gathering for the kids' last breakfast before they left to go home. It would be the perfect time to give Nellie back to her, and to tell her that he'd decided to stay in Aspen, that he couldn't imagine being even four hours away from her.

Because who the hell was he kidding, anyway? He loved the woman, no matter what her name was. He'd watched her with Brooklyn, he'd seen her save Nellie from a cruel owner, he'd seen her work her ass off for Aunt Elsie. So maybe she'd lied to protect herself, but she'd never been a fake.

Ruby may have been hiding, but so was he. They were the same, really. Running away from the past. Who the hell was he to lecture her on being honest? He hadn't even told Avery about his son like Bryce had asked him to.

He drove into the ranch's parking lot, noticing that Ruby's car wasn't there yet. She must be making a stop first. So instead of parking out front, he drove around to Bryce and Avery's driveway, following it up the small hill to where their house hid in the trees.

Scooping Nell under his arm, he jumped out of the SUV and muscled his way to their front door, trying to keep the dog from launching herself into the forest. "Easy, Nell. We'll find her soon." But first he wanted to take his own advice. Stop hiding.

He knocked a couple of times, still wrangling the dog.

Avery opened the door.

"Sawyer. Hey." She did a double take. "You have a dog."

"It's actually Ruby's dog." He nudged a foot into the door and opened it wider so he could get the rascal inside.

"I didn't know she had a dog," Avery said, giving Nell's head a good scrub. "What a sweetie. Wait until Moose sees her."

Right on cue, Bryce and Avery's massive Bernese Mountain dog bounded down the wooden staircase, slipping and sliding as he tried to find traction.

Instead of acting intimidated, Nell pranced right up to the dog. Immediately Moose lay down and rolled onto his back.

Avery rolled her eyes. "He's such a sucker for the ladies."

Sawyer laughed and followed her across the living room into the open-concept kitchen he'd helped Bryce finish out.

"Babe, look who's here," she called to Bryce, who was making a bottle for the baby. Lily cooed from the bouncy seat perched on the counter right next to Bryce.

Sawyer walked over to her, feeling the ache of his own loss acutely but fighting the sadness that tried to take over. He'd told Ruby to stop hiding and he had to do the same. He had to stop hiding from the grief, stop pretending his loss had never happened. And he could start right now.

"Can I hold her?" Sawyer asked, feeling tension climb into his fingertips.

"Sure," Bryce said, sounding surprised, but then he grinned. "She's working on filling her pants. Whoever's holding her has to change her. So be my guest."

"How bad could it be?" he asked, unclipping the straps that held her in so he could nestle her into the crook of his arm.

Bryce and Avery both snorted. "You'd be surprised," his cousin said.

Sawyer stared down at Lily's perfect face, those luminescent blue eyes, her dainty nose and puckered lips. She had tufts of hair, the same blond as Avery, and a chin that curved exactly like her daddy's. She'd already gained a couple of pounds. Her face had changed. "She's amazing." Somehow it wasn't as hard to hold her as it had been those first few times. Maybe because Ruby had inspired him to think about the future, to start dreaming about a family again. Maybe not a baby, but a family.

Avery peered over his shoulder. "Look at her stare at you. She loves her uncle Sawyer."

Not that he deserved it. A stab of regret forced a sigh. "I'm sorry I haven't been here for you guys."

"What d'you mean?" Avery asked, swatting his shoulder. "Sure you have."

"No. I haven't. I've hardly even spent any time with Lily." He'd held her once right after she was born, and maybe twice since, but it had filled him with an echoing hollowness and all he could think about was how much he'd lost. How empty his arms were. It didn't feel that way anymore.

He glanced over at Avery. Not because his next words would justify his absence in his goddaughter's life, but because he didn't want to hide it anymore. His son deserved more than that.

"Kaylee lost a baby," he said, steeling himself. "*We* lost a baby."

Avery's friendly expression gave way to an open-mouthed gasp. "What?"

"She was almost five months pregnant." He blinked against the burn in his eyes. "It was a boy."

Avery shot accusatory look at Bryce. She didn't like to be left out. "I didn't know."

"I didn't, either," Bryce assured her.

"How come you never told us?" she demanded. "God, Sawyer, we're your family. We could've been there for you."

"I thought I'd forget about it. If I moved on." But now he knew he never would. He had to acknowledge it for the loss it was. He had to let himself grieve the dream of having his son with him.

Avery's lips folded like she was trying not to cry, but it wasn't that convincing, considering the fact that tears dripped from the corners of her eyes. "I wish you would've said something. All this time I've been pushing Lily on you when…" The words trailed off and she shook her head at him. Or maybe at herself.

But none of it was her fault, the way he'd acted toward Lily. "I've been the worst godfather," he said, brushing a finger against the downy skin on Lily's cheek. "But I'll do better. I promise."

"She's lucky to have you in her life." Avery sniffled. "Just promise you'll visit her a lot. So she knows you."

Oh, right. He'd wanted to tell Ruby first, but he'd see her soon. "Actually, I'm not leaving." Damn, it felt good to say that.

"You're not?" Avery gasped again, this time through a wide smile.

"Chief offered me a promotion." Yeah. Like that was the reason. "Besides, Ruby is here. And I kind of like her."

"Now, that I knew. It was so obvious." Avery slid onto a stool. "Don't worry, we're having a girls' night tonight so we can discuss you and Ruby in great detail."

"Not sure how I feel about that." But he grinned. Because Ruby fit here. With Avery and Aunt Elsie and Paige. With him…

Lily opened her eyes and stared up at him. He held her up, blew raspberries against her tummy.

"Look, she's smiling!" Avery clapped. "What a sweet, smart girl you are, Lily," she cooed.

"She's not smiling," Bryce insisted. "She's too little to smile."

"No. She's definitely smiling," Sawyer shot back. "Aren't you?" he asked the baby. "You're smiling at Uncle Sawyer."

The front door whooshed open and Aunt Elsie rushed in, followed by a hobbling Thomas, who'd apparently decided to ditch the wheelchair against doctor's orders. "There you are!" His aunt charged across the room, huffing out breaths and fanning herself with her hand. "Ruby's gone! She's gone back to North Carolina!"

His body went cold. "Gone?" He thought about how

she'd almost packed up her stuff the other night to walk out
of his life. "How could she be gone?" He'd just seen her last
night…

"I stopped by her house to see if she wanted to ride
here together." Aunt Elsie steadied both hands against the
kitchen counter. "I never bothered to knock. The door was
unlocked."

Suddenly Lily felt too heavy in his arms. He handed the
baby back to Bryce.

"She left notes." Aunt Elsie handed him some papers.
"One for us and one for you, Sawyer. There's one for
Brooklyn, too."

He stared down at the first page, at his name scrawled
across the top.

I love you. That was all it said. "Shit." That made it
sound like she wasn't planning on coming back to tell him
in person.

"Read the one she wrote us," Aunt Elsie said.

He blinked so he could focus and flipped to the next
page.

Dear Elsie, Bryce, and Avery,

*I'm so sorry I had to leave without saying good-
bye. There are some things I have to take care of. I've
been lying to you all. My real name is Kate McPherson and I've been running from my ex-fiancé. He was
abusive and I was afraid of him, so I chose a new
name and drove until I ended up in Aspen. You have
been so good to me, and I'll always be grateful for
how you took me in and gave me a place in the world
when I didn't have one. I hope to come back to Aspen
as soon as I can, but first I need to confront my past. I*

*understand if you can't hold my job or the rental, but
I will always be grateful for what you've done for me.*

> *Love always,*
> *Ruby*

*P.S. If Sawyer finds a way for me to keep Nellie, please
take care of her until I can come back.*

Sawyer staggered as he crushed the note in his fist. He
couldn't help it. She was gone...

"What the hell is going on?" Avery snatched it out of his
hand and smoothed the paper, then held it up and read it.
"Kate?"

Bryce scanned the note over her shoulder. "That's not
good. Her ex sounds pretty dangerous."

"You don't even know the half of it," Sawyer said, panic
overshadowing the words. "He threatened to kill her and
cover it up."

"Oh, dear god," Elsie breathed.

"I don't understand." Avery murmured. "Why didn't she
tell us? Why didn't she ask for help?"

"I told her she had to stop hiding from everything..."
Dread seized his heart, squeezing the life out of it. It was his
fault.

But that wasn't what he'd meant. Not at all. He hadn't
meant for her to run back there on some kind of suicide mission.

Avery shook her head with confidence, attaching herself
to Bryce's side like she needed reassurance. "She'll be all
right. Surely he won't touch her."

Sawyer couldn't get enough air. The room was closing
in on him. "He's a cop. Her ex is a cop." Which meant he

had weapons at his house. He didn't have to explain that to them. They'd seen his Glock lying around.

Avery's face froze into a horrified expression. "You have to stop her then! We have to find her before she gets there."

Hands locked with tension, he dug out his phone and tried to call her, but it went straight to voice mail.

"Ruby. Don't go back. Please," he choked out. "Call me. I'll help you figure this out." Hadn't he told her that already? That she didn't have to do anything alone? Hadn't he made it clear to her that he'd be there for her? Sure, he'd been upset that she'd lied to him, but he understood why she'd done it.

"What can we do?" Thomas asked, holding tightly to Aunt Elsie's hand.

Sawyer looked at them, at Aunt Elsie, and Thomas, then Avery, and Bryce. "We have to find her."

Before she got hurt again.

CHAPTER THIRTY-TWO

Ruby glanced out the plane's porthole of a window, seeing the snow-capped mountains far in the distance. She'd been lucky to get a redeye flight from Aspen to Denver, and was now waiting to take off on the next leg of her journey. To North Carolina. The place where all her bad memories lived. And the only place where she could face every one of them so she could finally move on with her life.

On that mountainous horizon, the early-morning sunlight spotlighted the highest peaks, making them look postcard perfect.

Yearning swelled. She should've tried to explain herself in the note she'd left for Sawyer, but she hadn't known what to say to him. She still didn't. He'd offered her so much and she'd kept things from him. Things that had obviously hurt him...

"Please direct your attention to the flight attendant at the front of the plane." A flight attendant took her place a few rows ahead of Ruby's seat and held up the safety information card, smiling in that polite, plastic way. Ruby blankly studied the safety card still in the seat pocket in front of her.

Her phone chimed with an incoming call, which reminded her...she had to turn it off.

Yawning, she dug it out of her purse and checked the screen. Sawyer's number glowed back at her. Ducking her head so the flight attendant wouldn't see, she clicked *answer* and held the phone up to her ear. "Sawyer," she whispered, earning a glare for the woman across the aisle.

"Ruby? Where are you?" Even just the deep hum of his voice plagued her with goose bumps.

"Don't go anywhere," he said before she could answer. "Please. Come back and we'll figure this out together."

She swallowed against the mounting tears. "I'm on a plane." They'd sealed the doors. She couldn't get off now. And the truth was, he couldn't help her figure this out. He didn't need her dragging him into this.

"I love you, Ruby."

She knew that, she felt it in the warm rush that calmed her heart.

"God, please come back." The line scratched and made him sound so far away.

"Ma'am..." The flight attendant leaned down. "You'll need to turn off all electronic devices now."

"Wait!" Sawyer yelled. He must've heard. "I'm coming," he told her. "I'm coming to find you. Don't do anything until I get there. Okay? Ruby? Tell me you won't do anything until I get there."

But that was the one thing she'd feared the most all along...Sawyer getting hurt because he was helping her. "I'm not afraid." She was startled to realize the truth. "Sawyer, I'm not scared anymore. I'm ready." She was ready to look into Derek's eyes and tell him what he'd done to her was wrong. She was ready to make sure he didn't do it to anyone else.

"*I* have to do this." This was her fight. "Everything'll be fine," she said, signaling one more minute to the irritated flight attendant, because she had one more thing to say to this man who'd changed her life.

"I love you." Smiling, she said it again, loving the way it sounded. "I love you." In all the lies, the secrets, the things she'd hidden away, that was real.

Love had finally set her free.

* * *

"You sure this is a good idea?" Sawyer glared down at Nell. The dog stopped to sniff every ankle and shoe that passed by, and seeing as how they were at Denver International Airport, that was a hell of a lot of ankles and shoes.

"We *have* to bring Nell," Aunt Elsie insisted, tugging her hot pink zebra print carry-on behind her.

As if he wasn't already embarrassed enough by the ankle-biter attached to the leash. Not that the dog was ugly, but Nell wasn't exactly a manly choice. He'd take a boxer or a hound dog over a show dog any day.

"Think of that moment when Ruby sees Nell. Imagine how happy she'll be!" Aunt Elsie exclaimed, as though Nell was the key to Ruby's happy ending.

Uh...wouldn't that be him? He'd rather think of the moment she saw him. How happy would she be, then?

Not nearly as happy as he'd be to have her safe in his arms.

His aunt patted his hand, which was a feat considering it was waving all over the place trying to keep Nell's leash reeled in. Unfortunately, every time he put the dog in the travel crate, she howled like a banshee.

"Stop worrying about Ruby, dear. It will all work out," Aunt Elsie said, out of breath.

Stop worrying. She might as well have said stop breathing. "You heard what that asshole said to her." He belonged in prison. Deserved what he'd be forced to endure there, too. Maybe Sawyer could call in a few favors with some of the inmates...

"She's a smart girl with a good head on her shoulders. She won't do anything crazy."

"I know." Ruby was smart. But she was also hell-bent on confronting her past. Alone. And there was nothing he could do about it. Even though he'd packed everything he'd need in less than ten minutes, they'd had to wait for a flight out of Aspen, and now he had to be a good four hours behind her. Which meant he couldn't protect her.

"Maybe I should call the station out there," he said, tugging the dog to their gate. But the ankle-biter dug in its heels to stop and sniff another pair of leather shoes. Expensive taste, that dog.

"And say what?" Aunt Elsie shook her head. "You don't even know exactly where she's going."

Oh yes he did. He might've known her well only for a short time, but he knew Ruby would go straight to Derek Alders's house. She'd sounded different on the phone. Bold and fearless. *I'm ready,* she'd said. Which was why he'd had Vicki at the station track down the man's home address. It was scrawled on the piece of paper in his pocket.

He just had to get there.

"Everything will turn out wonderfully, dear," Aunt Elsie insisted. "I can feel it."

That's why he'd let her come along. Because she had the kind of faith he didn't, constant and unwavering. "I hope so."

He'd never hoped so hard in his life.

* * *

Ruby pulled the rental car over in front of the beautiful brick cape cod that had once been her prison. Built in the 1930s, it was old house, but it had been meticulously maintained. Derek had bought it as a fixer-upper and he obsessed over making it perfect. Not one brick was cracked. The siding around the top was a pure white, and red shutters accented every window.

A blanket of thick, green grass carpeted the half-acre lot. He mowed in a crisscross formation, which had become the envy of all the neighborhood men. The two dogwood trees—one on either side of the stone walk—were still blooming with white blossoms. Along the front of the house, a garden of the rosebushes she'd planted herself were starting to bud. It was the kind of house you'd stop to admire if you were passing by. Quaint and lovely. So well cared for that you'd never know what was happening inside those walls.

She'd gone to great lengths to hide it—the bruises, the fear, the shame. But those things couldn't stay hidden forever. She wouldn't hide them anymore. She would stand face-to-face with him and inform him that he could come after her if he wanted to, but then she would use every resource at her disposal to take him down. She would make his abuse so public that no one would be able to ignore it.

It's time. She'd spent a good part of the afternoon driving around, reliving the memories of her childhood, but she couldn't put this off anymore.

Surprisingly, she felt nothing as she climbed out of the car and made her way up the walk. Despite the sun and the clear blue sky and the sweet-scented humidity in the air, her body was encased in a dull, cold darkness. She stared only at the front door as she approached the house, not noticing even how her feet managed to navigate the steps.

Instead of ringing the ornate doorbell, she opted to knock, rapping her knuckles against the freshly painted red wood.

It opened and a woman stuck out her head. "Yeah?"

Ruby stared. The woman's long blond hair was pulled back into a loose ponytail. Her cheeks were sunken in and she had somber blue eyes. Even with the warm weather, she wore jeans and a long-sleeved blouse that draped over her thin frame. She was young, probably not a day over twenty.

Derek was with someone else.

It hit Ruby like another punch to the stomach. This girl was her two years ago. Except…the woman wore both an engagement ring and a wedding band.

Dear lord. She struggled to stay upright, teetering on legs that felt numb.

All this time…Derek hadn't been looking for her. He'd simply found someone else to abuse. "Sick son of a bitch," shot out before she could stop it.

The woman stepped out with one foot, most of her body still hidden in the door's shadow. "Can I help you?"

Inhaling, she found her bearings again, balancing herself. This was why she'd come. To stop him from hurting someone else. But she was too late. She blinked against the harsh sunlight. "Is Derek here?" she asked, keeping her tone polite.

"No. He's not." The woman seemed to be holding on to the door. Her head tilted like she recognized Ruby but was having a hard time placing her. "Can I tell him who stopped by?"

She swallowed past the emotion that jammed her throat and stepped onto the porch. "Does he hit you like you used to hit me?" Ruby asked quietly.

The woman didn't answer. She only stood there, shoulders as low and despondent as an old woman's.

"One time he came after me because I got home late from a shift." That was before he'd made her quit her job. "When I walked into the house he grabbed me and held a knife to my throat. I tried to get away and he kicked me in the stomach."

The woman's eyes closed. Tears ran down her cheeks, but she tried to close the door.

Ruby stuck out her arm and stopped her. "Listen to me. It's not your fault." Those words. She'd needed to hear those words so badly once. "He's sick. He's the one with the problem. Not you."

The woman's hand fell away from the doorknob. Her arms went limp at her sides.

"It'll never stop," Ruby told her. She remembered hoping. Surely he would get tired of it, eventually. Surely he wouldn't hit her forever. But he would've. "It's not just a phase. It's who he is and he needs to be held accountable."

"I didn't know what he was like before," she whispered. "He never touched me."

No. He wouldn't have made the same mistake twice.

This time he'd made sure he married the woman before he hit her.

Her eyes burned, but she fisted her hands. "I should've made sure he could never hurt anyone again. But I didn't. I ran." She'd never regretted that more than she did right now, staring into this woman's wide, empty eyes. "We can stop him. We can make sure he never has the chance to hurt someone else." She dug her phone out of her purse. "I'll call nine-one-one. We can both charge him with assault."

The woman's head shook. "No. He'll kill me."

"He's already killing you." That's how he'd made her feel for those two years. Dead inside. Like there was no light. What she would've given for someone to show up at her door and rescue her.

Ruby went to touch the woman's hand, but she flinched and pulled it back like she was afraid it would hurt.

Holding her breath, she looked closer at the woman's wrist. The skin at the edge of her shirtsleeve was smudged purple and blue.

"Have you had your arm looked at?" she asked, barely able to whisper. It was so familiar, that ugly damage. The evidence of a secret humiliation.

The woman shook her head. "No. Please. Just go."

She couldn't. She couldn't walk away and pretend she didn't know. Too many people had done that to her and she'd lost years of her life. She stepped closer to the woman. "He did that to me, too. At the hospital I told them I'd fallen and he'd tried to catch me. But he'd really yanked my arm so hard he broke the bone." She clasped her hand over her wrist, remember thing way pain had splintered through it. "That's all the proof you need." The bruises. "He won't be able to hurt you anymore."

The woman cradled her arm with her other hand, crying softly. "He'll be back any time."

"Good," Ruby said, dialing. "By the time he gets here, we'll have all the help we need."

And Derek wouldn't be able to hurt anyone again.

* * *

"Are you sure this is the right way?" Sawyer ducked his head and glanced out the driver's-side window. They were driving through a posh neighborhood with older brick homes and manicured lawns and young moms out pushing their babies and toddlers in strollers. "This doesn't seem right."

It wasn't exactly what he pictured when Ruby told him about her engagement. It was too pretty, too clean.

"This is what the map says," Aunt Elsie murmured, shaking out the map she'd purchased at the gas station and shoving her bifocals back up.

Nell looked up from Elsie's lap, but she was obviously exhausted from the traumatizing plane ride.

Sawyer's knee pumped. This was taking too long. "I think it's time to use the GPS." He'd already handed her his phone, but she insisted on using paper.

"Wait a minute!" she shrieked. Her head cranked and she looked back over her shoulder. "I think we missed our turn back there."

He tried not to grimace. She'd come all this way with him, she'd kept him positive, and she'd done most of the work with Nell, which, considering the way the dog behaved on the plane, made Aunt Elsie a saint.

"Yes, yes, yes." She traced her finger along a line on the map. "We definitely have to turn around."

"Roger that," he said, trying to lighten the weight that bore down on his shoulders. Slowing the car, he checked his blind spot and flipped a U-turn.

"It'll be the next left," she said. "I think."

Great. He swiped at his face. Between the stress and the humidity, he'd need a shower soon.

"You missed the turn!"

Damn it. He had to focus. They were so close...

Heaving out a sigh, he flipped another U-turn, heading back the direction they'd come.

"So you're sure—"

The sound of sirens cut him off. Louder. They were getting louder. He glanced in the rearview mirror.

His heart felt like it was clanking against his ribs. Three cop cars.

"Shit," he muttered quietly so Aunt Elsie wouldn't hear.

"Don't worry." She reached over to pat his arm. "I'm sure it's nothing." But her voice had lost the happy ring.

Sawyer pulled the car over to the curb, and the patrol cars flew past, lights flashing, sirens blaring.

They turned left a few blocks ahead.

"That's our turn." Even his chipper, eternal optimist aunt looked downright scared.

She didn't have to tell him because he already knew. That sick feeling had sunk into his gut, the one that told you something bad was about to happen.

He'd seen some bad shit as a cop. Not nearly what it could've been, thanks to Aspen's relatively low crime rate, but he'd been on the scene of a couple of fatal accidents, a suicide, a few ugly domestic disputes. And none of it made his heart pound as hard, or his stomach feel as sick as it did right now.

He glanced back to pull onto the road, but an ambulance

barreled toward them. He knew enough to know that was a bad sign. A very bad sign.

A split second after the ambulance passed, he gunned the engine, following behind.

"Slow down. She's fine," Aunt Elsie said over and over.

She's fine. In the midst of dying hope, he held on to those words to keep him afloat.

CHAPTER THIRTY-THREE

Sirens whined far the distance, but Derek's truck bounced into the driveway five minutes too soon.

"Oh my god," Ruby's new friend, Jamie, gasped. "He's here." Terror flared in her sunken eyes.

A surge of red-hot anger cleansed the panic that chipped away at her confidence. She'd felt that same terror so many times when she would see his massive red truck pull into the driveway. She'd run around the house, making everything look perfect, so afraid that one thing out of place would set him off. But she didn't fear him anymore. The sight of Jamie cowering inside the doorway reinforced her determination. She might've been weak when it came to Derek before, but now she had someone else to protect. And Ruby would make sure he could never force anyone to live in fear again.

"Go inside," Ruby told Jamie, noticing the woman had started to visibly shake. "Lock the door."

"Come with me," she pleaded. "We can hide in here and wait…"

But Ruby started to close the door. "The cops will be here in a few minutes." And besides that, she wanted to see Derek's face when he saw her standing there.

Jamie froze like she was torn, so Ruby gently pushed her inside and latched the door. "Lock it," she said as Derek came around the back of his truck.

Halfway to the yard, he looked up and saw her. His steps stuttered to a stop. "Kate."

At the sound of his voice, memories flashed, blinding her with images of Derek flying at her, raising his fist to hit her, bracing his forearm against her neck to strangle her. The images whorled with the present and rage iced her body over, making her feel unbreakable. She gazed down on him, heart beating wildly, building a violent force inside her. He looked the same. Tall and broad across the shoulders, arms rippled with muscle. His brown hair was still cropped into that crew cut that made him resemble a soldier, but his eyes had changed. They were worn and sagged like someone who'd been beaten by fatigue. Looking at his eyes reminded her he was just a person. A pathetic, miserable person who could no longer touch her. "Hi, Derek," she said, steady and in control. The same peace that steadied her voice radiated all through her. He couldn't touch her.

"What the fuck are you doing here?" He charged at her, but she stood her ground, somehow knowing he would stop before he got to her. In all the years she was with him, he never once raised his voice at her in public.

"Bet you never thought you'd see me again." A smile emerged at the shock in his expression. His lips were clamped but his nose flared with heavy breaths. He didn't know what the hell to do.

"Get off my property," he growled.

The sirens whined closer, fueling her courage, but he didn't seem to notice them.

"Why? Are you afraid the neighbors'll hear what a monster you are?" She stepped to the edge of the porch, looking down on him, taunting him with a smile. "Because I saw what you did to Jamie. And I called the cops. I'm not afraid anymore."

His jaw ticked. "You're a liar. You took off and as far as everyone knows, I was devastated. No one'll believe a fucking word you say."

"Maybe not." He'd looked at her that same way hundreds of times, angry and hateful, and it always used to scare her into silence. But now it made her stronger. "Jamie and I had a nice chat. She'd like a divorce, by the way." Once the police had charged him and the divorce was final, the woman would get everything. She'd be set for life.

"She won't leave me," he said with that snide arrogance. Like he was untouchable, above the law.

Was he? Oh, god. Would anyone believe them? "You broke her arm, asshole," she said, a tingling ringing through her fingertips. Her control was starting to slip. Blood burned through her veins, anger turning into something more dangerous, something that tempted her to jump off that porch like she'd jumped off the platform on the ropes course so she could punch him and kick him and hurt him the way he'd hurt her.

But those sirens. They blared louder and louder. The police would help them, right? They would knock him down…

Derek seemed to notice the noise, then. He looked left and right.

Three cop cars flew down the road and screeched to a stop in front of the house.

"By the way," she called over the sirens. "We reported an assault."

Derek wasn't looking at her anymore. He'd turned around. "They won't take me in."

"They will once they see Jamie's arm. Once she tells them what happened." They couldn't ignore both of them. She wouldn't let them.

An ambulance skidded to a stop right as the policemen jumped out of their cars. Two of them jogged over. The front door opened and Jamie stepped out. She'd changed into a short-sleeved shirt, making the damage to her arm visible.

"He attacked me," she told the officers through a sob. "He broke my arm."

Derek flew into a rage, screaming at them and swearing. He went to deck one of the officers but the man ducked, then wrestled him down to the ground. "Easy. Don't do anything you'll regret."

Ruby let out the breath she'd been holding. She reached over to squeeze Jamie's good hand.

The other officers gathered around them, firing off questions. Two EMTs bolted up the walkway.

But a shout broke through the chaos.

"Ruby!"

That voice. She knew that voice. Sawyer had come for her. The fury that had given her body so much power receded, draining away her strength. She only wanted to be in Sawyer's arms, to cling to him until she could stand on her own again. The world blurred in shimmering waves. Pushing past the men who hemmed them in, she floated down the stairs, scanning, searching...

"Ruby!"

From behind the police cars, Sawyer sprinted hard toward her. She tried to run across the grass, but her feet dragged like they'd been encased in concrete. So instead of running, she slogged until her legs lost power and she slumped to her knees. But it was okay because Sawyer was there, too. On his knees, holding her up in a sturdy embrace, kissing everything his lips could reach—the top of her head, her forehead, her cheeks, her lips.

She nestled her head against his chest to shut out the chaos around her. His heart beat so fast...

"God, Ruby. God." He smoothed his hands over her hair, her arms, her torso. "I thought he'd hurt you. You're not hurt?"

"No. I'm not hurt." She inched in closer, until he was all she felt, until his body became her shelter. Breathing deeply she inhaled his woodsy scent—the freshness of grass and sunshine—and she felt like she was home. "You're here."

"I'll always find you. Got that?" He smoothed his hand over her hair again, like he wanted to make sure she was really there. "So don't bother trying to outrun me again."

"I'm sorry. I'm so sorry." She shifted to her knees so she could look into his eyes, so blue and calming. Her heart sped up and this time it wasn't anger or fear fueling that pressure inside of her, it was a brand of passion she'd never felt before.

"Don't be sorry anymore," he whispered right before he brushed her lips with a tender kiss. "I've never been happier than I am right now."

"Me neither." It was over. The past would always be there—she couldn't erase it completely, but she didn't fear it anymore. It couldn't hold her back. "Thank you. For coming all the way here." For proving to her that she didn't have to face her struggles alone.

Sawyer held her shoulders in his hands, like he didn't

want her to run again, like he didn't want her to even move. "I'd go anywhere with you. And I'm staying in Aspen. Chief offered me a promotion."

Her hands shook. She was almost afraid to believe him. "But what about being a detective?"

"I never cared about the job," he said, stroking her cheek. "I was running away. But I don't have a reason to run anymore."

So he was staying. With her. Happiness ran all through her, so overwhelming that tears gathered and spilled over. "Sawyer..." She sunk against him and he held her there, head against his chest so his heart could beat new life into her...

"Yarf! Yarf!"

A sharp inhale stabbed her lungs. She braced her hands against Sawyer's chest and peered over his shoulder.

Elsie traipsed across the yard with that loving smile intact.

"You brought Elsie! And Nellie!"

"They didn't give me a choice." Sawyer scrambled to his feet and pulled her up, but he didn't let go of her hand.

Nellie ripped the leash out of Elsie's hand and leapt into Ruby's arms, whining and licking her face. "If you brought Nellie, that means—"

"She's yours. You were right." He tousled the dog's fur. "She had some old injuries. The vet said it was obvious she'd been abused."

"Nellie. Oh, sweet Nellie." She buried her face in the dog's fur.

"Excuse me." A police officer approached. "Are you the one who called in the assault?"

Sawyer steadied a hand on her back.

"Yes." She knelt and set Nellie on the grass, then stood,

stronger with Sawyer's hand on her. "He assaulted me multiple times a few years back. When we were engaged."

The officer nodded. "They're taking Mrs. Alders to the hospital. We'll need you to come down to the station to help with the report."

"Of course."

Sawyer's arm slipped around her waist. "I'll drive her."

The officer gave them the address and they all walked to the car.

"Everything'll be okay," he said, rubbing her shoulder.

And this time she believed him.

* * *

"Aunt Elsie would kill me if she knew I was staying in your room," Sawyer said, carrying in the last box from the storage unit he'd helped her clean out.

Before she'd left Cherryville, Ruby hadn't had the heart to throw away any of Miss James's things, especially not the pictures and little trinkets the woman had kept on her bookshelves.

"Elsie doesn't have to know," she said with a raise of her eyebrows, though something told her Elsie wouldn't mind. After a long afternoon at the station and then a quick stop by the storage unit, she didn't want to be alone. And since Elsie and Nellie had already headed to the airport to fly back home, Sawyer was her only option. Not that she minded. He'd volunteered to stay and help her deal with the things she'd left behind, so they'd found a cozy little inn on the edge of town, nestled in the beginning of the forest. It was quaint and intimate, the perfect place to sort through the memories of her past. And she was beginning to remember that it wasn't all bad.

She sliced the tape on another box and opened it. Books—Miss James had loved to read. She used to lend Ruby her old hardbacks, giving her the chance to escape into the stories. She picked one up. *Treasure Island*. She remembered reading that one. Mama had never gotten involved in her schoolwork, but Ruby's teachers always marveled at how well she could read. A smile radiated from her heart as she leafed through the pages.

A small Polaroid print slipped out of the book and fluttered to the floor. She bent to pick it up, studying the grainy image. It was the image of a younger version of herself, complete with that stringy hair and those knobby knees. She stood by Miss James, who must've been in her sixties then. Since she'd known her, the woman always had soft white hair that she'd kept in a braid down her back, and a rounded body that reminded Ruby of Mrs. Claus.

She stared down at the picture, tumbling back in time. That was the day she'd had to leave home. Her younger face was stark, like she'd seen something that had spooked her. The social worker had come knocking at the door, telling Ruby and Grady they needed to pack up some things and come with her for a while. It hadn't taken long because she didn't have much to pack, but on the way down the driveway, she'd asked if she could say good-bye to Miss James.

They took a picture, and Miss James had given her a copy, too, though she'd lost it somewhere along the way. Just before she left, the woman had knelt to hug her, and when Ruby started to cry, she'd wiped away the tears. "It will all turn out. Someday you'll find your happy ending just like in all of those books you read. You'll see." The words echoed back to her and filled her eyes with tears.

"You doing okay?" Sawyer asked. He'd been so concerned for her all day. "Maybe you should take a break."

He came up behind her and dug his fingers into her shoulders, kneading away all the tension that had built over the last hours.

"No, I'm fine," she murmured, but she lost one more car on the train of thought with each caress. She dipped her head forward so he could get at the knot that had been straining her neck. "I'm happy." Tired but happy. Her head dropped forward as she continued the massage.

"That's your old neighbor?" Sawyer asked, peering over her shoulder and studying the picture.

"Yes. That's Miss James." One by one the tears slipped down her cheeks. "She looked out for me when I had no one else."

His finger traced the name scrawled on the picture's label. *Kate McPherson.* "So your real name is Kate."

"Yes."

He rested his chin on her shoulder. "It doesn't feel right calling you Kate."

She leaned her cheek against his. "It doesn't feel right to be called Kate." Not anymore. "I'm such a different person now."

"It wouldn't be hard to change your name," he said, stroking her skin.

She turned to peer into his eyes, to feel that steadying peace wash over her. "Do you think I should?"

"I think you should do what makes you happy." He took the picture from her hand and set it aside. "After everything you've been through, you deserve to be happy."

"I want to do it, then." She couldn't think of a better way to honor Miss James. "Ruby James. It feels right."

"Ruby," Sawyer repeated with a heart-stirring grin. "Not sure about James, though."

"Why is that?" she asked, inching closer to him.

He shrugged as though he didn't know, but his eyes glimmered with a different story. "You might have to change it again someday. Don't want to have to do it twice."

She reached up her arms, lacing her hands at the back of his neck. His skin was so warm and wonderful. An electrical surge rolled through her heart. "And what would I have to change it to?"

"I can think of a possibility," he murmured, lowering his lips to hers, lighting the fuse of desire until it sparked low in her belly. One week ago she never would've dared to hope that she would be discussing possibilities with a man like Sawyer.

"I like possibilities," she whispered between the sensual movement of his lips against hers.

He pulled away, eyes heated with passion, and moved the boxes off the bed. "I love you, Ruby." He took her hands in his and tugged her close enough that she could feel his heart pound against her chest. Hers answered with a devastating longing.

"I love you, too," she said, already working at the buttons on his shirt. She couldn't be apart from him anymore. All she wanted was to be wrapped in his arms, enveloped in the heat of his body against hers, as he buried himself inside of her until she succumbed to the pleasure of being his.

"Make love to me, Sawyer Hawkins," she said, pushing him down to the mattress. He caught her hand and pulled her down with him.

This time, nothing would stand between them. No lies. No pretenses. Just him and her and the beautiful possibility of a happy ending.

EPILOGUE

"Slow down, will ya?" Sawyer chased Ruby up the steep switchback carved into the mountainside. Nellie sprinted back and forth between the two of them, ecstatic that she'd been let off the leash.

"You trying to run away from me again?" Sawyer asked. They'd done this same hike only four months ago, back when she hadn't even wanted to talk to him. Thank god things could change so much in the matter of four months. "You didn't like me much the last time we came up here," he reminded her.

"Yeah, and you wouldn't leave me alone." She stopped on the slope above him, hands pinned to her hips, cheeks pink with the crisp fall air.

He paused to admire her. Couldn't help it. She'd always been so beautiful, but now her green eyes glistened in a way they hadn't before, and her body moved with confidence and grace, as though a heavy weight had slid from her shoulders.

It had been such a busy summer for both of them—her working in the kitchen and him starting the new job. Besides that, there'd been a hell of a lot of details to take care of...he'd moved into an apartment downtown, and they'd both traveled back to North Carolina for Derek Alders's trial. At his encouragement, Ruby had sought counseling to work through the trauma of everything that had happened.

Even just thinking about the past few months made him tired. But it was a new season. Now the pale-trunked aspen trees were golden and shimmering against the blue sky. The bite in the air suggested that the first snowfall might not be far off. Far as he could tell, a new season was exactly what they both needed. They still had work to do— as Ruby kept telling him, healing takes work—but he was ready to take the next step with her.

Nellie bounded up to Ruby and plopped down in the middle of the trail, tongue hanging out.

Ruby knelt to give the dog some water and waited for him to hike up the slope and join her. "I'm glad you didn't leave me alone last spring," she said, eyes shying away from his like she had a secret.

"I couldn't." He slipped his hand into hers and they started out on the trail again, Nellie on their heels, as they passed into the shadows of the towering pines. "You're all I think about, Ruby." In between her long days at the ranch and his extra duties at the station, he'd made sure to date her as much as he could—bringing her out to dinner, taking her to the movies. Once, they'd driven up Independence Pass. And, yes, she'd slept over at his place a few times, don't tell Aunt Elsie.

But none of that had been nearly enough for him.

When she'd asked him if they could hike to the waterfall today, he knew it was the perfect opportunity. He'd gone straight to Bryce's house, because a guy needed a wingman when he went to pick out an engagement ring, and they'd shopped all afternoon until he'd found the perfect one.

"Are we almost there?" Ruby asked, gazing at the path ahead of them.

Why did she suddenly look so nervous?

"Not too much farther." One more uphill jaunt, then the trail would curve deeper into the woods and they'd be there. "Maybe we could go skinny-dipping this time," he suggested. "It'd be best if you could take off your clothes *before* you fall in."

He'd meant to make her laugh but her jaw tightened. "Um...probably not this time." She pulled her hand from his and walked faster, trying to outrun him again?

"But maybe another time," she called.

Was it just him, or was she acting weird? He caught up to her and tucked her under his arm so they were walking side by side. "What's up?"

"Nothing." But her eyes held that spark of mystery. "I just want to get there." Her boots continued to pound the trail like a gold medal was at stake.

Nellie sprinted ahead of them, barking and yipping.

"What's her deal?" he asked, but Ruby only shrugged and kept hiking.

By the time they'd made it up the last hill, he was out of breath. He followed behind her as the path curved. "Are you sure everything's o—"

A murmur of voices cut him off. He directed his gaze ahead them, but instead of seeing the waterfall, he saw a crowd of people.

Nellie tore around the group, greeting everyone before trotting to the pond for a drink.

Sawyer looked around. Seemed the waterfall was a popular place today. Elsie and Thomas stood with Brookie, who was balancing on one of the rocks. Paige and Ben formed a human chain with Avery and Bryce, blocking his view of the falls. And then there was...

"Kaylee?" What was she doing there? He stopped a couple of feet away, searching her face.

"Hi, Sawyer." She smiled at him—a real smile, and... were those tears in her eyes?

Confusion rolled in like a thick fog, but Ruby took his hands in hers and pulled him out of it. "What is this? What's going on?" His heart rattled in his chest. Something about the emotion gathering in Ruby's eyes. About the way everyone looked at him, somber and quiet. Waiting.

Ruby's hands caressed his as she peered up at him. "We know how much you loved Matthew."

Matthew. Just the name was enough to put him in a chokehold. Everyone told him he should think of the baby as Matthew. But for some reason, it still didn't make him seem real.

"And we wanted to do something," Ruby went on, steadying him with her loving gaze. "I asked Kaylee if we could come up with a way to remember him."

Kaylee nodded, then moved next to Ruby. "Matthew would've been the perfect name. Matthew Sawyer," she said, a hitch in her voice. "I miss him, too. I never thought I would, but I do."

A surge of emotion pushed up, too powerful to contain. Tears dimmed his vision. "Thank you," he said past the thick mass in his throat.

"We all agreed that this was the perfect place to create a memorial for Matthew," Ruby said softly.

Everyone parted to form a path down the center of the group, and Sawyer saw it, what they had been hiding. A granite bench perched on the slight swell of land close enough to the waterfall that, if you sat on it, you'd surely feel the cool spray.

He made his way down the path, in the center of all his favorite people. It was so serene, quiet and reverent, the only sound coming from the water that splashed and rolled over the rocks.

At the bench he stopped and gazed down at a gold plaque.

In loving memory of Matthew Sawyer Hawkins.
Beloved son who is forever in our hearts.

Though he'd been trained to hold them back, the tears wouldn't stop. They rained down, warm and relentless. "It's... incredible." Somehow he managed to find his voice, though the words weren't enough. Incredible didn't begin to describe it. It was the most beautiful thing anyone had ever done for him. He turned to Ruby, trying to tighten his jaw against the tears, but she was crying, too.

"Thank you so much." The carved stone bench did what he never could. It had given his son a place. One of the most stunning places he'd ever seen. He would always feel like a part of him was missing, but this made Matthew feel real. And no one would ever forget him.

Ruby hugged him, then stepped aside and everyone else took a turn.

Paige and Ben happened to be closest.

She threw her arms around him. "God, I haven't cried this hard since Ben made me watch *Marley and Me*."

"That was only two days ago, babe," Ben said, patting his wife sympathetically on the shoulder.

"So I'm a crier. I can't help it." She sniffled. "This is so beautiful. And you and Ruby are just so perfect..." She gulped a breath and shook her head like she couldn't say more.

"It's true." Ben hugged him quick and manly like, with a hearty clap on the back. "You two are great together."

"Couldn't agree more," he said, shifting his gaze to where Ruby stood cradling baby Lily in her arms with a look of bliss.

"Sawyer!" Brookie launched herself into the middle of their circle and squeezed him so hard his eyes bulged.

"I'm so glad you're here," he whispered, squeezing her back. Though they'd seen her two weekends a month for the entire summer, it hadn't been enough. Being around the ranch had done wonders for her, though. She laughed more easily and he noticed that faraway vacant look in her eyes less often. Still, if he had his way she'd be in Aspen on a more permanent basis soon. He fought the temptation to tell her so.

"I'm glad, too." The girl shot him the smile that never failed to unleash his protective instinct. "You'd be the best dad," she said. "Matthew was lucky."

His heart softened like melting wax. "That means a lot, Brookie. I hope to be a dad someday." Soon. Very, very soon. Both he and Ruby had already started the process of completing the requirements to become foster parents. Wasn't quite fast enough for him, but he knew it took time. "You're still gonna come up on the weekends, right?" he asked her. She'd started school a couple of weeks ago and Thomas wasn't sure how much time she'd be able to spend at the ranch.

"At least once a month." Her eyes went round. "As long as I keep up my grades," she added, glancing at Thomas, who confirmed it with a nod.

The man walked over, still sporting a brace from his leg injury and subsequent surgery. The brace was only for hiking, he liked to remind everyone. He caught Sawyer's hand and shook it. "Helluva place."

"Such a beautiful memorial," Aunt Elsie added, scurrying over like she didn't want to miss her chance to hug him.

"It means so much to have you here." He leaned down to kiss her on the cheek, grateful that she'd taken over as his mother when his parents were off gallivanting across Europe.

"We wouldn't have missed it, dear," she insisted before discreetly tugging Thomas and Brookie away as Kaylee approached.

The awkwardness that always seemed to cloud the air between them faded. For the first time, he realized that maybe Matthew's death had been harder on her than she'd let on. She just didn't know how to deal with it. He smiled at her. "I'm really glad you're here." He never thought he'd be able to say that to Kaylee, but so much had changed. He'd changed, and shared grief had a way of bringing people together.

"Me too," she said, nervously clasping her hands. "I'm sorry, Sawyer. I made a lot of mistakes..."

"*We* made a lot of mistakes," he said firmly. But he'd learned. And maybe she had, too.

Kaylee shook her head like it didn't matter either way. "I'm happy for you. You deserve the best."

"So do you." He hoped she'd find it someday, the kind of love he'd found with Ruby. The kind of love that was worth fighting for.

She squeezed his hand and moved on to chat with Paige.

That left only Avery and Bryce, whom he'd maybe hugged one other time in his life. After his first wife had passed away.

They might not have been the most affectionate in the family, but his cousin was his best friend. Always would be. He clapped him on the shoulder. "Thanks for offering up this place." It was perfect. He couldn't have asked for anything better.

"Matthew's part of the family," Bryce said, and his eyes were red-rimmed, too, if Sawyer wasn't mistaken.

"Someday his many brothers and sisters can visit this place, too." Avery leaned in for her hug, raising her eyebrows at him like she knew exactly what was burning a hole in his pocket. Which she probably did, since Bryce couldn't seem to keep anything from her. She stood on her tiptoes and directed her lips to his ear. "I'll round up everyone and get them to leave you two alone for a minute."

"That would be great." Because Ruby stunned him with her thoughtfulness, her sweet heart, and he was done waiting. Patting his shorts, he felt for the small box. Still there.

Squealing a happy "awww" Avery bounded away and collected Lily from Ruby's arms. "Hey, everyone."

When no one quieted, the woman stuck her fingers in her mouth and trilled a whistle that made Sawyer's neck hairs curl.

Silence fell over the group.

"Mom prepared the most amazing lunch for us back at the lodge." She pointed the group toward the path like a true social director. "Last one back has to do the dishes," she said, winking at him.

The stampede started, with Brookie and Nellie leading the pack.

Ruby took three steps before he hooked her arm and held her back. "Wait."

She wriggled out of his hold. "You don't want to do the dishes, do you?"

He slipped in front of her before she could race Brookie down the trail. "Trust me. We won't have to do the dishes." In fact, they might not even make it back to the lodge. He might have to take her back to his place first...

"But—"

He pressed a finger against her lips. "I can't believe you did all of this. For me." He didn't even want to imagine how much it had cost her...

"Sawyer..." Her head shook slowly, like she couldn't believe he didn't understand. "I love you. And this is nothing compared to what you did for me." She pressed into him, her curvy sexy body fitting so perfectly with his. "Because of you, I'm not afraid anymore. You helped me see this amazing future..."

Now she was just stealing his thunder. He silenced her with a long, slow kiss. The touch of her lips sent energy soaring through him, making him sure he could run a full marathon without getting winded.

That's what Ruby did to him. She revived him. She brought him to life.

Digging the box out of his pocket, he pulled away, and before she could steal the show again, he dropped to one knee.

That seemed to get her attention. Her head tipped forward and she gaped at him.

"In four months you've become my best friend." They'd bonded during those early tumultuous weeks, and now she knew him like no one else ever had. Somehow she still loved him. "I love your heart, the way that you take care of everyone…" He flipped open the box and raised it up. The diamonds encased in the simple platinum band caught the sun. "But I want to take care of you. For the rest of our lives. I want to give you everything. I want to make all of your dreams come true."

Breaths shuddered through her open lips. Tears dripped down her cheeks. "Sawyer. Oh my god."

"Marry me, Ruby," he said, memorizing the joy on her face. "Let's build the family we've always wanted." The family she'd never had.

"Oh my god," she said again, then sank to her knees. "Oh my…yes. Yes, Sawyer." She rested her forehead against his, her eyes so bright and alive. "I can't wait to marry you."

"Then let's do it soon," he murmured, kissing her lips. "So we can bring Brookie home." So they could make a home for her. "We can book something at the ranch later this fall." Knowing Aunt Elsie, she'd kick out all their guests to make it happen.

"Yes." She nodded, tears dissolving into laughter. "I'd marry you tomorrow, Sawyer. I don't need it to be fancy."

"Tomorrow won't give me enough time to plan the honeymoon." After everything she'd been through, she deserved the best honeymoon earth had to offer. He pushed to his feet and pulled her up, then tucked her under his arm and led her to the bench. They both sat, looking out on mountain-studded horizon. Already the tops of the peaks had been dusted with snow.

"Honeymoon." Ruby sighed like she'd been caught up in a dream. "I've never even been on a real vacation. Where we will go?"

"I'll surprise you." Maybe Fiji? Hawaii? The thought of spending an entire week alone with Ruby holed up in some beach hut reignited the whole skinny-dipping fantasy. "I'm thinking somewhere tropical," he said in a low voice, making sure it was close enough to her ear to give her some serious goose bumps. "So I can watch you walk around in a bikini for a week."

The happiness in her laugh filled him, too.

She peered up at him, joy blaring from her luminous, honest eyes. "I don't care where we go. As long as I'm with you. That'll always be enough for me."

He cradled her face in his hands, marveling at the beauty Ruby had brought into his life. Marveling at the power of something real and lasting. "That'll always be enough for me, too."

Fall in Love with Forever Romance

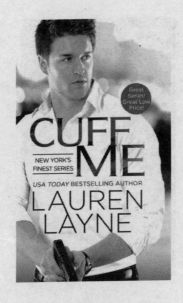

CUFF ME
by Lauren Layne

USA Today bestselling author Lauren Layne brings us NYPD's Finest—
where three Moretti brothers fulfill their family's cop legacy. Seeing his
longtime partner Jill with someone else triggers feelings in Vincent he
never knew he had. Now he'll have to stop playing good cop/bad cop, and
find a way to convince her to be his partner for life...

Fall in Love with Forever Romance

A BILLIONAIRE AFTER DARK
by Katie Lane

Nash Beaumont is the hottest of the billionaire Beaumont brothers. But beneath his raw charisma is a dark side that he struggles to control, until he falls in love with Eden—the reporter determined to expose his secret. Fans of Jessica Clare will love the newest novel from *USA Today* bestselling author Katie Lane.

Fall in Love with Forever Romance

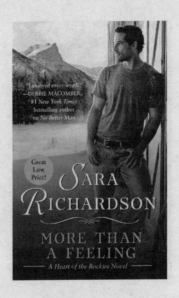

MORE THAN A FEELING
by Sara Richardson

"Charming, witty, and fun. There's no better read. I enjoyed every word!"

—DEBBIE MACOMBER, #1 *New York Times* bestselling author on *No Better Man*

Fall in Love with Forever Romance

An instant classic!
—RT Book Reviews
on *Dragon Fall*

NEW YORK TIMES BESTSELLING AUTHOR
KATIE MacALISTER
DRAGON SOUL

DRAGON SOUL
by Katie MacAlister

In *New York Times* bestselling author Katie MacAlister's DRAGON
SOUL, Rowan Dakar can't afford to be distracted by the funniest, most
desirable woman he's ever set eyes on. But no prophecy in the world
can ever stop true love…